Punky and Grump
In
The Ceaseless Chase
By
R.M. Bonham

ISBN 978-1-61225-399-2

Copyright © 2017 R.M. Bonham
All Rights Reserved

Cover art by Jeremy Britt

No part of this publication may be reproduced in any form or stored, transmitted or recorded by any means without the written permission of the author.

Published by Mirror Publishing
Fort Payne, AL 35967
www.pagesofwonder.com

Printed in the USA

This bizarre poetic endeavor goes out to my twin flame, Punk. May you always be a bright young thing, and may you always rebel, not to sell, but because "it suits you well."

To my mother, for always being my calm in the storm, and my relentless support.

And finally, to all the young ones out there lost in their own chaos, searching for the answers. They are already inside of you; just look to the bottom of the deepest wells you find, and never stop asking the questions that burn inside your mind.

I: Summer 2K12: The Seed

Smoke filtered its way from the ends of my lungs and out through my teeth, mixing with the day-old tequila that clung to my breath. Dazed, freshly eighteen, serving tables by the shore of South Carolina, and abiding by an unspoken code that allows curious minors to discover the grandeur of partying under moonlight. Staring into the side mirror of a girl's blood-red Mustang I see the reflection of looming leaves on the oak tree above. It's something of a treat the way its branches twist to cast shadows on us in the deep summer heat. I've found that working on the water in a vacation destination certainly brings an air of magic to the job. You can sense it in every whiff of the ocean breeze—in the way the wind blends the beach into a sweet perfume of sea salt, sunburn, and soft icecream.

    The restaurant that Fate brought me to sits on the far point of a marsh, and there's nothing like the pungent smell of muddy water to make it feel like home. It's fit with an open-air bar, a wood-fired grill, and a dock that lures the haggard fishermen in for a sip and a bite—the coveted kind of place that serves the same fish at night that was caught that morning, still squirming. Naturally, the staff is crowded with a bunch of hopeful, hormonal 20-somethings all trying to figure out our next step in Life. If they're like me, they're working to make some fast cash to pay their way through a mighty high American education.

    Carmen and I sat in her car across from the restaurant below that mangled oak, hiding our eyes from the entirely too eager sun at 2:38 in the afternoon. We awaited the arrival of every other soldier in our gangly armada with slightly identical hangovers and the proper medicine to cure it. As a group, we decided that this parking lot oasis was the perfect setting for us to come together before our shift to get high and wash away the night's sins. Smoke made the initial hour of dreaded pre-shift cleaning duties go by much quicker, too. I swear it. And *my*, is it a sight and scent for any bystander lucky enough to witness our ritual; a handful of cars passing thick joints, blunts, glass pipes, or whatever else we could find to smoke our precious green. And none of those bystanders have a word to say about it.

"Where is everyone?" Carmen asked with her head propped lazily against the headrest. Her cigarette was close to ashing itself, halfway forgotten between her two fingers.

"It's 2:41. Ya wanna just smoke it without them?" I asked, holding our white grape blunt in my own fingers. "Takes 12 minutes to burn through it."

An eruption of hollering rang out behind us just as Carmen began to mouth the word "yes," and we knew without turning a head whose voices they belonged to.

"Comin' in hot!" Steve and Nugget shouted as they ramped their black Mazda through the weedy gravel, barely stopping short of hitting the oak tree in front of us. Carmen squealed while I rolled my eyes.

"Y'all ready to get high, or what?!" Steve asked with alcohol reeling in his head and last night's smile stuck on his lips.

"Better not say, 'or what', cuz we've got too much to share for y'all to say no," Nugget said behind his thick square Ray Bans, putting the final touches on a blunt of their own.

"We wouldn't dare!" Carmen said as she handed me a hot pink lighter. I took the hint.

Just as I sparked the blunt a blue Dodge pickup clunked into the empty spot beside us. Dalton, Zander, and Tripp filled the seats in this one, and I could see a witch's finger joint in Tripp's hand.

"Laaaaadies," Zander cooed through beads of sweat and an open window, "ready for work?"

"Not quite," Carmen said, eyeing the blunt between my fingers, licking her eager lips. Content with the array of nearly half our crew, we lit each other in flames. Once a few rotations had passed Steve tilted his suspicious blue eyes up at me before saying,

"Rumor has it that you two were runnin' around holdin' hands at Hot Fish Club last night! I didn't get the pleasure of seeing it, but

I was busy dancing with Megan," he ended on a wink.

Carmen chuckled through a cloud of smoke before saying, "Wouldn't you like to know!"

"I saw it!" Nugget shouted from the Mazda.

"I did too!" Dalton said.

I burst into laughter before chiming in, "You wouldn't believe the reactions we got outta all the guys at the bar last night. The drunker the better."

"Yeah!" Carmen said, "An old gray man sat with his gin and tonic and gave us a spiel about never seeing two hot lesbians before. We didn't bother explaining that we weren't quite dykes."

"Just a couple teases," Zander said, playfully shaking his head and refusing the joint all in one gesture. "I'm gonna run inside a few minutes early while you guys finish your smoke."

"Tease?" Carmen started, with a slight air of annoyance. "Isn't that what you guys go to the bars for? To be teased? Because there hasn't been a single night that I've seen any of you captivate a woman."

"Ouch," Nugget said with an unwilling smile in the other car. "So, if you're not teasing, then what are you doing?"

"Just having fun, Nugget! Isn't that all we ever want to do?" I interjected. The wiles of Woman are such a mystery to Man.

"Oh, how could I forget! There was that song from the 80s that prepared me for this exact scenario," he joked.

"So, honestly," Steve started, "how many free drinks did that little hand-holding trick get you?"

"A few rounds of bourbon," Carmen said proudly, "but Lyla got the real treasure."

"What treasure? *Your* treasure?" Nugget joked. The boys and the girls—we all loved Carmen.

"That, too," I winked back at him, "but one of the cooks actually gave me a sack of weed. You're smoking it right now."

"What?!" Dalton yelped from the truck, "How did you pull that one?"

"It didn't take much!" I said, "He told us that he deals up and down the marshwalk when everyone parties after work. But before I could ask any questions he tossed a sack across the table and said to try some on the house."

"He was a little distracted by the idea of the two of us getting high and hanging all over each other, so I think we just helped feed his fantasy a little further," Carmen grinned.

"Yeah," I said, "I could tell by the way the moon hit the bag that it was at least an eighth, so I snatched it up, gave it a sniff, and put it right in my pocket."

"Un-fucking-believable," Steve laughed as he took one last puff, shaking his head. "Y'all always have it easy when you go out! I bet y'all wouldn't even have to bring money to a bar and you'd still get wasted."

"Hey, man," I said, "the world's a strange place! Sex sells, right? Even the sheer hint of sex is good enough for some to buy in. That's where we make our fortune," I giggled, grabbing Carmen's thigh.

"True! Unfortunately, true. Well, shit, here's to you, girls," Steve said raising the dead joint in the air, red beard catching a flash of white sunlight. "But it's 2:56, better cross the street or Miss Sheryl's gonna have a fit."

With windows rolled up and smokes snuffed out we walked two-by-two with the southern sun beating down on our black uniforms. That is unless we got sidetracked by the allure of ice-cold-cream when we walked by the yellow dairy stand on the road. Once we hit the double doors of the restaurant and felt the cool blast from the air-conditioner we all knew the game had begun. Every one checked which duties we were given and got to work without looking up for sixty minutes. Thank God, Allah, Yahweh, Buddha, Shiva, Kali, and Odin for the mind-focusing capabilities of marijuana.

By the end of the hour I was half-heartedly mopping the wooden floors and mostly gazing at the picturesque wall of windows in front of me. It's easy to be lost in a trance of fanciful daydreams with the way the afternoon sun glitters off those waters. Tripp, the newest edition to the busboy crew, caught the hard stare and interrupted.

"Hey, Lyla," he said sheepishly, "we're having a kind of house-warming party at our place tonight if you wanna come. Chill music, a fire, some beer pong. Ya know…" His voice faded. I saw the top of his disheveled mess of black hair as he looked down to the ground. He was fidgeting in the pockets of his grease-stained khakis—gestures you'd expect from a socially awkward genius type of character, who happens to be stoned.

"Yeah, yeah, I'll probably be there," I said glancing back from the view, "I might be able to grab a six-pack on my way over if Carmen wants to go with me."

"Oh yeeeahh, you're one of the young birds, huh?" He teased. "I always forget you're that young. Carmen's 21, right?"

"Yeah, she is. It won't be too hard to get her to be my date," I smiled.

"Yeah, you're the apple of her eye these days. Even if you don't bring beer we'll have tons in our fridge. I know Nugget and his girl are bringin' a case. My little sister's comin' down from Aiden, too. She won't bring booze, but maybe some weed?"

"Oh yeah? How old is she?"

"Same age as you. Her name's Scarlette. She's going to college next month—a place called Annabelle's College for the Arts. Which is an all-girls school. Which is a little hard to grasp. But I mean, she's kinda hard to grasp, too, so…" More fidgeting.

"Wait, what school did you say she's going to?" I asked.

"Uh, I think the name is Annabelle's College for the Arts."

"No way!" I said, "*I'm* going to Annabelle's! You know there's only like, 700 girls total on campus, right? What are the odds!"

"Whoa, you too?! Aren't you worried you're gonna get there and go a little gay," he laughed.

"Oh, don't you know that it's also an all-lesbian college? You might wanna ask your sister if she's got anything to tell you," I joked. "But what'd you say her name was again?"

"Scarlette. She's skinny, real pale, has long curly brown hair. Oh—and a silver nose ring."

"Mannnnn, I can't believe the coincidence. Make sure you point her out to me tonight!"

At exactly the right moment our conversation was cut off by the sound of other employees yelling "PRE-SHIFT! PRE-SHIFT! PRE-SHIFT!" Our own little version of a battle cry heard before the onslaught of war. Obeying the soldier's shriek, Tripp and I quickly parted ways to find where our respective battalion was gathered.

Once that battle song was sung we opened the floodgates to let all the waddling outsiders into our fortress for the night.

Let the summer evening beatdown commence.

***

"11:37 PM" were the green numbers that Carmen's Mustang read to me. I was sticky with sweat from a night in tourism hell. After a few impromptu shots from our bartender at work we managed to land ourselves in the parking lot of Tripp, Zander, and Dalton's apartment complex.

"Lemme smoke one last cigarette before we go up, yeah?" Carmen said as she lit her Marlboro. She knew I wouldn't say no.

Something about her drew me in like a hungry moth to fire. But maybe that flame is merely the cherry on the end of her cigarette, and I'm about to get burned. It's a fetishistic fascination with her nature; the way she slinks so elegantly out of her car with a case of beer in her hands and a sultry gaze in her seafoam eyes. The way the beauty mark in the middle of her back peeks out from under her voluptuous, burgundy mermaid locks. The way she exudes an effortless air of power when her summer wedges make her tower over everybody, including the guys. Or maybe it's the way all those same guys drop their jaws in awe and envy when they see the two of us lacing our fingers together, attention reserved only for the one whose hand we're holding. And maybe it's all of that. Maybe none.

I caught a glimpse of my post-work wardrobe in the mirror when I tore my gaze away from Carmen. It screamed "tipsy". Right after our shift ended I dashed out to my car in the hopes of finding a change of clothes before heading to the party. By luck, I found a royal blue crocheted tube top in my trunk that belonged to my mom during her prime era of 80s fashion. I ripped my greasy, seafood-smellin' shirt off underneath the oak tree, traded it for this retro half-shirt, and suddenly I was sitting shotgun next to Carmen on the way to buy beer. Nearly finished with her cigarette now, she climbed out of the Mustang with me following her lead. Stepping out onto the warm, hard concrete, I was reminded that I was still barefoot.

"You know," I said to Carmen, balancing delicately on the flat tar, "I think I hate wearing shoes *almost* as much as I hate wearing pants. Which is quite a bit, in case you didn't know already."

"Oh, dear!" She laughed, "Well you have to keep at least one of them for the party, and I wouldn't mind so much if you chose to ditch the pants." She said, grabbing my belt loops.

"I know you wouldn't." Flirt, flirt. "But for social ease, I think I'll stick to the bare feet."

House parties aren't my usual cup o' tea. It took two months for anyone at the restaurant to get me to go drinking with them, and Carmen was the deal-maker for that first occasion. She begged me, and how could I say no to a six-foot beauty with desire brooding in her eyes? Besides, small-talk is enough to bore me to death, and it's hard to get people to explore the deeper horizons of conversation in the wake of 56 beers and an endless competition of beer pong.

The second we got through the door of Tripp's apartment I assumed the wallflower position of watching it all, but participating in none. It was amusing to me, really, to experience an honest house party. I never wrapped myself up in the typical high school party daze for many different reasons--academia being the top. I was certain that I was gonna land a full-ride to a prestigious college, so the first time I saw a beer pong table was that very night at the boys' place. With rosy-cheeked fellows crowding the small walkway, Carmen and I tried to slip behind their table.

"Hey y'all, glad you could make it!" A smiling voice from the porch said, "Grab a beer from the fridge. I dunno what you like, but I'm drinkin' Landshark. There's all types."

Enter Dalton Sawyer—the gentlemanly type with effortlessly quaffed, dark hair and a buttery southern drawl that's like nectar in our ears. He always spoke with respect and ease, which naturally paved a path to the ladies at work. He was already on his third girlfriend of the summer, but who could blame them all for falling helpless to his song?

I saw Tripp, too, sitting on the edge of their striped couch not even bothering to look up from the video game on the screen. He just barked out a quick "HEY!" and that was it for a while. There were a few others scattered in the living room either lying on the floor playing cards, or sitting on the couch griping about the punishment we endured at the restaurant. It was enchanting to listen to everybody's chatter in their little circles while being involved in not one, single bit.

I grabbed the case of Shock Top from Carmen's hands and gave her a bottle before taking one for myself. When Tripp told me there would be a fridge full of beer, he wasn't lying—there was barely enough room for what I had left of our beer. Funniest thing about that fridge was the lack of anything edible. These boys were on a fermented liquid diet.

Carmen asked me to come out to the porch with her while she smoked a cigarette, so I followed her out to find three faces shaded in the dark, lit only by the pale glow of the distant neighborhood street lamps and the ends of their cigarettes. One guy wasn't smoking, though, just like me. I couldn't see the other faces very well, but I could tell there was a girl because of the shrill pitch of her voice. Carmen bumped my elbow to grab my attention and said, "Come on, let's take a picture." After six takes and freshly blinded eyes, we had two perfect shots of our crooked, drunken smiles.

"Perfect!" She said as she kissed me on the cheek before running inside to tantalize the others. Poor things.

Before I could make my way back inside, the third roommate of the modest estate walked out with a cigarette between his lips. Zander—what a wreck, this one. You could tell by staring into his once-sweet face that there was trouble toiling beneath the surface. His blue eyes were dulled from years of prescription drug abuse and lost love; shoulders slouched like he was trying to hide himself from the world. He tried to hook up with me on the 4th of July at a coworker's house while we were all sleeping on the same couch. I denied him, to his dismay, and we haven't really talked since. But when he saw me, he was loopy enough to say,

"Hey, heeeyyy pretty lady, how are ya? I didn't even know you were here." His eyes were all googly-moogly, so I could tell he snorted one of his beloved blue pills.

"You didn't know I was here? You're the one who's been locked in your room since we got here!" I joked back.

"I don't like having a lot of people around; they make me anxious. Hence, my pills," he said as he nodded his head in pleasant haze.

Right when he said that, I said, "Take a walk with me," before I dashed through the apartment and out the door. He followed after me as we stumbled down the stairs together. Dodging his kisses by darting in different directions in the road, I managed to make it to the bottom of discussing his addiction in a graveyard nuzzled among the apartment buildings. The tombstones surrounding us brought him back to the best friend he lost in Pennsylvania. Fast forward four years to the ripe age of 23, and the drug abuse was telling upon immediate evaluation. I stared at him with sorrow filling my belly as he spoke of how his friend was killed in a car accident, and that he hasn't coped well with not being able to give him that last "goodbye". It broke him down to alcoholism and rampant Xanax abuse. And here he is in Bloodmoon Beach, South Carolina, just trying to chase the low, numb the pain, and look out for big Love with a lonesome, starving, heart.

"I was engaged once," he said dreamily, "she was fucking gorgeous. Bleach blonde hair, a little lighter than yours. She had smile that could suck you in for years and a voice that sounded like Heaven." He paused, lingering for a moment on the magic of his past lover. "But after our friend died, I started spiraling out of control. I wasn't there for her the way she needed me to be, the way that she was there for me. She was supposed to move down here with me, and we were gonna start our life anew, together, ya know? All of that shit.

"But on the morning we were set to leave, I found out she packed up all her stuff in the middle of the night while I was nodded out on pills. I never got to say goodbye to her either. She changed her number, changed her address, got a new life, I guess… I don't know. People tell me she's doing fine. But that's the extent of it." He held his breath for a second, then repeated. "She's doing just fine."

He stared down at the ground, totally free of tears or any sure sign of heartache. Rather, an instinctive indifference flowed from him. He recognized that this was his Life, and he was stuck trying to make sense of it all by repeating his own tragedies to a near stranger. It was touching and thrilling, as sick as that sounds; but these are the conversations I live to hear—the kind where you get lucky enough and close enough to see someone's soft, writhing innards from the outside.

I took his hand and squeezed it tight, looked him in the eye for a second, then kissed his stubbly, sad cheek. Standing below the moonlight he cringed as he let a smile smear across his face, and I whispered to him,

"Zander, you can't be happy like this. I can see it just by looking at you. We all can. I mean, it might sound silly, but Life goes on if you try."

I paused as he cut his eyes at me.

"I *know* that's not what you wanna hear coming from someone younger than you, but you can't keep this up. It's sad for you and everyone around you, ya know? It's obvious. We all know every time you nearly fall asleep standing up at work. And you're still so young! All that's in your future is a lot of rehab and wasted years. You've gotta pick yourself up and keep truckin' through the shit." I said with a light laugh. "You have me, Tripp, Dalton, your family up north. You can't just quit. You have to always keep going up. That's the point, isn't it?"

"You're right," he mumbled, as if he'd heard it all before.

"Besides, you can't feel anything worthwhile if you're always numb," I said staring down at the scattered tombstones.

Still holding his hand, Zander squeezed mine back to let me know he heard me while another smile crinkled his face. I looked up at the moon shining down from behind the clouds and felt full, if only for a second.

Before letting go and walking away from him I said, "We gotta get back before people start making up stories about what we're doing out here."

He laughed and nodded in agreeance. As I walked away, he said, "Hey, Lyla?"

I turned to see him looking up at me the way a little boy might look at his mother, and he continued, "Thanks for that. You're a really great girl."

As he walked toward me he held my eyes with his own before leaning in to drop a kiss gently on my forehead. I smiled, and together we wandered back toward the party under the comforting glow of lamp light. Sometimes we just need to be heard, truly heard, until there aren't any words left to fog our bothered heads.

As we came back into the apartment, I noticed everybody was plastered. Dalton was lying on the ground gushing over the band on the radio, My Morning Jacket. He, Tripp, and Scarlette had just gone to see them in concert, and he couldn't stop raving about their transcendental psychedelic rock machine. I noticed a group had gathered outside, so I grabbed another beer before joining them. Walking away from the kitchen I thought I heard someone's voice and turned to look, but saw nothing.

Outside everyone crowded a huge blue hookah with pipes jutting out in every direction—another interesting first of the night. I managed to squeeze myself into a cramped corner while everyone waited for the smoke to start spewing. A tiny girl shoved her way through the bodies and sat down right in front of the hookah and started fiddling away with it. She can't be drunk; I know that much. Her hands were fondling too many delicate pieces with such ease that there was no way she could be. Beside her was a red-headed fellow who actually looked a lot like my own brother—all-American, Guy Harvey-shirt wearin, gun-shootin, football-watchin dude. Tripp walks up behind the two of them and says,

"Hey, did you get it workin, Scarlette?"

"UUUUUGGGGHHHH, noooooo," she said with a breathy sigh, "this was a free gift when I bought a purse, so I have no fucking clue what I'm doing."

Suddenly, it clicked, and I said, "Oh, man, you're Tripp's sister?!"

"Yeah," she said, "I tried to tell you that I liked your tattoos in the kitchen a few minutes ago, but you looked right through me!"

"Awh, damn, I'm sorry, I guess I'm a little drunk. I'm Lyla! Tripp told me that you're going to Annabelle's College next month too, yeah?"

Most of the conversation from that point became a blur. I remember that Scarlette and I were bonding over obscure indie-rock music that nobody else on the patio was interested in. The others were only there for the hookah, which she had gotten to work for five single puffs before it gave out again. Around 4:30 AM, Carmen came out of the abysmal apartment and grabbed my hand, saying,

"Come on babe, you think you're gettin' yourself home?"

We raced down the stairs, playfully dancing in and out of each other's reach the whole way. When we got down to her Mustang I leaned against the trunk to catch the nearly full moon and my breath. With eyes set to the glowing summer moon, I didn't even notice Carmen sneak up beside me until she wrapped her hand softly around my neck. She let out a little chuckle as she leaned in slowly, touching her lips just barely to mine, lingering, and inhaling the last bit of trembling breath left in my lungs. She dove in.

Her taste was tender and delicate. Sticky-sweet, like losing my head in a patch of honeysuckles. Our tongues and bodies swirling around each other's sparked an unspeakable thrill, dormant until an energy of shameless desire breathed into it. She gave my lower lip a tug with her teeth, and as I gently pulled away she only bit down harder.

"Does that hurt?" She asked, letting go of my lip.

With my smiling eyes glued to her emerald greens, I whispered, "There's no blood yet. I don't think you're biting down hard enough."

"Come here," she growled with eyes half shut, pushing me against the back end of her car. "I wanna taste it."

We collided again, this time with my claws tugging on the frayed ends of her tank top while hers held tightly to my neck. I let her sink into me as hard as she could handle, so that she might lick the blood leaking from my purple bite marks. Her sting was oh, so, inviting—enticing, sickening. Wrapped in a dark giggle, she let go of me before draping her arms around my shoulders, whispering

"You look so stunning in the streetlight…"

10:42 AM. Fuzzy red numbers on an unfamiliar screen. Face down on the pillowcase, mind swimming to meet something tangible. I roll over in a queen bed beside the queen siren, tangled in our endless web of white sheets. Groggy from the alcohol and molested by the sunlight in our fresh morning eyes, we laughed lightly together as we woke up to sober reality. We lay with deviant smiles, musing about the antics of the night before, awaiting a much-needed breakfast prepared by her roommate. Eggs, buttered toast, strawberry yogurt, and a peach blunt—in bed, at that. When the clock struck two, we readied for work together and remembered to grab some hangover weed for the rest to smoke before another disorderly evening. To my relief, my car was still parked in that lone, sandy lot from my abandonment the night before. And to my girlish delight, I realized my darkest fantasies with Carmen had blossomed into my own bouquet of decayed innocence.

II: Summer 2K12: The Warning

8:42 AM: Freshmen orientation at Annabelle's College after a grueling four-hour drive across South Carolina with my mom. The kicker is that she wasn't supposed to drive me here, oh, no! A mere two days before this moment I was hurled at a tree going 60 mph in my freshly paid-off Volkswagen Passat. A pearlescent olive green Passat with no insurance to cover a tree-accident, mind you. All I wanted was a quick road trip before continuing a life of concrete classrooms, borderline plagiarized papers, and books full of ideas coated in confusing filigree. It was clearly too much to ask.

This twangadelic-metal-jazz band, Dance Gavin Dance, was playing a show in Pennsylvania eleven hours away from Bloodmoon Beach, so in order to save money I decided to take the trip with a co-worker named Nikki. Since her family was only a short drive away from the venue in Philadelphia, I figured we could split gas and find a free place to crash. Having those bases covered, we left work at 11:18 the night before the show, grabbed some magic mushrooms from a bouncer on the marshwalk, got a case of Shock Top, and headed out on an all-night drive fueled by slight doses of ecstasy—the powder form and the natural form.

At 10:07 AM the next day we were parked at the town McDonald's of Lancaster, Pennsylvania trying to decide on outfits for the day. Our morning sky was colored with a hazy yellow tint and a strange feeling of discomfort from the nearby wasteland of factories. Faces that passed by on the sidewalk were devoid of any warmth; rather they were wary of our obvious foreign nature to the goddamned place. And I *do* mean that God damned that place, because it was nothing but a ghost town dubbed home by poor junkies and Amish recluses. Looking around, we saw nothing but empty dope bags littered across the pavement and their sick addicts looking for more. It was a hopeless pit of mankind, and we should have known right then not to eat our peanut-butter-shroom sandwiches. It was only my second time eating shrooms, but we decided there was no choice other than to split the huge bag directly in half and take a handful each.

"There's no time like now, right?" Nikki squeaked.

"This is the *only* time we've got! Here we go," I said nervously as I held up my sandwich to hers. We tapped crusts, as if to give each other a good send-off into the trip, and waited for the psychedelia to kick in.

"Hey," Nikki said to me after she changed clothes, "we need to get outta this place. And this McDonald's parking lot before I buy some—"

"Yes!" I said before she could finish her thought, "what are your suggestions?"

"Well," she said with a smile, "you know we're in Amish Country, right?"

"What does that mean?" I asked, sliding into my cut-off jean shorts.

"Well the Amish countryside is like, 3 miles east of here. Rolling green hills, horse-and-carriage families, strawberry farms. Sometimes they even have signs in their yards when they've made fresh pies!"

"Noooo waaay, really?! Well, we've got about 6 hours until we have to be at the show. Wanna kill some time out there?"

"Hell yeah!"

"Wait," I paused and cocked my head, "can you drive on shrooms?"

"Girl, I've driven all types of ways before. *You* drove here on Molly! Besides, the shrooms won't hit us for at least another hour."

"Okay, as soon as you think you need a break, lemme know. But I'm gonna be singing outta the sunroof until then."

"That's illegal!" She joked.

"Oh!" I scoffed. "Is that where we draw the line?!"

"Just duck if you see a cop, okay?" She laughed.

We coasted over the knolls of that forgotten land on our

sleepless Sunday afternoon with nothing but Dance Gavin Dance pumping through the speakers. I could tell the shrooms started taking hold by the intense euphoria and disregard I felt in my chest when I screamed their lyrics out of the roof. Another tell-tale sign was the "leaking," as I call it. For some reason, psychedelics make every orifice on the face leak; rogue tears leak down the cheeks, soupy snot from the nose, and drool from the mouth. It's a nasty facial affair, really.

Carriages full of pale faces passed as we drove by, staring with bewildered eyes as we looked back with a genuine mix of perplexity and awe. Snaking through their virgin hills I belted out some of my favorite verses in an emotional eruption, feeling my whole body brace the force of the wind as I raised my arms high out of the roof. I tilted my head back to let the air whip through my golden strawberry hair, shouting the lines,

"'Who has a plan? We hold out our hands in the hope for a free ride to successful endeavors...'"

I paused to look down at Nikki from above, and she stared with both hands on the wheel and both blue eyes on me. Then I roared.

"'Give my regards to all you shady fucks! Thorns in my fucking side! LOYALTY! HONESTY! TRUST! RESPECT! HUMILITY! SINCERITY! WE ARE ALL SO FULL OF FUCKING SHIT! WE ARE ALL! SO! FULL! OF FUCKING! SHIIIIIITTTTT!'"

In a dizzied frenzy, I sunk back into the car to notice Nikki shedding tears after my performance. An uneven voice flowed from her as she said she'd never felt such passion before. On the long, round-about drive back to the show, I smirked to myself while tears continued leaking down my own cheeks and hysteria set into my heart.

At 6:48 PM that night we sat with twelve minutes before the alleged concert was supposed to start. However, it can't be rock n roll without some complications, right? Fuckin' right. The vocalist of Dance Gavin Dance was a junkie like the rest of the poor town we were confined in, so the band had to cancel the show due to his "sickness". That "CANCELED" sign on the door of the bar sent me spinning. Our 24-hour concoction of Molly, insomnia, and shrooms was about to crash into me like the weight of a thousand cares I had forgotten.

"I don't believe it," I said, touching the soggy piece of paper taped to the rusted, iron door. "We came all this way, all this fuckin' way..."

"Awh, it's okay babe," Nikki said in her best motherly voice while rubbing my back, "it just wasn't meant to be."

I was to the point of tears, so Nikki drove me to a quiet back alley nearby to chug beers and bust bottles against the brick walls. Have you ever felt the release that comes with massacring a whole case of empty bottles? You should. My love for the sound of shattered glass blossomed that night and continues blooming to this day. We had to cut that escapade short, though, for we heard police sirens nearby and wanted nothing less than to go to jail in that state.

Drunk on Shock Top, sedation, and sadness, I sat in the passenger seat while Nikki drove to her "parent's" house. At the time, I had no clue that she was bullshitting me. The place we actually ended up was her ex's house—her heroin-addicted ex of seven years with whom she had a failed pregnancy and a failed engagement. Unbeknownst to my sad, sleepy self, I stumbled into what I thought was the comfort of a parent's home and found solace on the living room couch. Within two minutes, I was out.

***

5:55 AM. I was startled awake by some tall, lanky figure tugging on my arm while I was trying to sleep away our horrid day. He tried to pull my shirt off, but even in my stupor, I managed to divert his focus. As if he forgot was he was doing, he suddenly took me by the arm and pulled me outside to jump on a trampoline for half an hour. After he was satisfied with his number of failed backflips, he dragged me back inside to show off old photos of himself and Nikki.

Is this a brother? I asked myself.

Just when I was beginning to gain consciousness and question this boy's identity, he casually shot heroin straight into the swollen vein of his left arm. I swore I was dreaming until Nikki ran out of a hallway crying about something he said, or didn't—how could I fucking know. "What—the fuck—are you doing?!" Nikki wailed through her tears, "I woke up and you weren't there and now there's a needle in your arm?! What the fuck, Kevin!"

"Kevin? Like you're fucking ex, Kevin?" I said to Nikki with wide eyes. She didn't answer, and neither did Kevin. The needle that went into his arm sent that black-tar straight to his blood. He was nodding out on the ground while Nikki was a wreck above him, trying to force some sort of response outta his mouth. It was absolute chaos, and my messy mind couldn't figure out the flow of it all. I thought I was in the safety of her parent's home, only to be enlightened by needles in this guy's slum. I tried desperately to go back to sleep on the couch while the ex-lovers duked out their tragic past above me, but it was a failed effort.

After Kevin sobered up and Nikki simmered down at 9:56 AM, the only thing on my mind was some grade-A marijuana. Coulda been grade-B or C for all I cared. I ended up experiencing my first real-life drive-by drug deal in the ghetto of Pennsylvania. Crestfield was the town, and black was the strange dealer's skin. Brown was the shitty weed, and better was exactly how I felt upon inhaling it.

To my surprise, it was one of the quickest and easiest deals I've ever seen; drive slowly through a black neighborhood. Roll the window down when a man has stared at you for a second too long. Nod your head. He walks over. Whisper what you're searching for. Place money in hand. Drive down the street to the guy holding a basketball. There will not be a basketball goal anywhere in sight. He hands you an already wrapped dimebag. You both nod. Drive away quickly. But not *too* quickly.

Nikki and I decided to end the trip early that day and make an unexpected all-night haul back to Bloodmoon Beach. Without thinking, we left at a wonky hour that put us in Washington DC during rush hour traffic, a mighty fucking racket. Three hours behind schedule, my eyes were pulsating inside my head from the exhaustion setting in. At 1:13 in the morning we still had three hours to go until we reached the beach, and I could feel myself falling asleep as I swerved in and out of white lines on the interstate. I pulled over at a lonely gas station to get coffee and quickly realized I needed some version of sleep. I said to Nikki,

"I'm gonna nap for a little bit, or we're gonna crash. So just gimme thirty minutes, and we'll get back on the road."

She became frantic. "No, we *have* to get home!" She yelped. "We can't just sit here, we've gotta go. We're already so far behind schedule, let me drive while you sleep. I'm not tired. I can drive."

I agreed and nodded off in the passenger's seat while she hurried to the driver side. Unbeknownst to me until that night, Nikki was also a junkie and needed to get home to her crystal meth fix. On a positive note, I gained the sixth sense of always recognizing an addict after my Pennsylvania experience; their character is permanently on their sleeve and sometimes even in the ditch of their elbows.

Within a mere twenty minutes I was jolted awake by a violent thrashing of the car. All I could hear were the sounds of tires squealing and my own screams, yelling, "STOP! STOP, NIKKI, STOP!" I was certain this was the crash to end all crashes and refused to open my eyes. In my mind, we were still on the interstate where there were about to be eight other cars colliding into us at colossal speeds. She seemed to regain control for a second, but suddenly the back tire blew out and sent us spinning into turmoil again. I braced the grips on the side of the door, clenched my teeth together, and fell into a single moment of eerie silence while my car was suspended in mid-air. For that one flash of time, I felt entirely weightless before I heard a final boom,

BOOM,

BOOM.

When the noise quieted and the movement ceased, I opened my eyes. There wasn't much to see through the dusty, chemical fog floating around my head and the horrid ringing in my ears. My shattered windshield, a soft tap away from falling into a thousand shards, was but two inches from my face. The massive tree branch on the other side of the glass threatened to jab its way through to my skull. My knees were jammed into the dashboard, but all I could notice was the way the overhead lights flickered a pale yellow until they faded out entirely.

When the lights went black a sudden rush of panic swept over me as I imagined the car erupting into flames. I used my shoulders to bash into my door until it swung open for me to climb out. Regaining balance and focusing my vision, I noticed I was standing on soft ground, not a concrete interstate like the one we should have been on. There were no other cars around and no street lights either. All I could make out was the front end of my beloved car chewed up by a tree that was twice the size of her. It had to have been 300 years old, probably older, and I oddly felt sorry that we smashed its trunk so badly. Maybe the tree felt the same for me.

This unfortunate event happened in the middle of Nowhere, North Carolina—seriously. We were in a town called Godwind on a forgotten street that featured only a paint-chipped church, two abandoned farm houses, an old cornfield, wild stampeding horses, and that single astonishing tree. The emergency response team was a gaggle of burly men in denim overalls piled into an F-350 pickup, terrified and bewildered at the sight of us and my vehicle wrapped around the only tree in sight. It was unreal for everyone involved.

The strangest part about telling the story to others was the speculation as to why Nikki could have been traveling down that road. We should have been on the interstate the whole way home, but instead found ourselves wrapped up in an old tree trunk on a backroad in the backcountry. I told them I didn't know, though I wondered it myself. Most people at work who knew her better thought that she was trying to commit suicide. That, or searching for her forbidden fruit down forsaken roads. Whatever the case, I'm glad she failed.

***

"I looooooove your dress, girl! And those tattoos, oh *my*! Look at you! A half sleeve right out of high school?!" An enthused woman wearing khakis and a pink striped shirt burst out from behind the blooming rose garden, and I knew she was gunning straight for me. "Thanks," I croaked with sleep still in my voice as she approached. "I'll be covered head to toe one day."

"You think so?" She asked, eyes fully charged from the potion in her coffee cup.

"I know so!"

"Well, gooooood deal! Are you here for orientation?" She

asked.

"Yeah, I'm here for bootcamp," I joked with her. Really, a whole week of orienting to a school the size of one city block felt a little like overkill.

"Oh! Okay! Well, here, take a brochure! Welcome to the 2016 class of Pink Pumas! Don't worry, orientation is loads of fun. Dancing on the quad at 8 in the morning after eating an endless breakfast buffet? Hellooooo!" She bubbled with excitement and ran off, distracted by another group of girls. Note: avoid the coffee muggers.

"Good choice on the hot pink dress," my mom said as we walked away.

"Well, ya know, I thought it might just make the black and blue bruises on my legs look a little less shocking," I said.

"Sarcasm so early, huh?" She joked. "Those meds must be helping."

"Slightly," I said, taking a seat on a marble bench next to her. "Isn't this place gorgeous?"

Annabelle's College, CA 1884. Darbyville, South Carolina. Nestled in the only bustling piece of this tiny city, Annabelle's campus was built more like an exquisite, timeless fortress for us to romp all over. The aging iron fence spiked into the sky, enveloping the entire place in a wall of deep red bricks and black bars. Throw some green in there, too, from the native magnolias, to the towering pine, and the occasional oak. The dormitories, comforting in their antiquity and individuality, have been withstanding the drama of piercing summer heat and snowy winter ice for decades. Wilhelmina Hall, the grand entrance, was decorated with a stained-glass watch tower and a bronze bell to call to memory the days when it would toll. Tales and portraits of spirits past cling to the walls of that Hall, reminding us of the powerful men and women who made this enchanting place possible. My eyes landed on a marbled black fountain, rushing water flowing into a pool surrounded by an endless array of roses. Birds chirp to each other through gaps in the leaves above, singing sweet morning melodies.

And just like that, I'm Home.

"Yeah," my mother agreed, inhaling a deep whiff of southern

charm, "you sure picked a good one." Exhale.

The day of freshmen arrival on a college campus is a riot; we're ready to get the series of cheesy, endless welcoming events over with so that we can socialize with our new-found best friends. On the other hand, the parents are entirely too concerned with what we children will be eating for every meal and what rank the school holds in job security upon graduation. There are chances to meet up with our parents throughout the day during breaks, and I always found my mom apart from the others by the way she looked so cool floating down the sidewalk amidst panicked faces. She knows that her little bird has a strong will to fly, while the others are still trying to decide if they would've done better just to clip their baby's wings.

Right after lunch my mom caught up with me across the crooked concrete. As I was waiting for her, I watched two skinny freshmen walk under an oak tree and light up a couple cigarettes on the edge of campus. Annabelle's was a smoke-free school, so all the doomed nicotine addicts gathered on the sidewalk like ladies of the night. It was sad, really, as if the embarrassment of standing on the street could be enough to kick the habit. Those in charge clearly didn't understand the dynamic of misery's love for company.

I recognized one of the girls immediately as someone whom I had competed against for a scholarship just six months ago. She had distinctive Italian features wiped across her face and dark, curly hair that touched the smallest piece of her slender back. By the time my mom reunited with me she hadn't given the girls much attention other than a quick look of motherly disapproval.

"How's everything going?" She asked.

"Oh, just fine. Kinda boring, and I'm ready to get it over with so I can decorate that blank space in there," I motioned behind to the dorm.

I kept staring at the two girls, trying to recount why I recognized the other one, too. Her trim, white arms exposed themselves to the sun in her mint green tank top, and she carried a black fringe backpack that I could barely see under her mass of brown locks. Before I could carry on with my inspection, my mom scoffed,

"They can't even make it through a single day without a cigarette, huh? They should be out at all the expos they've set up for you guys, but they're just out here smoking the time away."

I laughed at her, slightly agreeing and further reminding her, "Yeah, I know one of them from the Presidential Scholarship competition. Her name's Mia, if I remember right."

Distrust and anxiety consumed my mother's face as she said, "Lyla, you've been surrounding yourself with *those* types of people since you could choose friends. It's time for you to make a change, and you don't need to be hanging out with the same kind of people anymore. You'd be smart to stay away from those two. Okay?"

A more genuine laugh came before I could say, "I can't promise anything! But don't worry, I'm trying for a fresh start too. I'll be fine, Mom. Really."

The back of my head rang with the echo of a deeper laugh that let me know my own Self didn't even believe what I was saying. With a sideways look of uncertainty my mom smiled the two cigarette smokers out of her sight and mind.

After all the anxious parents had been shooed on home, we were fed like cattle and sent to our respective pens before gathering at our first hall meeting as a hodge-podge family. Considering my birth into the world was the only time that I've ever been punctual, it'd be wrong to break that habit now; I walked into the study room on the 2nd hall in Leigh's dormitory, bombarded by a mass of exuberant, judgeless faces. Once again, I was forced to squeeze myself into the back corner of a crowd, and wouldn't you know that I ended up sitting behind the two girls whom I was instructed to stay away from?

The fragrant stench of weed flowed from their high school letterman jackets, a smell too familiar for my nose to ignore. When the Italian turned around she accidentally stared into my eyes too long, and I saw that they were bloodshot from recent smoking. Not only that, but I finally realized where I recognized the second girl from! It was Scarlette! Tripp's sister from the party in Bloodmoon last month.

"Y'ALL!" A staunch voice at the front of the room yelled. Charlotte Rhine, our darling, unstable hall monitor. "If you wanna get through this and out of the room, I need you to pay attention!" Just like a mother. Looked like one, too.

Her efforts fell flat, and the following hour ended up a sad attempt at subduing and informing carelessly excited girls. The minute we were released from that room, I hung back to let the crowd filter out enough so that I could follow behind the thin girls alone. As they left the room snickering to each other, I shouted,

"Scarlette!"

She whirled around to see my smirking face beaming at her and said, "Hey! I don't know you, but hey!" Something about being freshmen amplifies our overwhelming acceptance upon meeting strangers—a seemingly lost quality in the outside world.

I said, "Sure you do, I'm Lyla! We met at Dalton Sawyer's house about a month ago. I worked with your brother Tripp in Bloodmoon Beach. Remember?"

"Oh yeah! I told you that I liked your tattoos and you ignored me!" *That's* what she chose to remember from that night.

I laughed and said, "I didn't mean to!"

"That's so weird that you're here! Of all the possible buildings and all the possible floors that we could have been assigned," Scarlette beamed with a gaping smile.

"Yeah! Wild coincidence, huh? But listen, tell me how I can get in on some of this red-eye action."

She and Mia stared at each other wide-eyed in the middle of the narrow hallway before saying, "What do you mean?'"

"Oh, come on! Your eyes are redder than the devil's dick!" I said. Scarlette didn't like that one bit.

"Hey! Don't be vulgar!" She snapped before forcing a playful smile.

Mia giggled with me and said, "You tryna smoke?"

I nodded my head, said "Duh," and as they looked at each other with twinkles in their eyes it seemed they found the third lady to complete their trifecta. My own roommate, Tammy, has been on the phone with some boy since the moment I met her in our barren dorm room, so I didn't give it a second thought that she was being left out of the first night's christening smoke.

"Alright, we can smoke in my car," Mia said, motioning to follow her down the hall.

"Which room are you two in?" I asked, following the strip of dingy blue carpet.

"I'm not sure," Scarlette said. "What room is it, Mia?"

"222," Mia replied, "directly across from yours."

As we scurried down the stairs and breached the back door to into the summer's night air, I took a deep breath and imagined the charades that the next four years were sure to bring. In the same instant I heard my mother's warning to "stay away from those two."

I can't say that I heeded her words, but what I will say is this: Rebellion hatches in the soul at birth, and it only grows stronger and more infatuated with Chaos in Time. After eighteen years, it would be the highest blasphemy of the natural order to turn back on Rebellion.

III: Summer 2K12: The Loop

"I'm not dancing," Mia said, arms crossed, standing still with a pout.

At 8:38 AM we stood in the wake of Horus's brutal onslaught as his sun rose above our 19th century estate. It's the last day of freshmen orientation, and we're all having a hard time motivating ourselves to do jumping jacks across the dewy grass.

"Come on!" I yelled, flailing my body to the Proclaimers' "I Would Walk 500 Miles" song. "Just roll with it! It's the last day of this shit."

"Thank God!" she said, still refusing to dance.

Being the only group of 200 girls on such a pristine campus had a feeling of secrecy, a what-happens-in-orientation-stays-in-orientation vibe.

But every
single
day
for a week
we've been doing this same non-stop nonsense from 8 AM until 6 PM. The time in between our morning, afternoon, and evening sweat shops was filled with an endless barrage of classes on collegiate to-do's and not-to-do's, but the defiant minds of young ladies can't be bothered with the delegations.

Feeling a little brain-dead and thirsty for the games to be over, we were thankful when they cut the blaring radio. A squeaky blonde shouted out a corny "seize the day" speech over a battered megaphone, and the morning sweat shop was complete.

Disperse.

"Only like, four more seminars and we're home-free," I said to Mia, panting from the jazzercise. Pulling out my soggy green pamphlet, I read the options for the rest of our day.

"It looks like there's one called, 'It Could Happen to You,' which I'm not so sure sounds like a good idea."

We stared at our crinkled brochures together, secretly wishing for someone to whisper the word, "hooky".

"Hey, I found you!" Scarlette yelped from behind us. She was still in the sweats she fell asleep in the night before.

"I tried waking you up for breakfast, but you wouldn't move! Did you just get up?" Mia asked, slightly perturbed.

"Yeah," Scarlette laughed, brushing mahogany curls out of her face. "There was no way I could listen to that 500 Miles song again."

"Good thinking!" I said, returning my attention to the schedule.

"Y'all trying to figure out which ones to go to?" Scarlette asked.

"Yeah, there's one right after lunch where they're showing a documentary on the poverty line." I said.

"Wait, what's the poverty line?" Scarlette asked.

"You know, like, the line in the financial system where everybody under it makes such little money that they're considered to be living in poverty? It's a ridiculous percentage for a first world country like America. Right, Mia? How would you say it?"

"Something like that. Doesn't sound like my cup of tea, though," she shrugged. "The seminar called 'It Could Happen to You' is a theatre drama acted out by orientation leaders. I think I'm gonna go to that one," she said with a grin.

"Why don't we just call it even and not go to any of them?" Scarlette said.

Bingo.

"We've been to enough of these things in one week, and it's a beautiful day! I say let's start the weekend early." She suggested.

"Ohhhh, that's tempting. I like where your head's at!" I said

"Mmmmmm," Mia paused, "nope! I'm still going. Maybe we can go exploring through backroads or something after lunch and poverty talk?"

"Yeah, let's do that," Scarlette said, turning to me. "How 'bout you, Lyla? Whatchu think?"

"I think that I'm totally all for ditching the rest of the day. But it'd be kinda cool to see the poverty line documentary if all we've got is time to kill between lunch and dinner."

"Perfect! But right now I desperately need to go to the Kangaroo and get cigarettes. Wanna come with me?"

"Didn't you and Mia just buy some yesterday?"

"Yes, but she bought three, and I only bought one. What's your point?" She asked, digging in the pockets of her black sweatpants to find her keys.

"You smoked a whole pack between yesterday and this morning?"

"And, boy, could I smoke more!" Heavy on the cigarettes since sixteen, just like her roommate, Mia, and just like my roommate, Tammy.

"Damn, so I'm the only one, huh? My roommate is seventeen years old, yet, still finding ways to smoke cigarettes."

"You'll be a member of the smoker's club soon enough," she joked. "It's inevitable, if you're gonna be taking me on cigarette runs."

When we reached the parking lot where her black Jeep Liberty was parked, she tossed the keys at me and said,

"Do you maybe wanna drive? I got in this real bad accident last year and I've hated driving ever since. My mom also just got me this car, like, a week ago and I'm not comfortable in it yet."

Remembering the fresh wound in my heart carved out by the loss of my Volkswagen, my eyes lit up. A car to drive, but no gas or insurance to pay?

"Hell yeah!" I said. "I'd love to. I'll take ya wherever you wanna go, you name it."

"Will you?!" She asked with such disbelief. "Oh, good! You can drive my car anytime you want. In fact, when we go anywhere, you can just be my personal driver," she said with relief beaming in her eyes.

Despite her choice to sport sweatpants and an old gymnastics t-shirt I caught my first glimpse of Scarlette's desire for a glamorously rugged lifestyle. I saw that she carries her cigarettes not in the cardboard box they come in, but rather in a rose-etched antique case of her own. A delicate diamond and ruby bracelet hung loosely on her pale wrist, and the king of boots, Doc Marten, covered her feet in ox-blood leather. Given the option, I have a feeling she'd never labor the monotony of driving herself anywhere again. If this were the 1920s, she'd have a chauffeur named Winston that came running at the snap of her dainty fingers, providing as many vanilla Cokes and cigarettes that her thin body could handle. As I opened the driver's side door I think we both realized that I was to be her modern-day Winston, in a way, and she my degenerate glamour queen.

"Awh, shit," Scarlette said as she got in the car.

"What is it?"

"It says we've only got three miles to empty," she said, pointing to the screen above our heads. "Looks like we'll have to wait to do anything until Mia can drive, cuz I've only got enough for cigarettes and a gallon of gas."

"Good thing the Kangaroo's a block away."

"Well you have two options here." She said. "You can either pump my gas or go get the cigarettes so we can speed this up a bit."

"Ummmm, I'll pump gas, I don't know anything about cigarettes," I said.

"Shit!" She said, checking her pockets thrice over. "I forgot my ID, so it looks like *you're* the one getting the cigarettes. I'll get gas."

"Ohhhh, my first cigarette purchase" I said, pulling up to the pump. "What do I say?"

"Newport shorts in the box," Scarlette said, "don't get the soft pack."

It wasn't long after officially buying my first pack of smokes when Scarlette and I subjected ourselves to disheartening knowledge about the poverty line. Somber from such a heavy topic, we all rushed to the dining hall when the clock struck "dinner". One of the most captivating spots on campus, the Swan Dining Hall, showed off its crooked brick stones that lined the rose-dotted terrace. It's like being at home as the first class of 1889 the way the hall held on to her original look from the glory days. The doors are still standing tall with fourteen feet of cherry maple wood and ornate iron knobs that feel like you're twisting your way into a brilliant ballroom. Ancient chandeliers hung from the vaulted ceilings and rich white molding decorated the creamy green walls. Once inside the cafeteria, though, the high of stepping into a different era dies amidst the shoving of elbows reaching for flavorless spaghetti noodles. They sure tried their best to pull off an Italian meal, but it seems grandma's lovin' was absent from the kitchen.

"Can you believe they feed us this shit? And call it Italian?" Mia sneered. "My dad could cook better spaghetti in handcuffs!" Her hardcore Guinea father is rumored to make batches of the most exquisite pasta this side of the Atlantic, so we couldn't really fault her for being picky.

I laughed and said, "Hey, it's better than the slop they feed 'em in jail, right?"

She cut her eyes at me as they rolled into the back of her head all in the same motion. Mia's bad attitude was impeccable and unwavering, but somehow, rather amusing.

"Yeah. Riiiight," she sighed.

As I scooped my limp noodles and vegetarian marinara, I heard a voice say, "What's for dinner, y'all?" It was Scarlette, coming in late from smoking her cigarette and standing tippy-toed trying to see above everyone.

"Pseudo-Italian," Mia replied. "Or there's hotdogs and chili on the other side if you want that."

"*Nobody* wants that!" I laughed.

"Ick! No way, I think I'll make a grilled chicken salad," Scarlette said.

She scurried away to the salad bar, and I braced myself for the nearly impossible feat of finding us a table. Everyone wants their own seven-seater table to talk to only two or three girls. I guess it's some way of coping with the stress of such a huge transition and a mass influx of unfamiliar faces. We tried to be social by sitting with new people every day; we almost always had to if we want to eat during the allotted hour we're given. Realizing the pickings were slim I chose a place with some of the athletes where we all got the pleasure of learning that cliques in high school perpetuate themselves even in college. These girls couldn't be bothered to introduce themselves after we told them our names, and their body language evolved to shut us out entirely within a mere three minutes. We took their hints, shoveled food into our mouths as fast as we could, politely parted ways, and marched back out into the cooling southern air.

There's a ritual in the smoking community that involves a cigarette break after every meal consumed, and it seems I've grown accustomed to it in the last week. We'd leave the dining hall to walk over to the same old Oak tree that I saw Scarlette and Mia standing under during orientation. There was an oddly placed, yet useful concrete step that we called "the stairway to nowhere" beside the tree's roots. While they smoked their cigs on the stoop, I pulled out a tiny wooden box that held a bit of weed and a tiny metal pipe cleverly painted to look like a cigarette. I shoved the nose of the pipe into the box, packed it full of weed, and starting smoking it right there on the street. I felt Scarlette and Mia staring until Scarlette finally blurted out,

"Is that weed?!"

I smiled without confirmation and said, "If you smoke in public, people assume that it can't be weed. They think that you won't commit a crime in broad daylight with everyone watching. Ya know?"

Mia beamed and said, "I want a hit!" I handed it over to her before Scarlette could ask. She did anyways, and I gladly shared.

A little high, Mia said, "Hey, you guys wanna go for a drive through East Side Heights to see what's around?"

East Side Heights is a neighborhood directly across from our campus that used to house Old Money millionaires in Darbyville's safer area. Now it's a blend of lower-class tenants, the president of Annabelle's College, doctors, lawyers, businessmen, retirees, and regular Joe-Blows. The architecture was stunning, reflecting an era of Southern decadence in which home-building was an art that mirrored the souls living within the walls--lavish vaulted porches that wrapped around the homes paired with iron work that could make any blacksmith drool. Of course we agreed to a tour. The only problem was that we wanted to roll a blunt for the road, but we just finished the last bit in my one-hitter.

Despite the disappointment we were gonna head out anyways. At the last second when we were walking toward Mia's car, I said,

"Wait! I have an idea!" Their eyes questioned my scheme, but I continued, "I know where my roommate keeps her weed. It's shitty reggie, but it's a lot of it and she won't notice if I take a little bit."

I thought that they were going to scold me for thinking of stealing my own roommate's ganja, but they looked at me excitedly and said, "Yes! Go, go!"

I ran back to my dorm in Leigh Hall and, luckily, Tammy was absent. I opened up her desk to find the weed still sitting in a corner behind some pencils, whispering "take meeeeeee." I did, then swiftly ran back down to let my conspirators know that the game plan was a success.

We stopped by the Kangaroo to grab a peach White Owl cigar—the only brand of cigar that Scarlette knew how to roll a blunt with, and she would *only* smoke blunts. However, this particular Kangaroo didn't carry them, so we had to settle for an Old Dutchmaster cigar. Mia and I were keener on glass-pipe smoking, but we also weren't nitpicky. We simply thought that blunts were an easy way to waste a lot of precious greenery. But getting high is getting high is getting high. Scarlette always combatted our argument by saying,

"I'd rather be stupid stoned than half high. So I smoke blunts and only blunts." At least the girl knew what she wanted, right?

7:39 PM. As Mia's beaten down Camry cruised through sharp turns and perfectly groomed lawns it fogged up with dirty reggie smoke, and I felt an equally dirty smirk unfold across my face. It was prime-time for seeing that golden hour of setting sunlight bounce off the gigantic trees. I had never seen such thick forests of lush green brush like this before, because Bloodmoon Beach doesn't have many varieties of trees. In the upstate, though, anything could grow. And it did.

We whipped around a corner that greeted us with a tiny wooden sign and an arrow that pointed to the forest reading, "Nature Trail". It was like we all saw the sign in unison, and before Scarlette or I could say anything, Mia screamed,

"NATURE TRAAAAAIIIIILLLL!!!" and quickly cut to the grassy curb. In the back without a seatbelt, I skirted to the opposite side of the car from sheer velocity and yelled,

"Whooooaaa, Nelly!"

Mia parked and said, "So, we goin' in?"

"Of course we are!" Scarlette and I said at the same time.

We got out and found a small clearing in the thicket that led us to a wooden bridge suspended above a rushing creek. How pristine, I thought, to stumble upon this little piece of Eden so effortlessly.

Some of the trees were tacked with little plaques about what species they were and it was clear that this hideout was probably used as some sort of field-trip for eager elementary schoolers. In that moment, we were the eager elementary kids, and I knew we were having a much better time than all the girls stuck back at Annabelle's.

We had a piece of the blunt leftover from our abrupt stop on the side of the road, so we decided to light it up with the Earth. She seemed to condone, because the wind made no difficulties in our re-lighting it, and the heat seemed to disappear as the sun set off behind the mountains somewhere. We passed that last bit of weed underneath a canopy of leaves, and the once golden light that flooded the forest floor was now dimming to a deep blue. Any minute now, the paths would become so dark that we wouldn't be able to find our way back. Not to mention the mosquitos were fond of Scarlette's high-metabolism bloodflood. The poor girl was covered in bumps, so it seemed to be quitting time. We floated along the clay-colored ground back to the car, and the magic of watching the fireflies light up the forest was captivating enough to get lost in the woods all over again.

On our trek back to Annabelle's we were unaware that this ritual of driving through unfamiliar territory with a lit blunt was to become something much more than we planned. It was the first time that we had created a means of stress release from a day of heavy working with our minds, and it was nowhere near the last. Most every day that we could get our hands on some weed, we took off into the sunset after dinner to listen to music and ride. Just ride. Sometimes we couldn't find any weed, and that was all fine and well, but we couldn't do without the drive. We passed our precious Time by wandering through nature trails or dirty backroads, busy bouncing ideas off of one another. We were discovering the town and its many nooks and crannies that would shape us for years to come all while getting high on pure exploration of mind and matter.

Ever heard of a baby born by three women? Behold, the sacred Blunt Loop—budding brainchild of we manic wanderers.

***

A week later and we're up to our bloodshot eyeballs in assignments that can take all night to do right. Scarlette and Mia chain-smoke in their cars to make it through while I usually try to find a secluded nook on the third floor of the library to wallow in my academic misfortune. During the first few days of classes I even visited one of my greatest friends, Angel, in near tears about how much I had to read in one night. It was something like, 156 TEXTBOOK PAGES, and my head simply couldn't fathom why professors wanted to torture us kids like this. We are, after all, only kids. Or, at least they keep reminding us that we are.

In middle school they told us to choose a career path, and instead of asking, "Why?" we said "Okay, I wanna be a doctor. No, I wanna be a vet. Today I like sharks, let's do marine biology. Wait, no, I think I wanna be stay-at-home mom. Oh? You don't get paid for that? Never mind, let's go back to doctor."

An absurd amount of standardized tests later, we all find ourselves in this hyper-academic collegiate world that doesn't truly expose us to the Life lessons that we need to understand in order to be better humans. College certainly feels like a game of trying to figure out how to avoid responsibility rather than spending time actually understanding the given information. Quite frankly, that's the only way to get it all done in the time that we have, and nearly every college student could agree with me on that matter. Too much of anything is still too much. And college is much too much, much too much.

Mia and I both chose Creative Writing majors for our first path at Annabelle's, and luckily we had the same introductory writing course. We bonded over our love for literature and anything stemming from the written arts. Not to mention, we both loved tattoos. We gushed over having Harry Potter inspired work on our bodies—she with the Golden Snitch on her ribs and I with the Floo Powder's green flames on my arm. Our shared taste in alternative Indie bands like Say Anything, The Shins, and The Gorillas bridged any sort of personality gaps that there might have been, as music tends to do. Our dispositions were pretty similar anyways; that was obvious in our excessive use of crass language and deviant sexual humor. It tied us together in a way that Scarlette and I hadn't yet been knotted, and for a while it seemed that Mia and I would become like two peas in a pissy little pod.

Our last class of the day was our writing course, and it ran right up until dinner time at 5:20 in the afternoon. With only ten girls in the class, it got rather boring. One of the quirks I noticed being at college was that classroom engagement is a pointless modern formality; in the days of Socrates, Plato, and Aristotle, classroom settings were coveted because powerful minds could come together to throw their ideas back and forth to one another. In our world, nobody speaks up or joins a formative conversation because the only thing most students are worried about is reaching the other side of graduation in the least painful manner they can manage. Thus, very little conversation ever took place in the classroom; there was simply a dialogue between professors and the very few young philosophers still trying to uphold the ancient ideal, and I felt Mia and I were part of that.

Mia, however, is much more concerned with her academic reputation than Scarlette and I ever could be. You think we spend time stressing over which clubs to fill our precious two hours of free time? Oh, no! Our Time's spent chasing the feeling of becoming like wild animals that had escaped captivity; eighteen years of incessant parenting were suddenly and excitedly thrown away in exchange for sleepless nights, bad decisions, and zero need for approval from any authority type. No curfew, no need to tell anyone where we were going, and nobody to tell us whether or not our ideas were bad ones. It was a paradoxical feeling of weightlessness and decisive heaviness, as if the ropes that tied us to the anchors had finally been severed and we were left to swim out of our shackles alone; as frightening as it sounds, it's a cut that has never felt so goddamn intoxicating until now.

Speaking of cuts, my own roommate Tammy sure did need one. She's just barely 17 years old, and in the grand scheme of things it doesn't seem like one year would be such a gap from we 18 year olds, but this girl seriously needed that extra year before she came to Annabelle's. She was from a small town right outside of Darbyville that was essentially a redneck-ghetto-hybrid village. The kind of place whose drug of choice was cat-litter-made meth and whose beer of the night was Busch Light. Not a very enticing people, in my mind.

She's much shorter and plumper than me—a mere 5'1" in comparison to my almost 6' height. Her curly blonde hair touched the top of her shoulders and even showcased some pink streaks in the back. She had a tramp stamp and a couple of other poorly done house tattoos stuck to her body, and her Envy always tried to rag on the tattoos that I have. Her voice is sweet and southern, giving the false impression that she would treat you with some hospitality. Unfortunately for me, THIS. GIRL. IS. FUCKING. CRAZY. My mom should have told me to stay away from her instead.

I swear it's a constant struggle to get along with her; I smoked my only weed with her, I took walks around the block with her while I saw my first fireflies, and I even took her on outings with Scarlette and Mia. For a short period of time, it seemed that we would all be a nice quartet, but the three of us very quickly noticed her needy, self-centered, and destructive habits.

She almost always has a different boy in our room with her, and she barely ever goes to class. I mean, fuck, I'm on track to the Dean's List and I feel like the only way I'm making it is by going to class and turning in assignments. She won't even do that! The day I knew that we weren't gonna get along anymore, I walked into our room to see her making out with some dude on MY bed.

"What the fuck!?" I shouted. She wasn't startled. With his boney body straddling her, she peeked her face out from under him and giggled.

"What is it Lala?" She always tried to call me Lala, like a song. And I fucking hated it.

"Don't call me that, and get off my bed! Last thing I need is mystery semen on my pillow while I sleep." I cut my eyes at the boy, but I could barely even see his face behind his mess of a hairdo. Some scrawny emo-lookin' dude. Faded lime green hair that covered up most of his acne-ridden face. He didn't utter a word, and I could tell that they were both pretty stoned. They slowly got up and moved over to her elevated loft-bed, pretending nothing happened. That night when the boy left after hours of my trying to study, there was definite tension between Tammy and me. This was not how I envisioned my "new start" at college, so I tried to have a conversation with her to really dig at her heart.

"Tammy, I can feel that there's some shit between us, and I'd really rather not have our freshman year be this way."

"Well maybe if you weren't such an overbearing bitch, we wouldn't have any problems." This was outta left field, because she almost never saw or interacted with me since I was in class until 6:00 every day. Not to mention she was too busy making out with little boys during her supposed class time.

"Hey, there's no need for hostility! I want to know you. I want us to be as close as roommates can be, because we're gonna be sharing this space for a long time. I don't want this to be hard, but if you don't wanna at least try, it'll be much harder for you."

She turned around from her desk, looked me in the eye, and said, "You know, I don't really want any hostility either. Let's talk."

Success! Or, so I foolishly thought... She went on to ramble about how she feels left out of the group, because I'm clearly closer with Mia and Scarlette than I am to her. I thought her feelings were a little out of place, because it wasn't like we picked each other. We didn't even know each other's names before we met on orientation day. It was more like, "SURPRISE! YOUR ROOMMATE'S AN IMMATURE, SELF-CENTERED CHILD! HAVE FUN WORKING THROUGH THIS ONE!" I guess I just had to roll with it, right? I told her that we were roommates, and that we weren't supposed to be best friends. We were simply deemed "compatible" based on some bullshit personality test and were forced to make the best of it. Annabelle's had a very strict policy on roommate changes, so we had to come to an understanding—or else.

By the end of our conversation I felt that I finally got my message through to her; that I wasn't here to make her feel bad or to leave her out. We're here to get a degree and try to have as much fun with whatever spare time we have. I said I'd be there for her if she needed a friend, but not to expect so much out of a college roommate arrangement. I went to sleep that night feeling like I had broken through to the other side of her egocentric tendencies. The next day, though, she acted as if all of that was forgotten, and her instinctive animosity began rearing its ugly head yet again.

IV: Autumn 2K12: The Steal

It's a constant war with the Universe to stay High, and we were winning every battle. Our friendship and what we spent doing with it was obvious to everybody by week four, and suddenly the three of us were dubbed "Lyla and the Skinnies," like the badass band of beauties we think we are. We stand out—that's for certain. In a sea of proper, pristine southern belles we're probably the only three girls on campus that look like we live out of Goodwill, and we own it. We could take a 2XL men's winter sweater and make it look like we should be posing for the cover of Vogue. Scarlette kept a copy of their huge annual fashion issue lying on the cluttered floor of their room, so I should know.

Mia and I were spending a lot of time without Scarlette. The two of us got together to work on writing assignments while Scarlette grinded her hours away in the art studios. There were many a night when I sat inhaling second-hand cigarette smoke in Mia's passenger seat while both our pens fought fervently with our papers. Mind you, the car didn't move; Mia simply couldn't chain smoke inside her dorm, so the cars became second homes to work on our writing. Scarlette always knew that if we weren't in our rooms she could find our butts parked in that teeny tiny Camry. And most every night that we cooped ourselves in there, we could see her curls coming at us in the dark from a block away.

Scarlette's jealousy set in right before Mia left to go home for the weekend. She worked at a restaurant in her hometown to supplement her smoking habits, naturally. Sometimes Mia and I would joke about how we were the same soul in two separate bodies, and Scarlette just cut her eyes and growled,

"You guys are *not* the same person..." under her breath.

Anytime she caught Mia and me without her she had this sneaking suspicion that she was missing out on something good, and that we were purposely leaving her out of it. A trend, huh? Not the case! Mia and I merely meshed together so well in this early college daze.

When Mia left on a Friday morning to go peddle tables all weekend, Scarlette saw an opportunity to rightfully suck me into her vortex and away from Mia's. Everybody knows that in a group of three girls, there's always one that exists to get her feelings hurt and ego bruised. Scarlette saw that fate in her future, and she'd be damned if she let it happen.

Fridays were short days for everyone, THANK GOD, ALLAH, YAWEH, ODIN, BUDDHA, SHIVA, KALI, ETC. If we had classes at all, they were done before lunch. As we watched Mia leave while we scarfed down sub sandwiches in Swan Hall, Scarlette asked,

"So, whatchu gonna do all weekend?"

"Well, I've got some stuff I need to read for American Lit, but I'll probably do that in the library on Sunday night. You got anything to do in the studio?"

"Nope. Well, yeah, but I'm not doing it. It'll get done before it's due… You tryna get high all weekend, or what?"

"Uhhhhh, when am I *not* tryna get high all weekend? You wanna see what Tammy's got left in her drawer?"

"Sure! But I just bought a big bag of weed when I went home to Aiden last weekend, so I think we should be set."

"Well, you can't ever be too sure."

Up until I came to Annabelle's, I had never bought or seen weed in such gross quantities. I merely bought a gram or two from some stoner in high school for myself to enjoy. At the very most, I bought an eighth and thought that I'd never be able to smoke it all. But I'm learning that people like to have a lot, just to have it.

"I've got six grams, so we can add whatever you grab from Tammy's to the mix. That's twelve blunts! Maybe thirteen!" Scarlette squealed.

"Damn! You were serious when you said it was a big bag!"

"I'm always serious about my weed," she said. And she is. For a second I felt a little guilty that I was gonna smoke all this with her, because that's at least $60 worth! But if she was offering, you better believe I was taking. It's the chauffeur's salary.

"Okay, you done eating?" I asked, looking at her limp, half-eaten sub. "Let's go wander around before the sun sets and we get too lost."

"Yeah, let's go," and without skipping a beat, she was up and darting toward the garbage chute.

Even though we had been together for less than a month, it was already second nature for me to hop behind the wheel of Scarlette's Jeep. She kept her word of letting me drive wherever we went, and I looked forward to it, quite honestly. We drove across the way to our regular Kangaroo where we became familiar faces to look for in the night. One of the nicest cashiers, Miss Amy, was a stoutly middle-aged woman with dark black ringlets of dyed hair falling over her face. Her eyes were just as dark, but so full of a welcoming warmth—you could tell she was a mother. When we strolled in we heard her sweet, buttery voice call out,

"Well hey there, Miss Dutchie!" She was clearly talking to Scarlette, because I had no clue what that meant.

Scarlette smiled and said, "Heyyyyy, I'm back for more. I'll need... six? Yeah, six is good for now. Oh, and a pack of Newport shorts in the box, please."

She had bought so many Dutchmaster cigars in three weeks that Miss Amy decided to give her a moniker for it! I'm usually outside pumping gas like the Winston that I am, so this was a treat. From that moment forward Miss Amy always made a point to ask where Miss Dutchie was if she wasn't hooked to my arm.

We got back to the safety of Annabelle's secluded parking lot and rolled the blunts, because we were untouchable there. The Campus Safety at our school wasn't any sort of police force; they were simply there to make sure that we didn't get raped or mugged by the wandering homeless of Darbyville—not to enforce any "real world" laws. Plus, Annabelle's was a private school, and the police legally weren't allowed on the grounds unless our Campus Safety officers called them. Can I get a "fuck yeah" for loopholes in the system?

"I'm gonna roll three blunts now so we can just smoke them

back to back without having to stop, sound good?" She asked me.

"Sounds good to me," I said while I tried to attune my ears to the rap music coming from Scarlette's speakers. She obsessed over J. Cole while I obsessed over indie rock and heavy metal. It's an interesting blend of styles, to say the least.

"Here," she said as she passed me the baggie of weed, "break this down while I bust all the guts out of the gars."

Guts: (noun) nasty bits of tobacco that cigars are packed with. We exchange those flakes for tastier green ones.

Or, so I thought.

When I stuck my eager fingers into that bag I realized how spoiled I had been living in Bloodmoon. Our dealers were mainly surfer-brah white dudes who hung tapestries of Bob Marley in their living room while "Fast Times at Ridgemont High" played on repeat. Those guys only deal with dank—the east coast weed smoker's term for damn good weed. The highest grade of crystalized greenery you could get your hands on was the only type of weed I had smoked until I got to Annabelle's. When I expected to grab fluffy clouds of bud and instead got a brick of brown flakes, I was confused. The strips of weed that I pulled out of this bag were as dry and odorless as I had ever experienced, and quite frankly, I didn't know what to do when she commanded me to break it down.

"Uuuummmm…"

"What is it?" She asked.

"How do I break this down!?"

"Oh, honey," she said like a crooning mother, "look, you pull it apart in layers, like this…" And as she tried to give me a tutorial, seeds started falling out of her hands. Seeds were not only rare to find in Bloodmoon weed, but they were valuable, because if you got the right type of seed you could potentially grow your own.

"Whoa! Look at all those seeds!" I said with excitement. I started searching for the ones that fell to the ground when she said,

"No no, you don't want those! Seeds in shitty weed just mean that it's *really* shitty weed. You can't grow anything with them." Disappointed, I sat back in my seat while she said, "Okay, you got it? Just kind of rub it between your fingers until it flakes off."

"Uh, okay, I'll give it a shot." It took me way too fucking long to break this stuff down, and trust me, I haven't gotten any better at it in the years since. By the time she had three cigars busted down, gutted, and licked, I still had a while to go with the Mexican Cheech she assigned me.

"Oh, here, lemme finish that," she said, "you hold these gars so I don't lose them." I swear this girl is like a black hole. She could lay her fingers on something and suddenly that was the last you'd ever see of it.

Ever.

"You gotta watch for the stems, too," she said, "because if we tried to roll a blunt with what you've done, we'd have holes poking through all the gars! Oh, and the seeds. You don't wanna smoke a seed. It'll give you a terrible headache."

In that moment, the song "Colt 45" finally made sense to me. If you don't already know how it goes, I'll let you in on a cult favorite! The chorus goes like this,

"A Colt 45 and two ZigZags! Baby, that's all we need. We can go to the park after dark and smoke that tumbleweed. And as the marijuana burns, we'll take our turns, singin' them dirty rap songs. Stop and hit the bong like Cheech and Chong, sell tapes from here to Hong Kong. So roll, roll, roll my joint, PICK OUT THE SEEDS AND STEMS! Feelin' high as hell flyin' through Palmdale, skatin' on Dayton rims."

PICK OUT THE SEEDS AND STEMS. Who knew? I sure didn't.

After she stuffed three Dutchies with this stemmy, seeded weed she gave me the go-sign, and we were off. Driving down East Main Street with our windows wide-open, Scarlette said,

"Hey, truth or dare?"

"Dare," I said without question.

"I dare you to scream at that old man walking up there."

"What old man?" Sure enough, there was a scraggly looking gent moseying down the sidewalk on my side of the road.

"Wait, just yell?" I asked. She thought for a quick second.

"I want you to yell 'Take me hostage with your sausage!'"

"What?!"

"Don't make me double dog dare you!" She threatened.

I threw my head out of my window, looked him dead in his stoic, cold face, and yelled,

"TAKE ME HOSTAGE WITH YOUR SAUSAAAAAAAAAAAAGE!!!!!!"

It all happened so fast that I didn't even get to see the poor guy's reaction! Probably the most action he'd been begged for in years, though, so I'm sure I would have seen a nasty grin on his mug. Scarlette squealed with laughter in the passenger seat and managed to gasp long enough to say,

"Holy shit, I didn't think you'd actually do it!"

"You were gonna double dog dare me, and I couldn't let you think I was a pussy!"

"Hey!" She yelled as she stopped laughing. "Don't use that language, I don't like it. It's gross."

Odd set of standards.

We rode through East Side Heights as usual, but after we killed the first blunt we decided to venture far outside our comfort zone. Unknown territory is future found homeland, after all. We began riding through backwoods country roads that hid small towns with names like Clifton, Glendale, Clifdale, and Cowpens—a proud revolutionary war site, by the way! I remembered the name from the textbooks we read for ten years about the same old wars. Cowpens even painted a mural on one of their few downtown shops that depicted the battling Rebels and Redcoats! How novel.

"Man, this sure does feel like home," Scarlette said. There was nostalgia in her voice, and I could tell she was missing her own tiny town.

"I feel like I'm in a movie," I said as we passed an old rickety trailer with 6 different mutts running around in the endless grass. "I've never seen anything like this."

With the concrete tourist scenery that Bloodmoon had burned into my memory, my mind was wide open to replacing it with this quiet country. It's such a simple, slow-motion life that these people lived. Their homes were telling of the poor, early 1900s southern architecture by the way their doors were falling out of their frames and their iron railings were peeking out of chipped white paint to show their true blackness underneath. Their houses all had the same triangles-on-top-of-boxes look, that is, if they weren't the double wide trailers that we so often passed. Pickup trucks in every shade of red rust and dim blue were parked next to old sheds and older barns. There are grizzly country boys with their heads under the hoods of those beloved trucks, wearing flannels and stained blue jeans whose pockets held greasy, tattered towels. We drove under and over train tracks, through an old cobblestone one-way tunnel, and across a termite-ridden bridge with an ominous sign that read "WEIGHT LIMIT 2 TONS". There was a new experience around every corner, it seemed, and I was spellbound.

J. Cole was still pumping through the speakers, and I found that my ears grew accustomed to the beats with each new track.

"What's the name of this one?" I asked Scarlette.

"It's called 'Get Free'. One of my favorites! It's never been on an album. He just chose to do this mash-up, and it's perfect. Isn't it?"

"Yeah, it has a nice island feel. And the lyrics! The lyrics, man…"

Once we took the last couple puffs of the very last blunt things started to get dark. By "dark," I mean that the sun was setting, the roads were narrowing, and the GPS signal was fading. All the quaint houses began looking like facades that hid torture chambers, and I realized that we were fucked when the GPS coldly recited, "Signal lost."

I thought to myself for one more rap song, then decided to speak up.

"I don't wanna scare you, but I don't really know where we are," I said to Scarlette.

"It's okay, we have enough gas to drive our way outta it, right?" She asked.

I looked down at the gauge, and to my dismay, we were less than a quarter of a tank away from empty. Her Jeep burned through gasoline like no other car I've been in, so this was anything but comforting.

"Uhhh, not really…"

"Shit, are you serious?"

"You tell me! Look at that gas gauge!" I said, getting flustered.

"You know this car as well as I do!" Scarlette said, equally as flustered.

We passed a sign that read "River Road," and I remembered seeing that same name somewhere near our college.

"Hold the phone," I said, "I think I recognize the name on that sign, so we're gonna try following that road."

Scarlette calmed down and continued gazing out of the passenger window. I, on the other hand, was stuck imagining a cannibalistic scene from *The Hills Have Eyes*.

We reached a stop sign at the end of River Road, and I was disheartened, for we were nowhere near our familiar East Main Street.

"Well," I said to Scarlette at the stop sign, "what do you think?"

"You still don't know where we are?"

"Not in the slightest."

"Hmmmm." She looked to the left, then to the right. "Go left," she said.

I turned left, and for every stop sign that I came to after that, I *kept* turning left. Eventually (and thankfully) we found our way back home. After at least six left turns we were dumped right out to a road with a sign that read "DARBYVILLE" and an arrow pointing to home. We followed it all the way to the end, and sure enough, we were hit smack dab in the face with an intersection that connected us to East Main Street. That night ushered in the creation of the cardinal Blunt Loop rule of exploration: when in doubt, always turn left.

As I pulled into the closest parking space I could find, Scarlette said, "You know, I didn't wanna say anything, but I was kinda worried back there. I thought we were gonna be stranded out in the middle of nowhere."

"Really? You seemed so calm while I was imagining grandma chasing us, foaming at the mouth!"

"Yeah, well, maybe let's not do that much exploring after dark," she laughed.

"Agreed," I said, staring through the windshield.

"Hey?" Scarlette said, "You okay?"

"What do you mean?" I asked.

"You seem a little off. Not so chipper today, or something. Kinda somber. You sure you're alright?"

I didn't respond.

The last tinge of orange sunlight was burning away on the horizon, and I was hypnotized by the way the leaves above us had faded to black.

Speak.

"I don't know, man, I've been in a weird place ever since we saw that poverty line documentary."

"Oh…" she looked away. "What's got you feeling like that?"

"Did you notice that there were at least fifty chairs set up and only seven people showed? Us included?"

"Yeah?"

"It's just sad, you know? I think it's a direct representation of how important this issue is to everyone. Here, and in the rest of our society."

"You know," she paused, eyes searching for the right words, "that's what it's like in Aiden, for most people. It's the poorest town, because most of the farms aren't really in business anymore. When you ride around it's a loop of seeing the same poor black guys in tattered white tshirts and pants too big for them. But is it really that big of a deal? I mean, isn't America better off than most?"

"Sure, I think they said it was only something like 15% of America lives in poverty. But that isn't the point. The point is that there shouldn't be anyone living in poverty at all."

"What do you mean?"

"Do you know how wealthy the world really is?" I asked her.

"Not quite," she said, flipping the overhead lights on to see me better.

"A majority of the world's wealth is held by a select few powerful families or groups. They're called the One Percenters. Families like the Rockefellers, the Rothschilds, and the Waltons—ya know, Sam Walton? Wal-Mart? It's like here in Darbyville, where you can see homeless beggars and ghettos only a mile away from the riches of East Side Heights."

"But those people worked hard to get to that point, wouldn't you say they deserve it?"

"Yeah, they deserve what they've worked for, but when is it enough? Ya know? When does it satisfy them? They just have big pots of gold that they're sitting on long enough to keep their lineage rich for as long as they exist! And then there are some people who might've been dealt a poor hand in the Universe and they've gotta live on food stamps and shack up in a dingy slum. Or worse—government housing. It just doesn't feel right to me. I don't know how else to say it."

"So what should we do about it?" Scarlette asked.

"What *can* we do about it?" I replied.

"I don't know, my family's always been well off. I'm asking you!"

I laughed and said, "We're college kids, Scarlette, we're living in poverty too!"

"Yeah," she laughed, "but we've got as many cigarettes and marijuana that poverty can buy!" She grabbed a book to make a little lap table and began rolling another blunt.

Silence.

"Keep going!" Scarlette said, stripping the layers of weed.

"Keep going?"

"Yeah, gimme some of that Lyla-wisdom, I wanna hear it."

Pause.

Mull through the corners of the mind.

Speak.

"The Indians—and by that, I mean the Native Americans—have this legend about a tribesman who stole the wealth of the village and hoarded it for himself. In the beginning when they first built their village, the men would hunt in groups to bring back as much meat as they could for the rest of the tribe. And they would share what they caught, equally. They all ate well, drank well, and lived well for a while, right?"

"Right," Scarlette mumbled, sealing the blunt with her tongue.

"Well one day, this tribesman thought that he would go out alone to hunt for bison. He woke up before the sun, brought back as much as he could carry by himself, and kept it all in his teepee. He told nobody. After doing this day in and day out, he came to realize that he had to build a bigger teepee! So, he moved to the top of the hill away from the rest of them. Stronger, younger wood for bows, sharper rocks for arrows, and bigger storage. He continued hunting away the bison until the rest of his tribe at the bottom of the hill couldn't find any more food in the forest."

"Nuh-uh," she said, passing me the blunt.

"Yeah huh."

Inhale.

Hold.

Exhale.

"When the chief paid the lone tribesman a visit, he found the hoard of bison meat in the hut. Without anger, he asked if they might be able to have some in order to sustain. The tribesman declined, turned away his chief, and the village went hungry. The Natives thought it to be a serious mental illness that drove this tribesman to be so greedy. Not to mention selfish. So, if you look around at our world?"

Pause.

Stare at Scarlette.

"Well?" She asked.

"Well, we've all got mental illnesses. It's a sick, sick world we've got. Some of us have all the fucking bison meat, and still want more of it. Some of us are starving, asking for any semblance of help, and the government reluctantly gives it while those rich assholes keep hoarding more bison. And then some of us are in the middle with just enough, seeing both sides of the hill, wondering how it all happened."

Prolonged silence.

"Damn, Lyla." Scarlette said, surrounded by a circling wisp of smoke. "So our mental illness is excess?"

"Yes, you could say that. Excessive greed. It's kind of ironic, really. Because once we came to America, we got greedy and wanted to take what wasn't ours. We slaughtered all of our Natives, whether it be through disease or gunfire. And now we've all got this sickness that the Natives warned against. We can't trust our own fellow humans, ya know? And that's not right. That's sad. A species should look out for its own."

"And we don't." Scarlette said.

"I know," I looked down to my lap and laughed with half a heart. "But it *is* getting better. I believe that. There might have only been seven people in that auditorium, but there were still seven people. And there are 45 million others who know, first hand, of the poverty line. I have faith in Humanity, I think, and ya know… hopefully we figure it out, and we'll stop being so sick."

"Or not," Scarlette laughed.

"Or not!"

"Hey," she said, "Mia's not here all weekend… do you maybe wanna stay in my room with me?"

"Oh, please, can I?! My roommate stays awake until 5 AM playing farm games on Facebook and listening to dirty trap-rap. I can't stand that electric glow while I'm trying to sleep."

"Yeah, come on! I don't think Mia would mind. You've got her bed. Don't try to sleep in mine! I'm straight, I'm sure, I'm *not* curious."

"What the fuck?" I said, busting in laughter as we got out of the car.

"What?!" Scarlette said. "You never know! My mom made me recite that line to her before she left on orientation day!"

"You're a hoot," I said, "don't worry, I'll stay in my own bed."

Room 222, 10:48 PM. I sank into Mia's bed admiring her array of pop-culture posters from movies like Star Wars and Pulp Fiction. Amidst the pink quilt and the red pillowcase, I felt like a small child at a slumber party. Scarlette crawled into her little nest across from me, not before nearly tripping on her pile of clothes and crushing her laptop. She slid in to her bed hands first, feeling around for anything that wasn't a blanket. Another pile of clothes fell down to the floor, creating a new hill in the dormitory mountain range.

"Brunch in the morning?" Scarlette asked.

"Definitely."

Lying there with eyes shut I felt my insides swell with an intense euphoria. My breathing in sync with all that is Live and all that is Dead while a deep humming echoed inside my head. Despite the bad apple that lives in room 209, I've experienced the enlightening energy of this place; the shamelessness, the compassion, and the utter imagination in this people has come together to create the most amazing collection of young women I've yet to cross. I can feel the diversity in our characters, the excitement for our future, and the crazed obsession with changing how our world works. It took hold of me in a rush of peace and contentment that hadn't been rivaled since my first acid trip. The truly remarkable part of it all is that we've only just begun. We haven't learned a damn thing yet. But with all thy getting, I'll surely get understanding—or some version of it.

V: Autumn 2K12: The Conspiracy

Even though my heart's fond of most girls I meet here, there's a rotten piece inside of it that's being eaten away by my roommate. I swear she gets off on it. She barely ever lets me get a good night's sleep, her constant circulation through Darbyville's lesser suitors is tiring, and she's simply unpleasant! She's already been in trouble with the school for smoking weed inside our dorm (yes, *inside* our dorm), for having boys stay the night with her (which isn't allowed except for 5 weekends a year), and for blatantly avoiding class. If there's a naughty list at Annabelle's, she's on it.

She's become obsessed with dictating who is and who isn't allowed in our room, even though she whores herself around with the town's teenagers in the comfortable space of our 12 x 12 cell. Right now, she's got it out for Mia—claims that she makes her feel uneasy since Mia loves to call her out for the shit she spews from her mouth. During our homework marathon Mia and I were lucky enough to hear Tammy gloating about the $1,000/month check she gets from her dad's social security fund.

"Look at this iPod I just bought, y'all! It's hot pink," Tammy said as she held it up to us. Unamused silence.

"I don't have a whole lot of money left though, so I can't buy the new Nicki Minaj CD yet. I just cashed the check, like, two days ago, and it's gone already! Can you believe that shit?"

"Where the fuck did all that money go?" Mia asked.

"Eh, some weed. Some tattoos," she said as she pulled her hair back to reveal a keyhole and a matching key on her wrist.

"Okay, what else?"

"None of your damn business," Tammy snapped.

Mia and I are both self-made girls; we work for the money

we have and take shit serving people that we'd rather see *eat* shit sometimes. Since it takes us a whole month of weekend work to attain that kind of cash, Mia couldn't fathom that Tammy blew through $1,000 that had been handed to her only a few days prior.

"Well," Mia started, "I just think it's a little ridiculous that you were given $1,000 and wasted it. Some people don't even make that much busting their ass in a minimum wage job all month." Gloves on.

Round one.
FIGHT.
"Mia, get out of my room," Tammy said.
"I'm not here for you, Tammy, I'm here for Lyla." Mia said as she turned to me like this problem was gonna forget about itself.
"No, get out! I want you out." Tammy insisted.
Mia stared at her coldly for five whole seconds before calmly saying, "I'm not leaving."

Instead, she sat on my bed and pulled out a journal. I looked at Tammy, shrugged, and carried on with my writing too. Suddenly Tammy burst up from her chair in a fluster and nearly ripped our door off its hinges trying to get out. I could hear her next door in our CA's room and thought, "Oh, great, here we fuckin' go."

Before I could finish that thought, she stormed back in the room with the CA, Cheyenne, right behind her. A firm little hall monitor when she wanted to be, but like I said, Tammy's on everyone's shit list.

"What's the problem, y'all?" She asked.
Round two.
"We were just having a conversation," said Mia, "she took it the wrong way and now she's mad at me. I'm just trying to do this homework with Lyla."

"Okay, well... Mia, Tammy said that you're making her feel like she's being attacked and she's asked that you leave the room. Since this is her space, I'm gonna have to ask you to leave." Cheyenne didn't even want to listen to herself as she said that, but she had to do so for the sake of keeping her $300/month college job.

"Are you serious?" Mia asked.
Pursing her lips together in defeat, Cheyenne nodded, "Yeah,

I'm serious."

Tammy: 1
Mia: 0
Lyla: pending

Mia looked at me and snorted in disbelief, gave the second shrug of shoulders, and walked out of Room 209. Tammy stood behind Cheyenne, bobbing her head and crossing her arms against her body as if she'd won entirely. But when Cheyenne left the room and closed the door behind her, round three was upon us.

"What's your deal, man?" I barked. "She called you out for saying something stupid and you decide that she isn't allowed in this room anymore? You can't dictate that."

"Well I just did, didn't I?"

Deep breath in.

And out.

"Alright, I can see that our period of niceties is over, so here's what we can do. You keep to yourself, and I'll keep to myself. Also, think twice about doing anything incriminating. I have no qualms about turning you in."

"What is that supposed to mean?"

"Just that you might wanna reconsider where you keep your weed. Possession is automatic expulsion."

I smirked at her from my bed, shooting a smiling dagger straight into her head while her eyes flickered with sudden understanding.

"Is this really how you wanna play with me?" She asked.

"You pitched the ball, man. I'm just hitting it," I replied.

"Fine," she said, "prepare for your life to be a living Hell."

"Already there," I replied.

Stalemate.

Gloves off.

I grabbed my journal, stuffed it into my brown satchel, and disappeared to find Mia and Scarlette. We must have been on the same wavelength, because they were both standing in front of room 222, locking the door.

"You guys wanna get away for a minute?" I asked.

"Already ahead of ya," Scarlette said.

"Fucking cunt," Mia mumbled, pulling the key from the lock.

That's our Mia.

"I know," I agreed, slightly breathless from petty confrontation.

When we got downstairs we realized we had no gas and no real drive to sit through an extended blunt loop, so the Skinnies chain-smoked under the oak tree by the street while I paced and vented my woes.

"I don't think I've ever in my Life wanted to hit someone as badly as I wanna hit Tammy," I said.

"I don't know how you *haven't* hit her yet!" Mia said, "I'd strangle her."

"Don't give me any ideas," I joked.

"Hey!" Scarlette jumped in, "I have an idea!"

"What is it?" I asked.

"How about you just sit your grumpy little butt right down here next to me, right on this here stairway to nowhere, and enjoy a fiiiiiine tobacco product?"

"Nah, man, I've never smoked a cigarette before. I don't really feel like starting."

"Never?!" They both asked.

"Never."

"Well, there's a first time for everything, idn't there?" Scarlette grinned as she pulled out a single, slender menthol cigarette from her tin.

"It'll relax you, I swear," she assured me.

I looked to Mia for confirmation.

"Why do you think we're all so addicted?" She laughed. "Keeps us halfway sane."

Filter pressed between my lips.

Black lighter in Scarlette's hand.

Click.

Fire.

Inhale.

Immediate

explosive

hacking.

"Atta girl!" Scarlette said, slapping my back. "It isn't weed! You can't hold in the smoke!"

"Thanks for—telling—me," I tried through the coughing. Mia was laughing on the right, flicking her ashes on the pavement.

"GodDAMN!" I said, "I don't think my lungs know how to process this shit!"

"Oh, come on, it'll get better! Give it a chance," Scarlette said.

Usually we all have that one friend who acts as the Angel, and another as the Devil. In this case it seems that I've only got Devils by my side. After a brutal five minutes of delicately puffing their tobacco sticks, a final cloud of ash flaked off the burning end and signaled the death of the first cigarette. I sat on the edge of that stairway to nowhere, eyes squinted ever-so-slightly, head buzzing in a cool daze with my negativity gagged. The birds squawked their evening songs in the branches above, and the three of us silently sang along to their melodies.

"You know," I said while they both lit up one more cigarette in the dusky light, "I think I finally understand why you're all so addicted."

"For the sake of sanity!" Mia exclaimed.

For the sake of sanity.

***

I don't spend much time in room 209 anymore. I don't have the time to be there anyways; between looping with Scarlette and Mia I also juggle a full class load, eat three meals a day, work as a secretary for the economics department, and still visit my soul sister, Angel, in the Usher dormitory next to mine. We had gone to high school together and became very close during some of my darkest hours, and she's the only reason that Annabelle's was on my radar when I started looking at colleges. If we were gonna relate my Life to symbols in Buddhism, I'm the wild elephant that needs taming while Angel is the tamed elephant that helps guide me. Always has been.

I came to Angel this time for advice on how to go about changing roommates, because she was the CA in the Usher building and had a keen knowledge of the endless protocol. She handed me a form for a "complaint against roommate," which I thought defined our issues as well as a college degree defines true intelligence.

"What am I supposed to do with this?" I asked.

"Say exactly why you guys can't get along, what weird things she's been doing to get under your skin, and what kind of an outcome you want. Then give it to Cheyenne. She's your CA, right?"

"Yeah," I said as I looked reluctantly at the form, "how quick do you think I could get this sitch changed?"

"I don't know, really. I mean, they might not even approve you. They don't like to change roommates for freshmen because they want everyone to try to work through their problems. Ya know? They try to make it like... a learning and growing experience." It was clear she chose to wear her mom jeans today.

"This girl needs a lot more learning and growing than I could ever give her."

"You're right!" Angel admitted, "But you've still gotta do this."

I sat there with her and filled out the form and let her know I'd be back after I slipped it under Cheyenne's door.

"Hey!" She yelled before I left her room. "Hurry your ass, we're eating dinner with Victoria and the girls."

"Yes ma'am!" I yelled to her as I ran down the hall.

After I slipped the form under Cheyenne's door, I decided to go by my room to drop off my satchel. When I opened the door, I was dumbfounded by what I saw; my laptop on the floor, my speakers laying crooked beside my nightstand, and my cracked iPod under the bed. Not to mention, my blankets all in a tizzy even though I thought I made my bed that morning. I also didn't understand why all my stuff was on the ground, but I woke up late, so maybe I wrecked the place in a frenzy? Who cares. Since I was in a hurry I started picking things up off the ground but was rudely interrupted by my roommate mumbling,

"Maybe if you wouldn't leave the windows open, your shit wouldn't be all over the ground."

Tammy thought fresh air might poison her, so whenever I cracked my window on a breezy day, she threw a fit. Blamed it on some sort of lung disease, even though her lungs perfectly allowed for the inhalation of cigarette smoke. Suddenly I realized that my journals, *my journals*, were also on the ground. Pages bent and edges crumpled.

That's it.

That's the straw that's finally gonna break this camel's fucking back.

"You know, one thing I don't understand is why my bed is messed up, Tammy, because I swear I made it this morning." In that moment, I knew she had one of her punk slobs over and used my bed to showcase her filth. Didn't matter if she admitted or not.

I have never laid hands on someone maliciously in my eighteen year-long Life, but all at once I felt my face burning hot with the fiercest rage. My belly began turning with burning black coal and my palms clammed with sweat. She was saying something back to me that I couldn't hear, because my ears only caught the shrieks of wrath inside my mind. I was trying to breathe the fire away, but once I reached down to pick up my battered journals, I lost it.

In less than a second I was across the room and had that girl by the throat, saying over and over again,

"Is this what you want? Is this what you fucking want?"

Underneath the pressure of my grip, she said,

"Hit me, bitch, hit me," and with one hand on her throat, the other came rearing around my body to crush the side of her face. If I had it my way she'd be made of porcelain, and her shattered head would be all over the ground just like my journals. Like an alligator with prey stuck between its jaw I began thrashing her body around. I picked her up by the shirt and slammed her back down against her desk, smashing her lamp in the process. I did this all while her puny T-Rex arms tried desperately to make contact with my face. Realizing someone might hear the commotion if I went any further, I spit in her eyes before slamming her down one last, good time. I stared down into her fearful face, cocked my head, and let go.

As soon as I turned to walk away, she jumped up from her beaten desk, yanked a handful of my hair, and said,

"*You* did this! *You* hit me first! *You* touched me first! *You* put your hands on *me*!"

I whipped my body around, put my nose directly on hers to show her how small she is in my world, and growled,

"Oh yeah? Who do you think they're gonna believe? Dean's list? Or shit list?"

With a wink, I sauntered away.

Carefully shutting the door behind me, I took a deep breath and noticed an eerie quiet in the hallway. Luckily, it was feeding time, and almost nobody was in Leigh Hall during the scuffle. The whole thing lasted barely over a minute, but it felt like it could have been hours. In my disorientation, I heard a voice down the hall say,

"Hey! Wanna see the new clothes my mom just bought me?!"

It was Scarlette, and thank GOD, ALLAH, YAWEH, BUDDHA, ODIN, SHIVA, KALI that it was, because I needed a witness to say nothing happened in case Tammy tried to take this to the dreaded Corrections Court. If I was convicted of assault, immediate expulsion would follow.

"Yeah! Watchu got?" I said as she brought me to the edge of her doorway and showed off all these cute tops. I stared without seeing anything, though, because the adrenaline pumping through my veins had my mind focused on the story I needed to spin.

After a few "oooohs" and "aahhhhs" I said, "Hey, I gotta go, I told Angel I'd meet up for dinner. You comin'?"

"Nah," she said, "I don't think I'm gonna eat dinner today."

"Damn, more power to ya," I chuckled, "meet up later for a drive?"

"You know it!" By the time she said those three words, I was already halfway down the hall. I threw my hand up in recognition and sprinted down the stairs. She had no clue! Nobody but Tammy and I knew what the last couple minutes held, and I certainly wanted to keep it that way.

I made it back to the Usher Hall in less than five minutes from the time that I left. Angel, her friend Victoria and a few others were all waiting for me when I burst through her wooden door. They whooped for joy when I walked in, and we were off.

"Did you give your CA that paper?" Victoria asked. Being Angel's roommate, she had been given the details of my perils.

"Yep, slipped it under her door, because I think she's at dinner." Nobody could tell how riled up I was inside.

Calm and cool.

We walked toward the dining hall as the sun fell behind the campus skyline. The calming stroll and much needed fresh air was ruined by my sighting of Tammy on the far side of the quad. She was with some CA from a different dorm, rushing straight for the Campus Safety office. Regardless, I felt a misplaced hint of security no matter what was to come of this.

At dinner, I wasn't hearing any part of the conversation, and if someone spoke directly to me, I spoke back with empty disassociation. Before we were finished eating I felt someone coming for me out of the corner of my eye; it was my own CA, Cheyenne, and she was pissed—arms crossed, hip cocked. If she were a dog, I'd be seeing the hairs raise on her spine. Tammy followed behind her like an injured puppy, and the look on her face was nearly provocative enough for me to bash her skull again.

"Lyla, you need to come with me. Right now," Cheyenne said.

Play innocent.

"Huh?"

"Get up, let's go." She wasn't playing my game.

Is this about the roommate change form that I slid under your door?"

"No, get up, we're going to my room." She whipped her body around while Tammy bobbed her busted head at me, and I looked at the rest of the girls to say,

"Well, gotta go, guys. I'll let you know how this ends."

In Cheyenne's suite Tammy and I were officially summoned to Annabelle's Corrections Court. She had purple bruising along her throat, the side of her cheek, and along her back from being slammed on the desk. I had to tell Cheyenne about my whole day, start to finish, before I was allowed to go anywhere else that night. It was like a real-life crime had taken place, when the only crime committed was by that wretch when she put her prissy paws on my journals.

You don't fuck with a girl's writings.

Let it be known.

To my joy, they decided to move Tammy to a room in a totally different building until the date of our case a week later. I thought to myself, "I should have beat her ass long ago." She documented the bruises on her body, but that was the only evidence she'd have against me in court. And who knows whose hands made those black n' blue marks?

When word of the incident spread, the whole campus was aware of the unfolding drama before we made it to Corrections Court. Tammy's infamy had all the girls whispering, and like pure magic a rumor snaked through the halls, hissing that Tammy had put those bruises on herself in an attempt to get me expelled. All I had to do was relay the same exact story that she was spinning, and it became overwhelmingly easy for everyone to believe that she would harm herself in conspiring my expulsion. They were all too oblivious to the fact that they were actually being fed the Truth.

Once I filled Scarlette and Mia in on Tammy's potential fib, they loyally joined my fight.

"Dude, that girl is fucking nuts!" Mia said, holding a cigarette.

"I'm tellin' ya!" I agreed.

"How can she even think she'd get away with this? I mean, I saw you in the hall right as she's saying you were beating her up," Scarlette noted.

"That's what I'm saying!"

"What can we do about this?" Mia asked, now pacing. "How can we prove you didn't touch her?"

My wheels were already turning.

I glanced at Scarlette with a smile and said, "Well, there might be one thing we can do..."

"Me?" Scarlette asked. "You want me to go talk to administration?"

"I mean, I feel like you're my only chance at disproving this. It's worth a shot."

She hesitated at first, saying she didn't want to be associated with everything that's been going on with Tammy. Within a few minutes, she agreed and set up a meeting with the head administrator the next morning. She went as far as to tell them what a loving person I am, and that I'd never lay my hands on someone like that.

Oh, and that everyone in Leigh Hall thought that Tammy was clinically insane, just to add a touch of her small-town sweetness to my tainted Kool-Aid.

***

9:07 AM. I woke up early for the summoning, took the first shower I'd had in three days, set out to cover every single one of my tattoos, and paint my face with proper makeup. I put on my finest black lace dress, thick cream-colored tights, and one of Scarlette's more respectable burgundy pea coats. It sure is a blessing to share closets with another young woman of refined taste. Not to mention her uncle is a fashion designer in NYC, so she's got the most impeccable coat collection on the face of the northern hemisphere. Being a beach baby, I didn't even own a coat that could handle the upstate ice—or any ice, for that matter. The cooling autumn weather in Darbyville snapped on us the night before, and a bitter cold seeped into my bones regardless of the red sleeves that covered me. With gray skies and the threat of a hellacious downpour, I rushed over to the main hall where we'd be judged. I made sure that I wasn't only dressed for the weather, but also dressed to deceive the elders who held my Fate.

When I walked into the hall, the familiar face of a fellow writing major greeted me with a grin. She's the senior delegator for the Corrections Court this year, and she motioned for me to follow her inside a brilliantly decorated room. Antique wing-backed chairs draped in elegant velvets surrounded a table that had probably been in the Annabelle's collection since 1889. The team of people surrounding that wooden work of art was a mix of upperclassmen, Annabelle's alumni, and select administrators. They all looked up at me, smiled with their warmest suspicions, and asked me to take a seat.

"Okay, Lyla, are you aware of how this works?" The senior delegator asked.

"No," I said, taking a seat in a paisley-patterned throne.

"Since you are the accused, all you'll have to worry about it sitting quietly. The rest of the court and I have gathered our own evidence against Tammy's accusation, which we will present after she has presented her own case against you."

"So, I don't have to say anything?" I asked, bewildered.

"No, you don't have to say word. That is, unless you have something you'd like to add after we've gone through our evidence."

"Okay," I said, smirking. "Sounds easy enough."

9:59 AM. Tammy walked into the room a mere minute before the trial was set to start, smug confidence radiating from her blotchy cheeks. Before anyone delved into deliberation I already had them on my side; seeing as Tammy had no concept of how to dress for the occasion, her hot pink bra straps hung loosely on her bare shoulders. A sullied white tank top barely covered her cleavage, and the zebra pajama shorts she had on might as well have been panties. Her hair was matted in the back, as if she'd just rolled out of bed without grooming and expected everyone to believe she wasn't delusional. Needless to say, I was feeling righteous.

Lyla: 1
Tammy: 0

THANK GOD, ALLAH, YAWEH, BUDDHA, ODIN, KALI, SHIVA that this fabulous panel of women dug into their own research on Tammy's obnoxious behavior. Their first bit of evidence against her was a slew of tasteless photos and social media posts. One of particular interest showed Tammy wiping her ass on my pillow with a "death threat" underneath reading,

"If my roommate leaves her window open one more time, I'm gonna throw her outta that fucking window."

Not to mention the funniest Tweet of them all:

"I hope my god-awful roommate gets a flesh-eating disease that kills her slowly."

Had there been a camera in that room I'd have the essence of the trial captured in one single photo, which would have shown the shocked expressions those women wore as they read those Tweets. One woman who graduated in the class of '78 slowly reeled her head up from the table and glared at Tammy with disgust, and I knew there was no way she could redeem herself now.

Lyla: 3
Tammy: 0

With the odds stacked so high against her already, there wasn't much she could say to convince the court that our fight had actually taken place. She tried her damnedest, though, reciting hit-by-hit the ways I assaulted her. Her speech was strong and deliberate, and I secretly bowed my head to her for having the guts to continue defending herself after such crushing blows. However, it simply wasn't enough. She tried again to emphasize the bruises and marks all over her body, but the panel wasn't listening anymore.

There was a final piece of evidence that the judges were saving as a sort of tie-breaker, and it was beyond my wildest dreams.

The senior delegator stood to speak.

"On the day that Tammy claims Lyla assaulted her, Lyla left her work-study job in the economics building and visited Angel Haffing, the CA in Usher Hall. Lyla scanned her ID card in the Usher Hall at 5:02 PM. After talking with Angel, Lyla scanned her ID card into her own Leigh Hall at 5:13 PM. After dropping by her room, 209, she returned to Usher Hall to meet Angel for dinner."

Pause.

"The time it took for Lyla to punch into Leigh Hall, go to her room, and punch back into Usher Hall was only four minutes and thirty-six seconds."

Pause.

Confused glances from around the table.

Defeat in Tammy's eyes.

Delight in mine.

"Knowing this, it seems highly improbable that Lyla could have walked up to their room on the second floor, gathered her things, assaulted Tammy, spoken to Scarlette Bethesda, and returned to Usher Hall within four minutes."

Chaotic whispers.

Lyla: 4

Tammy: 0

"Lyla, is there anything you'd like to add to this statement?" the senior delegator asked.

"No, ma'am."

"Tammy?"

"No, ma'am."

"Okay. I'm gonna ask you both to step outside and wait in the lobby until we're finished deliberating. It shouldn't be too long."

I rose from my chair and sauntered out into the lobby with Tammy following right behind. Next to the grand piano under a golden crystal chandelier, I sat calmly and laced my fingers in my lap.

"What did I tell you?" I said, breaking the tense silence.

"Tell me about what?" She snapped.

"That they'd never believe you."

"Yeah, we'll see. You bruised my entire body. I can't fake these marks."

"I could have done you much worse."

I felt a deserved tinge of menacing darkness bubbling up under my brown eyes. Victory was floating around in there with the dark, too, and it made my lips curl up at the edges as my tongue pressed up against the crooked tooth in my mouth. I stared beyond Tammy, beyond my repulsion for her, and straight through to the success of my wicked scheme. Tufts of my freshly cleaned hair fell in front of my eyes as I chuckled to myself, and Tammy disappeared from my sight. She walked to the other side of the hall, found a chair up against a dim corner, and put herself in time-out. Less than five minutes passed before the senior delegator opened the door to call us back inside.

"Welcome back, ladies," she started, "let's get on with it.

"We, the women of Annabelle's Corrections Court, have reached our final verdict. We hereby dismiss the accusations made against Lyla Calders and motion for the immediate relocation of Tammy Belcher from room 209 in Leigh Hall.

"Tammy, you will be moved to the 5th floor of Eleanor Hall. You can speak with the housing authority after you've been dismissed to get your new room key. Lyla, you are hereby dismissed from this trial and of any accusations against you. Have a good rest of your week."

I beamed and tipped my head to all of those women in a final note of thanks, smiling not because they deemed me innocent, but because I had manipulated them into believing such. Scarlette's statement, my time card, the threats, and all of her past strikes with the college amounted to the case ruling in my favor and ultimately gaining freedom from Tammy's horrid coexistence in room 209. The elders thought that she was whacked enough to inflict those bruises upon herself, and that's how the story would live on. In the weeks following, she even had to back-track against her own word about the whole bit and told everyone across campus that the fight never happened, and that her plot failed. The irony.

She moved out of our room the night of the verdict without saying a single word to me. There was no need. She understood the lesson that a good ass-kickin' brings to sky-high attitudes. Sometimes people just need a swift choking to bring them back down to reality and the natural order of our society. If we were all too afraid to put someone in their place because of a legal consequence or otherwise, there might not be a solid spine left in humanity. The place that Tammy needed to be put just so happened to be pressed into her desk.

Amidst the empty space on her side of 209, I laughed to myself as I imagined the ways that I'd reinvent my brand-new dorm room. Perhaps I'll slide our two twin beds together and sleep like a queen. Maybe I'll buy psychedelic tapestries and flashing disco lights to transform the stained walls into a trippy haven. I could even replace the white lightbulb in my lamp with a fluorescent blue one and keep it on all night to lure weary young women back to their beds.

Silence.

Revelry.

This peace, brought to me by a rush of vengeance, has never tasted sweeter.

VI: Autumn 2K12: The Vortex

October Nine. Saturday. 1:42 PM. The demon has finally been exorcised from the sacred space that is Leigh Room 209, and I am finally beginning to pull it all together. I squeezed the two beds side-by-side to create a king size dorm set-up for Scarlette to spend as many sleepless nights with me as possible. The walls are plastered with various road signs that I've acquired in my journey, including one that I snagged in the middle of the night from a mountain-biking trail in the Blue Ridges. Others said things like,

"Slow children at play"

"Out of service, please call xxx-xxx-xxxx"

There's even a South Carolina license plate that I ripped off the obnoxious sports car, belonging to a boy who harassed Angel and me one night. And, of course, how could any sign collection be complete without a big red STOP?

As a backdrop for my Carolina King Bed I hung a massive burgundy and orange Buddha tapestry. Let us make no mistake; every college freshman needs a tapestry that signifies how Zen they believe themselves to be. I also have vibrant, fake flowers covering the window sill, because none of us have time to keep up with watering plants when we can barely water ourselves. The focal point that ties it all together is a dusty, white lamp draped under a piece of dainty, white lace. Just as I envisioned, I opted for a bright blue lightbulb and left it on 24/7 to glow for those women wandering through the night. It's like a sapphire version of Daisy Buchanan's dock light from *The Great Gatsby*. And wouldn't you know, "Gatz" was added to my repertoire of college nicknames soon thereafter.

"Aye, yo, Lyla— hoooooolyyyyy shit, my man! Look at your pad!"

Enter Miquia; a beautiful light-skinned black girl with the greenest Granny Smith eyes you've ever seen. Her hair was only slightly darker than her caramel skin, dangling in tight braids down to her collarbone. She's always wearing black wife beaters, slick basketball pants, and some fancy Nike kicks. We thought she was like the rest of the basketball team—gay. We were proven wrong by the way she's constantly gushing over a tall, dark man with deep brown eyes. Stereotypes can't help but make exceptions every now and again. She, too, graduated high school early like my ex-roommate, but she's far more tolerable than Tammy ever could be. Now that I was the Mac-Mama of our hall, it seemed everyone was stopping by to check out the new space.

"Yeah, man, isn't it nice?! Alllllllll mine," I sang.

"Duuuuuude," she said, oggilng the string of lights lining the ceiling, "this is dope! Definitely the best dorm I've seen yet! Are they gonna make you get another roommate?"

"Well, they told me I have to have one, because freshmen aren't allowed to have rooms to themselves. We gotta persevere through the torture of sharing a cage with a stranger, right?"

"Hell yeah, I heard that. But nobody could be worse than your roommate! That girl is fuckin' crayyyy."

"Oh, girl, you and me both know it."

"Ya know, I heard the stories," she said as she moved toward me and sat down on the bed. Did she really beat herself up to try to get you kicked out?"

"Sure did," I said with a smirk. If only Miquia knew, *really* knew, she'd be proud.

"I still can't believe that shit! I always had a hunch something was wrong with her."

"Yeah, I heard she's gone and dyed her hair royal blue now?"

"Yeah, shit looks ridiculous, man. It's anything but royal. Her little buddy dyed her hair bright red, too, so everyone's callin' 'em the Superheroes on campus. Lookin' like a jacked-up Superman split in two bodies."

"Ohhh, that's mean, but so good" I said as we broke into snickers. "But, it's already the middle of October. Most girls who wanted different roommates have completed the process already, so

I'm thinkin' I'll get lucky with a room all to myself. At least until Jan-term rolls around."

"Man, you got hooked up! If I ever need to get away from my own crazy roommate, can I crash here?"

"Of course, Mee-Kee, you're always welcome."

"Thanks, man. So listen, I've got this dude in Wellington who does tats. A bunch of the other girls on the hall are interested."

"What do you mean?" I said, squinting my eyes at her.

"Well, he says he's off tonight and lookin' to do some tattoos. So if you wanna come, Riley, Sam, and Emilia already said they're down."

"Uhhhhh…" I hesitated.

"I know he hasn't got shit compared to the dude who does your work. But you ain't even gotta get any ink! The other girls were just talking about how they wanted you to come. Ya know, as an authority or something."

"Does he have weed?"

Obvious question.

"Hell yeah. He sells too."

Obvious answer.

"I'm game. Is it cool if Scarlette and I just follow y'all over there?"

"Cool with me. Mia comin' too?"

"Ehhh, probably not. I think she's drowning in school work."

"Damn, I feel that. Well sweet, dude, you and Scarlette then! Just meet at my room when I text you."

"You got it."

Mia's growing colder and meaner with each passing day. My parents, luckily, divorced when I was in high school, but Mia and Scarlette's parents are both just beginning their split during our first year of college. Scarlette, keeping with Southern protocol, is highly adept at hiding her dirty laundry away and dealing with the stench internally. Mia, however, has never been one to deal with much emotion and has been taking her parents' split harder than any of us imagined. It feels to me like she's in a wrestling match with her misplaced guilt, her broken inner child, and her bulimia. She's started lashing out at everyone that crosses her path, like a rattlesnake coiled up to strike those unsuspecting ankles. The cynical behavior and fearless attitude that is so naturally "Mia" has become aggressive, to say the least. It's an ordinary fuck of emotions for most children of divorce, I'd say. As if Scarlette wasn't already digging her talons into my back, Mia's deepening trouble and general nastiness thrust her right into my lap. Just as Miquia left, sure enough...

"Lylaaa?" Scarlette said from the hall, sleep still clinging to her throat.

"Hellooooo!" I sang from my bed.

Her olive-green bomber jacket was falling off her left shoulder, like it wasn't ready to be up and awake either. Mascara bleeding around her eyes and color faded on her lips told the tale of an unusual sleep. She dragged her shabby beige boots across my crocheted rugs, tripping on them in the process and yelling,

"Oh, daggummit, I do that every time I walk into this room! You really need to get rid of those rugs. I might just die one of these days. Or worse; I could fall and fuck up my pretty face."

"No way, Jose," I said, "those rugs are the only thing keeping my delicate beach feet from being miserably cold in the morning!"

"Feet! Who needs 'em? I need my face!" She said, plopping down beside me and leaning her sleepy-headed curls across my shoulder.

"What's up, Punk?" I cooed.

"Oh, Lyla, I'm so tired. Mia was crying all night, so I stayed in my car and chain-smoked until 4 AM. I told myself I was gonna keep going until I either puked or fell asleep. So then I ended up smoking twelve, puked in the parking lot, then came inside. Thank God Mia was finally knocked out."

"Oh, God, that sounds horrible! Why didn't you just come over here?"

"I figured you wanted to enjoy your first night of freedom alone. But you better believe I'm showing up every night after this."

"Deal," I laughed.

"So whatchu wanna do today?" She asked.

"Well," I started, "we've been invited to a tattoo artist's house in Wellington."

"Who do we know in Wellington?"

"Oh, we don't. Miquia does. Riley, Sam, and Emilia wanna get some silly little tattoos done tonight, and Miquia says that he sells, too, so it'll be a good time."

"Sells? As in, the marijuana?"

"Yes, my dearest one. The marijuana."

"Well that's all you had to say! When are we going?"

7:56 PM. The sun is set and the cold is much too much for my outfit of choice; thin, patterned black tights, a body-hugging black dress, Scarlette's knee-length hunter green coat, and a pair of her battered black boots. I'm not so sure if my sea-drenched sensibilities will ever adapt to the frosty temperatures of the Carolina foothills. Needless to say, we dashed up the stairs to his apartment and out of the chill, eyes already bloodied from the blunt we smoked on the way over.

I have never been in the Projects before. Well—I *had* never been in the Projects before. I imagine what I felt upon entering that complex is the same emotion Dorothy felt when she realized she and Toto weren't in Kansas anymore. The brown bricks outside looked dingy even without exposure under sunlight, and the railings on the staircase were rusted to pieces, falling apart and morphing into toothy rods that ached for a piece of fresh flesh. The blinds that I could see on the stretch of windows were crooked and crushed, denoting a depressed air of Chaos. And yet, there was a delicious stench of weed wafting from inside that permeated the atmosphere outside his door. Not to mention the oh-so-familiar whir of the tattoo machine that rang through my ears.

Knock-knock.

Black face peeks through crooked blinds.

Unlock deadbolt.

Unlock turn-key.

Unlock chain.

Welcome.

"Ayyyyyye," he said in a deep rumble.

"Hey!" Scarlette and I both said.

"Yaaaayyy! You guys made it!"

It's Emilia. The tiniest little firecracker red-head fit with the sweetest face and the strongest appetite for trouble. She came barreling toward us with all 76 pounds of her body weight and stood on her tip-toes to wrap her fair, freckled arms around our necks.

"Yeah, how's it going?" I asked. "I hear you're gonna get poked, huh?"

"Oh, it's just a little one! It's my first one, actually."

"What is it?" I asked.

"It's 'Let It Be' on my wrist. Ya know, like the Beatles' song."

"Ahhhhh," I said with a shit-eating grin, pretending fully that I was interested. I guess I'm what you could consider a tattoo-snob. My first one stretched from my shoulder to my elbow, taking nine hours in totality.

"Yeah!" Another voice rang out. This time it was Riley, an all-American, blonde haired, blue eyed, horse racer from Carolina. "And I'm getting the name of my first horse on my ribs!"

"Do you have any other tattoos?" I asked.

"Yeah. It's a heart on my wrist."

It was getting harder to stay interested.

"I have only one tattoo," Scarlette said, trying to get involved.

"You have a tattoo?!" Miquia asked, appearing from the back of the apartment.

"Yeah, I got it when I was fifteen!"

"What is it?" Riley asked.

Instead of telling them, Scarlette took her fingers and tugged down on the bottom of her lip, revealing the word "secrets" in slightly sloppy black ink.

"Whoa!" I said, shocked since I wasn't privy to her tattoo either.

"Yeah, I was young and just thought it would be cool to have the word 'secrets' on my lip. I thought it would fade by now, but it's still good. Right?"

"Still says 'secrets', yep," I reassured her.

"Whooooaaa," the guy said to me, "I ain't even realized you had all them tats gurl, where'd you get 'em done?"

"Bloodmoon Beach," I smiled, "it's where I'm from."

"You from da Beach?! Maaaaaaan I luh the Beach. I go there wit my boyz all the time."

"Yeah, man, people love it."

"I'm guessin' you won't need any tattoos then?" The dude said with a laugh.

"No sir, but I am in the market for some of that green stuff you've got."

"Awh, yeah, notta prollem. Lemme do their tatz first, then we can go smoke a blunt wit my boi."

Little Miss Blondie was up first in the chair. She tucked her sheer white tank top into the strap of her bra, stretching tall to accentuate her bare rib bones. The sole piece of furniture in the place was a tattered tan sofa, and since there were five other girls crowded around watching the show, Scarlette sat on my lap. We stared at the slender black man as he laid the purple letters down with a stencil on the dead center of Riley's ribs. I could practically see her nervous sweat resisting a downpour, and when he flipped the switch to cut the machine on, she jumped.

One millimeter below the surface of the skin. That's all it takes to scar the body with an eternal ink—a sacred experience that fuses our usually separate body and mind into a united force, bracing the brunt of the finest needle points to endure the pain in masochistic harmony. With each dig of the needle pumping into the body at a speed unobtainable to the naked eye, there's a certain electricity that pulsates through your every nerve, every synapse. Any and all versions of filthy speech run through the mind in an endless string of vulgarities, only pausing when the buzzing quits. It's a terrible contradiction of a tortuous sensation and a wondrous relief that I've grown highly accustomed to, and mightily addicted.

9:24 PM. Each of the girls successfully made it through their scarring, save one who backed out after watching Miquia shed a tear. Nothin' like grade-A illegal house tattoos to solidify the inauguration of depraved college life.

"Aight, y'all two ready to smoke?" The dude asked.

"Fuck yeah," Scarlette said.

After he rolled a decently thick watermelon blunt, he motioned for us to come downstairs with him. Once outside, we were asked to step into a black Cadillac that looked like it'd practically scrape off the entire underside if the slightest bit of weight was added. The inside was plush, covered in black leather and wood grain on the doors. It was already full of smoke, and there was another stockier black man sitting in the driver's seat.

"Aye, y'all, wus up?" He sounded like he was slurring, and even though his NY Yankees hat made it hard to see his eyes, I knew they were barely open. "Ma name's Real. Who are you?"

"I'm Brittany," Scarlette said.

"And I'm Ashley," I replied, following her lead.

"Mmmmm, y'all are beauuuuutiful. Whatchu doin' after this smoke?"

"Going home!" I said. "We have a lot of homework to catch up on before Monday."

"Homework? Da fuck? Y'all go to skewl? You're way too pretty to be in college."

"Yeah, we go to Annabelle's," Scarlette said.

"Annabelle's?!" He instantly woke up, "So y'all gay?"

"Nnn—" I started, but Scarlette cut me off.

"Yes!" She said.

"Awhh, that's too bad," Real slurred, fidgeting uncomfortably in his reclined leather car seat. The tattoo dude sat in the passenger's seat next to him and lit up.

"You drinkin' dat drank, son?" The tattoo guy asked Real.

"Yaaaaahhh, nigga, sippin' on that Lean," he said as a murky chuckle escaped his lungs. A dangerous mix of jolly ranchers, sprite, and pharmaceutical codeine syrup—the black man's psychedelic.

The tattoo dude sucked his teeth in disapproval and said, "Nigga you crazy."

Puff, puff.

Pass.

Puff, puff.

Pass.

Repeat.

It took quite some time due to the inebriated condition that Mr. Real was held under, but we smoked three blunts with them and made out with an eighth's worth of dank bud before midnight. Not before much discussion and debate over being lesbians, though! I did most of the talking, seeing as Scarlette clammed up next to me just thinking about it. Remember: she's straight, she's sure, she's not curious.

***

"So where do you wanna go today?" I asked Scarlette when we awoke on Sunday afternoon. We stayed in her car until 4:17 AM chain-smoking blunts and cigarettes, musing over the fact that Scarlette flirted her way into an extra gram for us without paying for it. Sex certainly sells, even the sex that they don't necessarily agree with.

"I don't know, maybe let's go hit Target? I neeeeed some new black tights! All of mine have holes in them," she said as she plucked away at her leg to make a gaping hole even bigger.

"Yeah, cuz you keep burning 'em with cigarettes!"

"Noooo, it's not that! It's just, I don't know, they catch on things…" she said faintly. She was halfway right; being an art student doesn't allow for such fragile clothing to last very long. And she *had* to wear tights. There's no other Life for her except for the Tights-Life. She told me once that if she ever died young to make *sure* she was buried in tights, and I gave her my word.

"Alright, well, is it too late to go grab brunch first?"

Annabelle's served an endless brunch from 10-1 on weekends, THANK GOD, ALLAH, BUDDHA, YAWEH, SHIVA, ODIN, KALI. Unfortunately, it was 12:37 when I looked at the clock. I jumped out of bed, still in my clothes from the night before, and said,

"Get up, Punky Bruster! If we wait eight more minutes they won't let us in!"

"UUUUUUUGGGGHHHHHHH!!!!" She groaned, threw her legs in the air and gave a little kick, then followed after me, for I was already on my way out. No rest for the wicked.

I enjoyed a concoction of scrambled eggs, salsa, and home-fried potatoes for my weekend feast. Scarlette, on the other hand, is a true Southern Belle at heart and always made a blend of crispy bacon, buttered grits, and scrambled eggs. Once we downed our porridge it was time to head back to room 209 to make ourselves look presentable for a nice afternoon shopping—well, shop*lifting*.

When I was 15 years old, I visited the Mall of Charlotte in

North Carolina after going to the Carolina Rebellion music festival one summer. On that fateful day, I watched a friend of mine steal a hoodie right off the Hollister mannequin in a crowded hallway full of oblivious shoppers. Seriously—unzipped that thing, slid it off the lifeless plastic girl, put it on her own body, and kept going. I was shocked by how easy it was, because nobody seemed to notice! And even if they did, they surely didn't give enough of a shit to stop her. That day, I came home with over $700 in shoes, makeup, dresses, pants, shirts, bras, CDs, and Lord knows what else. A switch had been flipped inside my head that could never be turned off, and even now I'm not sure if that kind of exposure was a good thing. It's a lifestyle, really. Three years later and only one mistake made, my persona of a kleptomaniac has become an art form and a constant thrill.

Scarlette never stole anything, to be clear. It's all me, and always has been no matter the friend involved. We'd simply come up with a code word for something that their heart desired, and I'd come along to shove it into my satchel, my pants, my jacket, or my bra, for that matter. Looking back on it, it baffles me that nobody ever tried to stop me! Seriously, how could you believe that two young women leaving a store empty-handed with a fully-packed satchel weren't thieving heathens?

"Ohhh, look at these," Scarlette said as she pulled down a pair from the wall, "they have fit-slimming technology!" Even though her 105 lbs body couldn't be slimmed any further, she was mighty excited over those bad boys. I bent down to pretend I was looking at a pair of socks, looked both ways for shoppers, looked above for cameras, and delicately ripped the packaging off of them. Once bare, I shoved the teensy little tights into my satchel in one fluid movement and stood up to move on to the next.

"Did you get them?" Scarlette asked in an excited whisper.

"Ssssshhhhh, in due time, grasshopper," I replied.

"Ohhhh!" She began whisper-yelling at me through the aisles for hiding the spoils from her. I moved on to check out the selection of above-the-knee socks and managed to grab three pairs before leaving the area. We snagged a few more menial goodies before leaving Target that day, but not without my trusty shop-lifting ritual.

"Hold your breath as we go through the alarms, okay?" I whispered to Scarlette.

"Huh?" She looked very confused.

"When we go through the doors, ya know, with the sensors that they have to catch shoplifters? Hold your breath when we go through them." We were steadily approaching the doors at this point.

"Why?" She asked.

"Just do it!" I said.

She did, and as we both took a deep breath in we held it until we were all the way cleared from the doors. A rush of victory swept over me when we hit the fresh, mountain air, and I let my breath go with a triumphant release.

"What was that about?" She said to me walking towards her car.

"Just a superstition, I guess. I think if I hold my breath, maybe the alarms won't go off when they're supposed to. They haven't yet, in all three years of my mania."

"You're weird," she said, "so what all did we get?!"

"Hold it! I'll show you in the car!"

She could have died when I pulled out not one pair of tights, but *three* pairs of tights, all in her favorite color: the blackest black.

"Ahhhhh!" She squealed, "I didn't even see you take these!"

"Well that's the point!"

On most of these sprees I barely get much for myself. Mia needed a strapless bra to wear on a date once, and all she had to do was ask me to go with her to Walmart so that I could grab one for her. Done deal, man. I can steal almost anything I need for myself, but I practically owned all I needed and more by the time I'd been involved in petty(ish) shoplifting for three years. I coulda made a business out of it, I swear. Instead, I decided to make it my cause to raid only the big name corporate stores and offer up my earnings to my dearest mates.

These corporations that I speak of have thousands of dollars in their budgets for people like me; they make billions every year, what does it matter if I do them over for something they're paying for regardless? I feel that it's my social obligation to take advantage of the companies that do the same to their armies of overworked, underpaid employees, while they're busy over-paying their CEOs and exploiting countless foreign countries that make their already cheap retail even cheaper. I want to be the middle finger waving in front of their faces, pocketing their capital right from under their fat, stuffy noses. Since they're already paying for my criminal actions whether I committed them or not, I see myself as doing them a favor by fulfilling my duty as a corporate thief. As a rule to maintain my philosophy on thievery, I never took from locally-owned small businesses. Those were always off limits. It's only the fat, sick hogs that I wanna butcher.

If Angel, Mia, nor Scarlette wanted any of the treats I snatched? Well, I'd lay everything out in my dorm, invite all the Leigh girls over, and ask them if they saw anything that tugged at their heartstrings. They couldn't understand that I was simply giving away beautiful scarves and earrings and necklaces and handbags! Oh my! What sorcery! Their mouths hung agape, jaws swinging in the shock while trying not to let their smiles show. Once they realized I was serious, though, they had no trouble taking what I had to offer. My obvious proficiency in this type of Magick is how I gained yet another fond moniker: Robinhood. And you're damn fucking right—stealing from the riches to give to my bitches.

***

Midterms came upon us like a tsunami we tried to ignore. Scarlette and I experienced another one of our "firsts" together during that horrendous week: the first college all-nighter. What a mess; I had a 20-page short story to conjure up for my creative writing class and Scarlette had three massive art installations to finish. I have this firm belief that brilliance doesn't come at deadlines, and I had NOTHING brilliant floating around in my head to meet the requirements of this story—I mean it, nothing. I write incessantly, but my writings aren't fictional short stories. Rather, I attempt to articulate the ineffable beauty, humor, and provocative nature of Life and Love in our Youth, not fiction. Regardless, it's 7:16 PM on a Thursday night and the story was due at 10:30 AM Friday morn. Time to crack that whip.

We returned from a Blunt Loop full of discussion on the topic of sexuality, specifically how it was possible for me to be attracted to certain girls but to not consider myself bisexual. Amidst this conversation, Scarlette recited that beloved line that her mother conditioned in her head,

"I'm straight, I'm sure, and I'm not curious."

When Scarlette arrived to Annabelle's she had this uncanny theory that all lesbians were simply horny guys trapped in girls' bodies who would stop at nothing to turn a straight girl crooked. Now, that may the case for some lesbians, but not most. It was amusing and rather cute to see the fluster of her lezzie-fearing days. When she found out I had fooled around with a girl before college she was terrified that I'd try coming on to her! Little did she know that I wasn't a lesbian, and I certainly wasn't trying to get in her pants. I merely got caught up in a flirtation with an exotic flower blossoming by the beach. Who wouldn't?

After we drove ourselves mad chatting about the complexities of youthful sexuality, we parked back at our home and trudged our way across the leaf-scattered sidewalks toward the dorm. Noticing how brilliant the autumn blue sky was reflecting off my eyes, Scarlette interrupted my gaze by saying,

"So, you think you're gonna stay up all night?"

"Yeeeahhhh," I said with a breathy tone, "I'm gonna have to. That's the only way I'm gonna get this story finished in time. I'm so tired already, though. Mentally drained, ya know? Midterms are kicking my ass."

"Mine too." She said, picking up a golden leaf. "Well, I'll stay up with you if you want. I'll doodle and listen to music and stuff while you write. You want an Adderall?"

Scarlette has severe ADHD/ADD, so while all the other college kids were desperately trying to find some Adderall to "help them study," Scarlette was the lucky duck on campus who's prescribed the highest dosage to simply function in the academic world. It made her personality absolutely droll and zombified when she took it, but she made good grades and understood what her professors were lecturing. That's really all the institution cares about anyways. To hell with personality and charm! Who needs it in this age of manufactured behavior? When she doesn't take her Adderall, she's a riotous bundle of vitality that's energizing and damn near intoxicating to witness. She might not be able to pay attention to a single thought out of my mouth if her life depended on it, but that's the price I pay for teaming up with a rolling stone of mania! Sometimes I'd be telling her a story and all of sudden she'd bust out with something like,

"Did you know J. Cole grew up in Fayetteville, North Carolina? He's always making references to it. He never forgets his roots, and that's what I really like about him. He's an artist who made the big time, but he always remembers where he came from. Here! I'll show you a verse." Once her train of thought went in one direction you weren't getting that train to come back, much less stop. It was best to hop on the caboose and just ride it out till the next stop.

"What's Adderall feel like?" I asked her. I'm not a pill popper. I'm a weed-smoker and a psychedelics-enthusiast. Amphetamines are a new island of exploration.

"Well, it makes *me* feel hyper-focused and calm. And kinda empty. But that's because I'm ADD. It makes everyone else feel real jittery and wide awake and productive, I guess. Oh, and you don't sleep. Like, at all. You don't even feel tired. Or hungry! That's why I really like it. It helps me kick-start my diets."

"Hmmm…" I wasn't sure if I wanted her to take my amphetamine virginity yet, but with the glooming prospect of having to write a 20-page story, I said,

"Fuck it. Yeah, I'll take one."

With those words she slipped me a capsule from her bottle and I felt the cherry tighten just before the pop. Yet another first in Scarlette's presence. That bulky orange pill full of tiny, yet sickeningly powerful beads went down my throat and straight to my head within the hour.

Amphetamines are an odd bunch of chemicals. Adderall, after all, is just legal speed. They found a genius way to feed the hyper kids a supposedly illegal substance so that Big Pharm can stay Big. I felt an oddly warm, tingling sensation climbing up from my nerves, through my brain, and back down again. I was gritting my teeth together like a PTSD victim, and it seemed that the tighter I chomped down, the better it felt! And the thirst, ohhhh, the thirst is unreal; but trying to drink water is like trying to swim with clothes on—it just doesn't feel right. I knew I was creeping into dehydration, but I couldn't suck down that Life potion no matter how great the desire. And, of course, why else would it be called speed if it didn't fill you with an uncontrollable urge to talk until every possible English word had been uttered? My mind was running at 3,864,587 miles an hour and there was no option to slow down, only speeding up!

Led Zeppelin's "When The Levee Breaks" screeched from the corner of my bed. It's my ringtone. And who was it ringing me during such an episode?

"Hey, mom!" I answered, much more enthused than usual.

"Hi, baby girl! How are midterms coming along?" Just as enthused as always.

"Well, I've got a 20-page short story due tomorrow afternoon that I haven't finished yet, but I will! Don't you worry!"

"Oh geeze, what are you writing about?" She asked with a giggle in her tone.

"Haven't quite figured that out yet… but I will!"

"Oh, Lyla!" She laughed. She wasn't worried about me. I'm the girl who barely studied in high school and rarely stayed in class but still managed to place third out of 300 in academic performance. She knew I'd have those 20 pages perfect by 10:30 AM.

"So, you don't have any idea what you're gonna write the story about?"

I proudly said, "Not a clue!" then looked at Scarlette doodling to whisper, "I'll be right back."

Before I knew it, I found myself on the outskirts of campus wandering up and down the sidewalks, trying to pace away the sincere UP that I was experiencing. If only my mouth could keep up with how fast the thoughts were flowing through my brain, my mom would have heard a lot more out of me that night. Instead, all I remember clearly was telling her,

"Mom, I *know* that one day my writings will be some of the most influential writings of my generation. It's only a matter of time! Instead, I'm busy wasting time here to prove to someone else that I can write well! It's stupid! Do you know how much work they thrust upon us all at once? I swear they want us to feel helpless. I don't know why else they'd give our malleable, confused minds such heavy loads! It should be illegal, I'm telling you. This shit should be illegal."

It only escalated from there until I was in such a black hole of a rant that my mom couldn't get a word in edge wise. I looked at my phone to notice we had been talking for nearly 48 minutes—well, *I* had been talking for nearly 48 minutes. When I looked up, I saw Scarlette scuttling toward me from the dorm. I told my mom that Scarlette was walking up, so we exchanged our I-Love-Yous and hung up.

"You've been out here for so long!" She said as we stood below the pale glow of blue lamplight shining from my open window.

"Yeah, I got carried away. This stuff is making me feel real weird, man, I couldn't shut the fuck up talking to my mom."

"I know, I heard your voice from inside."

"Fuck, have I been that loud?"

She nodded her head at me as she put a lighter to the cigarette that was in her mouth.

"You want one?" She offered. "It'll make you feel good, I swear. Speed and nicotine go together like peanut butter and bananas."

"Sure," I said as I slipped one out of her pack. For the last couple of weeks, I'd been taking one whenever she offered. However, my lungs wouldn't let me inhale the smoke entirely. It was soothing just to puff on them every now and again. You better believe I was already feeling the holes in my lungs, though, because Scarlette smoked the most powerful menthol cigarettes the state could legally sell. After the first few drags I said,

"You were right, this is nice!"

"Told ya," she said as she plopped her butt down on the sidewalk. I plopped mine down right next to hers, and we finished our cigarettes staring at the gorgeous, white colonial southern home across the street.

"Did you write anything yet?" She asked me.

"Nope. Not a thing. My head's racing so fast that I can't even get one sentence out."

"What! What have you been doing these last couple of hours?

Just staring at your computer?"

"Yes! I know this stuff makes *you* focused, but it's making my mind race in circles so fast that I think I'm burning off the bottom layer of my brain. I can't keep track of a single fucking thought in my head. They all just keep blending together in a swirl of sounds that I can't recognize as anything from this planet."

"That's how I feel all. The. Time! So, whenever you get impatient with me or frustrated that I've lost something, remember how you're feeling right now. It's really hard to keep things straight in here," she said as she pointed to her head with the fingers that weren't holding her cigarette.

"Yeah, no kidding. This shit's no joke. I don't know how I'm gonna finish this story. Or begin it, for that matter."

"Write about me!" She said as she let a wave of smoke out of her mouth.

"Seriously?" I half-scoffed.

"Yeah!"

"What do you want me to write?" I figured it might be easier if she gave me a topic that I had to roll with. At this point, it was 10:06 PM, and Friday was fast-approaching.

"I don't know, anything. But make it good!"

Helpless.

"We'll see what I come up with," I replied.

"Awh, shitttt," Scarlette said, "I just realized I've only got one cigarette left. Ride with me to get another pack?"

"Yeah, sure. But when we get back I've gotta shut myself in that room until I come out with a finished product."

"Deal," and we're off.

Arms hooked.

Keys in the ignition.

Wheels on the ground.

Cigarettes in hand.

Parked.

Back to business.

Another two hours passed before I wrote a sentence that was worth a damn for this story. The words refused to flow, trapped inside of my head churning around with those orange beads in a havoc that can only be described as atrocious disorientation. Scarlette, whose body couldn't stay still, spent most of her time lying on my bohemian rugs drawing grotesque, abstract faces in a sketchpad while we both vibed to the same music.

Symbiosis.

***

10:14 AM. Friday morning. I finished that story exactly twenty-two minutes before I was due for class. I scrambled effortlessly to get the printers in the study room to work. It's as if they installed the lowest-grade technology they could just to force all the procrastinators into a premature gray. The story's a mess fueled by pharmaceutical speed, but it's finished—all twenty pages. I even wrote about Scarlette like she suggested! However, this was a story about hidden lesbian love in a backwards, small southern town. I painted Scarlette to be a rebellious debutante in love with an independent woman named Sarah, and she had no clue until the screwy story was already in my professor's hands. Scarlette fell asleep next to me around 5 AM while I tried my hardest to force words onto paper. I'll never forget how the glowing laptop made my eyes feel like they wanted to run away from my head. They certainly would have if there was a feasible way. I didn't sleep for two days after that, no matter how exhausted my body felt and how hot my eyes burned; Scarlette was a little too spot-on about Adderall's effect on the sleeping cycle, because there was none. Just a binge of relentless, artificial energy.

When we were heading toward her car for a loop after class that day, Mia and Scarlette asked me what I ended up writing for my story. With pride, I told them,

"Well, Scarlette wanted me to write about her! After 8 hours of absolutely no words coming to mind, I finally got it: a tale of two lesbian lovers set in Aiden, South Carolina, centered around Scarlette's upcoming debutante event and her crazy, alcoholic mother's inability to cope with her daughter's lifestyle choices."

Scarlette's body jolted around and all I saw in her face was a passionate combination of shock and vehemence.

"You did *what?*" She asked in disbelief. "You made me gay?!"

"I didn't make you gay! I made you a lesbian," I chuckled at her.

"You used my cigarettes, my style, my name, *my town*?! That's fucked up, Lyla. I don't like that at all. You'd better change my name."

"Oh, come on! You told me to write about you!"

"I said write about me, I didn't say make me a lesbian!" Mia was laughing all this time and not even trying to hide it, which made the situation no better.

"Quit laughing, Mia, it's not fucking funny!" She said with a rather long groan as she quickened her pace to get away from the two of us.

Maaaan, oh, Molly, was that an awkward Blunt Loop.

I did end up changing her name; instead of Scarlette and Sarah, the story became about *Elizabeth* and Sarah. Even with that fix she still wasn't very pleased that I turned her cigarettes and hometown into gay cigarettes and a gay hometown. Had I known her sentiments were so strong, I wouldn't have written her into a story like that. But, hey, she was with me all day and night for that trip through my hellaciously scattered mind, and without her as my inspiration it would have been a much deeper struggle to get those words out.

After that night and a few days' worth of Scarlette giving me shit, we spent our time continuing the transformation of Room 209 into a sacred space for us to erupt. Our nights were consumed with burning the midnight oil, AKA: the marijuana. We took more time to bitch and moan about our assignments than the time we spent doing them, and we visited the vending machine downstairs to fuel our deranged nights rather than the Swan dining hall. We converted that room from a nasty vortex into a serene trip all its own; one that is perpetually colored blue and refuses to slow down or conform to any passersby—and it seemed the trip was only getting wilder the further our friendship flowered.

VII: Autumn 2K12: The Rock

Scarlette grew tired of travelling the six-hour round-trip to Aiden just for some middie weed and a less than exciting time with her long-term boyfriend. During the last trip she made down there, he locked her in his apartment for two days and wouldn't let her leave. Clearly, that had to stop, so through a series of he-said/she-said connections, we managed to find a half-ass drug dealer named Big Mick. We called him Big Mick, because, as you can imagine, he was a BIIIIIIIGGGGGGG fella. In fact, upon our first meeting he introduced himself to us as Big Mick before ever uttering his true name. This boy was the Mac truck of mixed kids, weighing in at nearly 400 lbs and towering over us at 6'5". He deserved that name.

    The problem with Big Mick is that he isn't really a dealer, he's just the middle man; he knew where to get the weed from, but he didn't actually possess it. We didn't know it at the time, but the poor kid was homeless, and by necessity he had become a professional couch hopper at the ripe young age of 21. It was a ridiculous ordeal just to get some ganj through this guy, because we'd have to A) locate him on his endless walk through any given backwoods town, B) take him to his dealer's house that could be up to thirty minutes away, and C) take him to the house whose couch would cushion his tired body that night. Sometimes if he couldn't find a place to sleep he'd ask us to take him to a gas station, and we'd watch him trudge across the parking lot to disappear into the poorly lit country roads.

    It's nearly always an hour's worth of effort to get this little eighth baggie of weed in our hands, but it beat driving all the way to Aiden. We didn't mind too terribly at first, because Big Mick was a downright pleasant guy. He'd give us little insights into his life working at Subway, and for the most part he responded well to our conversation with some of his own. Most black dealers that we brought into our sphere were cold, cop-fearing, and strictly business-oriented. Big Mick, on the other hand, seemed to be trying to pass his days with as much of a smile that he could find, and we sensed a type of harmlessness in his character that way.

He helped us out one late day in October when we were on a mission to find some Molly, or, MDMA as I like to call it. When I was living in Bloodmoon Beach there was a girl I worked with who had a *pure* MDMA connection, which is extremely hard to come by these days with the amount of filler that the dealers put in the substance to make some extra cash. When I first met those tiny, yellow crystals I fell in Love upon ingestion—the feeling that pure MDMA envelopes you in is exactly what its street-form is named after: Ecstasy. Not the stereotypical "touch me everywhere, yeah, that feels good, put your fingers in my mouth" kind of ecstasy, but ecstasy in its rawest form: the rush of rapturous delight fueled by an overpowering state of sudden and lasting intense feelings. You fall into a frenzy of poetic inspiration that mentally propels you to the divine chambers of contemplation, and you never wanna fall out of it. It is one of the most beautiful and truest forms of psychedelic access to our inner-mind's workings, and I wish that everyone could experience that type of ecstasy at least once in their lives. Luckily for me I got to experience MDMA in all her glory before she was beyond tainted by the bullshit dealers scamming us for a dirty dollar.

MDMA is not a new drug; before it was synthesized in the western world by the chemist Anton Kollisch in 1912, ancient cultures were extracting a sap from the sassafras root to make a tea that created the same chemical reactions in the brain as does the lab-created form. Methylenedioxy-methamphteamine, shortened to MDMA, was first synthesized in the scientific community to find a replacement for a pharmaceutical drug meant to stop abnormal bleeding in the body. In the 1950s our very own United States Army commissioned a study of toxicity and behavioral effects in animals that had been injected with mescaline as well as MDMA. Why they didn't use humans for this study, I'll never know. But, when these lab tests were declassified in the late '60s it didn't take long for the scientific community to start advocating MDMA for medical use in the field of psychotherapy and psychoanalysis. For example, couples going through marriage counseling during the '70s were actually given micro-doses of MDMA during their sessions to uncover a sense of emotion that they had lost over the years. Lovers saw the actual *Love* in each other's eyes again, and it's remarkable that a little chemical surge to the receptors in our brains can achieve such emotional rejuvenation.

Sadly, like all good things, the government had to snatch Molly away from us and deem her "dangerous" to the general public if not kept behind bars; MDMA was declared an "emergency" Schedule I drug in May of 1985, but you better believe she didn't go down without a fight! A huge uproar came from the psychotherapy community in 1984 when the government warned the nation that there would be a preliminary hearing to decide if enough abuse was documented to make it illegal. There were three subsequent hearings that year, because that passionate scientific community was able to hold off the government with their overwhelming evidence confirming the drug as a progressive catalyst for clearing emotional blockage. Despite all their efforts, the government decided that there was simply "too much evidence of abuse" in at least 28 states. Whatever that means. It's heartbreaking to think about, really, because alcohol is *still* legal in the face of the rampant abuse and countless AA associations littered across our nation. But, I digress.

When Scarlette and I met across the grassy quad after class one day, I was hyped up on some strange form of the drug that some strange sophomore had given to me. Scarlette came running up to me when I began saying,

"Hey! Listen, this sophomore McKayla Weaver, the lesbian? The blonde one? The one who's always wearing tye-dye shirts and Bermuda shorts? Anyways, she saw me in the parking lot while she was in a frenzy of Molly. Can you believe she called me over to her car and gave me some?! I've never met this girl before in my life!" I said, still not really believing that a stranger handed me drugs. Or that I took them willingly.

"What?! I want some! Did she give you any extra?" She spouted off excitedly.

"Nah, it was only enough to swallow for myself, but lemme

tell you, her shit sucks. You aren't missing out. I know there's gotta be some Goodie Powder or something in this stuff. It isn't doing anything for me like the Molly in Bloodmoon Beach did. I'm just slightly excited and have this weird headache."

"Ugggghhhh, I still want some! What's it like?"

"Well, the pure stuff, pure MDMA, is heavenly. When I say heavenly, I mean it's the sweet nectar of the gods from which they drink at night to paint our dreams for us. There is no truer form of powerful emotion that could be found on earth."

"Wow. Sounds fucking great. When do we get some?" She asked bluntly.

"I'm not confident that anyone around here could produce some serious MDMA, especially after the shit that Weaver tried to pass off as Molly."

"Well that doesn't mean we can't try, right? Let's ask Big Mick," she said as she began typing away on her phone. To our surprise he texted back within five minutes and even knew exactly who to get it from! Score! He asked us to pick him up on the west side of town where he was wandering, and we drove back to the east side afterward to sit in a parking lot discussing the deal.

From the backseat of Scarlette's Jeep, Big Mick said, "So this dude, his name is Yoni. He a crazy-ass Greek muhfucka, so don't try ta get 'im down on the price, nah mean?"

"Yeah, I'm not trying to hustle him," I said, "but I want to make sure this stuff is good, ya know? Pure. I don't want powder."

"Well I'm pretty shur he said itsa rock, but I can't remember," Big Mick mumbled.

A rock!? That's THE purest form! If that was the case, we were rollin' in it, literally.

"Do you think he has heroin?" Scarlette asked, "because I really wanna try some heroin."

"HAIR-RON?!" Big Mick shouted. It was the most emotion I'd seen outta him in our weeks of acquainting each other. "You sayin' you never had hair-ron before? But chu want it?"

"Yes I do," Scarlette replied.

"No wayyyyy, dat's not a drug you 'wanna try' if you ain't neva tried it befo. People do dat shit cuz it's cheaper den da higher quality pill they after. Don't get into dat shit, it's not a pretty place ta be," he tried advising her.

"Yeah, I don't think that's a very good idea at all," I tried reasoning with her, too. But, who am I to judge what kind of drugs she wanted to experiment with when we had a homeless black man in our car waiting on a nutty Greek dude to give us a rock of MDMA? Right when we were throwing these ideas back and forth, a sporty little supped-up red Honda flew into the spot beside our Jeep. If this dude's character was anything like his driving, I knew we were in for some fun.

He jumped out of the car and immediately went up to Big Mick's window in the back. It was already down, and Yoni pushed his round, clean-shaven head inside and began mumbling and dabbing Big Mick in some sort of street-greeting. Eyes darting frantically, he caught a brief look at Scarlette and me and grunted, "sup" in a low gargle. I could immediately tell that he had taken some of the drug earlier that afternoon. Good news for us, because I like a dealer who's confident enough to eat their own product.

"So, how much you lookin' to get?" he asked me, staring toward the front seat. I guess being the driver subconsciously represented some authority to his mind.

"I was hoping for a gram; how much would you charge me for that?" I asked.

"Well, this shit's pure," he laughed as he shuffled around in his place, "so it would be $100 a gram." More good news, because that's how much it went for in Bloodmoon, which meant it was high quality.

"If I'm gonna spend that much money on it, I wanna see it first," I said.

"Yeah, sure, I brought a gram rock because I figured that's what y'all would want. We can break it into pieces if you want less than this, but here," he said as he handed over a small plastic baggie with black devil faces printed all over it.

The rock inside was fucking gorgeous; it looked like a blend of space glass and caramelized sugar, just begging to be licked. And, boy, did I want to! I held back my urge, though, and tried to contain my excitement at coming across a real-life pure, crystalized MDMA rock in Darbyville, South Carolina of all places. You can't ever let these dealers know that they've satisfied you, because they'll never stop trying to manipulate the deal after that.

"Alright, it *looks* really clean," I said to him. "Any way you'd go for $90?"

"Ehhhhh," he paused, "this is a pure rock! How about $95 this time? And next time, you'll get the $90."

"Deal," I said. I reached into my wallet to pull out 95 dollars, swiped it to him through the back window, and it was done. With the Molly in hand, my head began quivering as I imagined a passage into a world more enticing than the one I was experiencing.

"Hey, wait!" Scarlette yelled from the backseat. "Before you go, can you get me any heroin?"

Big Mick and I started crowing in disapproval as Yoni replied, "Yeah, what you lookin' for? Black tar?" It's like his long black coat full of drugs was scarce empty.

"I mean, I don't know, what do you think?" Scarlette asked while Big Mick shook his head vigorously right next to her.

"Wait, have you ever done that shit before?" Yoni asked, brow furrowed.

"Well, no, but I've never done Molly before, either, and you gave that to us pretty easily." She had a point.

"That shit's different!" Yoni shouted. Now he's got the point.

"I'm not selling you heroin, are you crazy? Is this girl crazy?" He asked, looking at Big Mick. "No way," he said, looking back at Scarlette, "people buy that shit because they're addicted. I'm not gonna give a pretty girl heroin, sorry."

"Awh man, come on!" Scarlette tried pleading.

"Nawh, trust me, dog! That's not shit you wanna get started on. Once you're hooked, you don't come off it unless you go to jail or you die. I'm serious," he said with a hard stare at Scarlette. "But I gotta go guys, I'll catch y'all later. Lemme know how you like that stuff," he said as he dabbed Big Mick one last time, nodded at me, and hopped right back into the speed-racer that he jumped out of minutes ago. Watching him disappear around the corner, Scarlette said in her best pouty princess voice,

"He's not a very good dealer. He wouldn't sell me what I

wanted."

"For good reason!" I shouted, "you gotta start with the small stuff. If you try everything else on the list and decide you still wanna try heroin, or meth for that matter, go for it. But if a dealer didn't even feel comfortable about making money off your heroin sale, that should tell you something. In my eyes, it looks like we need more dealers like him."

"Yeah, I guess. Looks like Molly's the first on the list!" She said, distracting herself from disappointment with the prospect of an ecstasy ride.

Big Mick was still sitting by Scarlette when she pulled out her Newports, gave him one, and lit up. While they shared their smoke in silence behind me, I caught him still shaking his head in astonishment, and I grinned.

***

I wanted to save our Molly rock for Halloween, the sacred Samhain that has always been dear to my Irish heart. Scarlette, however, was not one for patience, so she relentlessly questioned me every day as to when our trip would be. Realizing she wasn't going to give up the game until the precious Molly had been won, I gave in and promised that we'd take it the coming Friday after classes let out and all the other girls had gone home for Fall Break. It was only a four-day weekend, but there was a free Annabelle's bus trip headed to Charleston for a Citadel football game that Saturday. Seemed like a fun, free college experience with plenty of forbidden boys nearby, so we signed ourselves up for the bus-ride and signed our souls away to a Friday night in Neverland.

When the clock struck "Friday," Scarlette wasted no time getting straight to the point. While we were eating lunch that afternoon, she said,

"So we're taking it tonight right? I mean, like, now. We're taking it right after lunch." She grinned through her spaghetti noodles.

"No way!" I said. "I see what you're trying to do! We'll take it when the sun starts to set, and it'll last for about 9 hours. I promise, we'll have plenty of time in the vortex," I assured her.

With a little pout, she accepted, and we went on a Loop to kill time instead. When we got back from the Loop, though, the suspense had just about shoved a stake through her heart.

"Can we pleeeeeeease take it now? Please, oh, please!" She said, tugging on my arm like a small child.

"Fiiiiiiiiine, ya big ole baby!" I groaned with a slight smile. She started skipping around in her place, dancing with her arms and shoulders while I rolled my eyes into another dimension.

Since I was the buyer of the Molly, I was naturally her keeper as well. I made Scarlette shut her eyes and turn her body around while I grabbed an old boot box from the top of my closet. There were a bunch of odd keepsakes littering the empty space, like little motivational notes that Angel had given me and pieces of my journals that had jumped ship during tireless writing sessions. Excavating the tiny bag of Molly from the bottom, chills shivered their way from the base of my spine all the way to the tip of my skull.

Sweet anticipation.

"Okay, so we're not gonna take all of this at once, but we're gonna crush it up in the bag so we don't make a mess later," I advised her.

"Wait, why aren't we taking it all?" She asked, a little offended.

"Trust me, if this is pure MDMA, we won't be needing half a gram each to ourselves. We'll test it out and see how it goes."

I took my beloved wooden one-hitter out of my satchel and began using the blunt end to crush the rock into lickable yellow crystals.

"Wait!" Scarlette said.

"What?!" I asked, startled.

"Well, you know I'm gonna wanna take a lot of pictures of this. And I look ugly," she said, staring down at her sweatpants and boots. Don't you think we should get cute first? Ya know, play with our clothes and put on a cool outfit?"

"Ya know, you're right!" I said, putting the bag of Molly down. "Meet back here when you're all done. Don't forget to be comfortable! Things might get weird."

I believe if you treat your Life like a ritual and make sure to dress the part, too, then the magic of a ritual won't be far behind. It took me three full sweeps through my closet before finally deciding on a sheer ankle-length olive green dress. Since the weather outside was less than warm, I chose crocheted maroon leggings to wear underneath and put on Scarlette's beige boots. I draped myself in golden teardrop earrings, an old-school bronze stopwatch necklace, and the most ornate golden septum ring I owned. Over-top of the slinky green dress, I wore a copper brown leather jacket that had industrial zippers scattered all over the body. Since I got lucky with the straight-haired genes of the family, all I had to do was brush it out and tussle it a bit with my fingers before my tri-colored locks were ready for action. A little extra mascara on the eyes, and voila.

"I hope you made a good choice!" I heard Scarlette from the hall, "Because if we're gonna be taking pictures of this we've gotta be complimentary!"

"Take a gander, what do you think?" I asked, arms spread wide open, twirling my body in slow motion for her.

"Ohhhh, very chic! Very 90s, meets steampunk, meets Hindu goddess."

"Look at you!" I said.

"Like what you see?" She teased, spinning in slow motion for me, too.

Scarlette knew how to dress impeccably, no matter the actual condition of the clothing that covered her. From the toes up, she was wearing her Ox-blood platform Doc Marten boots that paired perfectly with her sheer leopard-print black tights. It wouldn't be Scarlette if there weren't a few rips and nicks in the fabric, of which she had plenty. The skirt she chose for the occasion was a tight black mini that had silver studs, spikes, and beads decorating the whole piece.

"Flashy skirt, man!" I said, reaching out to touch the spikes myself.

"You can call me Queen Badass from now on," she said, nose in the air.

"Oh, please, I'm the Queen. You can be my successor in the case of an unfortunate event."

To complete the look, Scarlette wore a simple low cut black tank top tucked into the studded skirt. For warmth, she had her father's letterman jacket from the 70s—black, gold, and white tattered suede with a capital "A" for Aiden and the number "41" from football glory days. Her deep brown ringlets fell down on her shoulders in a calculated wreck, and her eyes had just been inked with a fresh peppering of makeup.

"Now we're ready," I said to her. I shook a couple fingers worth into the palm of my hand and held it gently while I did the same with hers.

"How am I supposed to snort it when it's in my hand like this?" She asked.

"Oh, no, no, no, honey. Contrary to popular belief, the best way to take Molly is by licking it off your hand! It isn't cocaine, you don't wanna snort it. It just doesn't hit you the right way."

"If you say so," she said with stars in her eyes. She was dazzled by the expectations she had built up for the night, while having no earthly clue what her mind was about to show her. With our hands held clumsily above our chests in the middle of room 209, I held mine out to her in an effort to cheers good luck to the trip we were embarking on, and she did the same.

"Well, here it goes," I said, "you ready for this?"

"Yes!"

"Okay, let's go!"

With those words we both dived nose-first into our anxious palms.

One big lick.

Quick swig of water.

Wincing eyes.

Swallow.

The bitter gems swam their way through our throats, buried themselves into our stomachs, and seeped their way into our bloodstreams within the hour. Upon swallowing, I felt the pupils in my eyes grow large enough to black out the honey-brown that Scarlette had once seen. Staring into her eyes, I saw the same reaction mirroring my own. Blast off.

VIII: Autumn 2K12: The Rock, Part Deux

"I don't feel anything," Scarlette said with a sigh. It had only been 30 minutes since we lapped up those pretty little crystals.

"Just give it a little longer, I swear it's gonna hit ya," I assured her as I flung my body onto the bed.

"Can we take morrrre?" She asked.

"We don't need more yet, just wait!" I said, sitting up to grab her hand in between my own. "I promise you, I'm not trying to jip you out of your first Molly experience."

"Okay, well, can we go to the art building right quick then?" She asked, squeezing my hands. "I think I left my phone charger there."

"Yeah, hop up, let's go."

Since Annabelle's houses less than 800 students, they built only four parking lots for us to shuffle around and play musical cars. One of the largest lots was beside the art building, so there was always a chance to chat with a familiar face while everybody came and went. The ones we met in the parking lot this time were those of McKayla Weaver and a girl named Velma. Everyone knew McKayla as Wavy, a name she took up in the creation of her very own electro-hippie trance music. Ironic, because Wavy is the girl that gave me that sub-par MDMA a week ago. I waved to her obnoxiously from across the parking lot, and she gave a nod across the way. She turned to her friend to say something about how I drove her around on a wild binge, I'm sure.

"Is that Wavy Weaver?" Scarlette whispered to me.

"Yeah, that's the girl that gave me that shitty Molly in exchange for driving her around the other day!"

"OOOOOOooooOOOOhhhhh! Wow, yeah, when I asked

people where to get weed from they all told me 'Wavy.' But I never knew that's who they were talking about."

Wavy interrupted the ah-ha moment by walking up to say,

"Look who it is! Nice to see ya again, man."

She reached her hand out from under her tye-dyed hoodie to give me a smooth handshake with the geekiest smile spreading across her face. Despite Wavy's excitement, all I was noticing was her friend's beguiling demeanor. You see, Velma is what we call a stud—an LGBTQ term for a lesbian who's practically a man with a vagina. Dresses, speaks, acts, and thinks with a masculine perspective—must be a what we call a man. It was all in the way she presented herself.

"This is my good pal, Velma. Velma, meet..." and with a struggle on her face she squinted her eyes at me to ask, "Lyyyyylaaaa?"

"Yeah! You got it right. I'm Lyla," I said with a chuckle. I guess the Molly held her memory hostage. "Good to meet ya," I said to Velma.

"Yeah, you guys, too." She spoke gently, but firmly. Her brown eyes were masked with thick-rimmed glasses that blended into her buttery, cocoa skin. Inviting, yet stoic. She was dressed head-to-toe in black and red coordination; black slacks, a red men's Polo, a black blazer, and red and black Jordans on her feet. She even had a matching red and black New York Bulls hat that she wore backwards on her bald scalp. She's a stud, alright.

"I'm Scarlette," she said to them both. "Everyone told me that you were the one with the weed connection, but I never knew where to find you," she said to Wavy.

"Awh, man," Wavy said, "you coulda just paid a visit to the music building! That's usually where I am. Ya know, mixin' them beatz." She broke down a little beat-box routine for us, and I was surprised by her oral expertise, dare I say.

I laughed, then looked to Velma. "You go to Annabelle's too?"

"No, I just graduated this past May."

"Oh, what was your degree in?"

"I triple-majored in music production, Spanish, and philosophy," she said coolly.

"What the fuck," I started, "where do you work now?"

"Don't laugh," she said as she rolled her eyes and kicked the air near the ground, "Payless Shoes."

"WHAT?!" Scarlette and I both shrieked.

"Well think about the job market out there," she said, "there isn't much opportunity for a music-playing, bi-lingual philosopher." It's sad to say, but she's right. The job market post-college is shit. Pure shit. I won't put the usual "bull" in front of it, because not even bulls deserve to be sullied by America's capitalist monster.

"Goddddddd, that fucking sucks," I whispered.

"Ohhh, yeah it does. I spent six years here, and I've got student loans out the ass. Peddling shoes isn't gonna pay those bills, ya know?"

"SIX YEARS?!" Scarlette and I yelled once again in unison.

"Yeahhhhhh, maaaan," Wavy said, "she ain't no super-senior, she's a super-*duper*-senior! Six years in this place, and three degrees!" You could tell they were best friends.

"How did you stay here for six years?!" Scarlette asked.

"This is a great place," Velma said to us, "and I wouldn't have chosen to graduate from any other school in the world. Really! Sure, the rules are a little strict and you see the same faces day in and day out, but I had 700 ladies to make the days go by faster," she said with a sinister giggle.

"Yeah, I guess that would do the trick," I laughed. I caught myself being careful for Scarlette, because she was still mighty stand-offish when it came to the lesbians, especially studs like these.

"So, what are you guys getting into tonight? You tryna hang?" Wavy asked us.

"Well, we have to go to the art building to see if I left my phone charger there. And we took some Molly," Scarlette blurted out.

"Ohhhh SHIT!" Wavy and Velma said together.

"What, my stuff got you a little taste and you decided to go for more?" Wavy asked me with a wink.

"Yeah, we ended up getting in touch with someone who found a pure rock!" I told her, "So here we are."

"How long ago did you dose?" Wavy asked.

"It feels like hours," Scarlette said.

"It was only 45 minutes ago!" I laughed.

"Damn, man, you're gonna be feelin' that soon!" Wavy said. Little did she know, I could feel the euphoria swelling in my veins right there in the parking lot.

"Well, we gotta go see Mary and Ashley anyways," Velma reminded Wavy, "why don't you two do what you gotta do, we'll go do our thing, and we can meet up in a bit to smoke or something?"

"Yeah! I'm down," Scarlette said.

"Yeah, sounds good, just shoot me a text whenever y'all are ready," I said to Wavy.

***

Before long our heads had shot way past the 9th cloud and onto the umpteenth. It's hard to get a grip on what's swimming around in there, but it sounds something like,

"Fuck, man, our generation has the potential to be *the* generation to make some sort of impact, I mean, we gotta restore some kinda honesty! You know we've been warring since the dawn of fucking time and we still can't get a grip on the fact that we aren't getting anywhere with it?!?! All the same land, different rulers, different times, same blood, same deceit I can feel it more and more and more with each new face around me, the thirst for an honest society, a tried-and-true set of people, I think we are thee generation that could be like WHAT THE FUCK EVERYBODY, quit this shit, let's make Life what it should be: HONEST HONEST HONEST, and why the fuck are we doing all this fighting in God's name? don't we know God doesn't like war? Or maybe God does like war and that's the issue, right? because if God is the reason there's all this war and death and hate then God's a piece of fucking shit, right? what kind of God would let that happen? why can't we be more honest, 'with all thy getting, get understanding,' ya know, what a beautiful feeling this all is, sensational, my GOD, look at how the leaves go from that dim hunter green to a golden dandy yellow, and then that true verde! Ohhh…"

Trying to keep up with my deafening inner monologues, I faintly heard someone calling out from behind us. I turned to see that Wavy and Velma were trudging up the hills along the quad, gunnin' for a smoke sesh.

"How you guys feelin' now?" Wavy asked.

"Great, I'm feelin' great! My chest feels like it's heaving with happiness, real happiness." Scarlette squealed.

"Yeah! So Velma," I said while the four of us moseyed over to the car, "I've been thinking a lot about what you said about the job market being shit and all, and I've been on this whole wanting-to-be-a-tattoo-artist kick, and, I mean, what I'm really trying to ask is, do you feel like you fucked up by following what you wanted to do instead of focusing on what you were gonna do after college?"

She let out a quick laugh before saying, "Don't get me wrong, I know it sucks dick that I'm working at a shoe store with a $180,000 worth of degrees in my pocket. But I put six years into exactly what I wanted to learn and who I wanted to become. Some of my professors are my best friends now, and I even house sit for a couple of them when they go on vacations. My life won't always be spent as a shoe salesman, but right now, it is. I get by with a little help from my friends," she said shooting a smile to Wavy.

She paused her story to unlock the car for everybody. Naturally, Scarlette and I hopped into the backseat while Wavy took the passenger's. When we were all safely within the confines of yet another Toyota Camry, she said,

"The biggest lesson you've gotta learn while you're at college is to be true to yourself about what you want in Life. I know that sounds cliché and overplayed, but take this for instance; I'm a dyke. Ya know? It's obvious. I like to dress very masculine—men's shoes, men's pants, men's shirts, men's hats, men's underwear, you name it. But during a big recital in my sophomore year, I decided to try to dress like all the other music students. I went out and bought a nice skirt, pantyhose, heels, some dainty blouse. Sounds normal, right? It was anything but.

"I looked hideous, and I was beyond uncomfortable. It was like seeing Santa in a speedo on a Hawaiian island. Just wrong! Oh, and the breeze coming up my skirt? Hell no! Hellllllll nooooooo. I dunno how y'all do that. Anyways, you could see the lack of comfort in my recital. I was horribly rigid and tense and played the worst performance of my life to date. After the recital, one of my closest professors pulled me aside and said,

'Velma, pardon me for saying this, but that was awful. I've never seen you so miserable playing music. And what are you wearing? Really? Don't take this the wrong way, I understand what you're trying to do, but this isn't you.'

"She was right," Velma continued, "I realized how atrocious I looked trying to be a graceful little girl, when really, I'm a bad-ass stud, and I like it that way! I learned that in order to cope best with what Life throws at you, you gotta always strive to be the best you. You can't try to be someone or something else, because you'll do a terrible fucking job. You have to wake up every day and push yourself to dress in your own style and walk your own path as naturally as it comes to you. You never know who you're gonna meet along the way, and you don't wanna be a half-ass version of yourself when you meet the person who could make your wildest dreams come true."

I couldn't tell if her speech answered my question, but I also couldn't remember my question to begin with. But I'll tell you what, it's absolutely empowering to know that Velma is still so full of hope after spending six years on a triple-degree to work in retail.

"Do you think being at Annabelle's made you more of a lesbian? Or do you think it just made you feel comfortable being who you are? I'm sorry if that's too personal, I'm just really curious." Scarlette asked.

Oh boy.

"Annabelle's doesn't make you more of a lesbian," Wavy answered her, "but if you're already a little bi-curious, trust me, this place will bring you over to the rainbow side of our world for sure!"

The car erupted in a roar of laughter right before Scarlette blurted out, "I'm straight, I'm sure, and I'm not curious!"

"Hey, man, don't worry, you're not really my style," Velma joked with her.

For nine hours Scarlette and I kept our butts parked right in Velma's backseat while we relentlessly talked her to near death. We weren't leaving until she kicked us out, and oddly enough, she never tried to. She didn't seem at all bothered that we were rolling on Molly and tumbling so fast through our thoughts aloud. I think she found us amusing—two naïve freshmen, so interested in dissecting the secrets of the world around us. We rode to her house so that she could get her bowl to smoke in, and Scarlette tolerated it at first. But since she's an all-blunts kinda gal, she refused the second bowl and instead asked,

"Velma, would you mind driving me to the bank and the gas station to get some blunt wraps? I don't wanna be difficult, but I can't get high off of bowls. I don't think I know how to smoke them, honestly. And I'd like nothing more than to smoke a nice fattie right now."

"Yeah, sure," Velma replied easily. She was such a calming and comforting energy to be around. Her smile was as soft as her voice, and her lack of annoyance with us was a godsend. She was even open with talking about the complexity of lesbian sexuality, which was fun to talk about in Scarlette's presence and her budding curiosity to fathom that world.

"I don't understand your sex," Scarlette started to say, "I mean, this is all very new to me still, this gay world. It's kinda scary to me because I'm secretly worried that the lesbians are plotting to come after me and corrupt me, but I'm trying to open my mind to it. I am, I really am! It's just, I mean, I come from a really small southern town where everybody knows everybody and NOBODY there is gay. It's all about God in Aiden, and I've never even been around a lesbian to know how to act with them or how they act with me. Does that make sense?"

"Girl, you ain't gotta be scared of us! If you're not scared of guys, you shouldn't be scared of lesbians," she said very matter-of-fact. "Our sex really isn't too complicated either. Typically, in a lesbian relationship there's a penetrator and a receiver, just like in straight sex. Me, for example, I don't like to be penetrated. At all. But I like to wear strap-ons and give it to the chick I'm with."

"Ahhhhh!" Scarlette shrieked and covered her face. "I'm sorry, I never knew that, and that's an odd visual," she said with a laugh.

I was laughing too, but my eyes were glistening with compassion as I said,

"Velma, I know she sounds shocked by all of this, but it's really beautiful to see her open up and ask you questions about your sexuality. She's still kind of skeptical of lesbians, but listening to her try to shut that discomfort out is awesome, and I'm glad you're the one helping her with it." Sentimentality is on full-blast during a Molly trip, and this one was a textbook trip of tasting such emotion.

Velma smiled, nodded her head in agreeance, and said to Scarlette,

"Speaking of your whole backwards-southern-town notion, I feel you on that. My church is that way. I'm from here, from Ferndale actually. In this tiny town, we can all smell each other's dirty laundry and have no problems gossiping about the odor. I've always been a tomboy, so when I got older and started showing signs of being a lesbian, people started showing 'concern' for me. My parents were never against me or how I acted, but once they saw that the tomboy phase was turning into a lesbian lifestyle, they were worried. They started telling me I needed to dress more feminine, that I needed to buy a weave instead of keeping my head shaved, and that if I didn't quit soon people would start thinking bad things about me. I wasn't worried, but I wanted my parents to be proud of their kid, ya know?
"

"We all do," Scarlette said.

"Yes, yes, I agree," I said.

"Well, things just went from bad to worse. During my freshman year at Annabelle's, my church pastor called me in for a meeting one Wednesday night. He and another woman that watched me grow up in that church were sitting inside waiting for me on one of the pews. Nobody else was there, and I had that immediate sinking feeling in my stomach when I saw their faces.

"Long story short, they straight-up asked me if I was a lesbian. I was floored, because I knew that telling them the truth could get me kicked out of the church, but I also didn't feel like it was something to lie about! I didn't need to be lying about who I wanted to fuck, or why. It's ridiculous. But to them, God hates the homosexuals. I don't believe that, but they do. It's the Baptist philosophy. And they're my "leaders". I couldn't lie about it, so I told them that I was indeed a lesbian. In less than a heartbeat they started giving me a passionate spiel about how I could be saved and that I could recover from the sin that's consumed my life. They told me it's a matter of disease in my heart, and that through God, all my pains could be cured.

"I decided that rather than arguing, it would be better for everyone involved to pretend that I believed I could be cured of my 'sin'. It broke my fucking heart, man, because I knew that if they were coming to me about it, then all the other church members had to be talking about it too. This was the church I had been going to all my life, and I couldn't imagine just walking away from it. I'm a lesbian, yes, but I am still in that church *every* Sunday. Unfortunately, being in my house of God never felt the same after that talk with them. I felt ashamed, even though I knew I had no reason to be ashamed! And I felt wronged by society, too. Just because certain humans feel uncomfortable with who I'm sleeping with, they decide that they have the authority to say someone as benevolent and all-encompassing as God gives a shit about something so menial. It's wrong to humiliate someone for being who they truly are. It's just wrong," she said solemnly as she looked out of her car window.

"Wow," Scarlette said, "I can't believe they tried to give you an ultimatum like that."

"Yeah, that sucks," I started, "humans just have the hardest time understanding that attraction to a soul is a matter of their energy, not their gender. It's all about the energy! A masculine woman has a masculine energy, and a straight woman who senses that masculine energy is going to feel some type of pull. It's natural. Whether it be a sexual pull or a platonic pull depends on the energy of the person within. It's a balance, a yin-yang type of game. If the yin to your yang just so happens to be someone of the same sex, who's to say that's wrong? We're all just trying to find the energy that balances ours out, and I don't know why it's so complicated for organized religion to accept that. Buddhism and Taoism seem to be doing just fine in the modern age. When will the Abrahamic traditions get on board?"

"I agree," Velma started, "it's all in the energy. And on that note, we're gonna smoke another blunt. Cool with that, Scarlette?"

"Fuck yeah, please!" She said enthusiastically.

We met up with Velma and Wavy around 6:08 PM earlier that evening, and Wavy had to call it quits before midnight since she had to take a trip with some friends the next day. It was 3:12 in the goddamn morning before Velma finally kicked us out of her car. She had a 10 AM shift at Payless that morning and figured she needed sleep before battling with the public. I couldn't tell you what we talked about for most of that time that night, but I know every second was spent gabbing and exploring all the ways we've experienced humanity. After parting ways and giving profuse thank-yous for dealing with our non-stop conversation, Scarlette and I walked away from Velma's car with arms hooked and eyes as wide as could be. It was a night of insight for both of us, and I could tell we busted down some walls in Scarlette's tight, Christian mindset. Spending nine hours in a car with a new-found friend was not my vision for how the night was gonna go, but I couldn't have asked for a better first Molly trip with Scarlette. Psychedelics like that open your eyes to all the glorious connections that Life effortlessly manifests right under your nose, and we could see them all.

We wandered back to room 209 with the pale blue light greeting us upon entry, thankful for the bed that awaited our shaking bodies. It felt phenomenal to stretch out on that plastic excuse of a mattress as Scarlette said,

"She was really great. I'm glad we met her, and I'm glad we spent our whole trip with her. I love Molly. I've never been so open to that lezzie stuff before. Never even wanted to ask questions about it or anything."

"Right?" I said. "Now, let's get some shut-eye for our trip to Charleston tomorrow."

"Ohhhhh! I'm so excited! Citadel boys in military garb, and tailgating, and big, strong football players! Oh my!" She squealed.

I laughed, because Citadel boys were not my cup of tea, but I was still excited to experience such an event at the south's premier military academy.

"Yeah," I said to her, "don't you ditch me for some football player!"

"Oh, I wouldn't dream of it," Scarlette said.

"Good answer," I replied, "now close your eyes and I'll see ya in the morning light."

***

We tried. We could *not* close our eyes. And trust me, our frazzled maniacal minds wanted nothing more than to be turned the fuck off. With the sun intruding upon us at 7 AM I realized that it was round-fucking-two of an awful amphetamine restlessness.

"Oh my Goddddddd," Scarlette groaned from under the covers, "I just want to sleeeeeeeep! My eyes won't even stay closed for more than five minutes."

"I know," I sighed, "it's like they're operating on a spring method; as soon as you try to close them, they pop right back open."

"I'm so miserable," Scarlette said with a little weep in her throat, "my head hurts, and it feels fuzzy. My mind stopped going through 1,000 thoughts in a minute, and now it's just stuck on one thought that won't quit."

"I can't stop thinking about Velma," I said to her, "that's the one thought that my head won't fucking give up."

"What about her?" Scarlette asked.

"Nothing, really, my inner voice just won't shut up with her name. It's saying Velma-Velma-Velma-Velma-Velma."

"That's weird, you crushin' on Velma?"

I laughed obnoxiously and said, "no way, she was just really interesting, ya know? And meaningful."

Ignoring that last statement, Scarlette said, "We *have* to find a way to sleep. We need more weed, we need it. We've only got one blunt left and I know that won't be enough."

"Yeah, but I spent all my money on the Molly, and you don't have any left. So, all we've got is that one skimp. We have to use it wisely."

"UUUUUUGGGGGHHHHHHH!" She yelled, kicking her feet around like a child, as usual.

"I'm gonna put on some shamanic drum-beating and see if we can at least get a couple hours in. The bus leaves in three hours, so set an alarm," I said.

For the next three hours, there was little sleeping. There was a lot of tossing and turning and moaning and groaning and hating the decision to take so much Molly, but we were able to get about ninety minutes of sleep—heads still reeling and trying to run away from our bodies. When my alarm went off at 10:30 AM, I didn't even have time to complain before Scarlette said,

"We are *not* fucking going to Charleston."

"FUCK no," I agreed. Thank GOD, ALLAH, YAWEH, BUDDHA, SHIVA, ODIN, KALI that she didn't want to go either. My body quivered a little as I crawled out from under the covers to grab my phone. Checking my messages, I was slightly alarmed that I had eight texts from this boy named Brandon. He was just a horny 25-year-old trying to hook up with as many young Annabelle's girls as he could, and I happened to be the apple of his eye during my freshman year. I forgot that weeks ago he had asked me to go to a wedding with him, and in my stupor I totally neglected that the wedding was this very morning.

"Ohhhhh fuuuuuuuuuuuuck," I said in overwhelming defeat.

"What is it, honey?" Scarlette asked.

"I was supposed to go to a wedding today."

"With that old guy?" Scarlette asked. Twenty-five seems a bit old compared to our eighteen.

"Yep. With that old guy."

We looked at each other in a distraught pause before bursting into hysterical laughter.

"No fucking way you're going to that wedding!" Scarlette chimed.

"NOOOOOOOO fucking way," I agreed. I sent a few quick little sorry-I-forgot messages to my boy, and in my heart, I knew it would be at least three months before he got over this cut. And it was, but who cares? Definitely not Molly-crashing Lyla.

"Well now that we've established we aren't going anywhere today, we need to smoke weed," Scarlette insisted.

"You wanna go ahead and try to smoke the last one?" I said.

"Yeahhhhhh," she huffed out, "let's go."

There has never been so much grief spilled out into that Jeep other than when we were trying desperately to get high and make all our incessant babble disappear that day. We were grumpier than Snow White's cranky dwarf and pouting harder than a five-year-old that didn't get her pony. Ridiculous, if you could have only seen it! Everything seemed to go wrong for us—we ripped the first cigar we bought, the weed was nowhere near enough for the pain in our bodies, we ran out of gas, and we just couldn't seem to get comfortable anywhere we were. It's as if the certainty and pure elation of a Molly trip is destroyed by the total lack of conviction and discomfort that follows in the crash. Don't get me wrong—the trips I've taken through MDMA have always been exactly what I needed without a crazy drop off the cliff. This time was different, though, and the plunge back down to reality was really messing with us.

We tried smoking in the back of an Annabelle parking lot behind a dumpster, sitting on a plush white blanket under some trees; it was one of the worst ideas we've ever had! To stage a picnic and smoke a blunt in broad daylight, post-Molly trip, on school grounds? Ha! But I'm telling you, it was a fury of grey melancholy and we didn't give a damn about anything except inhaling that weed and trying to simmer down.

"What are we doing?" Scarlette asked, sweat dripping down her cheeks, "we should be driving the loop, not sitting here under a tree at school."

"You're right, I don't know why we thought this was a good idea," I said, putting the blunt out with barely a laugh. We ended up scraping together $2.36 in loose change for some gas and took off into the country.

"LLLLLYYYYYYYYLLLLLAAAAAAAAA," Scarlette whined from the passenger's seat, "I'm so FUCKING uncomfortable!" She squirmed around in the leather and kicked her feet at the dashboard before saying, "Why is she doing this to uuuuusssss? I feel like crying," she said as a tear nearly escaped from her eyes, "and I *would* cry if I could, but I can't even muster up any tears!" Luckily for her, or maybe unfortunately, our real sense of emotion had been stolen from us by a crushed up rock. I bet we could have smoked sixteen more blunts before we were satisfied, but that was a lesson for us in weed conservation as well as the true meaning of the word "crash" when it comes to psychoactive drugs.

"Hey," she started, "do you think we could get Big Mick to find us someone to front a little weed until I get my allowance next week?"

"It's worth a try," I said, "give him a call."

She did.
He agreed.
We screamed.
Acquired the weed.
Relief.

After we had another gram in our possession, we rode out to an abandoned farm twelve miles from Darbyville. Dodging the rusted metal remnants and jutting wooden fragments, we carried the white blanket and the blunts up to the second floor of an old hay barn. As we laid on the crooked, splintered floorboards watching the smoke go up with the draft, our stresses left us with each inhale. Passing the weed back and forth without the slightest word, we were thankful that if we were going to feel this much pain, at least we were toughing it out with a sympathetic familiar beside us. It was one of the nastiest comedowns I've ever witnessed, and it took us two whole days of resting and resetting before our bodies and minds felt back up to speed. Needless to say, we were more than thrilled to kick Molly out of room 209 after that trip. And we never called Her again.

IX: Winter 2K12: The Unraveling

The careful stealth that I had perfected over the years and had become so proud of was diminishing into reckless abandon—and fast. My secrets started revealing themselves, and it was only a matter of Time before Scarlette and Mia caught on to the deceptive dark brewing a storm inside me. Tammy, by her own accords, had been expelled from Annabelle's, and I was too excited to share the real story of the ass-kickin' as soon as I heard she was gone. Naturally, I ran to Mia, because not only did I think that she would find the humor in all of it, but I couldn't tell Scarlette yet; she had been brought into the lie as a witness, and I didn't want her to know that I dooped her into that job. Not yet.

"Are you fucking serious?" Mia said with zero praise in her voice. I decided to tell her while we were doing homework and chain-smoking in her car.

"Yeah! Are you kidding me? First, she forced you out of the room, then she started fucking in my bed, and then fucking with my things? My journals, Mia, my journals." I thought she'd at least sympathize with that much, being a writer herself.

"You know she just got expelled, and your bullshit case probably had a lot to do with that," she said as she bobbed her head at me, just the way Tammy used to do.

"Are you saying it wasn't deserved? She shits in a plastic bag and puts it on her CA's doorstep, and yet, she isn't a bit crazy? Even if she didn't beat herself up, we all know that was her shit in that Ziploc."

"I'm saying that there was another way to go about it rather than lying," she said coldly.

"Maybe," I said, turning back to face the windshield so as not to catch her disappointed eyes, "but I tried that, remember? I went through all the bullshit processes on how to get a new roommate, and they wouldn't listen to me. What's done is done."

"Yeah, sure," Mia said, staring at the journal in her lap.

From that point on Mia was much harsher with me; she didn't seek me out for a random hangout sesh, we rarely spoke in class, and she always carried this hint of suspicion whenever I was near. I began to push her away, naturally, because I realized that letting her in on my diabolical scheme was only making my darkness ever-apparent—and it wasn't pretty.

While Mia was distancing herself from me after catching a real glimpse of my soul, there was one girl on the Leigh Hall that was only trying to get closer to me. Emilia is her name, the one who got the silly "Let It Be" tattooed on her wrist. She's the offspring of a millionaire Alabama preacher who would stop at nothing to enable his daughter's incessant alcoholism and endless partying. She's the total cliché preacher's daughter, right down to the multiple abortions and begging Daddy for money at the end of the week so that she could finish a "school project" only to spend it traipsing through every frat boy in town. She spent more time at the co-ed school down the road than she did at ours, but that's beside the point.

The point is that Emilia finally started catching on to the true ways of Robinhood; she knew that I had been stealing all of the jewelry and clothes and handbags and shoes from around Darbyville, and one day she came into room 209 with the sweetest smile full of shit, and said,

"Look, I know where you get all that stuff from."

"Huh?" I questioned, looking up from my laptop

"All the stuff you give away to the girls around here," she started whispering since the door was open. "I know that you steal it. And I know which stores you steal it from."

I paused and stared at her, brow furrowed. I hesitated a moment in an attempt to gather the possible avenues I could take this before saying,

"Okay? So, what are you trying to tell me?"

"Well," she said with a sinister grin on her face, "I want you to do something for me. And if you say you won't do it, then I'll go to all these different stores and tell them that I know the girl that's been stealing all their merchandise."

Fucking great.

As if swiping from corporations wasn't already risky business, now it seems I'm getting blackmailed for the good deed of giving some broke college girls a taste of free glamour. That's a preacher's daughter, for ya.

"Are you fucking serious?" I scoffed at her.

"Yeah, I'm serious," and without skipping a beat, she went on to explain her predicament.

"Here's the deal: my daddy gave me $400 to buy two sun dresses and hats for the upcoming Kentucky Derby. I need that money to buy beer and Molly for this weekend's party over at Centennial College. So, I need you to steal me two dresses from this nice boutique downtown. Don't worry, I can get the hats myself."

As if that was a relief. The shop she wanted me to steal from went against all the rules I had built my empire upon; it's a locally owned boutique with highly expensive, yet stunning handmade dresses. Owned by a fellow woman, this shop was not made to be tainted by Robinhood. This woman even donated some of their profits to a charitable organization in the community. FUCK, right? The mighty huntress had become the hunted and it looked like I had to fight for my life on this one. It was steal, or be given up as the thief that's been robbing all of Darbyville's major outlets. Stealing seemed to be the only logical action to take.

Once we were at the boutique, I was only seeing the world through tunnel vision. My objective: grab two dresses as soon as humanly possible, AND GET THE FUCK OUT. I covered up all of my tattoos by wearing a long sleeve shirt and maxi skirt, pulled my hair up into a disheveled bun, and wore my glasses so that I would seem totally unrecognizable if the shop owner ever caught on to what I was doing. Turns out, Emilia visits the boutique frequently every time her family comes to visit her in Darbyville, and she and the owner were on a first-name basis. Wonderful, stealing from a friend, too!?

"Danaaaaa!" Emilia squealed when we walked through the door. "It's so good to see you again!"

"Oh, Emilia, what a surprise! I wasn't expecting you for another couple weeks!"

"Well, you know the Derby is coming up! So, Daddy sent me in here to pick out a few options and send him photos before I buy anything. You know how picky he can be," she said as they both giggled. I'm sure Dana could notice the pained anger stuck on my face, but she turned to me anyways and said,

"Oh, is this a friend of yours, Emilia?"

"Yeah! That's my friend Rachel. She goes to Upstate College, but we met at the bar the other night and hit it off immediately! So I asked her if she wanted to go shopping with me today." I had to give it to the girl, she was damn good at lying on the spot.

"Oh, how sweet! It's lovely to meet you Rachel."

"Likewise," I said with a grimace.

"Well, girls, I need to go unpack some of the new items we've got. They're absolutely beautiful, you must try some of them on for me, Emilia! I have yet to see them on some real flesh! But in the meantime, you peruse the store, pick out anything you might even remotely fancy, and hang it up in your dressing room. Now don't try anything on without me!" With a sweet smile, Dana turned her heels and went skipping to the back room. That was my que to begin.

As we wandered the place, Emilia whispered to me when something caught her eyes.

"Ohhh, this would be nice, don't you think Lyla? Remember, size 0!"

Right, FUCK YOU, I thought. But, better news for me, because size 0 meant less fabric, which meant maybe a less obvious sign that there were two dresses in my obnoxious silver tote bag. After going through the tiny boutique, I managed to snag Emilia two wonderful dresses that would fit her stupid fucking Kentucky Derby image. Just as I had shoved the second one into my bag, Dana came out of the back room glowing with anticipation to see Emilia try on all these different pieces.

"Are you ready, sweet pea? Show me what you picked out!" As they went through five different picks, Dana turned to me to say, "Oh, Rachel, you didn't see anything you liked?"

"No, ma'am, that's not the case! I love it all! It's just, I won't be going to the Kentucky Derby, and I'm just a broke bartender trying to pay for school. There will come a day when I wear a hat to the Derby, though, don't you worry!"

"Oh, I'm sorry to hear that. But no matter! At least you know your limitations, right dear? I was never very good at that," she snickered to Emilia.

If she only knew how far past my limitations I actually was, I don't think she'd be so friendly. While Emilia took her sweet time trying on her clothes, Dana began giving me odd looks. She started looking a little too hard at my bulging tote back and noticing my anxious demeanor. Because, let me remind you, I was entirely out of my comfort zone with this heist. Before I knew it, Dana was wandering around her own store with a scowl on her face, picking up two empty clothes hangers from her displays. The empty hangers let her know only one thing: the dresses that belonged on those hangers had conspicuously disappeared within Emilia's visit. I saw her grab the second empty coat hanger, and as she pulled it off the rack she looked up directly into my eyes. I could see the lava about to burst from her own, spewing across the boutique and onto my face, burning off every inch of precious skin I had to cover my shame. She knew what I had done, and she knew why my bag was bursting at the seams.

Intense burning sensation.

Intense shiver.

Paranoia?

No.

Pure panic.

My heart beat rapidly and in an instant my palms got the clammy-cold-sweats. I grabbed my phone out of the bag, pretended like it was ringing, turned to Emilia, and said,

"Hey, I'll be right back, my mom's calling me."

Out of the corner of my eye, I saw Dana begin to open her mouth and I heard her heels clicking ferociously to stop me, but Emilia distracted her easily by asking her opinion of a horrid yellow dress.

I stepped foot outside her shop, took ten shaky steps to the left until I was out of her view, looked both ways for cops and other authority, and I took the fuck off. I bolted down Main Street through the barrage of towering 18th century buildings, and as soon as I got to the closest alley, I darted behind the wall. My heart was thrashing inside of my chest, my throat, my head, my eyes, my fucking mind, screaming at me, telling me what a fucking idiot I am. No way I was going to jail for this girl over bullshit blackmail. No fucking way, man.

Deep fucking breath.
Exhale.
Sharp Inhale.
Hold.
Peek out.
FUCK.

Dana's standing outside. A mere forty feet away, I might as well be invisible. She had her hand shading the sun away from her eyes to try and find my dirty feet scraping the ground, but I was already out of sight. I saw her slap her hip in defeat and walk back inside to likely bitch at Emilia for bringing a thief into her store. As soon as she did, I took off through my fair share of shady alleyways until I had cut across town and made it over the iron gates to Annabelle's lawn.

It was only a mile back to the school, and it took me less than ten minutes to make it back to sacred soil. Right as I set foot onto the grounds, Emilia pulled up to the sidewalk in her white sedan. She paused in the middle of the street to keep up with my sidewalk strides and said,

"Hey! Did you get them? Dana knew what happened, but it's a good thing I told her you went to a different school, huh!"

"Fuck off," I said to her.

"What?" She asked nervously.

"FUCK. OFF. You nearly got me arrested because of your own goddamn selfishness. This is NOT what I steal for—little debutants who wanna blow their parent's money on booze and drugs," I said while reaching into my tote to pull out her dresses. If only I was a size 0, I probably would have kept them. But I wadded them up, tossed them into her face and said,

"If you ever try to pull any shit like that again, ohhhhh. Mark my words, Emilia, it'll be your ass. And not a fucking word of this to ANY. ONE."

Her doe eyes suddenly widened, and I was the pair of headlights shocking her into realizing she narrowly escaped kissing the pavement. With her mouth agape, and my teeth gritting against each other I her,

"Do you understand?"

"Yeah, I— I got it," she stuttered.

"Wonderful." I stared into her eyes for another moment before slamming my fist on the top of her car and turning my back to walk away from her. Into the sunset, might I add.

The only thing running through my head was the tired questioning of a voice, wondering how a good thing had become so far twisted—how in trying to share the wealth with my fellow college girls, I was used and abused for my power by the richest, bitchiest one. If she had caught on, who else had? Dangerous times to be a thief when the veil of secrecy is wearing so thin.

***

Before we knew it our first semester at Annabelle's was over. THANK GOD, ALLAH, YAWEH, BUDDHA, SHIVA, ODIN, KALI. The air outside was brisk and barely icy, but nice enough to still roll around with the window down and the white winter sun blazing down. Since I was carless, Angel and I carpooled in her little red Mazda to get back to Bloodmoon Beach during our school breaks. It allowed us for hours of peaceful, quiet if we so pleased, or hours of muddling through our psyches in a small car. With the weight of finals removed from my shoulders, I remember riding home with her that winter break feeling like I was on top of the world rather than being crushed underneath it. I wished I could tell Atlas what that weightless feeling was like.

Because of my distancing from those who may see my true deception, I sadly missed one of the most important days of Scarlette's adult life: her debutante ball. In Scarlette's deep southern roots there lies a tradition in which the young belles reach a point of peak maturity, and in that year, they debut as a true Southern Belle.

It' a coming-out type event, if you will; a revealing of the woman she has spent so much time and lipstick becoming. The debutantes of the evening wear beautifully simple and modest white gowns with white satin opera gloves stretching behind the elbow. They drape themselves in the most dazzling diamond jewelry and pink Barbie doll lips you've ever seen, and then they take the ballroom for an elegant first dance as a woman next to a strapping young gent. It's a striking southern tradition that hasn't died out in the face of globalization, and I hope for the sake of southern culture that it's never tossed aside.

    I knew Mia was going to the ball, and I didn't want any chance of quarrel or secret spilling. Reluctantly, I stayed away. Rather, I spent the whole month of December parading around with Angel in Bloodmoon Beach, shoplifting anything I could touch. You'd think my little scare back in Darbyville would cool me down a bit, right? Not so, not so.

    It's easy to escape with a ton of goodies when the Christmas shopping crowds are already out of control; I wasn't even a blip on the radar to security that month, when I should have been their primary focus. Covered in baggie clothes and armed with the same silver tote that almost got me caught, I managed to thieve at least $4,000 in goods that season. Not just for myself! Oh, no, that wouldn't be the way of Robinhood. My mother's, brother's grandparents', and friends' gifts were all acquired within that month-long shoplifting spree, and I feel no shame about that. I'm sure none of them did either. Not to mention, I was in such a belligerent stupor for the entire month because I turned back on my truce against Molly; I brought the bag with me and took spontaneous licks every now and again. That sure did keep the creative thievery flowing.

    I lost the bag of Molly in a KFC one night five minutes before they closed. Pretty sure the counter clerk had more than fried chicken for dinner that night.

    When Angel and I came back to Annabelle's on January 2nd, we pulled into the parking lot at 8:16 PM the night before our classes started back. The air was icy and lifeless, but the nearly full moon lit our whole drive back. Luckily, we weren't the only ones showing up at school a little late, for as soon as we pulled into a parking spot my passenger's side window took the brunt of excited, forceful fist blows and muffled squeals. I opened the door only to be tackled by both Scarlette *and* Mia in a flurry of affection.

"Ahhhhhhhh!" Scarlette squealed as she wrapped me in a tight hug, "We missed you so fucking much! Why didn't you come to the Debutante ball?! Oh, Lyla, I wish you could have been there. I looked so pretty!"

"I'm sorryyyy," I said wholeheartedly, "but I had to work. You know how it goes, man."

That was a lie.

"She really did look so beautiful, Lyla," Mia said.

"Yeah, she straightened my hair and everything! Oh, and Mia finally let me do her makeup! She looked amazing, too!"

I turned back to look at Angel, who was quickly unpacking her bags from the trunk. She took my stuff out, tossed it on the ground, grabbed her own, shot me a quick, "love you," and headed off to her dorm. She had official CA business to take care of, so I shouted, "love you too!" and turned back to the animated friends I hadn't seen in a month.

"Hey, we've gotta go on a Blunt Loop," Scarlette said, "I haven't been out on a loop in way too long. You comin'?"

"Of course I'm coming!" I said.

"Mia, you in?" Scarlette asked her.

"Duh," she shot back.

"Then let's go!" I said. Scarlette hooked on to my right side, and Mia hooked on to hers. Lyla and the Skinnies back at it, regardless of my fear that they might catch on to my ever-growing deceitful heart. It didn't matter that night, though. We were celebrating our last night as free women before having six-hour long classes for the next month.

You see, since we're an all-women's private school, we don't operate like most colleges. We had the fall semester, the spring semester, and an awkward in-between semester dubbed Jan-term; during Jan-term, you only take one single class that could last anywhere from five hours to eight hours a day depending what you signed up for. We got lunch breaks in between, and it only ran four days out of the week. After those grueling and gray four weeks of

January, we got a whole four-point credit on our transcript and a four-day break before gearing up for a full spring semester. It was halfway torture and halfway recovery—there's no other real way to describe it.

The Loop that night was especially heart-warming for me, because not only were my two minions so excited to see me, but because I had just started talking to my high school sweetheart again. You know, that one boy that you just never could say goodbye to no matter how many "breakups" you had or how many years flew by? Yeah, that's this guy.

His name is Tyler Brooks, and we've been through more heart-wrenching and heart-pumping experiences than you'd probably care for me to share with you. He was the first honeyed apple of my heart's eye, and he was a tough one to let go. He seduced me with a silly sense of sarcastic humor that kept me giggling throughout our six-hour nightly conversations. His round cheeks were always rosy, setting off the emerald green that glowed in his eyes. With shaggy dark brown hair swooping across his forehead and curling around the bottoms of his ears, how could a hormonal teenage girl resist? We knew each other even in middle school, but it wasn't until the summer before high school that we actually started our puppy love affair.

I still remember a day during our freshman year when I brought him a mini-cake for his 15th birthday that October; there was turquoise blue icing, black and green sprinkles, and a gift-bag with a metal band shirt inside of it. He was wearing my favorite hoodie—a black and white striped zip-up that had pops of red and black filigree patterned in between. Since I was always caught wearing the shortest of shorts, I was freezing by the time we met up for second block break. That favorite hoodie of mine usually laid on my shoulders once he saw my shivering body and felt my chilled, purple hands. We were simply entangled within each other not only physically, but emotionally and psychologically, too. He was my first real Love, and once we feel that Love for the first time, we can't help but think it was the only Love we were ever supposed to feel in the first place—the only Love that's pure. The older I get, the more tainted and hideously complex I see that Love has become in the hearts of those around me. For the sake of wanting to preserve that first, innocent type of Love, we keep going back to that one.

Haven't you ever wondered at the notion of divorcees running back to their high school lovers? Yeah, so have I.

I can hear Mia and Scarlette in the front seats listening to The Gorillaz and going on and on about how they don't wanna start classes the next day. I wasn't really there; it's just where my body happened to be. I was inside my phone where Tyler and I were texting back and forth, discussing his upset with the fact that I was in Bloodmoon for a month and didn't tell him. To be quite honest, I didn't think he would have cared if I was right next door to him, much less in the same town. Like I said, we've been through some heart-wrenching ordeals, and he has absolutely no reason to keep in contact with me. Yet, he always does.

"So you were here for an entire month, and you waited to tell me until you were back in Darbyville?!" His message read.

"Yeahhhhh, I didn't think you would have wanted to see me anyways!" I replied.

"Wrong!"

"Well, excuse me for thinking otherwise! I'll come see you next time I'm down there?"

"When's that gonna be? A year from now?" He responded jokingly.

"Haha, maybe, because you know I don't have my car anymore, right?"

"What?! What happened?"

"It got totaled. Some meth head trying to commit suicide—ran into a tree. Haha. Not funny, but I can't help but laugh."

"What the fuck is your life haha," he wrote.

"Yeah, you're telling me."

"Soooooooooooooo..."

"Soooooo, what?" I replied.

"So how about you borrow a friend's car and come here tonight?" He asked.

"What?! Tonight? I have my first Nazism class tomorrow morning at 9:30!"

Yes, you read me right: Nazism. At a liberal arts school, you can teach a class on just about anything. Oh, and the real kicker? The class was being taught by a 60-year-old Jewish man.

"Skip it!" He was always such a bad influence when it came to blowing off official business.

"Are you kidding me?! No way anybody's gonna let me take their car all the way to Bloodmoon and back in the middle of a winter night!"

"You don't have to tell them where you're going! Just say it's a family emergency haha."

"No way!" I replied.

"Oh come onnnnnnn. Don't be a pussy."

"I'm not being a pussy! I just know that's impossible!"

"Okay, well if you don't wanna be a pussy, you can at least be a kleptomaniac and steal a car? I know you like your stealing haha," he planted that idea on purpose. He knew my inner klepto couldn't say no to such a grand opportunity to steal.

"Who the fuck do you suggest I steal from? I'd need the keys, because I don't know how to hotwire a vehicle. The only keys I'd be able to get ahold of are Scarlette's or Mia's. Definitely not Mia, she's too sharp."

"Well what about Scarlette?" He wrote.

He had a point. What about Scarlette? I mean, she's constantly losing things; this was the girl could lose only one shoe out of a pair for three weeks before finding it under a dirty mountain of clothes. She's scattered beyond belief, and if she can't find something, she just assumed that she must have lost it somewhere and gives up without much of a fight. Plus, I've been driving Scarlette's car around since day one of college, so I felt I practically had part ownership in the damned thing.

Dangerous business.
Dangerous business.
Risky business.
Fucked business.

Because Scarlette's looking more and more like my next victim with each second waning away.

"Hmmmm. I guess Scarlette's car couuuuld work. She's really tired, and we're smoking a blunt right now, so she'll be even more tired. I'd probably be able to get the keys and get to you by 3 AM."

"3 AM?!" He asked in disbelief.

"Yes, 3 AM! It takes four hours to get to you! And it's gonna take me a good minute to even get these keys from her."

"Alright, so you're gonna do it then?" He asked.

"UUUUUUUUGGGGGGHHHHHHHHH," I typed, "yeah, I think I am. Goes against everything I stand for when it comes to stealing, but I think I am."

"Good! Hurry up and haul ass! Haha."

"Shut up!" I typed, "I'll get there when I get there. You can't rush betrayal!"

Dante Alighieri reserved a special circle in Hell for those blackhearts who betrayed their benefactors, and I knew exactly where Robinhood was headed after this heist: the frozen lake in the Ninth circle where Satan sits close by to remind us of the treachery that lived, died, and continues living in our souls—forever. There, the sun doesn't shine golden rays behind lofty clouds, nor does it warm your cruel skin, nor does it grace you with its life-light for even a second! The sinners are condemned to a perpetually motionless state, stuck in a bleak and destitute underworld where they are suspended in contortion while being unable to speak so as to prevent the deceit of any others. And to think that the Christians see Hell as a landscape burning in a perpetual heap of flames! If only they knew fire was just one of the many punishments Hell hath to offer.

I damned Robinhood to an eternity under ice that night, and sometimes I hear her call out to me from the depths of my soul, longing for me to break her out of the everlasting frost. But I keep her down there, ignoring her pleas by drowning her in sheets of sharp ice and double-crossing corpses. Despite her insistent cries, she knows she cannot be let out. She would surely be my demise if we were ever to reunite. She knows it. *We* know it.

So in that deepest circle of Hell, Robinhood will remain.

X: Winter 2K13: The Deceit

.

11:38 PM. I was able to snag Scarlette's keys from an appalling pile of half-full coke bottles, empty cigarette packs, and worn clothes in her dorm room. It was easy, really; I simply waited until she was passed out from smoking consecutive blunts then shuffled my feet around the pile quietly so as to not disturb her slumber. It wasn't long before I heard the familiar clinking of her keychains, bent down for the snatch, clasped them tight in my hand, and slipped out of the room without her or Mia detecting my presence. It's amazing the unspeakable things that happen with eyes shut.

Before I left Annabelle's I made sure that room 209 was locked. Scarlette had a tendency to come into my room at night whenever she couldn't sleep considering she always left her Newports, her weed, or her keys with me. To pay homage to the sanctity of clichés, let's just say that girl would lose her fucking head if it weren't connected to her body.

Door locked.
Check handle.
Sprint down hallway.

I wanted nobody to think I was gone. Only one glitch in the plan: I've finally caught myself a roommate in the absence of winter break. Administration was afraid I wouldn't get the "real college experience" if I spent the rest of the year in solitary confinement, so they stuck me with someone who also couldn't stand their original match. The lucky one to share the splendor of room 209 with me is named Destiny—a real petite, athletic girl from the Philippines. She was cute as a bow with deep, dark hair longer than her belly button. Her dark skin and dark eyes complimented the light that always shone from her bright smile. She was a musician in her spare time, which was rarely at all, because she plays tennis for Annabelle's. We hadn't spoken much at all, so it's not like I can count on her to vouch for my absence on her first night's stay in the palace.

Oh, and did I mention she's a fire dancer, too? My new roommate is a tennis-playing, guitar-slaying, fire-breathing Philippian.

I hopped into Scarlette's oh-so-familiar Jeep only to see that the poor needle on the gas gauge was below the empty notch, and the monitor above my head read,

"0 miles to empty"

"Well, fuck!" I yelled to the gods.

Scarlette's Jeep cost a whopping $60 to fill up, and I would have to do that twice to get all the way to Bloodmoon and back. $120 to see Tyler for an hour? Doesn't seem like a worthy trade. But I'm eighteen, hormonal, invincible, and still hungry for contact with an old flame. So, of course, I can't let a pesky lack of oil get in the way of my revving engine.

As if stealing Scarlette's car to drive an eight-hour round trip in the night wasn't already bad enough, I realized that both of her debit cards were in the pouch attached to her keys. Now, because Scarlette trusted me with her Life enough to drive her around all the time, she also trusted me to buy her cigarettes, snacks, and Coca-Colas whenever she didn't feel like going inside the Kangaroo. Naturally, she'd hand me her debit card and say, "1994" so that I could buy what she needed. Since she's a privileged little belle, her parents give her an allowance every week. I knew that her mom had just given her an allowance, because it's Sunday, and the money always comes on the weekend.

Before I had time to talk myself out of double-dipping into deception, I was already at the gas station using her debit card to fill up the gas tank for the car that I had stolen for the trip to see an old lover. It isn't like I felt that Scarlette deserved it, or that she wouldn't mind, or that I was entitled to her money and her vehicle, but you could say there were voices in my head trying to make me believe them. The selfishness and denial that it takes to achieve such a feat are psychologically imperative to come out whole on the other side.

After pumping $57.78 in gas, I got back in the car to see that I had three messages from Tyler. One after the other, they read,

"So you're really gonna do this?"

"Lyla?"

"Oh my god, you fell asleep didn't you?"

I giggled to myself and replied,

"No, I didn't fall asleep. Yes, I'm really doing this. I just filled up gas, so I should be there around 4 AM haha. Don't you dare fall asleep waiting on me."

Click.

Seatbelt on.

Chirp-chirp.

Response.

"What the fuck?! 4 AM?!" Tyler replied.

"Yes!! It took me a long time just to wait on her to go to sleep! Take it or leave it, because I'm fucking over a good friend for this, and if you're gonna be asleep, I'm just gonna turn around and tell her that I filled her tank up for her when I couldn't sleep. And that's gonna sound fucking weird."

"I miiiiight be asleep haha. So, haul ass!"

"You better not be asleep, I'll drag you out by your bad ear!" I replied.

"Well hurry the fuck up then!" Tyler wrote.

I laughed, shook my head, and put the car in drive. Before pulling onto the interstate out of Darbyville I noticed six cops—an omen, perhaps? Irony, certainly; here I just committed grand theft auto, and not a single person around had any idea. What the public saw was a girl driving in the middle of the night; what I knew is that I was driving a car after I had stolen the keys off a girl at her most defenseless hour. It's a fucked up world that just keeps on spinning, because people like me can't quit dirty dancing with the cosmos.

As Tyler suggested, I was hauling my ass. On the interstate in South Carolina, the speed limit is 70 mph at best, but I was going nearly 100 mph. Since Scarlette didn't have much in the way of musical selection, it was J. Cole that I was listening to the whole way down to Bloodmoon. Not bad, but also not my first choice. Gimme something with a little rock in the roll. I felt my betrayal with every beat that played through those speakers, so I shut it off to not be further reminded of the shit storm I'm in.

About an hour away from Darbyville, I came barreling down a hill going 93 mph with a joint in my mouth. You see, I also snagged some of her weed and rolled a nice fat one for my trip. Strike 387. Flying down the hillside I opted for the fast lane so as to avoid a semi-truck and a sedan going the correct speed limit.

Dart around.
Smoke inhalation.
Hold.
Exhale.
Blue lights.
Blue lights.
Behind me.
Blue fucking lights.
Blue fucking lights.
Blue fucking lights!
Behind me.
Fuck.
FUCK.
FUCK FUCK FUCK.

My stomach dropped down to my knees, I swear. Or imploded within itself, I don't know. Do I swallow the joint? Do I shove it up my cooch? Can't throw it out the window now, because his camera will catch that shit, and once he finds it, off to jail I go for grand theft auto and possession of marijuana. This is Karma coming back to slap me in the fucking face without any sort of grace period. Man, She waited NO time to turn this shit back around on me, and now I'm definitely regretting these poor goddamn choices and my degenerate behavior.

I rolled the window down reluctantly, thinking it may be my last breath of fresh air before being locked inside yet another cell. The officer walked up to my window, shining his blinding flashlight straight into my eyes, causing me to squint and look away. Thankfully.

"You wanna tell me why you were going so fast?" He said with the tone of any stern policeman wearing a big-billed hat.

Great. Can't even flirt my way out of this one.

"I'm sorry, sir, we were on a hill and I just wasn't paying attention to how fast I was going. This isn't my car, so I'm not really used to how it behaves," I said.

Maybe honesty really is the best policy. If I told him up front that I didn't own the car, he can't immediately think it'd been stolen.

"Well whose car is it?" He asked.

"It's my hallmate's car. I'm from Bloodmoon Beach, and there's a family emergency. I don't have a car, so I asked around until I found someone that would let me use theirs."

"Well, I'll tell you one thing, your friend sure does like marijuana," he said as he flashed his light all over the interior of the car.

My heart started racing—no, more than racing. It was fucking traveling at the speed of light. I hid the joint underneath some crumpled receipts beside the console, and I was praying that he wouldn't search the car. There was a baggie in the glove compartment, and I knew I was fucked if he either found that baggie or just looked dead into my eyes to see how bloodshot they were.

I laughed nervously before saying, "Yeah, you're right, she does."

"Well if this isn't your car, do you know where the registration is? Go ahead and give me your license."

I handed him my license while I shifted my back to block his view of the glove compartment and search for the registration. And what do you know? No registration! Of course Scarlette didn't have registration in her car. She probably had no clue what car registration was to begin with. I'm sure her mom probably told her, "here, this paper is important! Don't lose it, and put it in your glove box." Scarlette, I'm sure, nodded her head, and threw it in this dump with the layers of dirty clothes, dill pickle chips, cigar wrappers, past weed baggies, and other muck that shouldn't be kept in a vehicle.

"Uhhhh, sir? I can't seem to find the registration," I said as tampons and trash started falling out of the glove compartment. I looked at him with sad puppy dog eyes and a wrinkled forehead, and he asked me,

"Well who does the car belong to?"

"Her name's Scarlette Bethesda, but I think this car is registered under her mom's name, which would be Nancy," I said nervously. I was praying to God, Allah, Yahweh, Buddha, Shiva Kali that he wouldn't look up the registration, see Nancy's name, and give her a ring. That was the last thing I needed—for Scarlette's own mother to know that I stole her vehicle in the middle of the night.

"Alright, well you hang tight while I go check it out," he said as he walked away in his taut gray hat to do his official business.

I pulled out my phone to text Tyler, saying, "Just fucking got pulled over while smoking a joint in a stolen car, I'm so fucked, I'm so fucked, I'm so fucked."

He replied quickly saying, "Ohhhhh balls, that fucking sucks! Lie your way out of it!"

"I am!" I wrote, "But I stole this fucking car! He could take me to jail! Not to mention I was already going nearly 25 over the speed limit!"

"Well that's your fault haha," he replied, "you shoulda just gone the speed limit, speed racer."

"YOU were the one who said you might be asleep! I was tryna book it so that stealing a car wouldn't be a waste!"

"Whooooaaa, can't pin this on me now haha," he wrote.

"Whatever, he's coming back, better pray to your God that he doesn't find out I stole this car," I typed quickly before I slipped my phone between my trembling legs.

"Alright, here's the deal: I've got you a ticket here for speeding. Keep to the limit, and by no means go over even a single hair, you got that?"

"Yes, sir," I said in my meekest school-girl voice. I'm sure he got off on it.

As he walked away to his blue lights, still blinding me in all three rear mirrors, I looked down to see the damage done on the little blue slip of paper.

"$395," the ticket read, "for minor traffic violation." And that was just a speeding ticket.

"GodDAMMIT!" I said aloud. I pounded my fists against the rim of the steering wheel before I laid my fuming head on it to spit the fire out of my heart. I guess I wasn't cute enough nor convincing enough to get the let's-pretend-you-were-only-going-five-over rate. But, hey, it could have been a lot worse; I could have been thrown in the back of the cop's car riding along with those blue lights in horror with the impending doom of facing grand theft auto charges. Karma bit me in the ass hard enough to make it hurt, but she didn't bite hard enough to rip away my lively flesh, and for that, I must be grateful.

4:03 AM. My ordeal with the police cost me precious time. I had a mere hour before I needed to be back on the road to make my 9:30 class, and I found myself questioning if this is at all worth it as I pulled into Tyler's suburban pocket. I winded around the streets of cookie-cutter houses, rusted basketball goals, and "BEWARE OF DOG" signs before parking at a familiar spot of ours by the community pool. As I stopped in front of the iron gates surrounding the water, I looked up to my left to notice the playground that had been a sort of secret-trading-post in our younger age; when Christmas came around my mom, brother, and I began the ritual fudge-making of the season, and I always laid a nice, fresh bag for him on the edge of the slide in the dark to satisfy his midnight sweet tooth. Sometimes I'd write him letters and leave them on that same plastic slide to read the next morning at the bus stop. It's such a game to be young and in Love, and now more than ever I wish the game could still be as simple as leaving surprises on slippery red slides.

In the midst of my nostalgia, a furious knocking pounded on the passenger side window. My heart squirmed a little and sunk down to the pit of my stomach as I plundered around in the dark to try and unlock the door for him. Without thinking about how atrociously messy the car was, including the passenger seat, I opened the door to let him in, and he just stared down.

Down at the seat.
Back at me.
Down at the seat.
Back at me.

"Uhhhh," he said with a laugh, "how do you expect me to sit down in this?!"

"I told you she's a messy girl," I anxiously laughed back as I reached out my hand for his, "but we don't really need to be in this car, do we?" I said suggestively.

"No, you're right, I was gonna take you to this house on the corner anyways."

Just like old Times.

He was holding onto the top of the car, letting his head hang low as his lips curled into the sweetest grin. His black hood was keeping the wind from ripping through his ears, as well as balancing out his innocence with a touch of gloom. Those familiar eyes shone like green gems under the glare of overhead lights, promising one final night to live in the reflection of our past. My doubts about the trip being worthwhile faded away entirely when I saw their flicker.

"What house on the corner?" I asked with laughter still in my voice.

"Come on, I'll show you," he said as he cocked his head in a motion for me to follow.

My mind's eye flashed back to a time when we were but two young teenagers, forced to walk around neighborhoods in order to get any sort of "privacy". He used to live in a part of town that was only a short walk from the beautiful marsh that separated us from the ocean, and there was nearly always an abandoned house waiting for two delinquents to break in to. He and I were those delinquents. On afternoons that we spent moseying through isles of myrtle trees and ponds, we'd find a hollow house that we'd never been in and a window that was mistakenly left open. Naturally, we'd bust that window open while one of us kept watch on the surroundings, and in we went, giggling and twirling around the barren skeleton of a home. Those early teenage years were magical, because we were still young enough to search for mischief and uncharted territory, but we were old enough to be excited by the wrong-doing of such.

Tyler had a way of sneaking behind me to grab my hips, causing me to squirm from his tickling touch, and gently pushing me up against a wall to ravish me like no one else. We were virgins when we met each other, and we remained such even after our first go-around; but that didn't stop us from stripping our clothes and exploring our bodies in other ways.

I hopped out of Scarlette's car and scurried to catch up to Tyler, who was already halfway to the house on the corner. When I caught up to him, I asked,

"How do you know you can get into this one?"

"Well, my friend's mom cleans houses in this neighborhood,

but she doesn't have a key to this one, so I know it's unlocked," he whispered back.

"Wait, nobody's living in it?" I asked.

"No!" He chuckled, "you think I'd take you to a house where people are fast asleep?"

"It would be a thrill," I said jokingly.

"Maybe for you!" He said as he crouched his body low while softly twisting the doorknob, listening for any unexpected raucous inside. Together we heard a pop, and a creak, letting us know that we were yet again successful in our ability to sneak into empty houses.

I swear it was déjà vu all over again when I walked inside the place; the sliding glass doors edging the vacant living room allowed for moonlight to spill onto the wooden floors, illuminating everything in a navy haze. The echo off the empty walls was mesmerizing, for each footstep I took sounded like there was an army following behind me. I wandered around for just a moment, in awe at being inside another home that wasn't mine, wasn't his—wasn't anyone's. There were but four walls, forgotten and found, meant only to be the walls of our playground.

If only for a night.

Tyler broke through my hypnotic state by doing the same old thing: catching me by surprise from behind, only to crash my body into a wall while he crashed his lips into mine. With my eyes closed tight and my hands gripped around the back of his neck, pulling at the long tufts of his brown hair, I saw those stars swirling in my head; you know, those stars that only shine when your own mind can't believe what it's experiencing—this ecstasy of Love and a deep soul connection. We still have it.

We yanked and tugged on one another, taking turns at who was up against the wall and whose neck needed biting, whose hair needed pulling and whose body needed groping. In our euphoric dance we toppled to the floor and I climbed on top to bury my face in the crook of his neck, licking and teasing and nibbling the soft ends of his ear. His panting grew deeper, faster, harder, and suddenly my jacket was off and tossed aside. My dress was the next to go, and before it was even over my head, I felt his strong hands squeezing my breasts so tight that I swear he was trying to rip them off and keep them forever. But he knew I liked that, so I just laced my hands over his and we squeezed together, drawing moans out of each other with each heartbeat.

He tossed me over on my back while I began shedding his layers, starting with his hoodie first. Underneath revealed a wrinkled white V-neck T-shirt, the irresistible style of his choice. I refrained from taking that layer off for a moment, choosing instead to claw my hands up his back, scratching my nails into his skin so that he won't forget that night for weeks to come. Again, his breaths grew heavier and hotter, but all of a sudden, a light flickered on in the house.

"Fuck!" Tyler whispered.

"What the fuck is that?" I whispered back. It was coming from down the hallway that led to various bedrooms and the garage door.

"Quick, what time is it?" Tyler asked as he pounced off of me to grab his jacket and toss me my dress.

"I don't know, probably around five?"

"FUCK!" He yelped, "My friend's mom gets up at 4:30 to come clean the empty houses!"

"What?! She's in here?!" We were still whisper-yelling at each other as we ran to the front door from which we entered.

"No, but she's about to be! She comes in the side door in the garage so that people don't just see some random lady walking into an empty house."

I struggled to throw my clothes back on as we were trying to escape being seen by his friend's mother. Still putting one arm in my coat, I raced behind him. The very second we flung ourselves out into the winter night's air, we heard a door open from the inside of the house. I shut the front door ever so carefully, and we ran all the way to that black Jeep by the pool. Another three seconds in there and we would have been caught, clothes disheveled, and Tyler's boner still raging.

Now that our panting had gone from pleasure to fear, we were jolted right out of our intimacy and faced the inevitability that we had no more time together, for I had to get back on the road.

"Well, fuck," I started with a giggle, "nothing like a nice run in the morning, huh?"

"Speak for yourself!" Tyler laughed back, "Do you have to go like, *right* now?"

"Yeeeeah," I said reluctantly, "I probably should."

"Five minutes?" He asked.

I lit up like a firefly.

"Five minutes."

He pushed me back against the car and kissed me like it was going to be the last time he ever did so, and again the stars started swirling around my eyes. Before I knew it, the five minutes had passed, and he pushed himself off of me.

"Alright, now go. You don't wanna be late for Nazi class," he said as he opened the front door for me.

"I know. But I'm gonna miss you," I said with sadness in my eyes as I climbed up into Scarlette's car.

"I'll miss you too, but I'm always with you, right?" He said as he hung onto the car frame, hood above his head, just as it was a mere hour before.

"Right," I replied.

Just before he shut the door I blurted out, "I love you."

He looked at me with those blazing green eyes and kissed me on the forehead, then again on the lips before he said, "I love you, too. Now go, go! Drive safe, and don't get another ticket!"

"Yes sir," I said with a smile on my face.

He shut the door, tapped the window twice for good luck, and sent me on my way. As I drove off, I looked down to see that it was 5:01. Four hours to get back to Darbyville, then another six hours of classroom time to start the school day. I'm fucked.

After driving for nearly an hour and a half, reminiscing on the short, yet wondrous hour I just spent with Tyler, I realized I was starting to doze off on the highway. The sun had finally made his appearance, and the sky was as blue and as clear as Winter could make; but their beauty combined with the blasting beats from the stereo weren't enough to keep me awake. I decided that a stop for coffee was inevitable after four different cars honked at me for drifting into their lanes. Luckily, Dunkin Donuts was but a hop and a skip away, and I ordered the absolute largest vanilla iced coffee that money could buy—Scarlette's money, mind you. With coffee in hand, I slurped that sucker down as fast as I could and tossed aside the coupon pamphlet they handed me.

I hate coffee. I do. Caffeine propels my body and mind into a state of flustered fuckits. The jitters start setting in soon after, and hours later my eyes burn and my throat tastes awfully bitter and sugared. It's a gross cocktail—coffee, sugar, and milk. But I drank it. A third of it. And I didn't doze off again the whole way back to school. Success! Or, so I thought.

I parked the car near the same spot that I stole it from and looked around to make sure nobody could see that I was getting out of Scarlette's car. When the coast was clear, I hopped out with a smug smile on my face—the kind of smile when you've completed a mission that was deemed nearly impossible. And I did it. With iced coffee in hand. Now all I had to do was return Scarlette's keys to the pile of clothes that I found them under, and nobody would suspect a thing.

Right?

Say it to me.

Right.

When I got back to room 209, Destiny was straightening her hair before she had to be at her Beatles class; that's right, I opted for a class on Nazism while she opted for a class on the love-rock band of the Hippie era. Annabelle's is not your typical college. Or is it?

"Hey!" Destiny said with a perky smile, "where you been?"

"Grabbin' coffee, but I don't like it very much," I said. "You want it?"

"Helllll yeah, I love coffee!"

"Great! All yours," I said as I looked at the clock. 9:24 AM. Six minutes.

"Damn, class starts in five, I gotta book it, but I'll see you later! You gonna come on a loop with us after?"

"Yeah, but I've got practice again at 5:30, so it has to be before then."

"God, your life as a college athlete sucks," I said jokingly.

"Tell me about it!" She said seriously.

I booked it out of the dorm and nearly ran over three people with my bicycle in my frantic effort to get to class on time. I'm notoriously late for everything; I'd like to think that the only time I was ever early was when I was born six weeks before my due date. But, I didn't want this professor to know my habits just yet. I made it with maybe ten seconds to spare, and as I sat down in that metal chair surrounded by only six other Nazi-curious faces, I felt I had accomplished one of the biggest heists of my Life.

I was wrong.

***

When my class let out at 4:28 PM, I rushed back to room 209 so I could try to catch up on the sleep that I threw away the night before. Instead of coming back to an empty room, as is usually the case, I came back to an intervention type scenario; Destiny sat on the edge of her bed, Mia was by the desk at the end of mine, and Scarlette stood pacing the room as I walked in. Immediately I knew something was up.

"What's up, guys?" I asked with a smile on my face. Maybe if I was smiling they'd throw out any suspicion.

"We know you stole Scarlette's car last night," Mia blurted out.

Those were eight words I definitely did not want to hear, especially out of Mia's mouth. I felt my inner Robinhood begin to tremble as she whispered to my psyche and told it, "Oh, fuck, I'm outta here! You can handle this, right?" And off she ran to leave me alone and deal with this fuck-up all on my own. I didn't even have a whole day to soak in my triumph! Now I had to do damage control and piece together how in the world they found out I had stolen it. I got back just in the nick of time, but I guess that wasn't quite good enough. The only thing that came to mind was to deny, deny, DENY.

"Huh?" I asked with a puzzled look on my face.

"Lyla," Scarlette started, "did you use my car to go to Dunkin' Donuts this morning?"

"No?"

Fuck. Dumb response. Clearly, she knows something.

"Well, where did you get the coffee that you gave to Destiny?"

"At Dunkin' Donuts." I looked toward Destiny to see if she was going to react at all, but just as I did, she buried her head in her shoulder.

"And you didn't use my car?" Scarlette asked.

"No!"

"Then how did you get to Bloodmoon Beach last night?"

"Wait, how do you know about that?" I asked.

Mia butted in and said, "Because you told me that you drove all the way to Bloodmoon last night to meet some boy."

In my elated state upon arriving to campus this morning, I had forgotten that I told Mia about my middle-of-the-night trip to Bloodmoon. Why I felt like that was a good idea, I don't know. But I told her that I had borrowed a Jordan's car to get all the way down there, not Scarlette's.

"Yeah, I did, but I took Jordan's car to Bloodmoon Beach. That's how I got the Dunkin' Donuts this morning."

"So, if we asked Jordan if she let you borrow her car, she'd vouch for you?" Scarlette asked.

"Yes!" I said instantaneously. This was turning into a fucking train wreck, and I was about to suffocate in the burning flames that I lit with my own tongue. Of course, Jordan wouldn't vouch for me! I was just praying to God, Allah, Yahweh, Buddha, Shiva, Kali that they hadn't already asked Jordan if I used her car.

"Well, I don't know what to think, Lyla," Scarlette said. As I looked into her eyes I saw how hurt she was, and instantly my heart broke to know that I had taken such advantage of a girl who respected me to the point that my betrayal brought tears down her cheeks.

And she knew.

I knew.

Mia knew.

Destiny knew.

We all knew.

Still can't quit.

"What do you mean?" I asked. Just can't give it up. Gotta see the lie to the end.

"I mean, you say you used Jordan's car, but there were Dunkin' Donuts coupons sitting in the floor of my car when I went out to smoke this morning. And I don't eat Dunkin' Donuts. I like Krispy

Kreme."

"How do you know those coupons didn't just get tossed in there from someone else one day?" I asked like a blubbering idiot.

"Sure, that might be a possibility. But there's something else," she said as she finally took a seat on my bed instead of pacing around me.

"What is it?"

"My mom called me this morning and said that my debit card had been stolen."

"Huh?"

"She said my card was stolen. I didn't believe her at first, because she always thinks my debit card gets stolen. But she told me that there was a transaction for $57.76 at the QT gas station at midnight. And I never go to the QT. I *always* go to the Kangaroo. But I know you and Angel go to the QT."

FUCK FUCK FUCK.

"Well maybe it *was* stolen," I tried to reason with her. As if Reason was a god present inside of me.

"Yeah, but there's another thing; the card was also used at a Dunkin' Donuts an hour away from Bloodmoon Beach at 6:30 this morning."

"Oh...well that's a wild coincidence." I still couldn't give it up. I was caught, there was no getting around that or lying hard enough to convince her otherwise. I slipped up in my thievery. I didn't think about the fact that Scarlette only goes to the Kangaroo and that her mom checks her bank statement every morning. But, I guess when it's her mom's own money, she has to keep up with how her daughter spends it. It's just that it wasn't Scarlette spending the money this time.

"Lyla, just tell me you did it. We'll get past it and I won't be mad at you for it. I know you'll pay me back for the money you took. But just tell me you did it."

"I didn't, though," I said while staring at the ground, shaking my head back and forth. My body trembled all over, and this hot wave of rage, sorrow, and embarrassment draped my whole body in sweats and aches. This is why we can't look into the eyes of the ones we've betrayed; our conscience doesn't allow for such deceit to come naturally. We can't peer straight into the eyes of the people we love while telling them such falsities—it simply isn't a human.

"Lyla," she said with tears welling in her brown doe eyes, "please."

I couldn't look at her. I put my head down and stared at my lap, letting out a nervous laugh as I did so. I looked back up at her, if only for a brief second, to say,

"I didn't steal your car, man. I don't know who did. But it wasn't me." The voice that let those words come out of my mouth had such an arrogant tone about her. Such a goddamn entitled cold flowed from me. I don't know which Lyla this is, but I'm not sure I've met her before.

Those words hung on a fine thread, suspended in the air, weighing their heavy bullshit on my weak shoulders and Scarlette's, too. I wished I could go back to the moment I walked into room 209 and admit everything, up front, step-by-step.

What's done is done.

Scarlette stared into me for seven long seconds, and I could hear her soul screaming at me, begging me to just let down and admit my wrong-doing. I stared straight back, and I know she could hear my own soul screaming about I-don't-know-what, really. But it was making a horrendous racket all the same. She finally broke the stare and gave me a final, defeated,

"Okay."

She got up off the bed and rushed out of the room with no hesitation. Mia sat back for a moment longer, just to shoot me a look of utter disapproval and a slight grin at the idea that I had finally been caught in a pathetic web of lies. Destiny didn't leave immediately, because room 209 had become her room, too; but she definitely pretended like she had to get to practice fifteen minutes early and scurried away before I even had a chance to say anything to her. The air was more than awkward between us when the Skinnies left—it was contaminated. Soiled. Tainted. Polluted by my own putrid attempt at hiding my obvious betrayal.

As soon as I was left alone in that room, I heard nothing but the cacophony of tortured pieces of my Soul, gearing up for war. That night a battle began between Lyla, Robinhood, and all my hidden personalities that would rage for seven whole months until Robinhood finally surrendered and accept her Fate in the deepest, cruelest circle of Hell.

I've heard the winters are unbearable there.

XI: Spring/Summer 2K13: The Hiatus

"Oh, fucking Christ, this hurts," I winced through sharp breaths.

"No, don't say that, Lyla! I'm next!" Angel said from behind the red counter.

"It'll be over in a minute, baby!" Raph said.

Raphael, the skeezy owner of the Red Aces tattoo shop in Darbyville. He had dark hair, quaffed like a Latino Elvis. He wore baggie 90s jeans with metal chains draped around his waist, paired with some sort of black t-shirt that showed off his plethora of traditional Japanese tattoos. Luckily for us, his parents made their way into Florida from Cuba way back when, and now he's running a tattoo shop in upstate South Carolina. It's 11:29 on a Friday night in March, I just turned nineteen, and there's a needle in my ass. Angel, Victoria, and a guy named Ginger stood in awe on the outer edges of the booth where Raphael bloodied my bum with black ink.

"It's making my whole leg and back twitch, Ang, it's fucking weird!"

"Alright, alright, baby, you're done!" Raph said, patting my ass.

"Thank God," I said, lifting myself from the tattoo bed. It was covered in a thin puddle of sweat, even though I only laid there for three minutes.

"Oh, that's gross. I'm sorry about your bed, Raph," I laughed.

"Lemme see it!" Angel said.

"Hold please!"

I walked over to the full-length mirror, stared at the reflection, and squealed when I saw my branded ass; Angel's crooked handwriting, in all caps, inked the black letters that read "ANGEL".

Just ten minutes before we ended up at the tattoo shop, we were all piled into Angel's Mazda, smoking a mighty generous bowl.

When asked what I wanted to do for my birthday, I told her that we were already getting high, and it was 10 PM! Nothing else was open for the night in Darbyville.

"Except the tattoo shop," Angel said.

"Well, yes, except the tattoo shop."

"Let's get tattoos," Angel said, matter-of-factly.

"Okay!" I said, "You payin'?"

"Depends," she said, "what are we gonna get?"

"Wait, you're really gonna get one with me?" I asked through the smoke.

"Yeah, girl! Let's get matching ones."

"Seriously!?"

"Yes!"

"Okay!" I agreed, "What do we get?"

She paused.

"How about our names. In our handwriting. On the other one's ass."

I couldn't control myself, I had to laugh.

Victoria chimed in from the backseat, "What?!"

Ginger laughed as he hit the bowl.

"Fuck YES, let's do it," I said to her.

"You guys, that's so silly," Victoria said.

"Yeah it is, but let's go! Nineteenth birthday ass tats!" Angel hollered.

So here we are. After spending at least twenty minutes deciding on which handwriting sample to use, we decided to try one last time with eyes closed. We covered each other's eyes with our hands, put pen to paper, and wrote out "Angel" and "Lyla". Whatever way this try came out, that's what was going on our rears.

"Awh, what the hell, Lyla?" Angel said, looking at my handwriting.

"What's wrong with it?"

"It looks like it says 'Lyle'! You can't even see the 'a'!"

"Oh, whatever, it says 'Lyla'! And you can't say much, yours is in all caps like a small left-handed child!"

"It clearly says 'Angel' though!"

"Oh well! No turning back now," I winked.

And there wasn't. I turned right into the needle and was left with Angel's name tattooed on my body. If they didn't think I was a lesbian already, this would surely raise some questions.

"Come on, honey, it's your turn now!" Raph said to Angel with a thick accent.

"Okay, Lyla, squeeze my hand!"

"Yes ma'am," I laughed, coming to her rescue.

Raph flipped the switch.

Machine whirred.

Needle trembled.

Skin ripped.

"Holy shit!" Angel said as she gripped my hand tighter.

"Told you!" I laughed.

"You can really feel it all the way in the back! It's like a single nerve that—fuck! Ow!"

Her sweat-drenched fingers couldn't be stronger the way they crushed my clammy hand. I was thankful this wasn't child birth. Once she was finished, she climbed off the table and slid down to the floor.

"I'm glad that's over," she said, eyes wild behind her blue glasses.

"Check it out!" Raph said.

"Oh, kiss it for me, first!" Angel teased.

Raph got down on his knees without even a question, pressed his brown lips to a pucker, and laid a fat one right on Angel's ass cheek. She giggled and jumped a little, while I laughed at the hilarity of the night.

"Look, it does say 'Lyla'!" I said to her, looking in the mirror at her moon.

"It does not! It says Lyle!"

"Well, guess what?" I asked. "You'll always be conscious and able to tell people that it's your friend Lyla's name!"

"Yeah, yeah, whatever." She laughed, "I can't believe we did this."

"I can! It's only fitting. You know that song called 'Nineteen With Neck Tatz'?"

"Yeah?"

"We can be nineteen with ass tatz."

Raph laughed behind us as he put away his ink and cleaned up the station.

"You guys like 'em?" He asked. "I'll be honest; I've never agreed to do ass tattoos for people. I almost told you guys no. But, how could I?" He grinned.

"Right! How could you? But, really, thanks a lot. This was a perfect way to quell the boredom. What do we owe you?"

He shook his head and threw up his right hand in dismissal.

"Nothing?" Angel asked, shocked.

"Nah, my birthday gift to you, Lyla. It was nothing! And call it even for letting me kiss your girl's ass," he laughed.

"Awh, thanks, Raph! I really appreciate it."

"Yeah, don't mention it. Now go have a drink or something!"

"I'm nineteen, Raph!" I reminded him as I gathered the crew to leave.

"So what!" He joked.

"So, I'll see you around!" I said, waving with my back to him.

"Happy birthday, honey!" He reminded me.

We left the building with my arms around Angel and Victoria and Ginger straggling close behind. There was only one clear plan of action at this hour of night.

"Denny's?" Angel asked as she unlocked the Mazda.

"You read my mind," I said.

"Wait a second, guys," Victoria said as she climbed in the car.

"What is it, little Victoria?" Angel asked.

"You know, you got these tattoos pretty impulsively. How do you know you'll be friends forever?" She chuckled.

Angel and I let the moment linger.

We took one solid look at each other, and then Angel said,

"We don't,"

"But at least we'll know we were," I finished.

I grew closer to Angel and her roommate Victoria as I drifted further apart from Scarlette and Mia. Like I've said, Angel is the tamed elephant that always has my best interest at heart, fights for me like a sister, and fights *with* me when I'm fucking up. She's part sibling, part mother, part daughter on the rare occasion that she needs guidance, and part, well... angel. She' been my ride-or-die since I was fifteen years old, accompanying me on midnight tramps through Bloodmoon's beaches and early morning trips to Denny's. And, of course, advising me on how to heal my soul after throwing myself into a psychic pit of vipers that I bred for myself.

You wouldn't imagine she'd be such a guide by looking at her; she's the cutest, perfectly plump girl with the curviest, softest bosom my head has ever laid on! She's always dressed in thick, colored glasses and nearly-neon clothing, whether it be in pants, dresses, or shirts. Her hair's a vibrant violet color that takes me nearly six hours to dye perfectly, but it's always perfect. You can only imagine how we looked in public! Her glowing purple head grabbing attention while my tattooed arm and leg caught the others.

Angel knew as well as Scarlette did that I had stolen her car that night, but she wasn't going to call me on it and she certainly wasn't going to force me to apologize; over time, however, she dropped hints on the matter, letting me know there was a way to fix the hole that I had ripped open in my friendship. Ignoring her hints, I went along strengthening my friendship with her in such ways that people had no choice but to assume we were an Annabelle's-certified lesbian couple. We'd take spontaneous night trips up to visit our friend Tawnie at a college deep in the mountains of North Carolina, where I'd get drunk and ditch everyone to jump across rocks on a raging river. Those woods incited a riot within me, causing me to jump off suspended bridges, twenty feet above the river, full of shitty alcohol. Yet, I always stuck the landing on a slab of rock below. There was one poor, sweet soul who followed every one of my steps, sober, in an effort to make sure I didn't crack my head and drown alone. To this day I don't know what compelled him to act so righteously.

We spent a lot of time shoplifting, of course. Robinhood hadn't been thrown to the Underworld, yet. In fact, with the Skinnies gone, Robinhood came out with the hungriest appetite to date. There's no one around to call on her deception now, so what else was there to do? Besides, I needed all the money I had to buy weed, not clothes and toiletries. It's all about the priorities.

Speaking of college, did I mention that Scarlette and I are in two of the same art classes this semester? Well, since I changed my major to studio art, we have a drawing course and a design course together. How goddamn awkward; as if being in the same class of ten people wasn't bad enough, we also have easels *directly* across from each other in drawing class. So, when our subject matter is set up on a table in the middle of the room, sometimes Scarlette and I catch eyes because we've gotta stare in each other's direction for the entire three hours of class. Not only that, but we have to critique each other's work during our weekly review. What a karmic punishment.

 I know that all Scarlette wants is for me to admit that I fucked her over. She even tried to remain friends for a couple weeks after the deceptive ordeal, but I couldn't do it. It was like I could feel Robinhood laying claim to my mind, and She couldn't stand the thought of being caught in defeat. That said, I pushed Scarlette away with as much cold heartedness that I could muster. Hatred is a powerful motivator, and I figured if I could just convince Scarlette that it would be better for her to hate me it'd be easier for the both of us. Had I swallowed that sick pride, the cut still would have hurt her, but at least I could have stitched the wound rather than letting her bleed out.

 They say hindsight is 20/20, and my present vision is, at best, 280/20.

 By the end of my first year at Annabelle's, Angel and I made a plan to not return to Bloodmoon Beach for the summer; she got a job as a summertime CA for the dorms that house the summer school kids. I, on the other hand, got the privilege to be a "camp counselor", meaning that when they rent out the campus for events like JROTC camp, author's association retreats, or music camps I'm one of four girls who make sure the dorms are spic and span for their arrival. I also got a job working downtown at a rancid sports bar to rake in some real cash flow. It wasn't my first choice of employment, but it's honestly one of two places in town that would hire me with my ever-growing tattoo collection. The camp counselor job only provided me with an apartment to share with Angel and two other girls, free of charge. Not such a bad set-up when combined with working at a bar that's only a fifteen-minute walk away.

 Angel and I eagerly moved into the Heathers apartment building once school was out of session. The luxury of this apartment is unprecedented— we each have our own rooms! Granted, they're only eight-foot cubes, but it's a wonderfully modest privacy. Angel and I shared a wall between our rooms, naturally, and we wasted no time making ourselves at home. With a full kitchen at our disposal we fantasized nights of freshly baked lasagna and bowls of crisp summer salads. It's as if we went from dorm-children straight into the land of single, independent ladies, and we like it here.

"Hey, Ang," I said, unpacking boxes of knick-knacks.

"Yeah?" She shouted back from her room.

"I wanna go get some fresh flowers to put in my window, you think we can take a trip to Walmart?"

"Yes! I wanna get some groceries, too. We'll finally get to cook!"

"Right! We have to get an infinite amount of noodles. Just lemme get this box unpacked and we'll go."

We showed up to Walmart in our usual get-up; Angel's wearing a navy-blue dress with yellow bicycles all over it, and I'm wearing a long white skirt and a crop-top. Gotta let the skin show.

"Are you gonna push me in the wheelchair?" Angel asked, already touching the handle of the chair.

"I don't think I can say no, can I?" I asked.

"Nope!" She said as she plopped her little bottom into the seat. "Take me away!" She commanded.

"Yes ma'am!"

Sure, we're single independent ladies! But the child is still fully alive inside us, you see?

"Angel?" I said, noticing two boys staring us down as we entered through the doors.

"What is it?"

"Do you see those two boys gunnin' straight for us?"

"Yeah, you think they're coming over here?"

"They sure look like it," I said as they closed in.

"Hey, ladies!" They said from five feet away. Knew it.

"Hi!" We both said, still pushing the wheelchair.

"Do you mind if we talk to you both for a few minutes?"

"I guess not," Angel said. "What do you wanna talk about?"

"Well we wanted to take some time to ask you if you know

about our Lord and Savior, Jesus Christ."

Immediate laughter ensues. We can't help it! I grew up without a religious direction, thankfully. After taking some classes, I threw myself head first into the Buddhist and Hindu faiths, seeing as they're the only religions left on Earth that seem to make sense to me. I tried the whole Christian-thing when I was a teenager, but it rubbed me the wrong way. Angel was a devout philosopher, though, and loved nothing more than the chance to hear a religious pitch at Walmart.

"Are you serious?" Angel asked them.

"Yes," the brunette boy said, "why are you in that wheelchair? Are you hurt?" He asked with sympathy in his throat.

"No, I'm not hurt," Angel laughed, "I just like for Lyla to push me in the wheelchairs."

"Really?" The puffier blonde guy asked. "So you're not hurt?"

"No," Angel said, "but I wanna hear what you think about God. Go ahead, we're listening."

They weren't ready for us. Angel and I got off on talking about religion, and these two Christians fell into our lap to debate their God against Allah, Yahweh, Buddha, Shiva, Kali, and Odin. The whole ordeal turned into a question of whether or not their God is the same one that all humans pray to, and if he is all-encompassing or singular in his power. The two of them had opposing views, which was especially amusing, because they hadn't gathered a proper argument to withstand the minds of two amateur theosophists. Before we knew it, fifteen minutes and a little embarrassment had gone by and the blonde boy decided to end the ordeal with a bang.

"Well, listen, we really like what you have to say. It's good to be challenged in one's faith. But my father is a preacher. We're from South Africa, and we're doing a tour of the United States right now. He'll be preaching in your town all weekend, so if you'd like to come, we'd love to have you," he said, slipping us a white sheet of paper with the location and time.

"It's been a… fun chat," Angel said, taking the slip of paper. "Maybe we'll see you there."

The boys wished us a God-blessed day, and left to search for their next victims. I'm sure they would have skipped over us if they knew that they'd become ours.

"Lemme see that!" I said to Angel as they walked away.

"We can't go tomorrow night," Angel said, "but we can go to the one on Sunday?"

"You really wanna go to this?" I asked.

"Lyla. The Universe literally just handed the opportunity to us. I think it would be good to experience someone else's practice for a moment."

"You're right," I said, pushing her through the crowded aisles. "What time do we need to be there?"

"Four o'clock," she said.

***

3:38 Sunday afternoon. We arrived to the abandoned Shriner's Club building early in case of a huge turnout. Remembering to dress modest for the occasion, I wore a floor-length black dress and threw my hair in a tight bun. My sleeve of tattoos was showing, but I figured I could make a good impression and show them that tattoos aren't just for medieval heathens and prisoners. Angel wore a black and white striped dress and orange tennis shoes, just to remind them of our favorite time of year.

Upon entering the dingy red doors, we noticed a sea of empty fold-out chairs before the grand stage. Only ten people were floating around the room, mingling and perusing the tables of various religious books that the preacher wrote himself. There was a crazy array of pamphlets, too, with words like "prophecy", "end times", and "salvation" written all over them. We hadn't even had a chance to sit down before the blonde boy came marching up to us.

"Hey, ladies, glad you could make it!" He said with a smile. I didn't like what was in his blue eyes though.

"Yeeeahhhh," Angel said, smacking her gum.

As he walked away to help his father set up the stage, a short haggardly woman with frizzy, gun-metal gray hair approached. She had the wart-ridden face of a witch paired with the limp of a gimp, and she had her dull eyes set on us.

"Hi, y'all, how are you doing today?" She said softly. Her voice told the story of an age-old relationship with cigarettes.

"Just fine, how about yourself?" I asked.

Angel was silent.

"Oh, I'm wonderful. But I can't wait to see what kind of work the Lord brings tonight. Have you all been saved?"

"Well, not quite. We're here to just explore other people's religious views," I said politely.

"Yeah, we relate more to Buddhist philosophies," Angel said.

"Is that right? So, you don't know about our Lord and Savior, Jesus Christ?"

"Oh, I know him!" I said with a smile, "You could say we're studying the belief."

"Well I believe that you two can still be saved," she said, grabbing my arm. "The Lord works in wonderful ways and I truly believe after tonight, the two of you will leave here singing Jesus's name."

"Thanks!" Angel said quickly. She's trying to shut it down before it goes any further.

"Now, let me see your arm," the woman said to me.

She grabbed me without a response, turning and twisting and rotating my arm to get a good look at it all. She noticed moons, roses, and a huge eye with the Hindu Om in the center. She twists my arm just a little longer before saying,

"My, my! This is quite an arm! But I don't see Jesus on here?" She said, glaring up at me, searching for the reason why.

"Yeah, you're right! Jesus is not here," I said, shaking my head and staring down at the arm along with her.

"Hmmm. Maybe He will be one day," she said with an upturned nose. Thankfully, she ended on that note.

"Okay, now let's sit! Before anyone else comes over," I whispered to Angel.

We chose a seat in the middle of the crowd next to an aisle for an easy getaway. By the time the event started at least 35 people showed up, which was surprising. There was a scrawny, hunchback old man pacing in the front, wearing blue jean shorts, suspenders, a plaid button-up, tall white socks, and sneakers. His image alone is enough to describe the type of folk who showed up to this religious rally. A tall man with dark hair got on the mic to speak, and I only assumed he was the preacher. He told us that before he started his sermon, there were local gospel musicians who were going to lead us in singing worship.

"Cool," I said to Angel, "just the experience we wanted, right?"

"Yes," she said, staring straight ahead, still smacking the gum.

"You're nervous, aren't you?" I asked her.

"Little bit," she said without blinking.

Three black women dressed in white robes entered the stage and set up at their preferred instrument. One of them took drums, another on the guitar, and the final on the mic. For an entire hour and a half, these women jammed together and belted out some ear-shattering notes of worship for Lord Jesus. It was incessant, and the loud banging and shrill squealing eventually got me so bent out of shape that I wanted to leave. My ears were nearing the threshold just outside the impending burst of the drum.

"Angel,"

"What?" She asked.

"Let's get outta here."

"No way."

"Why not?! I'm about to scream *with* them!" I whispered.

"Because that would be rude! We came here to experience something. This is the experience," she said, daring me to challenge her.

I didn't.

"Fiiiiiine," I said, slinking back in my seat.

The old man with the suspenders and long socks was in the front, screaming and jumping up and down over and over again. He kept yelling,

"Yeah, ladies! Sing it! Sing it, ladies! Oh, my Lord! Jesus, God!"

Then he proceeded to jump up and down some more, throwing his hands around and yelling, "Yeah! Yeah! Yeah!" Half of me was waiting for a heart attack. The other half was glad Angel made me stick around.

When the preacher finally took over the mic, I had this odd flashback to a documentary I watched on Jonestown—the settlement where preacher Jim Jones created a cult-like religious group then offed them all in one night with poisoned punch. The man standing on the stage in front of us resembled Jim Jones to a tee, and his sparkling white teeth looked like they hid some stains to me. He began preaching after welcoming us all here, and before long I couldn't understand a single word he was saying! He started preaching quickly, going through PowerPoint slides of verses that he had on the wall behind him. It was hard to keep up with his speed, but I could at least understand the words. The further he dove into his sermon, though, the less his words sounded like English and more like a frenzied psycho-babble. Just as my confusion was growing, I heard a woman behind us speaking something like Spanish, but also something a little like Latin. She was crying, too, whispering to herself nonstop.

"Angel, what the fuck is that? What the fuck is that?" I asked, grabbing her leg.

"I think it's Tongues, Lyla. That woman is speaking in Tongues."

"Wait, what? Like, the language that all the crazy snake people speak?"

"Yeah, the Pentecostal church."

"Wait… is this guy a Pentecostal preacher from South Africa?" I asked.

"He must be, because he's speaking it too!" She whispered.

Just then, the man to the left of us starting rocking in his chair, arms crossed over his chest, eyes closed, tongue speaking languages entirely foreign to Angel and I. The whole room quaked with a rapturous wave of insane whispers as the preacher's voice got louder and louder.

Sudden silence.
Ringing from the mic.
Sobbing from behind.
Preacher turns.
Locks eyes.

The preacher noticed a group of three boys sitting in the front row of the crowd. They looked like high schoolers—tall, skinny, athletic, and wearing backwards hats. They seemed to be laughing and whispering to each other, and the preacher caught them having fun. He got down from the stage, cornered in on them with the mic, and proceeded to ask them how they were doing. They nervously responded with inaudible whispers, and the preacher lost it.

"Can you speak in Tongues, boys? Huh? Tell me, do you understand what I'm saying up there?"

The middle boy nodded his head.

The other two didn't move.

"So you can speak Tongues, then, huh? If you can understand me, you can surely speak it. Lemme hear you—" he started commanding them in Tongues, and I couldn't understand a damn thing sliding off his sinister lips. He got louder, started puffing his chest up like an animal and hitting the side of his head. The woman behind me was now yelling in Tongues, squealing after every other sentence. The rest of the room was in an uproar, shouting in whatever language would fall out of their mouths. It wasn't long before the three boys had the right mind to stand up and leave the situation, and if I hadn't had Angel, I'd be right there with them. We were watching a preacher all the way from South Africa bully three teenagers in a language that no one but he could speak. Maybe I'm wrong, though. Maybe they're all communicating with each other, and us sinners are out of the loop.

After the poor high schoolers ditched the scene, I grabbed Angel's leg again and said, "Can we *please* go now?!"

"No! Not yet!" She said.

It wasn't long before the preacher transitioned from his psychotic end-of-days rant into what he called "The Healing Hour". Women and men alike lined up in the center of the aisle, begging this man to bring the power of Christ into their bodies and heal their physical ailments. The first man who approached was the one sitting beside us, rocking. He was limping as well, and when asked what bothered him, he pointed down to his ankle to say that it was broken. The preacher announced the illness to the crowd, asked for some spiritual help in the form of yells, and laid his hand upon the forehead of the diseased. He closed his eyes, lowered his head, and spoke into the mic another string of excited slurs. At the climax of his spell, he smacked the man directly on the forehead, and back he fell. Women crowded around the man, wiping his forehead and yanking on his body. When he stopped shaking and came back to the room, the man jumped up and kept jumping. Up and down, up and down. His ankle, so it seemed, had been miraculously healed.

"As if it was broken to begin with," I whispered to Angel.

"Sssshhhhh," she said, still smacking.

When I looked back up at the scene, I noticed the preacher's snake-like eyes zeroing in on my bewildered brown ones. He smirked with his mouth open, sweat pouring down his red face, and began walking through the crowd of people.

"Lyla, Lyla, what the fuck, he sees us."

"Yeah, I think he's coming for us," I said.

"Fuck no!" And before I could say anything else, Angel had jumped from her chair and was trying desperately to escape the sickly crowd around us.

"Wait!" I said, catching eyes with the preacher just before he bashed a bunch of chairs to clear a path.

"Angel!" I yelled. I could barely see her. There were so many bodies crowded around us now, and she was darting all over the building trying to get out. I took the hint of the preacher and started barreling through chairs, knocking them over into the others. I made a beeline for the door, while Angel found herself stuck in a circle of old black men. They surrounded her, and she panicked and stood still. They looked down at her, chuckled, and said,

"Lady, lady, you're going the wrong way!"

"LYYYLAAA!" Angel shrieked.

"This way!" I yelled to her from the other side of the chairs. She pushed through them just like I had, knocking her knees the whole way.

"Lyla, come on, go, go, go!" She said as her purple hair flashed past me. She burst through those red double doors and ran down the steps to the parking lot. I was right behind her, knocking chairs back into the crowd so as to prevent anyone from coming after us. We sprinted all the way to her Mazda, and just before jumping inside we looked back at the building. The double doors were both opened, full of faces on top of faces peeking their heads out to watch the fiasco. The preacher parted the sea of bodies and came out to stand on the stoop in front of them, arms crossed over his heaving chest.

"It was nice to have you girls," the he said in a creepy tone.

"Remember," the tongue-speaking woman said, "He loves you."

"Oh, God," I said to Angel.

"Get in the car," she commanded.

I did.

Doors locked.

Windows up.

Keys in her lap.

Eyes dead ahead.

"What the fuck was that?" I asked her, staring at the people in the doors.

"I have no clue." Angel said, staring into Oblivion. "Other than the most terrifying event of my Life."

"Yeah, I'll fucking say so. Tongues?! They were speaking Tongues?!"

"Yeah, I don't know what to fucking tell you."

"Well let's get the fuck out of here then! Pedal to the metal, let's go!"

She agreed, and we skirted out of that parking lot and back on to familiar land. We turned the radio off and sat in an abysmal silence for five minutes before we hit a stop light.

"Can we go get vanilla milkshakes? Please?" I pleaded.

"Fuck yeah, we can go get vanilla milkshakes."

"Thank God," I said.

"Thank Satan. God and I aren't speaking anymore."

***

Remember Big Mick? Ever since Scarlette and I took our split, I never saw him. But what would you know, the day I started serving at the bar downtown Big Mick came walking through the front door. Naturally, I was excited to see him, because I thought he was a good dude! He's still that big ole wandering teddy bear who brought me the joys of marijuana when in need. To see him now, though, was a shock; he lost a massive amount of weight, got a good haircut, and had a Bruno Mars kind of swagger about him. We hugged instantly and laughed at the coincidence of it all, because he just so happens to work with me as a dishwasher. Since I didn't have a car I walked to and from work every day, but thanks to the advice of every one of my customers, they let me know it's a bad idea to be wandering around Darbyville after dark. Big Mick agreed profusely and offered to walk me home.

Every.

Single.

Night.

Then he'd walk all the way back to his friend's house two miles in the opposite direction. Sometimes we'd even take a detour through one of my favorite graveyards behind Annabelle's for a midnight smoke, or we'd scale the library building to smoke on the roof while we watched the city lights burn through the sirens and gunshots. Eventually after spending so much time with Big Mick, I learned the truth about his couch-hopping homeless 22-year-old lifestyle, and all of a sudden, he was sleeping in my 8x8 apartment room. It's easier just to say we're dating than to say,

"Well, I'm keeping a roof over his head and feeding him when he doesn't have any money. He's smoking me out whenever I ask, walking me home at night, and we occasionally have sex." He's not a bad guy at first glance, and I generally had a wonderful time in his presence. But over time his nasty, lifeless colors ran all over me.

Toward the middle of the summer in late July a decisive moment hit me when I became the target of all the "mean girls" at the bar. I didn't play into their silly games or their middle-school gossip, and I was trying to read "The Tibetan Book of the Dead" while they were Facebooking during slow hours. Naturally, I became a target for their feeble minds to prey upon. I let them fuck with me for two straight days before I tried to talk to management about their ridiculous behavior; before I knew it, I was walking out on a full restaurant, in the middle of my shift, flicking the "manager" off as I walked out the front door of his restaurant. I realized that I could sacrifice my happiness to continue working at that job, or I could sacrifice my financial security and have a wonderful summer.

I thought to myself, "money comes, and money goes. So I'm

gonna let this money go." I walked home that day in the sweltering southern heat prouder than I had ever been, and I called Angel immediately to tell her the good news as I stepped across the concrete sidewalk.

The next week of our lives Angel and I spent travelling to and from North Carolina every single day—we dubbed it "NORTH CAROLINA FREEDOM TOUR 2K13," and it was one of the best weeks of my Life. The inherent drive I have inside my heart to travel and explore every corner of the Earth was reawakened that week as we spent hours driving to Charlotte, Cherry Grove, Asheville, and Boone. There's nothing like draping yourself in the sweetest sundress, putting your rockstar shades on, and cruising down the interstate with the sun in front of you and the mountains beside. Obsessed with Whole Foods Supermarket, we visited their headquarters in Charlotte, NC where there's an entire parking garage underground and an escalator for the carts! We stopped at itty-bitty valley towns with hippie shacks colored in tye-dye, got lost through mountain highways and waterfalls, pouted over lack of weed, and groaned over having an hour's drive until the next Whole Foods. It wouldn't be a true trip without the fear of jail time, though; we nearly escaped being caught by mall security when I fearlessly and idiotically grabbed a purse Angel wanted and ran straight out the exit doors of Nordstrom! It was riotous! And, my, did that escapade ignite my burning desire to travel more.

See more.

Feel more.

Do more.

Be more.

In the month that followed, we managed to torture ourselves by taking a trip to the Humane Society—of course we brought a kitten back to a college apartment complex where pets were an illegal commodity. Oh, and the campus administrator lived in the apartment unit directly beside us; her closet was separated from Angel's room by a single, flimsy wall. Needless to say, we eventually got caught with her, and I got caught sneaking Big Mick into the apartment every night and letting him stay there even while I was gone. It was such a mess, and we were asked to pay a bunch of bullshit fines for all of our violations. But what did we care, really? We did what we wanted, unapologetically and regardless of whatever rules tried to bind us down.

Angel developed a serious bout of depression by late August, and while we were sitting in two bean-bag chairs in the middle of a Target aisle she said to me,

"I think I'm dropping out." It was hard to take her seriously with the hot pink plush that she was sitting on as customers walked by with puzzled eyes.

"Wait, what?!" I didn't see that coming. Angel has always been a prime advocate of Annabelle's.

"Yeah! You know, our trip to North Carolina really put things into perspective for me—about how I want to be living and how not to waste time doing anything that makes me unhappy. Frankly, I'm not happy here and I haven't been for a long time. This isn't where I want to be. And Bloodmoon isn't necessarily where I want to be either, but I definitely don't want to stay in school. I keep thinking about how classes start in two weeks, and how fucking horrible that sounds."

I laughed before saying, "Yeah, I get that. But you really think leaving is going to help you in the long run?"

"I *know* it will," she said with confidence. She was always the "knowing" type; she knew what she knew, and she didn't dwell on trying to change her mind or reason herself into a different opinion. She's the instinctive woman who knew how to let live and let die. Annabelle's had died in her heart, and she didn't want to carry that carcass around any longer.

"Damn," I said softly as I looked at the white tile floor beneath my feet.

"You could come back with me, you know," she suggested.

"I can't go back!" I immediately blurted out. I didn't even think about it, but that's the honest answer. Bloodmoon is not a place of nostalgic comfort for my mind nor my heart.

"Why not?"

"Well, first, my mom would fucking wring my neck if I dropped out. I've always felt like the disappointment to her, I can't prove her right again. And, I don't know, I just don't feel like I'm done here."

"Lyla, are you kidding me?" She said as she whipped her purple hair around.

"What do you mean?"

"I know why I don't want to finish school, but what were you thinking even starting college?! Ever since I've known you, your only dream has been to travel the world and to write. You should be working in restaurants making bank, then jetting off to wherever your next destination is! What you want out of your Life, college isn't going to give you. You're trying to fit yourself into a box that just isn't made for you; you've got way too many round edges, not corners."

I was speechless for at least thirty seconds with the silliest smile on my face, because I knew she was right. But I had never really thought about it, I guess. We're bred to understand from an early age that if we don't go to college, we'll be bums in the streets or worse—flipping burgers at McDonald's. Since I've been a highly academic student my whole Life, nobody ever told me that there was another option to living other than going to college immediately after high school. I repeat, NO ONE TOLD ME I DIDN'T HAVE TO GO TO COLLEGE. It was expected. How could someone with such high test scores and grades forego college?

"You're right," I finally said to her, "but there's no way I can go back to Bloodmoon."

"Yes you can!" She assured me, "I can even see if my dad will let you stay with us."

"Oh, NO! The second my mom finds out I dropped out, didn't tell her, and decided to live with you instead of her? She will disown me forever," I joked.

"Lyla, you can do whatever you want. Be here now, remember? Don't plan a future that you can't control. You don't dictate how Life happens, you just dictate how you react."

One of the most significant teachings we've learned together is to "be here now", as the Buddha says. We've had to remind ourselves to live by the moment, being present in each fleeting second, and squeezing the Life out of it rather than worrying about planning a future that hasn't happened yet or dwelling on a past that can't be altered.

Our debate about the pros and cons of my staying at school continued well into the night. I shed a lot of tears, and she shed only a few. We even made a chart of the different aspects of dropping out or continuing, but that didn't help very much. I went to sleep that night heartbroken because my little Angel-baby was leaving, but she managed to sneak into my room and grab my journal. She wrote me the longest, sweetest letter about how I shouldn't stress about my decision; if I'm not ready to leave, I'm not ready to leave, but that she will always be there for me to support me and pick me up when I've fallen back into that venomous pit. I cried when I woke up the next day to read everything she wrote, and it was then that I realized I simply wasn't finished with Darbyville. It really isn't about college, because Angel made me see that I could care less about my scholarly affairs. I merely knew without a doubt that I had other business in Darbyville that needed explored before I could spread my wings and fly away from this place. We're not done with each other. Not yet.

Angel left Annabelle's ten days before my sophomore year was scheduled to begin, and it was wretched having to help her pack up her car and watch her drive off to Bloodmoon Beach. She'd become my backbone, my rock, my elephant, my strength, my partner in crime, my guide, and my other half. She's the fire under my ass, as I'm the pain in hers, and we have the tattoos to prove it. I experienced deeper sides to myself than I realized were possible to reach through the sisterly Love and support she gave to me, and now I'm left to move into a different dorm room with only Big Mick standing by me.

Nothing left to do but to let live what should live, and let die what must die.

XII: Summer 2K13: The Mercy

I let Big Mick's influence over my Life die away as soon as Angel left, but only for a few weeks. It wouldn't be long before I was reminded of his homeless state and the impending cold weather that autumn would surely bring. In those few weeks that he disappeared from being an obligation of mine I hurled myself even further into the Buddhist practices; I ate a strict regimen of rice crackers, hummus, grapes, quinoa, and yogurt. They say that in order for yoga to properly benefit the body your stomach should be filled in ratios; the lower quarter should be food, the next quarter should be water, and last half should be air. It works wonders! With that ratio you're never too bloated to bend your body into a fleshy pretzel.

The monks also sleep on the ground, straight on their back, and only sleep enough to get their required REM sleep; as soon as that's achieved, they immediately wake from the dreaming state to go into a six-hour meditation, regardless of what time it is. Supposedly 3 AM is the golden hour by which your soul speaks to your psyche, so they'd usually be awake all through the night. I attempted to follow their example and slept on the hard maple floor in my new dorm room for 3 nights, and each time I awoke, I hopped up for meditation. However, I usually always dozed off while sitting straight up. I'm no monk, but boy, I tried. Regardless of how difficult certain aspects of Buddhism were for me, I was constantly reminded to keep treading the waters through the lessons of the Buddha:

1) Do not go by reasoning, nor by inferring, nor by argument. A true disciple must know for himself.
2) That being present, this becomes; that not being present, this does not become.

3) Suffering is the essence of Life, and the end of Suffering is the essence of mastering Life. It is just Ill, and the ceasing of Ill.
4) Suffering exists because of human beings' desires within the world, their problems through trying to attain those desires, and the dynamic of coping with the outcomes.
5) Buddhism signifies entire equality; men and women alike can both be enlightened.
6) ALL individuals should proceed toward enlightenment through confronting his or her individual situations rather than comparing themselves to others.

"Therefore, O Ananda, be lamps unto yourselves. Betake yourselves to NO EXTERNAL REFUGE, but hold fast as a refuge to the Truth. Work out your own salvation with diligence.
Buddhism is devoid of authority, ritual, speculation, tradition, and the supernatural. We focus only on intense self-effort, because we are given the path to the end of suffering, and so we tread it!"
And, of course, the Buddha's Eight Noble Truths teach us that in order to function in this Life properly, we must have:

1) The Right Views
2) The Right Intent upon manifesting those views
3) The Right Speech during conversation
4) The Right Conduct in every-day doings
5) The Right Livelihood in acquiring your daily bread
6) The Right Mindfulness in every minute
7) The Right Concentration on your goals
8) The Right Effort to achieve them

Even though I can't function on merely three hours of sleep and endless meditation, I still manage to practice yoga and meditate on Buddha's lessons and Eight Noble Truths in the Oakland cemetery each day. Since school hasn't started yet, but the summer camps were all done, I had to move out of the summer apartment and into the Allen Dorm that has become my new home for sophomore year. I'm the only one in the entire three-story building, so to combat the lonely hours, I spend time with the past souls in the hillsides.

Cemeteries have always been a place of peaceful serenity for me, seeing as they're the only places on earth where Life and Death come together in perfect harmony. The Oakland cemetery has been around since the late 1700s and held every type of body from collegiate affiliates, southern aristocrats, fallen war heroes, foreign immigrants, children, and all others in between. Whole families that are dead to the rest of the world live on together in a 10x10 grassy plot, and there's something inherently beautiful about that. The sprawling hills serve as a shore full of empty shells covered only by sands of grass and twisting oak trees, and what an enchanting place to be! where Life and Death continue to play in a distant realm not yet visible to our human eyes. Can you think of a quieter place than a field full of dead memories? Full of past lives, past energies perhaps still lingering all around, whispering tales of the Otherworld. I have always treasured what it feels like to be among it all, and luckily for me, this cemetery is only a five-minute walk from the Allen Dorm.

It's this time spent lying beside tombstones when I find myself sinking deeper into my psyche, bringing out the demons and the angels in a war of internal revelations. I've begun to see clearly all of the ways in which I'm inhibiting my own growth and how I've hurt those around me, and it didn't take long before my own personal Buddha said,

"You've gotta find a way to make things right with her again."

The external, third-dimension-dwelling Lyla replied,

"I know, but where do I even start?"

"You start by apologizing," the quiet voice said.

With only one week left until Annabelle's was back in session, I sat myself down at a cherry wood desk in my new dorm room, put pen to paper, and began pouring everything out. With the creaky wooden windows wide open, the birds sang songs of retribution while I wrote how sorry I was that I took advantage of Scarlette's kind heart the way that I did, and how my own vain ego wouldn't allow for me to back down after I had been caught in that sick lie. I told her how much had changed inside of me and how much Love I have found in my own soul in the last seven months without her friendship, and that I wanted nothing more than for her to know how truly devastated I am that I destroyed our friendship for my own selfish gain. After five pages of writing this letter, I finally finished by saying,

"I don't even expect you to forgive me. I hope that you do, and I hope that we can carry on our friendship like we had before. I love you, and I am so, so, SO sorry that I ever hurt you like that. If you want to talk, here's my number…"

I sat back and read the letter over and over again, making sure that I wrote the words just right in order for her to feel my heart. When I felt satisfied with committing it to my conscience I tucked it away in the drawer of my desk for safe keeping. That letter is a reflection of myself with my heart on my sleeve, bleeding freely, and that sort of vulnerability is what it takes for people to see your true nature—the internal flame of compassion that is unwavering in the face of such conviction and honesty with oneself. I'm not even sure if I'm seriously going to give Scarlette the letter, but I know it's there if I ever want to.

You know, the experiences we have and the memories we keep are all that we truly have in the end. They are our only friends and our only enemies when there's nobody but ourselves to talk to; even when there are more enemies than friends inside of our heart, those shadows shape us into the blissfully bold and brash brilliance that we are. Whoever that person is will emerge when the time is right, and I'm just hoping that it might be my time—my time to come forth as the bleeding heart that I so naturally am. But, as Buddha has taught me, you cannot rip the skin off the snake; the snake must molt the skin in its own time. That is the rate by which spiritual evolution happens.

This bleeding heart of mine is only looking to spill its Love over everyone that I touch, even though Love is the sole emotion that one can feel both alive and dead within. Ecstatic and devastated, at home and at war. But if you're honest with yourself and open up your squinted eyes, you'll see that Love is *everywhere*. Just like those Christians say. Could it be that Love is my God? Love is in this rocky wooden chair when I sit to write. Love is in the golden evening sunlight bouncing off the towering tree trunks outside. Love is the sound of heavy drums and mesmerizing guitar riffs chanting from my stereo. Love is looking down at the brown, crunchy grass beneath this foggy window and knowing that our own roots are under it, tangled within all those others. Love is anywhere and everywhere that we choose to see it! The murder of crows jetting to a nearby tower? That is also Love. The clouds above them that dot the sky to create a patchy white and blue painting? That is also Love. The milky, yet lively, green water in the distant creek that ripples in the wind?

Love.

Love.

Love.

And Love deserves to infect all. Love is to regret nothing past and embrace everything to come as a part of a much bigger, better plot for the universe, and how can you argue with any of God's or Allah's or Yahweh's or Buddha's or Shiva's or Kali's or Odin's inner workings? You cannot. We are all but a blend of dust and Divinity, and it's our decision to figure out which end of the spectrum we'd rather fall on: the dusty? Or the Divine? All things in the Universe are good and divine in some manner, even the ignorant and the sorrowful. But it's up to our own heads and our own perceptions to be able to see it in whichever way we'd please: Divine, or sorrowful.

I'll take the Divine.

***

10:56 AM. Late August. I walked through the musty back door of the Allen Dorm to see a string of girls dropping their suitcases as their old roommates ran to embrace them in a tackle of affection, while the boyfriends drop to the wayside to pick up the fallen luggage. Squeals and yells of different names were being shouted all across that familiar grassy quad, and the budding roses blotted the landscape with a touch of sparkle that reflected the reunion of everyone around them. The ancient trees lining the sidewalks swayed their branches in whimsical rhythms, creating a lofty ballad fit for such a delightful event. It's certainly the happiest that these girls will feel for the entire year ahead of them! That first day always tastes the sweetest when your lips have forgotten how revolting the journey through college can be. The bitterness of Life bites through our flesh, tough and searing; but the sweetness sedates, divine and misguiding.

As I danced my way through the merry crowds, it warmed my heart to see how much these girls missed each other and the kind of outpour of Love they've created. Classes start in the morning, but that's no matter; now I'm on my way to a friend's dorm to take a trip down to a local river before the chaos erupted the next day. As I walked up the sidewalk to trek across campus, I came upon Angel's old Usher dorm. Reminiscing on the times we spent inside that building together, I almost didn't notice the black Jeep that parked directly beside the entrance.

A Jeep.

A black Jeep.

A necklace hanging in the mirror.

Scarlette.

Scarlette Bethesda.

She must have just arrived at school and in her frenzy decided to park "illegally" in the alley way that separated the dorms. I stood smirking in the middle of the sidewalk for a few moments, trying to make up my mind on what my next move should be. Coincidences don't just happen; they're put out there for us by the Universe. So, the fact that I happened to be walking by the Usher Dorm at the exact moment that she had arrived to school couldn't be ignored. Fate is a sneaky lady, and nothing she facilitates is out of place—ever.

Before I had time to doubt myself, I turned and sprinted all the way back to my Allen Dorm. I darted through girls and various parents with arms full of notebooks and lamps, hopped over protruding tree roots and rose bushes, and hurtled over pieces of the brick courtyards that lined the dorms. I punched my code into the brick building, ripped open the door, and sprinted even further through the winding hallways and double-stepped it up the three flights of sunken stairs; you see, the Allen Dorm is the oldest standing dormitory on Annabelle's campus. It's just a tiny brick building that's housed upperclassmen since the 1890s and had been built to resemble something more of a home than a uniform cinderblock prison. The wooden walls were painted a mint green color while the aging wooden staircases were covered in hunter green carpet. When you set foot on certain steps, you'd swear the builders were drunk when they created the place! But the character in that building cast a fine shadow on all the others across campus.

  Once I hurled myself into my room I grabbed the letter out of my desk and raced back through the hallways without even bothering to shut my door. I repeated the process of whizzing in and out of the obstacles standing between me and my mission. When I got back to Scarlette's car I was relieved to see that she wasn't standing anywhere outside, so I walked right up to the driver's side, lifted up her windshield-wiper blade, and made sure the letter was tucked tightly underneath it. I looked around one last time to see if anyone I knew was around, and seeing that the coast was clear, I smiled to myself and skipped away to my friend Katy's dorm. All I have left to do now is wait.

  I ran through the halls of Katy's dorm, too, panting from the whirl I just took all over campus. When I finally found her room I nearly ran right past it, and everyone inside started laughing.

  "Robes, is that you?!" I heard Katy call to me. I ran back and grabbed the sides of the door, breathing heavily, and said,

  "You know it's me if I'm running! I'm always late!"

  "Yeah, I know!" Katy laughed. She's probably a foot shorter than me, but has the tallest personality and the biggest heart to match. She's a CA now in a freshman dorm that she's living in, and a few of her new mates were gathered around her.

  "Oh, Robes," she started, "meet Hannah, Shannon, Tatiana, and Ellie. Everyone, this is Robes. She's fucking awesome."

  "Heeeeyyyyyy!" Everybody cheered.

  "Wait," Hannah said, "is Robes your real name?"

  "No," I laughed, "Lyla is my real name."

  "We gave her the name Robes during freshman year, because she always wore the coolest Kimonos around the hall."

  Everybody rang out with infinite questions. Everybody except for the one they call Ellie. She captivated me the instant I set eyes on her. With honeysuckle blonde hair curling down to her shoulders and an enticingly curvaceous body, I couldn't help but stare. I looked at her eyes, and this mischievous innocence radiated from the glacial blue glow inside. A few faded freckles brushed her cheeks in a bronze sheen while her silver septum ring dangling from her nose focused my attention toward her lips, which were a luscious pastel pink. There was something about her meek demeanor that charmed me, too, and as I bowed my head at everyone's praise, I could only look at her while I did so.

"Alright, so you guys ready?" Katy said as she interrupted my daze.

"Yeah, man!" I shouted out with everyone else cooing in agreeance.

"Okay, Robes, I know you don't mind adventure, so since there's only enough seats for the fresh meat, would you mind hangin' out in the back?" Katy has a little Ford Escape, so there was just enough space for my long body to fit in the hatchback. And she was right; I didn't mind a little adventure, so I complied without hesitation.

The river that we came to is one of the scenic spots that Scarlette, Mia and I would always pass on our Loop; there's a run-down, sunken-in, barely-standing Redneck Riviera bar across the street from the river, and there are always cars in the parking lot and Bud Light signs lit, despite the voices inside your soul telling you to stay away from the abandoned shack. On a hot summer's night, we found the parking lot packed and the river empty. Good news!

We all gathered around on the bank and kicked sand at each other, racing off in different directions to see what hidden treasures we could find. I started rock hopping all across the formations, ditching my shoes halfway through. Before I knew it, everyone else was falling in line behind me, trying their hardest not to get their shoes wet. Since I was barefoot I practically ran across those rocks until I came as far as I could and decided to pop a squat on a jutting rock, letting my feet plunge into the slow-moving water below me. I stared off into the distance at the glittering movement of the sun's glow bopping across the ripples in the water. The shadows from the surrounding trees began to cover the farthest end of the river in a cooling shade, and blue sky began to fade into the warm hues of descending daylight. I breathed deeply and tilted my head back, soaking in the perfection that Mother Earth so graciously shares with us day after day. When I opened my eyes, I looked down at the water and thought,

"I wanna be *in* that."

My inner voice said, "So get in!"

"Yes, ma'am!"

I gently pushed myself from the rock I was perched and into the cleansing rush of the river. How weightless it feels to be floating along a moving body of water! You begin to drift with the ebb and flow of Life's organic nature rather than fighting to figure out the next move, and it's as if all the knots in your soul are smoothed out in the tumbling of the water's gentle force. The river carried me down past all the bands of rocky beds, and as I floated close to the bank, I looked back to see how far the river had taken me; all the other girls were staring at me from a football field away, waving and jumping to make sure I was okay. I whooped and hollered to let them know I was just fine. But to my surprise, there was one girl missing from the rest, and she happened to be hurling down the river toward me! It's Ellie, and it seems that she found the genius in my ways.

The rest of the girls doubled back down the hill of rocks to get closer to us near the bank, but we weren't even thinking about getting out! As soon as Ellie reached me, I laughed and said,

"You too, huh?"

"Yeah, you looked like you were having so much fun! And I was right!"

"I know! Perfect swimming weather. Perfect sunlight. Perfect temp."

"Yeah," she said as she wiped the water off her face, "but my jeans are getting kind of heavy! They're weighing me down."

"Take them off!" I said instinctively, "I'm taking my skirt off, too!"

"Okay!" She agreed. We both took off our bottoms and threw them toward the bank where Katy and the girls were.

"What do you think you're doing?!" Katy yelped.

"You *know* I love an adventure!" I shouted back at her. Ellie waded beside me, giggling all the while.

"You took your clothes off?!" Katy shouted in disbelief.

"They were weighing us down!" I shouted.

"You know I don't have any towels in my car!" Katy yelled.

"It's okay, just strap me to the roof!" I joked back.

As she and the others chittered back and forth about our absurdity, Ellie and I turned to look at the opposite bank of the river covered in lush trees instead of paved highway. I looked at her and said,

"I'll race ya!"

I started swimming as fast as I could to the opposite side. It only seemed like it was a few strokes away, but it was a tiring trudge to beat the current and reach the shore! About halfway there Ellie squealed and said,

"Look! There's a rope hanging from that tree!" And sure enough, one of the neighborhood rednecks tied a sturdy piece of rope around the oldest tree in sight, fit for anyone to take a jump and fly straight into the river.

"No fucking way!" I said in sheer elation. "Let's go!"

When we finally reached the bank, we were bottomless and soaked from head to toe, exposing our bright bras like a wild wet t-shirt contest. I stared up at the tree and asked Ellie,

"Have you ever done this before?"

"No way, have you?" She asked.

"Nope," I answered. And just as I did, I heard Katy's shrieking from the other side, yelling,

"WHHHHAAAAT ARE YOU DOOOOOIIIIINNNG?!"

"IT'S A ROOOOOOPE SWWWWIIIIINNNGG!" I yelled.

Just as I finished bellowing back at her, a young father and his much younger son came out of the woods behind us! They were in their swimming trunks, but were still dry, so I could only assume that they were the ones who had constructed this rope swing.

"Whooooaaaa," the too-tan mustache-sportin' father said, "niiiice eenk!"

I knew he was talking to me, because all my tattoos were showing now—even the one on my ass.

"Thanks!" I laughed, "excuse our attire, we weren't prepared for this."

"Nawt uh prawblim hun," he said, "y'all ever rope swang befo?"

"No sir," Ellie said with a chuckle, "can you show us?"

"Shur!" He bellowed, "Mah son heer 'ill show ya the ropes, if ya know wut I meen!"

Before he could go any further, that little spider monkey of a boy climbed up the slanted tree trunk, grabbed a hold of the rope, and jumped off the large knot on the outside of the trunk. I swear he flew 40 feet in the air before he let go! And just like that, he bombed down into the depths of the river so hard that I'm sure even the mud-dwellers felt his plunge.

"WOOOOWW!" Ellie and I said in unison.

"Awl right, wich one 'o yew is next?" Papa Stache asked.

"Do you wanna go first?" I asked Ellie, just to be polite.

"Nuh-uh!" She squealed, "You go!"

"Yes ma'am!"

Carefully, I climbed up the side of that massive sapling, knees weakening with each step I took. I climbed out onto a branch in order to grab the rope and placed my two hands right above the knot at the top of it. I looked back at Papa Stache and asked,

"Like this?"

"Yea, hun, now jus' juuuump!"

"Okay! Here it goes!"

I kicked my whole body weight off the middle of the tree's knot, clutching the rope in between my thighs as I soared into the air. At the peak of my swing, I looked up again at that fading evening sky and let go all in the same second. My body and gravity tangoed together all the way down to the surface of the river, then SMACK! I left the airy element to drown myself in the watery kind. The quiet of the underworld held me in that river during a dazzling moment suspended in time. I let my body linger in the cooling river flow long enough for the sounds of the outside world to come back to me after the ringing in my ears cheered me on.

As I emerged from the muddy depths and broke through to the air, I looked back to see Katy and her minions howling. I howled right back, as the feral pack of wolves we'd become. Suddenly, another howl came from behind me—it's Ellie! Just as I looked toward her, she was jumping off the tree and dangling in mid-air. She managed to twist her beautiful body into a backflip, giving her more cool-points than me for the creative execution! As she came back up from the water after having sunk down into the abyss, she and I laughed hysterically. She swam across to meet me at the halfway point in the river, and we both turned to give a wave and a shout to Papa Stache and Boy Stache, saying,

"THAAAAANK YOUUUUU!" In between our hoots. They waved back as Papa Stache prepared for his descent into the river, and we began swimming back to shore where our friends awaited us.

When we got close enough, I saw Katy standing with her hip cocked, tapping her flip-flop like a mother.

"You guys are fucking nuts," she said as she let out a little snicker.

"But fucking fun!" Ellie shouted. It seemed her modesty had been replaced with confidence! A 40-foot dive into water will do that to a girl.

"Yeah, well, get ready to air dry!" Katy said, "I've got the glass hatch open in the car, you both are riding in the trunk on the way home!"

"Awh, come on, I can't ride on the top?!" I asked playfully.

"I will not be responsible for your death!" Katy shouted.

When we got back to the car I was thankful that I kept my phone hidden in the back instead of attached to my wrist. I situated myself among all the old clothes of Katy's and wet clothes of mine and Ellie's before grabbing the phone from my wallet. When I checked my notifications, it said I had five missed calls from a random phone number and two texts. My heart starting racing with anxiety, because I was sure it was Scarlette. When I opened the first text, the only piece I read was,

"Hey it's Scarlette, everything is okay—"

Before I read any further I dialed the number back immediately. As it rang, I swear my heart was in my throat and I couldn't hear anything other than the dial tones in my ear.

"Lyla?" A voice on the line said.

"Scarlette?" I asked back.

"Hey, this is Mia's phone, because I didn't have your number anymore. But listen, I'm not even mad anymore. I knew you stole my car and I don't care, I really don't care!"

"Really?" I asked, voice cracking and tears welling in my eyes.

"Yeah!" She said, "Everything's okay. We're okay, we're okay.

Of course, we can still be friends. I didn't even read the letter that you left on my car at first."

"Well how did you know it was me then?!" I asked between tears.

"I just knew it had to be you! I mean, I've read it now, and it's all okay! We're cool, I swear it. It's all done, so let's just start over."

"I'm so happy to hear you say that!" I squealed, "I don't know if you can tell, but I'm crying right now. I'm crying I'm so happy."

"Awhhh, Lyla!" She said with a sure smile. "Where are you? Let's hangout!"

"I'm almost back to school! I just took an unexpected plunge in the river by that sketchy bar. Did you know there's a rope swing hanging from a tree out there?!"

"What! No way, did you jump off it?!"

"Hell yeah I did!"

"That's awesome! Okay, well, call me when you get back to school, do you still have my number?"

"Yeah, I gotta go put some clothes on though because I'm soaking wet and half naked, so I'll call you when I'm presentable."

"Okay, hurry-scurry," she said, "I love you!"

"Okay, okay, I love you too!" I replied. As I hung up the phone a huge wave of joy passed over my whole body, causing me to shiver with excitement. More tears trickled down my beaming cheeks, and Ellie turned to wipe a few away and ask me,

"What's wrong?"

"Nothing!" I replied. "Absolutely nothing is wrong."

***

Scarlette and Mia told me to meet at the smoking stoop by the oak tree on the edge of campus. As I turned the final corner and beheld only a grassy lot that separated us, I noticed Scarlette's curly head staring straight in my direction. When she saw my long-skirted silhouette drudging through the tall green grass, she jumped off that stoop and ran! I started skipping along, too, holding my skirt in one hand and my wallet in the other. When she was ten feet from me, I stopped running to brace myself, for I knew she was going to tackle me like I had seen all the other girls do earlier that day.

"Oh, Lyla!" She said as she pounced on me and wrapped her legs around my back. I wrapped my arms around her back and twirled her around just like the lesbian couple everyone assumes we are. I tripped on a tricky tree stump, though, and down we went, toppling over into the grass and laughing the whole way down.

"You bitch," she said with a grin as she playfully punched my shoulder.

"Yeahhhh, I know, man! I'm sorry!"

"I know you are," she said, "come on and sit with us while we have a smoke."

As we walked over to Mia with our arms hooked, the final rays of the sun's daily allowance faded into the black night and the crickets began singing their lullabies. The moon was rising just above the dark tree lines, emitting a magical orange glow behind hazy summer clouds. The other girls wandering the campus behind us were but distant caricatures of whimsical laughter, and as their cheers hushed I thought back to when Angel tempted me to leave Annabelle's; my instincts paid off, because I knew I wasn't done here, and my heart felt at ease knowing that I followed my gut and repaired this once-in-a-lifetime friendship.

"What's up, man?" Mia said, taking a break from puffing on her Marlboro.

"Hey, how's it goin! How've you been?" I asked.

"Oh, I'm great now, I think…" she said.

I looked at Scarlette for some answers as to what that meant, but she gave me none.

"What do you mean you think?" I teased.

"Well, I tried to kill myself last semester and got sent to a mental hospital when it didn't work," she laughed and took another hit of her cigarette as if what she said was no big deal.

"What?!" I shouted.

"You didn't hear about that?" Scarlette asked while Mia was laughing at my reaction. I don't know what she thinks is so funny!

"No, I didn't hear about that!"

"Yeah," Scarlette started, "last semester we were walking out to her car to go for a loop, but she just started throwing up in the parking lot. She wasn't making any sense and her voice was really weak. Finally, I asked her if she had taken anything, and she told me ate a whole bottle of Tylenol."

"Whaaaaat?" I said with eyes wide, "are you serious, Mia?"

Again, she laughed, "Yeah, but it's not a big deal. I was in a really bad place. My bulimia had gotten worse and I was only 94 lbs. I got depressed really bad," she paused for a puff, "but after my body pumped all that shit out, the school sent me on a medical leave and my parents checked me into a mental hospital." Another puff, "I fucking loved it there, man! Everyone was batshit crazy, and I just sat back and wrote about it all. I could have stayed there forever, but I figured I should get my degree before I become a full-time loony."

Before we all split, it was clear that Mia was falling into a dark place. Just weeks after we all started our freshman year at Annabelle's, Mia confessed to us in a drunken stupor that she's bulimic. While Scarlette and I starved ourselves on spinach leaf diets for a week at a time, Mia's weight loss choice was to eat a gallon of icecream and puke it all back out. Her parents' divorce only got more complicated, she was loaded with the most rigorous academic class load, and her hot Italian blood just couldn't handle all the pressure she was getting from herself and from her family. On a bad night with a full bottle of Tylenol beside her bed, she decided to see if she could stomach one final meal—good news is that she couldn't.

"GodDAMN," I said in awe, "no wonder I didn't see you around for that last month, huh?"

"Yeah, off to the asylum they sent me!"

"Wow. Well it's good to see you're still standing! Or, sitting in this case."

I could feel Scarlette staring at me on the dark sidewalk. She finally broke the stare by looking to the ground and saying,

"Yeah, it's been a weird fucking time since you ditched us. I spent the whole summer living in Aiden at my parents' old house doing mushrooms every day with a bunch of country boys."

"Whoa!" They were surprising me all over the place. When I met Scarlette, the only drug she had crossed off her list was weed—she's clearly moved on to bigger and better things!

"But enough about us, we wanna hear about you!" Mia said,

lighting another cigarette and giving one to Scarlette in the process.

"What about me?!" I laughed.

They both looked at each other before Mia blurted out,

"Why'd you do it?"

"Why did I steal Scarlette's car?" I asked meekly.

"No, we know why you stole it. Why did you lie so hard about it? You know we knew the entire time, right?" Scarlette said.

"Yeahhhhh, I know," I said, "I guess I was just embarrassed, you know? I was disgusted that I could do that to you, and I was even more disgusted that you saw that side of me. I know it sounds silly and cliché, but I never meant to hurt you with all of that. It's just, I couldn't stand the idea that not only did I fuck up so bad on the execution of covering up the obvious tracks, but I know how highly you thought of me. And I didn't want that to change. I wanted you to keep seeing me as this incredibly righteous human being that tries to do the best for everyone around her. But, I fucked up. I lost my judgement for a while and I wanted to make you hate me so that it would be easier for you to move on from the friendship."

"Yeah, I get that," Scarlette said, "and I wouldn't have been mad about it if you would have just been honest with me when I asked you. Do you know I went to your room in the middle of the night when you stole my car? I was shocked to find it locked, because you never lock your door! I knew something was wrong, because I woke up and wanted a cigarette, but I couldn't find my keys."

"So, you came to my room thinking you left them in there?" I asked.

"Yeah! But when it was locked, I just decided to go down to my car. I thought that maybe I left the keys in there."

"And you couldn't find it, could you?" I smirked a little.

"No! I looked everywhere! My contacts were all blurry and it was dark and cold, and I could barely see anything, but I couldn't find my car ANY. WHERE. I finally gave up and just went back to sleep. But the next morning before class I decided to check again in the daylight."

"And?"

"And my car was back in the exact spot that I know I checked the night before. I got in to smoke a cigarette and saw those Dunkin'

Donuts coupons and thought to myself, 'I never go there,' but didn't really think much of it until I saw Destiny walking down the hallway with an iced coffee as big as her whole body!"

Mia and I erupted in laughter before I said,

"Oh, shit! So, I was caught before the morning even started!" I joked.

"Fuck yeah," Scarlette said, "I looked at Destiny and asked her where she got that coffee from, and she told me that you gave it to her before you went to class."

"Daaaaaaaamn!" I could only muster up respect for how perfectly the Universe played that scenario. Nothing is a coincidence.

"Not even two minutes later," Scarlette continued, "my mom called freaking out that my card had been stolen. When she told me all the charges and got to the Dunkin' Donuts part of it, I asked her where it was. She told me it was an hour outside of Bloodmoon Beach, and that's when I knew for sure that you stole my car."

"Wow," I said shaking my head, "I can't believe you didn't at least try to beat the shit out of me," I teased.

"Speaking of beating the shit outta someone! When were you gonna—" Scarlette started.

"I told her about Tammy," Mia said, cutting Scarlette off.

"You brought me in on that lie, too, and didn't tell me!?" Scarlette spouted off.

"I didn't know if I could trust you yet!" I shouted, smiling.

"And you thought you could trust Mia?! You know she told absolutely everyone about that story after we weren't speaking to each other!"

"Yeah, but it backfired on me!" Mia said, "Instead of everyone thinking you were a bad seed, they all thought you were a badass and that Tammy deserved it!"

"Aha!" I cackled, "She *did* deserve it! And I *am* a badass!"

"Oh, don't you start!" Scarlette said with the ferocity of a mother in her voice.

It's such fun to laugh and play with them like this again. Lyla and The Skinnies have been raised from the dead—or so it seems. To forgive and forget is a mighty selfless trait, and while Scarlette may never forget that I betrayed her that night, she was able to effortlessly find it in her wild heart to forgive me for it, and it's one of the most generous acts of kindness and Love that she's ever shown me.

"What time is it?" Mia asked.

"Time for you to get a watch," Scarlette replied.

"Oh, fuck off!" Mia said.

"Is it time for a loop?" I asked.

"Fuck yeah!" Scarlette said, "You drivin'?"

"You know I am," I said with a gleaming grin.

Together the three of us rode off into the moonlight together, whipping around those oh-so-familiar lightless roads that my soul dearly missed. Passing the torch of Life back and forth to each other we snickered and chittered about the foolish places we'd found ourselves in while we were apart—Scarlette with all of her trippy mushroom-eating excess and Mia with her hilarious stories about sexual encounters with cooks in a restaurant freezer.

In the midst of all the commotion I instantly appreciated how each memory in Time fluidly passes from one to the next. If you think of it like this; material things, like our bodies, are composed of cells, atoms, and particles to make something physical and tangible. Consciousness, however, is composed of *moments*, and every one of them casually and continuously connects to the next, perfectly linking the past and the future in an odd place that we humans call the present. Very few of us choose to keep our minds focused in the present, much less are those of us who are able to actually live in the present. It's usually because we're too focused on building a future or reconstructing the past to be able to take what Life throws at us and honestly savor what we're given. But in this moment with Scarlette and Mia, I feel I finally understand what Buddha meant when he said to "be here, now." All we've got is this present moment, for the past is but an illusion that we cling to in our minds, and the future isn't ever guaranteed. But this is Life—our Life. We've just gotta take what we can get when it's given to us, and enjoy it for everything it's got. There is no other way.

XIII: Autumn 2K13: The Debate

"I'm shaving my head," I said to Scarlette in the lunch line on an October morning after swimming class.

"Oh, you mean like mine?" She asked. When Scarlette and Destiny became closer after we split, they both shaved the left side of their heads. Everyone wanted that I'm-so-edgy-but-I've-still-got-long-hair look. However, that is not the style I'm going for—I mean total buzz.

"No way, Jose." I said. "Shaved. Like, shaved-shaved."

"What the fuck!?" Her face looked as if she'd been slapped. "Lyla...no."

"Why not?!" I know I'm doing this; ever since I signed up for swimming class three days a week, my unnatural tri-colored had become much too unruly. Every time I left the pool with what should have been sopping-wet hair, the last eight inches of blonde were dried to crunchy bits because of the damage I had done from dying it for so many years. There was no brushing it out, and even if I *did* manage to untangle that mop I had to douse the ends in five different hair products to keep it from looking like a mangled mess. It's frustrating and ugly, and I didn't want to deal with it any longer.

"Lyla," she paused, "...that would look hideous. Please don't do that, oh my God, please don't shave your head."

I couldn't help but laugh at her genuine concern for my aesthetics.

"Too late," I laughed, "Angel already planned a trip up here, and we're gonna have a ritual shaving of alllllllll the hairs on my head!"

"No way..." even more horror filled her shining brown eyes.

"Yes way!"

"But why!?"

"A lot of reasons!" I said. She sounded more like my mother than my punk best friend. "One, because I can't fucking deal with this atrocious muddle of crunchy hair every Monday, Wednesday, and Friday. It's worse than a shaved head would be!"

"Wrong!" She shrieked.

"Two: you know I've been into Buddhism lately. I mean, I gave up *all* my jewelry, all of it. I stopped stealing, I've been meditating and doing yoga day in and day out, I've—"

"Are you trying to be a monk?" Scarlette interrupted.

"No way!" I said quickly, "I'd have to give up a lot more than just my hair and my jewelry for that. But my point is that I've been getting into this whole idea of non-attachment, and I think it would be a really good exercise in detaching myself from materialistic notions if I got rid of one thing that's supposed to make me naturally desirable as a woman."

"I don't think it's the hair that makes you desirable or not, I just think it would look really bad. I mean, do you, Boo, but it worries me. I'm scared you're gonna regret it after it happens and wish you had all your hair back. And then what are we supposed to do about it?!"

"No waaaaaay," I reassured her, taking a bite of my bland baked ziti. "I'm excited for it! I mean, look at this face," I said with a cheeky grin, "how could you not love this face?! Look at the symmetry!"

"Yes, you're gorgeous, Lyla! But I'm nervous! You know I love to take pictures with you, and what are we gonna look like when you're bald?!"

"We're gonna look top-notch, is what we're gonna look like!"

"Uuuuuugghhhh. When is Angel gonna be here?" She asked with a touch of annoyance.

"In two days," I said with a touch of pride.

"You're shaving it in *two* days?!"

"Oh yes!" I said happily, "but don't worry, I'm cutting it to my shoulders and dying it fire-engine red tonight as a final dye to end all dyes. Only natural hair from here on out."

"Ohhhhh myyyyyy, Lyla. Well, more power to ya, I guess. That's what I'm supposed to say, right?"

"Ha! Sure, that's what you say."

"I can't believe you're doing this," she said, staring at the cup of Coca-Cola in her hands.

"Hey, what time is it?" I asked.

"Time for you to get a watch, bitch!" She said as she slammed her cup on the table before playfully darting away to the trash chute. Never fails.

Two days later as I was walking to my dorm, I noticed a vibrant purple-headed woman wearing red and white polka-dotted skinny jeans, a navy blue and white striped shirt, and glittering silver Ugg boots. There's a round navy leather purse with gold studs strapped around her arm, and I recognized it immediately as the one that almost got me in trouble; who else could it be other than the notorious Angel?

"ANGEEEELLLLL BABYYY!" I screamed out behind her as she was struggling to find a way into my dorm building.

She whipped her body around and squealed all in the same motion, yelling,

"LYYYYYLLAAAAA! Oh, I'm so happy to see your stupid little faaaaace!"

We ran to each other and hugged as if it had been six years rather than six weeks we'd been without each other. Naturally at an all-women's school, we have our fair share of lesbian flings; everyone automatically assumes that when you spend so much time with another girl and shower her in loving affection that you must be sleeping together. Furthest from the case with the two of us.

After we embraced and shook each other around like little dolls, we spent the afternoon with her old roommate Victoria and a few other girls who were assigned to "watch over me" while Angel returned home to Bloodmoon. We got high all day long before the sun went down, but once it did, it was show time. Or, shave time.

Angel sat me in the wooden chair in my dorm room while the three other girls all sat on my bed in a nervous line. No one but Angel and I thought this was a good idea—we were genuinely stoked to get rid of this evil that I call hair! As I sat in that chair, Angel got the clippers ready and said, "Alright, Lyla-Delilah, I'm gonna shave directly down the middle first, so you can't back out of it. Or it'll be reeeeeeal ugly lookin! Ready?"

"Oh fuck, oh fuck, oh fuck," I said between laughter, "yeah, yeah, I'm ready! Do it!"

The buzz from the clippers whirred after Angel flipped the switch and the girls sitting on the bed started groaning with anxiety. I had my hands up saluting rock 'n roll with my devil horns, and Angel happily put that blade directly to my scalp and whizzed the red hairs right off my head. I felt the clippers vibrate through my whole body, tingling the base of my spine and the edges of my lips. As she cut through the middle, like she promised, I let out an excited roar while I felt the falling hair tickle the tips of my shoulders, arms, and anywhere else it could land. There's an absolutely perfect picture floating around somewhere that shows me in mid-roar, Angel mid-shave, and the other three girls each displaying their own versions of absolute terror; one with her hands in her mouth, the other covering her eyes, and the last wincing and wrinkling her entire face. It's the epitome of every emotion running through our bodies—and fucking priceless, too.

***

"LYLA?!" Scarlette shouted from behind me. "You did it!"

"Heeeeyyyyy, what's up Punky Bruster! Of course I did it!"

"Wow," she said with wonder brewing in her eyes as she stood still in front of me, "I never thought I'd say this, but it looks so fucking good." She was shaking her head in disbelief.

"Right? I told you so!"

"Oh come on! What girl on earth can pull off a shaved head? Other than a blue-dark African woman? Or Sinead O'Conner?"

"Me, mutherfucker!"

"Seriously, Lyla. It's so elegant. You look like a powerful woman. I was wrong. I was dead wrong."

"Daaaaamn right," I said, "I *feel* like a powerful woman. But man, it's the strangest feeling when the wind blows—I can feel it blowing between every. single. little. strand. It tickles, kinda!"

"My brother actually told me that once," she laughed, "now you know what it feels like to be a boy!"

"Oh, shut up!"

We finished our dinner with Mia, who loved the haircut too, and when she went off to go play with her international debate team, we decided to go on a Loop. Not before I grabbed a to-go plate to take to my hidden monster back in the dorm, though.

"Alright, I'll meet you at the car," I told Scarlette, "I have to take a plate to Big Mick before he goes to look for a job."

Big Mick came back into my Life like the stray puppy dog that he is—unable to find refuge with any of his so-called friends or family. I was the last decent person he knew, so he spent his days cooped up in my dorm room like a filthy secret, for I'd be in serious trouble with the school if they found out I was hoarding a homeless man and feeding him food from the cafeteria. But, hey, if he wasn't going to eat the leftovers, who was?

"He's *still* staying with you?" She asked.

"Yeahhhh, he doesn't have anywhere else to go. I feel for him; I don't really know what else to do about it. If I were down on my luck, I'd want someone to believe in me."

"It's just weird, don't you think? That his own family won't take him in?"

"I know, don't make me think about it," I said, "I'll be at the car in five."

Scarlette didn't know it, but I'm about to drop another surprise on her—no pun intended; I've been seriously thinking about dropping out. I know that every college student thinks about it at one time or another, but Angel's words have been echoing in my head ever since we had that conversation sitting on beanbag chairs in Target. I took a swimming class hoping it would help keep me calm and centered, but all it's done is make me want to spend my days swimming rather than studying. The moment of inexplicable Truth came when I was sitting in a class dubbed, "Religion in America," which chronicles every branch and tiny little leaf of Christianity that the Pilgrims spread throughout the land, leading up to the present day. Let me just say that the span of Christianity in America is absolutely absurd, because the only reason we have so many denominations in our country is because two men living in the same colony disagreed on one miniscule detail, typically based on power struggle, and decided,

"Well, fuck you *and* your church, I'm making my own religion, and God's gonna like us better!"

This went on for hundreds of years until finally, we have over 250 Christian denominations in this pilgrim land. It's ridiculous, and trying to keep up with it in textbook formation was just as awful to do as it was to listen to lectures on the matter. Nobody ever speaks up in class, because none of us understand what the fuck all this is for, or why it mattered. The professor, therefore, filled the entire 100-minute duration in a white cinderblock classroom talking to an LED screen full of lengthy words meant to only confuse people into thinking that weighty words mean righteous religion. On one of these particularly drab and depressing days cooped inside that place, I looked to the left of me to see the three tiny 2x2 windows that give us a glimpse of the world on the outside; it was early autumn, so the sky was a blue that matched any pure patch of cerulean paint, the trees that lined our campus swayed in the wind, shaking their leaves about and letting the golden ones drift away down the pavement. The cars on the nearby highway were rolling along leisurely, taking their time through the sleepy, yet lively town. I saw two birds playing tag with one another and darting in and out of branches to trick their chaser—and it was like a freight train hit me in that vision, with the words of Walt Whitman painted on the front, reading

"As I wandered through those empty roads, I saw a sight which displeased my soul. I never liked the school houses; they always looked more like prisons to me."

And that was it. I couldn't hear the professor's drone any longer, and a switch had been flipped inside of me that could not be turned off. I accepted my Fate—that college was never the right place for me to begin with, and that I had to find a way to get back outside, to get back out into the tangible world that I could experience, learn, and grow from. I understand that everything I'm being taught is lined with a coating of bullshit-biased-brainwashing, and I can't keep living a life of reading page after page of books that I will surely forget, of writing report after report that take upwards of ten hours to write. All for what? An expensive piece of paper at the end of the four years that says,

"Congratulations! You have mastered the art of being told

what to do without question! You are qualified for training! Now continue working for the system for the rest of your Life. Don't forget to pay your taxes and your $80,000 student loan debt. Oh, and good luck finding a satisfying job in this market. Thanks for buying in!"

Remember our friend Velma? Yeah, me too. I refuse to end up like her—six years in a prestigious college only to graduate and work at a shoe store.

They say that experience is the only way to master the art of living, really. And it is! Experience is the only way to know Life, to love Life, to *live* Life. In the words of Aristotle, "much learning does not bring intuition…" nor instinct! If we possess nothing of either quality we are just mushing our heads with nonsense that we cannot truly understand or apply to our lives, because we cannot personally, spiritually feel it in our bones. And if we cannot feel it, what real authority do we have on the matter? We become like machines, being fed information and spitting it back out when the exam is slapped down on the cold, hard desk in front of us.

The answer is that we simply don't have any authority or understanding about Life's magic just by getting a college degree. The true magic of becoming mature and ready to take on the world only ignites the soul when you become the authority of your own life. And, well, instead of being taught that *we* should be that authority, we are thrown into subservience in the face of power that we're told we must obey if we're to be successful in this Life. We've got to obey the authority of our parents that birthed us, the police and the laws that control us, the government and money that rule us, and the psychic agitators that try to seep into us.

But if we could only stop to question all of that, we'd realize that we are the authority of our own lives. There will, of course, be others that try so desperately to tell us what they know is better or worse for us, and how to gain money, notoriety, or fame if we could only follow their step-by-step procedure. But no two people are going down the same path in the same manner, and some of us are looking for something that money, notoriety, or fame cannot grant. So how in the world could anyone else ever claim authority on the proper way to live a Life?

They can't. And we shouldn't let them. I knew sitting in that classroom staring out at the other side of that cinderblock wall that I couldn't stay another week, let alone another semester in that setting of dubious, boring obedience. The only person who could convince me otherwise would be Scarlette, and my, would she try.

"Lyla, what the fuck? You can't drop out," she said, not even slightly worrying about the prospect as she rolled a blunt. It was clear from the way she spoke that she dismissed it entirely.

"Why not?" I asked with a nervous smile. I didn't want to hear what she had to say, but I knew I needed to hear her out.

"Because, what are you gonna do? Move back to Bloodmoon? You can't leave me now, and you're already two years invested into it. What would be the point?"

"Scarlette, I can't do this shit anymore. I can't. I've never been more depressed in my entire Life than being at this school; I don't wanna get up in the morning, I've stopped going to classes, I eat my weight in horrible cafeteria food every day. I can't help it that my soul has grown sick of the institution. I've been trying to pretend like it's just a hard semester, but I'm taking easy classes that I absolutely love! Except for that stupid Religion in America class."

"Well you changed your major to Religion, why don't you just go back to being a studio art major with me?"

"No fucking way, I'm not an artist. Not that kind. I can't paint or sculpt or anything the way you and all the others can."

"Wait, isn't there something in Buddha's Truths that talks about setting goals and achieving them?" She had to hit me with the Buddha.

"Well, yes, but without suffering! I'm fucking suffering!"

"It's not that bad! Come on, you have a place to live, food to eat, and you're getting a degree. The very thing we came to do, right?"

"But I don't wanna do it anymore, Scarlette. That's the point. I feel like I'm suffocating. Besides, the food isn't all that great. They get discounted, nearly expired prison food for us. Emilia told me that."

"Oh, whatever! What's the alternative, Lyla?"

"I don't know." I said, simmering down from the escalation

and staring through the windshield. "I honestly don't know. I can't go back to Bloodmoon—I'd only be retreating if I did that. But I can't be here anymore. It doesn't feel right. I'm not happy, and I don't wanna waste anymore of my youth being unhappy. It isn't fair to myself."

"Okay, I'm gonna say something and it's gonna sound harsh, but I want you to try to listen to me," Scarlette said, putting on her mother-hat. "Life isn't about being happy, Lyla. Life is fucking hard. And it's hard work too. Do you think anyone likes to be in college? No! We all hate that we have to do this. But we do it because there is no other alternative. If we want to be successful and have less stresses later in Life, we have to do this now. Later we get to be happy, if everything goes as planned."

"No," I said shaking my head profusely, "no, I don't agree. Life shouldn't be like this. Life *should* be about happiness! Because if we're not happy, we're fucking doing it wrong, man. Who decided that in order to be successful you've got to have a degree?! It's a ridiculous notion that we have to get rid of. Some of the smartest people I know and that the world knows are either college drop-outs or college foregoers. Don't they always tell us that Einstein sucked in school?"

"Yes, they do," Scarlette said, sealing the blunt.

"Because school sucked the genius out of him! He and other people like him decided that their pursuit of happiness was different from what was laid out in front of them, and that's what I want to do, too. I can't be stuck in this box anymore, I have to get out and see what other shapes I can make. Ya feel me?"

"Sure, I feel you on that. But instead, why don't you try getting a job so you don't feel so cooped up here?"

"I've *been* trying," I said, "I've applied to nearly every restaurant in this town, and nobody's biting. It's frustrating, because I feel like it could help. But I just can't seem to find anyone to hire me."

"Well don't give up," she said as she rested her hand on my shoulder, "you'll find the perfect job soon. But, please, don't drop out. I can do it without you, but I'd rather not," she said, staring straight into me. The eerie silence in her Jeep was unusual, and I immediately felt the weight of the air around us. I just shook my head back and forth before resting my forehead on the steering wheel, sighing deeply.

"What if I just take a leave of absence?" I asked.

"What's that?"

"Basically I'd cancel out this semester and start over again in Jan-term like nothing ever happened. I could blame it on the depression, stay here in the dorm and wait it out, then hit it again in January. I'm ahead of graduation schedule, anyways. I can take it."

"But, Lyla! There's only a few weeks left! We've passed midterms, you just have to make it to finals. I bet you have all As, right?"

"Well, yes, but I automatically fail based on how many classes I've missed."

"What?! You haven't been going to class?!" There was anger in her eyes. Just like a mother. I'm waiting for the steam to start spewing.

"Well, not lately! I told you!"

"Oh, Lyla, what a mess. Well, alright, maybe taking a leave of absence would be better. But talk to your professors and see if they can just excuse it? Give it a little while longer." She was trying her best to be helpful before her fear of losing me kicked in.

"How much longer?"

"At least two weeks. Promise me two weeks. Everything's gonna turn out just fine, I swear it."

"Alright, alright," I sighed, "I'll give it a little while before I make a decision, okay? I just wanted to give you a heads-up. And also give you a chance to change my mind," I said.

"Well did I?" She asked.

"Not quite," I smirked. "Now let's get to that Loop!"

***

Two weeks after our debate on happiness, we were driving back from a lavish Goodwill trip with bags full of dashikis, weird red feathered blazers, jean coats, and various articles of black clothing— Scarlette's color of choice. We passed a building that usually looks like an abandoned Indian restaurant, but this time we noticed a ton of construction going on inside as well as out. Before it was merely a grey brick building. Now it's being repurposed with turquoise metal doors and yellow siding from various railcars. The pieces of the wall that weren't covered in metal were sponged with lime green, teal, baby blue, and red paint. It was beginning to look like a rad place, and in my admiration, I managed to catch a banner hanging on the corner of the building that said,

"NOW HIRING COOL, FUN, HARDWORKING PEOPLE!"

Before I could say anything, Scarlette squealed,

"Look, Lyla! Turn around, they're hiring!"

"Already on it, Punky Bruster!"

I whipped the car around in a bank parking lot and scurried across three lanes of traffic to pull into the place; when I got out of the car, I was thankful that I was wearing a flowing teal skirt, white tank top, and beige shawl that covered all my tattoos. The only visible thing to throw them off now is my bald head. I saw a man that looked like an authority figure, because he was wearing a collared shirt and wasn't doing any of the dirty work. He, kind of like me, was entirely bald—Mr. Clean bald. He had a salt and pepper goatee fit with a metal cross on a chain around his neck. His stern brown eyes sunk underneath his broad forehead, and for a moment, I was intimidated.

"Hi, are you the manager here? I saw your sign and I wanted to fill out an application."

"Yes, I am," he said with a deep bellow, "I'm Justin, the general manager. Give me just one second and I'll find where I put those darn things."

He walked away, and I was still standing on the brick ledge outside of the place. I looked back at Scarlette in the Jeep and gave her a quick thumbs-up, as did she back to me.

When he came back with the application he told me to bring it by anytime, to which I replied,

"Give me just a minute and I'll fill it out right here!"

I ran to the car to get a pen and had the application in Justin's hand within five minutes. Turns out the place is a local concept that blended together fresh, organic ingredients in wild Mexican inspired tacos, nachos, sandwiches, and margaritas. He told me training wouldn't start until the week before Halloween, so I had a little time to wait on a call back. I left feeling great about the whole thing, crossing my fingers that I had finally found a job to distract me from the dormitory blues.

"Maybe I should get a job, too," Scarlette said as we rode back to Annabelle's.

"Yeah? You don't really need a job, though, do you?"

"No, I don't need one at all. But ever since I started smoking loud, I have no money left at the end of the week to do anything or eat anywhere. And I can't keep eating chicken salads at Swan Hall. Plus, my brother's girlfriend keeps making snide comments about how hard she works. I kinda just wanna get a job to throw it in her face that I can work hard, too."

"Hell yeah, get a job there with me then! I don't even know what the place is called, but restaurants are easy to work in."

"I'd have to be a hostess or something," Scarlette said, "there's no way that my scattered brain would be able to keep up with everything you servers do. Someone would ask me to get them ranch, and I'd bring back a Sprite because I zoned out while they were talking."

We laughed and continued joking about restaurant mishap before pulling up to Annabelle's. We noticed a group of degenerates, including Mia and Big Mick, lounging around on the benches at the makeshift smoking section.

That's right, a real smoking section. Girls started getting harassed on the streets when they'd smoke, whether it be by a bum looking to snag a free cigarette, or a creepy old man in a rickety van asking if they wanted to go for a ride. A group of upperclassmen petitioned hard enough against the administration to get a designated smoking section for us, and while they tried to fight it they finally had to agree, because our chances of getting snatched off the street were growing by the day as the seedy community spread word that naïve, unsuspecting girls stood alone by the road at all hours of the day. They granted the smoking section, but left it up to us to construct it. You should have seen these girls wandering campus to gather lonely, unused wooden benches to create a seating area. Someone even managed to find a large stone trashcan with a metal ashtray on the lid, like one of those that you'd see in front of a gas station. It was a quaint little area that was right beside Scarlette's dorm, so we got out of the car to join the rest of them in some afternoon conversation and show off our hideously gorgeous new clothes.

"Hey sexy ladiiiiiies," one of the girls said as we walked up. They had rowdy rap music playing and Big Mick was sitting there in the midst of it just bobbing his head, swaying in his red t-shirt and camo shorts. He reached his long arm out to me as an offering to take his hand, and I did as I stood behind him with the other on his shoulder.

"Hey, babe," he said in his soft, country voice.

"Hey, you. Guess what? I found a place you can apply to! I just did."

"Yeah, where at?" He asked blankly, staring at the pile of clothes that Scarlette was modeling.

"Right down the road! Remember that old Indian place? Take a walk down there while I run to grab my mail. The guy that I talked to was Justin, and he's the general manager. Middle-aged dude with a bald head and a goatee. Seriously, go now."

"Yeah, I'll go," he said before asking the girls to bum one last cigarette for the walk down. He kissed my forehead and disappeared in the distance, just as he always does.

I left Scarlette with the gaggle of smokers to walk down campus to get my mail. The post office is inside the student building where companies are constantly setting up booths to prey upon the interests of all of us, and this day is no different. I walked through the doors to see a goofy looking man with a helmet of shaggy, curly brown hair and a lumberjack beard nearly down to his chest. He had these squinty blue eyes that looked like he was always stoned, no matter the time of day. To continue with the lumberjack motif, he was wearing a red and brown plaid flannel and some faded out Levi's. I recognized him as Kenny Crit, Darbyville's very own small-town celebrity. His brother owned one of the best restaurants downtown— a place that I had tried to get a job at months ago—and the only reason I knew him was because he'd come into the awful bar I worked at to drink after hours. People around me broke into whispering,

"Oh my God, there's Kenny Crit, there's Kenny Crit! You think he's single yet?"

As I walked by Kenny, he smiled at me and lingered around his little booth. I decided I'd talk to him on the way out. It was worth a shot, right? I felt like I practically knew the guy already. I came up behind him and said,

"You're Kenny Crit, aren't you?"

He turned around in surprise and beamed this ludicrous, toothy grin that reminded me of a dirty car salesman. He said,

"Why, yesssss, that's me! And you are?"

"I'm Lyla," I said reaching my hand out for a shake, "Lyla Calders."

He grabbed my hand in both of his, shaking it genuinely and saying,

"Lyla, it's so nice to meet you! Now tell me, are you looking for a job?"

"Actually, yes!" Two in one day?

"Well, great! I'm involved in this new project with my brother, Willis Crit. You've heard of Crit's downtown, right?"

"Oh yeah," I said, "great place!" Even though they won't hire me.

"Yeah, yeah it is! This new concept we're going for is gonna be like an American chef-inspired twist on Mexican favorites. Have you ever worked in restaurants before?"

"Oh, yeah. I'm from Bloodmoon Beach, right by the inlet, so I have a lot of experience in fast-paced service."

"No way! I love Bloodmoon! So, then you're pretty set, because those restaurants down there are madhouses in the summer time."

"Yeah they are! But I'd love to work for you and your brother. Where did you say the restaurant is?"

"Well, we're actually finishing construction on the place right now. It should be up and running in the coming weeks. Do you remember where the old Indian restaurant on East Main Street used to be?"

Again, I'm floored by Life's infallible perfection with bringing together what's necessary when the time is right. There's a reason I haven't been hired by anyone else in recent months, and the Universe seems to be rewarding my patience by letting me know that this is exactly where I need to be, considering the restaurant that I just applied to is the very same one that Kenny Crit wanted me to work for.

Coincidences.

Are.

Not.

Real.

Fate wins.

"No way!" I said, "I just filled out an application down there not even thirty minutes ago!"

"Wow! So you're already one step ahead! Did you speak to a man named Justin? He's the general manager."

"Yeah! He told me you guys were hopefully starting training the week before Halloween."

"That's right, wow!" Such cheesy speech, this guy had. "Well I'll definitely make sure to talk to Justin myself and give him the thumbs up on you. I love the tattoos, the nose piercing, the shaved head, the overall *style* you've got going on—you're everything that we're looking for in our team, and I think it'll work out beautifully having your experience with us."

"Oh, so I don't need to worry about covering my tattoos or taking out my septum ring?" I asked excitedly.

"No way! We want you to be yourself, and if this is you, we'll take it with open arms."

"Perfect!" I said as I caught myself jumping a little. What a relief that I won't have to cover myself the way I did in Bloodmoon.

"Well, Lyla," Kenny said reaching to grab my hand one last time, "we're looking forward to having you and I'm so glad you stopped to talk to me. We'll be giving you a call in the next few days or so, be sure of it!"

I stared back into his slanted blue eyes and bronzed cheeks, feeling my own warm with rosy delight. As I bid him goodbye and walked toward the door that led to the grassy quad, I couldn't help but squeal once I got outside. I started running all the way to the smoking section where I noticed Scarlette still was. I couldn't wait to tell her about the uncanny coincidence that of all the days for me to randomly check my mail it was the day that Kenny Crit was killing time in the student center to scope out future taco slingers. Everything appears to be seamlessly falling into place, and I might be starting to feel like I won't be dropping out after all.

A sinister voice inside my head awoke with that thought and whispered softly, but surely,

"Don't fool yourself, little girl."

XIV: Autumn 2K13: The Dropout

"Scarlette, you have *got* to get a job with us at this place! It's the best restaurant I've ever been a part of!" I sat at my desk with the windows open, studying the new menu that I got for training week. Big Mick sat on my roommate's bed, pretending to study the menu, I'm sure. Scarlette, lying across the bed next to me, had her legs propped out of the window, letting the wind waft her naked feet in the autumn air.

"What's so great about it?" She asked, eyes lost in the bright blue sky outside the dorm.

"Well, first of all, it's fucking rad! Second of all, they use all-organic produce and locally sourced meats. Third, they have a zero-waste policy, meaning that they recycle and compost absolutely anything and everything! Can I get a hell yeah for saving Mother Earth?"

"Hell yeah," Big Mick mumbled from the corner.

"That's neat! Scarlette said, sitting upright in the bed, "but do you think they really need anyone else now that they're already training everyone?"

"We're only three days into training, and you're gorgeous. I bet if you talk to Kenny Crit he'll hire you on the spot."

"But I've never worked in a restaurant before!"

"It's okay! It's easy! Just wear a low-cut shirt when you go in!" I teased.

"I was already thinking of that," she laughed, "but I don't wanna go in before Halloween, because I'm going to a party at Centennial College and I can't miss it. It's my first frat party! I could meet a future doctor! Which means potential husband!"

I busted out laughing and told her, "Oh, yes, *that's* a must!

Don't worry, you have plenty of time to entice Kenny Crit after Halloween. The last day of training is on November 1st, but I won't be here, because I've gotta go to Bloodmoon to see my family."

"Okay, then I'll definitely talk to them after Halloween! We're gonna take over Bubba Burrito and make this shit work, aren't we, Lyla-bird?" she asked.

"Damn right!" I said, smacking my hands together.

Halloween is fast approaching, but the only plan I've got is to finish training at Bubba Burrito. On Halloween night, the restaurant's going to have a mock opening in which the whole staff is split into two parts; half of the kitchen will come in to cook the food, while the other half will come with their friends and family to act as pretend-customers. The same goes for the servers and the bartenders too, because while half of us come to eat the other half acts as if they're serving the general public. It's a great concept, because it allows for all of us to get a feel for the flow of the place and how the food, drinks, and service work together for Darbyville's newest, coolest restaurant. The inside looked like the cuerpos from the Mexican Day of the Dead threw up all over the walls; there were abstract paintings of skeletons wearing sombreros, metallic sculptures of intricate sugar skulls, old bison horns mounted to wooden plaques, and the coolest mismatched, rusted steampunk light fixtures hanging from the ceiling. The walls were painted vibrant colors just like the outside of the building, and the lights were dimmed to offset the high energy of the upbeat indie and classic rock music that blasted the speakers.

"What a place!" I thought. I'd only ever worked at Denny's and a simple beach shack, so I was floored that such an interesting idea came straight from the minds of five southern friends living in the middle of nowhere. Since I wouldn't be able to be there on the second night of the mock opening, I had to play server on the night of my favorite holiday: Halloween.

We had signs up outside of the restaurant that said we weren't open for the general public, but the buzz about Willis Crit's new place spread like wildfire through the tiny town, and the people of Darbyville came out in masses when they saw the lights blazing and cars in the lot. Halloween night was absolute and utter chaos; we couldn't tell who actually worked for us and who happened to just be a local foodie, but we turned away *nobody*. We sat these people down in the midst of taco mayhem, served them organic margaritas, fed them blue corn chips and queso, and tried our damnedest not to let the ship sink while having a blast.

The rush of working waterfront in a tourist town is all I've ever known in a restaurant, and I loved being in the midst of the turbulent industry again. The people that I work with are amazing, too. It was like Kenny Crit managed to find the most down-to-earth people in town to be the image of Bubba Burrito, and we all laughed and joked together to get through the night. Everyone was decked in their Bubba Burrito tees, but each person had their own style to work with; some had short ballerina skirts with converse tennis shoes while others wore a colorful flannel and blue jean shorts with their taco t-shirts. We were allowed to be exactly how we wanted to be in that place, and it was beautiful to see how well the town's folk responded to it. Little ole southern Darbyville hadn't ever seen anything like it, that's for sure.

Around 9 o'clock, the bosses decided that it was time to roll the mock opening to a close. The people of the public were floored when they learned that all they had to pay for was their alcohol. Since this was only a practice run, their meals were on the house! Even though a few people started trickling out, we were still jam-packed. I began to wander around the restaurant checking everyone out, seeing how they responded to it all. When I walked outside to the patio, though, I found myself caught in a stare-down with a complete stranger.

He was sitting at table 72, seat three, surrounded by four other friends that I didn't pay attention to in the slightest. I laid eyes on him, and it was like a bolt of lightning straight from Thor's hammer came crashing down to my head, bursting with colors that I had never experienced before as it shattered through my skull and into my mind. He was in mid-laugh when I caught him in my gaze, throwing his head back while his beer sloshed around the glass in his hand. He had skin pale as a ghost, but cheeks rosy with boisterous pleasure. His brown eyes were nearly black, and they shone with a mystical darkness that reeled me further into his realm the longer I looked. I noticed a loooooong black ponytail tied behind his head, curling around itself all the way to the small of his strong back. He was *huge*, —at least 270 lbs, towering over six feet, covered in scattered black tattoos that looked like he had spent his last few years in prison. His plump red lips were surrounded by a deep brown goatee and a Jack Sparrow-looking mustache, feeding this mermaid's secret desire to fall in love with a rowdy pirate. He was absolutely nothing like what I would usually find attractive in a man, but every bone in my body vibrated with an intensity that I couldn't ignore. He was the most beautiful and most grotesque creature my soul has ever recognized, and I just *knew* that this wasn't the first Life I'd seen him. I felt beyond compelled to speak to him, and luckily, he was almost out of beer! There's my que.

As I approached my knees felt weak, but I managed to smile as I laid my elbows on the edge of the table and said,

"How's it going, guys?"

He looked up at me, and I could tell he was immediately thrown off. I'm sure it's my lack of hair, my vivacious tattoos, and my oversized dangling turquoise Grecian earrings. I'm a sight to behold, that's for sure.

"Everything's great, how 'bout yourself?" He asked, taking the lead and holding his beer out to me in a gesture of welcome. I swear I didn't look at anyone other than that gorgeous, foreboding man, and it was quite obvious that I was only there for him.

"I'm great! But your beer looks a little low, can I grab you another?"

He stared at me for a second longer than he probably meant to, squinting his eyes ever-so-slightly to try to understand where I had come from and why I wanted to cater to him. My heart beat inside my ears.

"Yeah," he said, eyes still squinting, "yeah, I'd like that."

"Dos Equis?" I asked, eyes twinkling.

"Yeah, Dos Equis Amber," he said as I raised myself up from the table to go to the bar. His answer let me know he has good taste, too! I walked five feet away, keeping my eyes on him as he did to me, and I could see the curiosity budding in his eyes. Just like me, I could tell he was searching for the place that he's seen me before. But that place isn't here.

After I dropped his beer off and continued with my medial server duties, I was determined to slip him my number. Never in my Life have I been so drawn to another human being, and the instant his eyes met mine I knew I was doomed to a string of days filled with dark fantasy. Suddenly, the restaurant flow went hay-wire and it took me some time to get back to the server station and write my number on a napkin. Excited beyond belief I walked back out to the patio, and to my dismay, the beautiful man that I was so enticed by was no longer at table 72; he's gone. Nothing but empty beer glasses and dirty taco plates covered the table that he and his friends were gathered around, and my stomach sank to the concrete floor.

Utter.

Devastation.

The most striking man of my Life walked right out of it and I didn't even get to tell him my name.

Rats.

I walked back to Annabelle's after we closed the place up that night feeling great about the success we had at the restaurant, but feeling down that I couldn't get to that man fast enough! I watched the sky as a hazy orange moon came rising above the blackened tree-line, and I immediately forgot my grief as I remembered that Halloween night is upon me! I hadn't made any plans because I was so focused on perfecting this new job, but I was hoping I could get back to Annabelle's in time before Scarlette left for her frat party.

When I turned the corner to walk through the wrought-iron gates at Annabelle's entrance, there were ghouls and goblins and princesses and zombies wandering all over campus! We always held a Halloween party at the Alumni House across the street, and everyone was scurrying through the clear night to make their ghastly appearance. Amusement filled my heart as their unabashed laughter filled the air, and I began darting across campus to find Scarlette before she, too, disappeared into the night.

Luckily, I found her smoking at the stoop on the street with a few other ghouls. She was wearing the cutest little cow costume, fit with ears, a dress, and a tail that she had made herself. She's very creative when it comes to Halloween costumes, which made me proud of having a best friend who refuses to play into the slutty, too-tiny cliché cop and nurse outfits. When I finally got close enough for her to realize it was me, she ran up and wrapped her arms around me in an eager embrace.

"Oh, Lyla, I wish you were going with me!" She said, refusing to let go of me. She clung to my neck, dangling her skinny legs to the sidewalk.

"Me too," I said sadly, "but you'll have a good time! I think I'm gonna go to the Alumni House party. My roommate dressed as Batman, and I thought it would be funny to just dress in my normal attire and call it 'Batman and Lyla', what do you think?"

She started laughing and said, "That's so lazy and nonsensical, so yes, do it! But how was Bubba Burrito, did you have fun?"

"OH MY GOD, SCARLETTE, I MET THE MOST BEAUTIFUL MAN OF MY LIIIIIIFE!" I said, yelling out into the trees above us, arms flailing around in a wild passion.

"No way! Did you talk to him? Did you get his number? What does he look like?! Tell me, tell me!"

"He looks like a mix between Johnny Depp in Pirates of the Caribbean and a Viking God, and I think I'm in looooooove! But I didn't get to give him my number or anything, because the restaurant got really crazy. I talked to him for a second and managed to give him another beer, but that's as far as it went. And now I'm doomed to never see him again," I said, looking at the ground and kicking the tree stump in defeat.

"Awh, honeyyyyy, maybe he'll come back in to eat some time! Don't lose hope! He sounds kinda scary."

"He *is* kinda scary, Scarlette! That's exactly why I want him!"

"Like, the good kind of scary? Or the, I'm-gonna-eat-your-babies kind?"

"No, no, this is good! Maybe. I don't know! I don't even know who this man is. Other than the Love of my Life." I said excitedly.

"Then you'll have to see him again!" She said as she hugged me in equal excitement.

"Yeah, you're right," I said. "But, hey, I have an idea!"

"What is it?" She asked in between puffs.

"Wanna go to the church pumpkin patch in East Side Heights and steal some pumpkins to throw at old buildings?"

"Are you serious?!"

"Hell yeah! Nothin' like some good Halloween mischief! Come onnnnn, we didn't get any pumpkins this year! And what are they gonna do now? They're gonna take them all to the dump tomorrow! Let's go before you get picked up for the party!"

She looked up at me for just a second longer than usual before snuffing her cigarette out on the pavement and saying,

"I fuckin' love you, let's do it!"

I smacked my hands together and held out my arm to lift her up off the stoop. We clasped palms just like little girls do and took off running in the direction of her Jeep. Luckily for us its black coat of paint covered us in an inconspicuous shield in the dead of Halloween night. We rolled up on the street that ran behind the church, because we had found a secret alley that led directly to the church's backyard. We only knew where it was because of our many weekend morning walks where we'd stumble upon this concealed alleyway to smoke a blunt or two. It's covered in overgrown trees from the neighbors' yards and ivy that had taken over the fences on either side, so it made for a great sneak access to our pumpkin patch.

"Alright, alright, park here!" Scarlette whispered.

"Yeah, now listen, we need little ones if we're gonna smash them against a building. BUT, I wanna grab a huge 15-pounder just for shits and giggles."

"Oh my God," Scarlette said as she gasped and rolled her eyes. "You're nuts, but fuck yeah, let's do this shit, Pumpkin Queen."

We got out of the car and shut the doors quietly, snaking our way through the canopy covered alley to the glorious sight of an unattended field of pumpkins. There's nothing more beautiful than the glow of an orange moon reflecting off of orange gourds, am I right? We giggled like children, frolicking through the sea of Halloween magic. Poor Scarlette's little cow ears kept falling off every time she bent down to grab another pumpkin! Soon there were eight or nine pumpkins stacked in her awkward little arms, while I tossed three little ones inside of my satchel and made my way toward the perfect Pumpkin King—it *had* to be 15 pounds! Scarlette was ten feet from me, snickering so hard that she sounded like she was wheezing in between opportunities to catch her breath! I couldn't stop laughing either, but suddenly we heard a loud voice about 30 feet away, yelling out,

"HEY! What do you think you're doing?!"

I looked up, but the moon had cast a huge shadow behind the church where this man was standing, so the only thing I saw in the dark was the radiant red tip of his burning cigarette. He hadn't made a move, yet, because I'm sure he thought we would just drop the pumps and go. Not so, sir, not so!

"OH SHIT!" I yelled out, "Go, go, go!"

Scarlette was already on the move before I finished the last word! I had *just* put my arms around Papa Pumpkin when the man called out, but I wasn't leaving without him! I picked it up and booked it in the opposite direction, running right back down the alley from which we came. By the time I got to the car, Scarlette was already in the passenger seat with a lap littered in little pumpkins and the engine running. She busted the driver's side door open for me, grabbed Papa Pumpkin, and tossed it in the back seat. I hopped in with one foot on the gas and the car in drive before I even had my butt in the seat, and we were off! When we realized we had gotten away with it and that the man wasn't on our tail, we squealed in a chorus of victory.

"That was fucking AWESOME!" I said while slapping my hand on the dash.

"No way, that was really fucking scary!" Scarlette said, "...but also fucking awesome! I can't believe we almost got caught!"

"Do you think it was someone who was put specifically on pumpkin patch duty?" I said jokingly.

"I mean, it would have to be! Why else would he be out there hiding in the shadows, smoking a cigarette?"

"Yeah, it seems odd, but I guess that's the only way to ensure that no heathens like us take the pumpkins in the middle of the night."

"They failed," Scarlette laughed, "and I *cannot* believe we just did that! At a church, of all places! Hell is waiting for us." Her cow ears had fallen off her head in all the commotion, but fortunately they sat on the floor below her.

"Oh, come on, Hell's *been* waiting for us! Where is the one place on Earth that you can find the most sinners?" I asked.

"Ummmm, the bar?" She said, confused.

"No! A CHURCH, silly!"

"Lyla!" She said, crossing her arms in disapproval. The Christian roots run strong in this one.

"Hey, at the very least we actually let that guy feel important in his guarding of the pumpkins! One of the best Halloween stunts I've ever pulled," I laughed, "so where are gonna smash all these gourds?!"

"Well," she paused to think, having just pulled up to the Annabelle's parking lot, "what do you say we smash them against the student center?"

I've never seen so much mischief in Scarlette's eyes, but in that moment, she was the primary sinner of the two of us. Stealing from a church pumpkin patch *and* defacing school property?! The student center is the perfect choice, because that's where all the administration works throughout the week.

"Oooooh, I wasn't thinking about the school, but I like where your head's at! We're gonna have to wait until you get back from the party, though, because the student center is in the middle of campus and there are too many opportunities to be seen. Let's say, 3 AM? Everybody will be either knocked out in their beds by then or too drunk to notice what's happening. Think you could be back by then?"

"Oh, yeah," she said. "What about the big'un in the back seat?"

"We're gonna paint him! And put him right outside your dorm building on that little marble bench that sits between the rose bushes."

"Fuck yeah!" She agreed, shuffling in the passenger seat. "But I gotta go, Addie keeps calling me, so I'm sure she's waiting outside the dorm. I'll call you when we get back!"

"Alright, Punk. I'm gonna run over to that party and eat some bangin' cupcakes to prepare for this midnight mayhem."

"You do that. Love you!"

"Love you too! Be safe! Don't get roofied!"

"I won't!" She screamed, running off with little cow ears

bouncing.

On the morning of November 1st, I woke up to drive to Bloodmoon Beach groggy from sleeplessness and an excess of celebratory Samhain smoking the night before. Annabelle's administration woke up to a beautiful mural of slung Pumpkin guts, shells, and seeds strewn across their beloved student center windows. Someone looking at that masterpiece felt a blend of astonishment and resentment, thinking to themselves,

"This is why we need some fucking cameras around here."

***

When I came back from Bloodmoon that on the night of November 2nd, I remembered that Bubba Burrito was scheduled to open for serious business on November 4th. Heeding my advice, Scarlette took it upon herself that very day to talk to Kenny Crit about being a hostess! She got the job no problem, because like I said, he was helpless to her drop-dead gorgeous appearance and the cleavage peeking out of her black tank top.

"He stared at my boobs the entire time," Scarlette laughed with a hint of disgust, "and it was so obvious! He'd start to ask me a question, but the words faded out of his mouth because his eyes got stuck on my chest. It's hilarious how easy it is to baffle a boy."

"Even when they grow up, they're still slaves to just the mere *idea* of sex!" I agreed, "But hell yeah, I'm excited! When do you start?"

"I go in with a couple other girls for training tomorrow, but I guess I'll be working on opening day, because he gave me a schedule already!"

"Fuck yeah! This is gonna be so fun with you working there, too. We can have late-night dinners together. And carpool! And look like the cool kids on the block." I fantasized.

"I know it! So how are you feeling about everything? Do you still feel like you wanna drop out?"

"Well... I kind of don't have another choice at this point. I was supposed to write a massive research paper on Hinduism and its relationship to the environment, because it's a fascinating part of their religion. Buuuuuut, I didn't. And I haven't been to Religion in America in at least a month."

"Lyla, what the fuck?!"

"I know, I know! But if I stay through the whole semester, my GPA will drop from a 3.8 to something embarrassingly low, because I'll fail every class except for swimming. And if it drops, I lose my scholarships. If I lose my scholarships, I can't stay anyways."

"So, what are you gonna do?"

"I'm gonna take a leave of absence, like I planned. I have to go talk to the dude who's in charge of granting that, though. I have an appointment with him tomorrow."

"And you'll just come back to classes in January?"

"Yep! They'll wipe out the record of this past semester as if it never happened, and I'll come back for Jan-term when I'm over it all. *If* I get over it all."

"Don't say that! It's a 'when', not an 'if'! Nothing lasts forever, Lyla." I can tell she's perturbed. I looked up from below and smirked at her with a deviant smile and asked,

"Hey, what's the time?"

"TIME FOR YOU TO GET A WATCH, BITCH!"

Exactly the response I was counting.

"WRONG! TIME FOR A LOOP MUTHERFUCKER!"

I slapped my hand on her thigh twice, motioning for her to hop up from my bed and get a move on. She did, we looped, and we slept. When I awoke the next morning, I went straight to the "drop out office," and got approved for my leave of absence. All I had left to do was go through two sessions of exit counseling and get all ten administrators to sign off on the process. Counseling was interesting, because all they had to do was ask me why I wanted to leave and make note of it so that they could either fix the problem or evaluate a trend among students who quit. The woman who listened to me talk was actually very supportive of everything I said; she told me that she knows I'm quitting because it's too hard—my grades told her that. But she was the first person I had come into contact at Annabelle's who believed that sometimes college isn't right for everyone. We bonded over the fact that nobody bothers telling kids that college doesn't have to be the only option, and that since we aren't told there are other avenues we can explore, too many of us are sucked into the collegiate realm without much introspection as to what our hearts truly desire. All of a sudden two years and our sanity slip by and we've got $40,000 worth of debt and nothing to show for it except our own certainty that college was not made for our kind.

Tuesday, November 4th, 2013 is the day that I signed the paperwork to officially take a leave of absence from Annabelle's, and myyyyyy did it feel good! But wait, that good feeling can only last two seconds! When I got the final sign-off from a head administrator, she heartlessly said to me,

"Alright, now you have 48 hours to move all your things out of the dorm and return your key to Student Life." She didn't even look up from the paperwork when she uttered those words.

"*What?*" I asked sharply.

"Well," she said taking a deep breath, "once you signed that paper, you're no longer a student here. And legally, our housing agreements are for students only." She looked back down at her Southern Living magazine.

"But I've already paid you for this semester's room and board. You aren't going to refund me the last month of the semester that I don't live here, are you?"

"No, that's not how it works."

Fucking.

Livid.

And homeless.

I went through ten administrators and none of them bothered to tell me that I'd be kicked out after I took the leave. I thought that because I paid for the semester already that they couldn't kick me out. After all, there were only a few more weeks left. What would it hurt to let me stay here while I waited for Jan-term to start?

"So you're telling me that I'm homeless now and there's nothing you could have done to tell me that I'd be immediately kicked off campus?"

"Lyla, it isn't like that, it's— "

"No, I can't just leave here, Miss Damingo. I have a great job, and if I leave right now, I surely won't have a job when I come back. I can't go back to Bloodmoon, because I *need* this job to be able to pay for any schooling that I continue after the leave. And I'm trying to buy myself a car and get my mind back on track, and I'm coming back in January anyways! Isn't there something you can do to let me stay here just for three more weeks? Please?" I realized I was at my end—my moment of desperation in a desperate time.

"Legally we cannot let you do that," she said coolly, peering over her thick rimmed glasses with a stoic severity in her eyes.

"Are you kidding me? I'm telling you that I have nowhere to go and that you will be putting me out on the streets, and you're okay with that?"

"I'm not okay with that, but this was your decision."

"My decision to forego classes for the next three weeks. My decision that nobody bothered to tell me would result in being kicked off campus entirely. For Christ's sake, it's only three more weeks!" I shouted.

"We could get in serious trouble if we let you stay here while you aren't technically an enrolled student."

"Who's gonna know? Tell me that. Who's gonna know? Nobody." I said with a silence.

"But you'll know that you just royally fucked me."

I ripped my body up from that chair and stormed out of her office with tears welling in my eyes. I couldn't believe that nobody bothered to tell me at any step that as soon as I signed that paper that Annabelle's was no longer my home. You'd think that would be a major point in the procedure, but it appears that not everyone has a functioning brain. They confirmed to me that the collegiate world is only a money-making scheme; it isn't about the students, it isn't about the knowledge and insight you're supposed to gain, and it surely isn't about making sense. Money is the name of the game, and that made me fucking sick.

Scarlette came to my room after her painting class that day and found me packing up all of my things. There wasn't much; it could all fit in the back of a car. But when she walked through the doorway, she said,

"Where are you going?" Eyes wide with fear.

"Well, I got my leave of absence. But now I'm fucking homeless. They have this bullshit legal agreement with some bullshit agency in some bullshit distant land that says they cannot house anybody who isn't an enrolled student. Therefore, I'm no longer an enrolled student! I have moved my way onto being a homeless college dropout."

I started crying. I couldn't believe that this is the system we live in, and that this is how we treat the people who are just trying to piece Life together in the best way that we know how.

"Oh, Lyla," she said in the sweet, comforting way that she always does, "now what are you gonna do?"

"I don't know. I sent Big Mick a message telling him what happened, because some of his stuff is in this room too. He said he's gonna try to find me an apartment somewhere. That's really the only option I have. I can't go back to Bloodmoon. I can't tell my mom that I've done this, she'll be beyond let down. I have to coast until Jan-term and pretend like I've been going all along."

"Well where are you gonna put your things?"

"That's what I was gonna ask you... do you think I could put them in your car?" I asked sheepishly.

"Oh, Lyla, where are you gonna sleep?!"

"Well, that's another thing," I said carefully, because even I can't believe these words were about to come out of my mouth, "can I *sleep* in your car too?"

"Oh, honey, of course you can," she said, petting my prickly bald head. "I'll sleep in the car with you! It'll be fun, like a sleepover! We'll find you a place to stay, don't worry."

Just like that, I went from being an A+ student to being a homeless dropout living in the back of a Jeep. It only took 6 hours. Funny how Life can flip in an instant, huh?

That night when Scarlette and I were lying scrunched up in a pile of my own wardrobe, pillows, and blankets with our feet propped up on a stack of books, I felt happier than I have this entire year. The hours that Scarlette and I spent listening to shitty pop music, Manchester Orchestra, and J. Cole, smoking blunt after blunt and cigarette after cigarette are some of the most weightless hours I have ever spent living. It's like I was in this strange purgatory of Youth's dark corners—like I didn't exist to the world, and that her Jeep was the only place I felt I could be calm enough to truly see the divine play that's weaved throughout our lives on Earth. I watched as the smoke billowed up to the grey upholstered ceiling and realized how menial this all is; that there was a much bigger scheme at work behind the doors that I couldn't open yet, and I felt that warm fuzzy sensation of contentment fill my belly.

Not everyone young is reckless, careless, or homeless. And above all, we are not directionless. There is a path of direction that we're following, it's just one that nobody can predict, and that is what drives the authority absolutely mad. I'll gladly be their driving force of madness any day.

***

After three days of sleeping in a makeshift bed in the back of Scarlette's Jeep, I got a phone call from the agency where I applied for my first apartment. On the way back from work on the first opening day at Bubba Burrito, Big Mick and I stopped at our regular Kangaroo to grab a chocolate banana Naked Juice and noticed somebody moving out of a decrepit brick building cloaked in trees next to the gas station. I never gave that building much thought, because from the outside it looks entirely abandoned; lights were never on, ivy branches grew over the dusty glass windows, and paint was chipping off of every pillar, door, and window ledge that the eye could see. It's at least an eighty-year-old building, which would put it at being built around 1930. As I walked into the Kangaroo for our nightly juice, Big Mick stayed behind to talk to the man who was inside the moving truck. When he met me inside, he had an application for the apartment in hand.

"Here," Big Mick said to me, "I know this company, they'll get back to you in two or three days. You ain't got a record, right?"

"Not reeeally," I hesitated, "but where's the apartment?"

"Right here!" He said, grabbing the Naked juice to take the first swig. "It's tha brick buildin' we always thought was abandoned. It's actually an ole house that got split into four units. I jus' went up and looked at the place he's moving outta. Pretty fly, Ly. Fill out the app and bring it to the agency tomorra mornin'."

I'm thankful for Big Mick to tell me what to do in this scenario, because I didn't even know how to go about getting a place to live. The location of the apartment couldn't be better! Directly beside our frequent flyer Kangaroo, only a block from Annabelle's, two blocks in front of my beloved Oakland Cemetery, and a mere twelve-minute walk straight down East Main Street from Bubba Burrito.

When I got the phone call, I borrowed my generous Guatemalan friend's car and shook nervously all the way to pick up the key. I had become the proud renter of Unit 4 in that barely standing building, and I couldn't wait to see what it looked like inside.

On the morning that I picked up that key, Big Mick was at Bubba Burrito working the lunch shift and Scarlette was in classes, so it was just me, myself, and I to take the first look at the apartment that would become my sacred space to sort through all the insanity plaguing my mind.

Upon entering the building, I clunked up four brick steps that led to an old white wooden door colored a musty brown from all the dirty hands coming in and out. One of the glass panels in the door was busted out; looked like somebody got locked out of the building a time or two. The door squeaked and echoed loudly when I walked inside the empty foyer, noticing the odd shade of Kelley green they chose to try to cover up the stains on the walls. The steps that circled up to the second floor were solid maple wood, and with each creaky step I took my heart pounded with excitement. There are some moments in Life that are so paramount that they go on to act as snapshots for our mental video montage; the moments that have a mystical quality to them and send a sharp tap into our mind's eye to let us know to pay attention, because what we're about to see will change the fabric of our Life forever. This was one of those moments.

In the tallest corner of the foyer, a huge flake of green paint fell off the wall and onto my shoulder, but I couldn't be more amused. I already loved the character that this place had, and the apparent shiftiness didn't deter me one bit. I've got a place to live now that nobody can take away from me; a shelter to rest my head at night that isn't just the back of my best friend's car. And how could a nineteen-year-old college dropout's first apartment be anything less than messy?

When I slid the key into the latch my I heard my heart beat in my throat. To my surprise, I didn't even have to turn the key, because the door was so warped from years of use that it didn't entirely close anymore! I merely had to push the door open, and when I did my eyes lit on fire.

The room that I entered was absolutely stunning! And huge! The size of a decent living room with a massive opening to the right that led into another large room. As I surveyed the surroundings I took in the cream-colored walls and high ceilings. There's beautiful white molding lining the tops and the bottoms of the walls where it created a stellar contrast between the deep wooden floorboards. To my surprise, the windows in this place are nearly the size of the walls and allow for every drop of natural light to pervade the whole room! The windows looked out to the parking lot of the gas station, but you could only see it if you got up close to look down; otherwise you were staring out into a slew of ragged tree branches and ivy leaves, which is mighty enchanting. There's even a patio outside my second story apartment! A mighty fine one, too, and I instantly got a flash of nights that Scarlette and I would spend passing blunts back and forth watching the commotion of the cars coming and going on East Main Street.

When I walked through the rectangular opening, the apartment just seemed to be getting deeper and deeper! At only $375 a month with water included, I couldn't believe how big this space was. My mom was paying for an apartment that was smaller than this one back in Bloodmoon that was costing her over $800 a month! I lucked out, I tell you. From the middle room of the apartment, there's a quaint dining area separated from the rest of the living space by a vaulted archway. I snaked around the left of the dining area to find a massive kitchen fit with a back door that led to yet *another* brick patio out back! This is absolute Heaven for southern girls who loved natural light, big windows, and porch sittin'. The sink in the kitchen looked like it hadn't been updated since the 1930s, and the water that poured from it ran bright orange with rust from the old pipes for a few minutes before it finally ran clear.

"Step one: buy a faucet filter," I said aloud.

I opened the fridge expecting to find some sort of pest

scurrying around inside, but to my surprise it was the cleanest part of the apartment! Nearly spotless, so it was obvious that the past tenant spent almost no time in the kitchen. Must have been a boy.

I walked back out to middle room of the apartment to explore a long, skinny hallway that led to the only technical bedroom of the place; the hallway itself had a door that shut off from the rest of the apartment, but the room at the back had its own door as well. Passing through the hallway, I found the bathroom to the left and an adorable little hole built into the wall directly opposite from it. Turns out, the box that was built into the wall was made for telephones back in the day! The cord that would have connected to a phone was still in the corner of the box, covered in white cream paint from the lazy maintenance men. There's a tiny slit underneath the hole that was used for old phone books, which couldn't have been thicker than a modern-day magazine. For the first time in my Life I have fallen madly in Love with an empty space.

The bathroom had an antique medicine cabinet mirror that sat above the oldest pedestal sink I have ever seen. It used to be white, I'm assuming. But through years of wear and tear and makeup and hair, the sink had layers upon layers of thick, chipping white paint that previous tenants thought might rid of the stains. The only light in the bathroom didn't turn on via the switch that was on the wall; you had to yank on a metal string that came down from the 12-foot ceiling to turn on a bulb above the old mirror. The shower needed some work; I looked at the warped pieces of plastic holding onto the wall by nails and saw layers of black mold peeking out from behind. Nothin' a little bleach can't take care of.

I honestly have never experienced a place with such quirky character, and as I walked out of the bathroom I walked through to the empty bedroom and marveled at what I've accomplished. Last night I was cramped inside of a black Jeep, smoking blunts with my best friend in a cluster of college knickknacks. Now I find myself sitting crisscross-applesauce in the bedroom of my very first apartment, right on East Main Street. I thought of how I won't have to share a twin-size bed with Big Mick anymore, or try to sneak him into the bathrooms for a shower at 3 AM. I thought about how Scarlette would react upon seeing this place, and how many nights we'll spend tramping all over these floorboards. I began laughing almost explosively, and suddenly I found myself wet from spilling tears of retribution; they tried to take my opportunities away, but my own luck and a twist of Fate had my back.

The night was fast approaching, and because it's a Friday afternoon, there wouldn't be any electricity to light the place for three days when the sun went down. With about $800 left in my bank account, it was time to hit the dreaded Walmart for some supplies to make it through the weekend. Not to mention a trashcan or two, because while this place is adorable, this place is also covered in human piss and dust and bugs and mouse poop. I'll never know how, or why. All I know is that it's time to clean this shit out and make it mine.

What's it feel like to be a college dropout, you might ask?

Like I've tricked them all; like they tried to fuck me up and trip me over a few hurtles, but they didn't know I was wearing my moonboots. I've still got my books, my brain, my thrift-shop wardrobe, my laptop, and my candles. I've got a full-time job, I've got the astounding tattoos on my body, and the barely visible tufts of hair on my head. I've got my best friend back, I've got my mom convinced I'm still going to class, and I've got a renewed sense of living fully. I've got everything I could ask for, and now I've even got a solid place to keep it all safe. As far as Annabelle's goes, I've got a 3.8 GPA, and I'm still on track to graduate early as long as everything goes according to plan come January. I'm just a ghost to the institution for a time and a more complete woman to myself. That's all.

So, ask me again what it's like to be a college dropout at nineteen.

Fucking brilliant, I'd say.

Fucking brilliant.

XV: Autumn 2K13: The Catalyst

Thirteen candles.
Two twin mattresses.
Two red duffle bags.
Four pillows.
Three blankets.
My blue-lit Gatsby lamp.
A pile of books.

    I had more books than anything. It took me three whole days to get the place clean enough to call it a living space; piss crusted every inch of the bathroom floor, and the toilet seat was frightening with its disgusting discoloration. That bathroom nearly killed me dead on my hands and knees, scrubbing mold and urine out of a tile floor. Not to mention the seven bottles of Draino it took to clear out the muck in the shower. I'm serious, seven whole bottles. Consecutively.

    It was almost as if a construction crew used the apartment as a hangout pad between jobs with the way plaster and dust littered the floor. Dirt, dead spiders, live spiders, cobwebs, death webs, and the occasional Palmetto bug, too. Here in the south we joke about the beloved Palmetto bug being our state bird, but don't worry; they're just finger-long cockroaches with wings.

    I heard the door creek open while I was sweeping the floors for a third time. Before I could turn around I heard Scarlette say,

    "Whooooaaa, I swear all I did was try to knock and your door just opened!"

    "Yeah, it does that," I said laughing. "But check it out! What do you think!?"

    "Oh, Lylaaaaa," She said, eyes lost in creamy walls and creative imagination. "It's gorgeous! It has so much potential! Kinda dirty, though," she said, looking at an already-full trash bag.

"I'm working on that part! You shoulda seen it when I got here. Oh, and I won't even pain you with the details of the bathroom. Just know that you'll be able to eat off the ground when it's all said and done."

"And I won't," she laughed. "Oh, excuse me, but is that a porch I see right there?" She said with an embellished southern accent.

"Yes ma'am, it sure it!" I said in my best, but not as convincing, southern drawl.

She reached for the crystal doorknob and opened the portal to my perch above the city. The porch called her back to the sharp memory of romping throughout her family farm in Aiden. The days of rocking in chairs with the elders, sipping sour lemonade, and running aimlessly through fields of open grass. Scarlette grabbed the white wooden railing outside slowly, paused, then exploded,

"Holy shit, Lyla, I can't believe this whole place is yours! Look at this porch! I haven't even seen the rest of it, but I don't even care. I'm here to tell you, right here, right now, this porch is worth it all!"

"Even the piss and the vomit on the floors?"

"Ew, vomit too?" Her animation died instantly. "That's disgusting. You cleaned that up right?"

"No, I figured you'd want to give it a little whiff before I get rid of it."

"Yeah, and I figured you wanted tooooo go fuck yourself, so uh, yeah, show me the rest of the house!" She said. She's got jokes. She gushed over the high ceilings, the archway, the back porch, the telephone nook, the bathroom, all of it. Just as I expected! Her absolute favorite part, though, was being a hop and a skip down a flight of stairs to being at the front door of the Kangaroo. 24/7 Newport cigarettes, dill pickle chips, and Coca-Colas.

"It's darling, Lyla. I'm so proud of you! You did it all by yourself! And it only took three days of living in a car." More jokes!

"Aha! Aaaaand it's so close to school! Riiiight? I told you dropping out wouldn't be so bad!"

"You haven't dropped out, don't say that! It's a leave of absence, right? You're going back in January, right?"

"Yesssss," I said with a sigh, "I'm going back in January."

"Okay." She said glaring, "Don't you fucking drop out."

"I won't, Mom, geeze! But, hey— "

"What is it?"

"Can you tell me what time it is?"

"Time for you to get a watch," she said so simply.

"Oh, fuck you, what time is it?!"

"Seriously, get a watch. It's 3:48."

"Damn, already?! You work tonight, right?"

"Yeah at six. Don't you?"

"Yeah, but I gotta be there at 4:30 and still have to shower all this shit off me! Do you think you can gimme a ride so I'm not late?"

"Yeah, gurl, but you gotta hurry scurry. I'm trying to go on a loop before I have to be there."

"Oh, you sneaky dog! Showing up high already?" I asked, stripping my clothes on the way to the bathroom.

"Lyla, it's tacos. Show up high always."

"Touché."

4:28 PM. She got me to the edge of that door with only two minutes to spare, and I came barreling through with adrenaline pumping for the first official Friday night run. The whole place was buzzing with that anticipation of our performance for the weekenders rushing out to their dates. The rush doesn't start until nearly six, usually, so I decided to keep myself busy by doing bullshit chores. These can include, but are not limited to, filling ice bins, bringing up clean glasses, sorting silverware, stocking sodas, and filling salts and peppers. Thrilling, right? Well, by 5:24 there was honestly not a single chore left to do, and with only one table in my hands I decided to help bring food out from the kitchen.

I stood facing the stainless steel food fortress watching every avenue; the tortillas steaming on the grill to the left, the raw shrimp sizzling as they hit the flat-top, and the endless chomping of the computer printing out food tickets. The boys with their clinking spatulas make small talk about gambling films, sport, and women. They argue about music and who does it better: the metalheads, or the classic rockers. Lost in their commotion, I almost didn't notice the man on the very end of the line, nearly out of sight. If it weren't for the thin sliver between the stainless steel, I wouldn't have caught those same dark eyes that hypnotized me days ago. He looked up to check a ticket, and underneath that blue and white bandana I felt something pierce my chest as I recognized who they belonged to. My heart shuddered and my stomach jolted and my head tickled and my spine ached and my knees felt shaky and my hands felt clammy. My face was showing only symptoms of shock and awe, and my body was doing the same. Every molecule in my makeup was surging on this wavelength that I'd never been to before, and the only zone I was in was his.

"Hey! Hey, you! What's your name? Come on, take this guac to table 41! Let's go!"

Chef's in my face, and boy, was his red! Startled out of my spell, I blushed, apologized, and grabbed the board of mushed avocado. I practically ran out of the kitchen, breath quivering up and down. Up and down. Up and down. Just as Fate would have it, that beautiful bandana-wearing boy that I met during the mock opening is actually an employee, and not just some street-walker. What a sneaky bitch, that Fate.

Just as I dropped off the guacamole, I circled back to the server station and met Scarlette as she walked through the door to clock in. Thank GOD, ALLAH, YAWEH, BUDDHA, ODIN, SHIVA, KALI, because this momentous discovery could not wait.

"Scarlette, Scarlette, Scarlette!" I said in excited whispers, clutching her skinny arms.

"What, what, what?!" She asked in equally excited whispers.

"Scarlette, remember last week when I told you I met the Love of my Life and I was doomed to never see him again?"

"Yessss?"

"I was wrong. I was dead wrong. He's here. He's in the kitchen, Scarlette, he fucking works here. He's here, he's here, he's here."

"What! She said, now clutching both my arms in her hands. "Oh my God, which one is he? I have to go look."

"Go, go! He's the one on the very end, to the left. In the blue bandana."

"Okay, I'll be right back!"

She whisked away in her rockstar uniform: black tights ripped so badly that there was barely any fabric left, black sequined mini skirt, ox-blood Doc Martens, and the Bubba Burrito tee. She sure did dress for her part as the face of the restaurant. She is the first person these people see, after all.

I stared at the kitchen door until I saw Scarlette's curls come bursting through. She darted right over to me, a look of confusion clouding her cheeks.

"What is it?" I asked.

"You're talking about the dude who literally looks like a pirate, right?"

"Yes, who else could I possibly want in that kitchen? The douche-bad chef?"

"He even has those big earring thingies you like!" She said, trying to cover up the fact that she thought he was revolting.

"Yeah, the gauges! I knowwww. And the pirate thing! You know I've always loved Johnny Depp. And Johnny Depp as Jack Sparrow beats all else."

"Yeah, yeah, sure, but something really weird just happened," she said, eyes looking wild.

"What?"

"Well, I walked back there, and I had to pretend I was doing something, right? Well, I went to the sink to wash my hands. That's when I turned and got a good look at him."

"Yeah, and?"

"Well, he was staring at me, too. And I tried to look away, but I could feel he was still staring at me. So I looked back, and he was pointing at his eyes."

"Huh?"

"He pointed at his eyes, then he pointed back at mine. Then he motioned with his fingers to his lips, like he was smoking a joint."

"What!" I said, excited.

"Yeah! And then he mouthed the words 'do you smoke?' and I nodded my head. He held up a finger, wrote his number down, and gave it to me." She said, holding her palms out with a single ripped piece of prized paper, seven digits, and the name "Sid" written in the corner. She was smiling with the tip of her tongue licking her sharpest fang, eyes full of accomplishment.

"Noooo fucking waaaaaay," I said, grabbing the paper.

"Fucking way! We're gonna hang out with him tonight!" She said, grabbing my hands and jumping up and down.

"Wait, what?!"

"He says he wants to hangout after work! I asked him if I could bring my best friend Lyla, and he asked who you were. I told him the chick with the shaved head and all the tattoos. He smiled, and told me to bring you, too."

"Wait, wait, wait, isn't this a bad thing?"

"What do you mean?" She asked.

"Well, he gave *you* his number. Don't you think he wants you if he's asking you to smoke when he just saw your red eyes?"

"No way, I'm not his type at all. He's way too ugly and scary and huge for me."

"Hey!" I barked.

"Hey, what?! You *like* ugly things! And scary things! He's perfect for you."

"Okay, so, wait. What you're telling me," I paused, breathing heavily, "is that you and I are hanging out with Sid Vicious. Tonight?"

"Is that what we're gonna call him now? Sid Vicious?" She said sarcastically.

"Yes, I think it's the *only* name to call him." Equal sarcasm.

"Really? Because I was thinking we'd call him Spydawebs, on accounta that web he's got tattooed on his elbow." She said, staring into space and tapping her chin.

"Ohhhh, I think I like that one better! Spydawebs it is. So we're hanging out with Sir Spydawebs. Tonight. Fucking tonight." I said with my eyes wide and ready to fall out of my skull.

"Wait a second, we're forgetting a very big part of all this," she said.

"What is it?"

"What do you plan to do about Big Mick?"

"Oh fucking Christ, I totally forgot about him." I said, rolling my eyes and sinking my head.

"What do you mean you forgot!? Isn't he your boyfriend?"

"NO!" I said without hesitation, "he's my homeless stray

dog that I can't get rid of. I'd humanely put him down if I could." The other servers bustling around us shot me strange looks. Good thing they couldn't quite understand the context, considering he's an employee of this place.

"Well you can't do that! But what do we do if he's really at the apartment?"

"I'll tell him to get the fuck out and go somewhere else! I don't know. I'll figure it out, I'll figure it out. For now, I'm worried about being in the presence of this divine man, Punky."

Big gulp.

"Oh, honey, get excited! At the very least, we'll get free weed. And that's sumthin' to be excited for!" Scarlette hummed.

"At the very least, I'll faint," I said, squeezing her hand and walking away.

Gotta sling burritos for five more hours before anyone thinks about fainting.

Just five hours.
Just five hours.
Just five hours.
Just five hours.
Just four hours and fifty-nine minutes.
Just four hours and fifty-nine minutes.

***

Four hours and fifty-nine minutes passed and left me in a puddle of anxious sweat as I started sweeping my section of the restaurant. I only had twenty more minutes of chores before I was released to race home, shower, and exchange these black skinny jeans and yellow tee for something a tad more beguiling. The kitchen, having to break down entirely and make itself look brand new every night, lets its soldiers out much later than we front-of-the-house folk. I knew I'd have at least an hour to scoot Big Mick out of my house, scoot myself into some enticing clothes, and scoot that fine-looking man into my empty abode. It's the final countdown.

"So I hear I'm coming over to your place tonight," a thunderous voice attempted saying softly. I looked up to see Mr. Spydawebs clutching a yellow metal chair in my section, leaning slightly forward and tilting his bandana'd head of hair up at me. He was smiling just slightly, his shady eyes penetrating my chest where I searched to find any semblance of sound to usher up through my throat and out of my mouth.

"That's what I hear, too," I said with a tender tone, broom in hand and still sweeping crumbs. Can't ever let them know how interested you are, or the whole thing could be killed in less than a second.

"So tell me your name, then," he said, still smiling.

"I'm Lyla. Lyla Calders," I said, half curtseying with the broom. "And you are?"

"High Priest Sid Wotanson Francesco Bickley Acid Freak," he replied, "but you can call me Sid."

"Well, Sid, that's quite an introduction, but you're gonna have to tell me what all that means later! You know where my place is, right?"

"Yeah, uh, your friend told me. A brick building right by the Kangaroo. Unit 4, right?"

"Yes sir. I'll see you tonight, then," I smiled, eyes twinkling brighter than I cared for him to notice.

"Yeah," he said, lingering on that last syllable and trying not to let his delight show. "I'll be there within the hour, I hope," he said, tapping the chair twice and walking coolly past me. I looked down to avoid exposing my elation, sweeping up the same crumbs that I'd been pushing around for two minutes. All I could think about was what I was going to wear!

I practically ran down East Main Street to my apartment, dashing up the stairs two at a time until I burst through the already open door. Big Mick was standing in the barren living room talking on the phone and jumped, startled by my rush.

"Hey," I said panting and racing past him to the bedroom, "what are you doing tonight?"

"Uhhhh, nothin, why?" He mumbled.

"Because, I'm having some people over and I need you to leave. Go down to Wild Wing or something and get yourself a drink."

"But chu been tellin' me I gotta pay you back, right? But chu want me ta go drankin?"

"You'll pay me back; I know you will. I just need the place for a while tonight. It's a girl's night, and you know all we're gonna be doing is discussing the likes of you men," I tried convincing, taking off my uniform and scurrying to the bathroom.

"Aight, I get tha hint. I'll be back real late. If I come back," he halfway threatened. Then the door slammed. Thank GOD, ALLAH, YAWEH, ODIN, SHIVA, BUDDHA, KALI. Quite easier than I expected.

Scarlette had clocked out much sooner than me, and she was out getting her late-night loop before she planned meeting me back at the apartment. I tried showering the taco stink off my skin as quickly as my hands could scrub when I heard the front door creak open again.

"Puuuuuunk, is that you?" I called out through the downpour above my head. "I'll be out in just a minute; this stench is impossible!"

It wasn't Scarlette. She would have yelled out to me, tossed her keys and coat on the ground, and shuffled her big bad combat boots across the wooden floor to sit on the toilet while I finished showering. Instead, I heard slow, deliberate footsteps pounding across the floorboards, pausing every now and then to survey the surroundings. I stood frozen under the hot water, knowing there was only one other body those steps could belong to.

"Hello?" I called again.

"Hey, it's Sid. I was the first out tonight since I was the first one in. I, uh, brought us a few beers." He yelled awkwardly from the living room.

Shit shit shit shit shit shit.
Shit shit shit shit shit.
Shit shit shit shit.
Shit shit shit.
Shit shit.
SHIT.

"Oh! That was so much quicker than I was expecting! Hold on, I'll be out in a sec. But, uh, my clothes are in the bedroom, so excuse my towel-dress, please!" I laughed. I was mortified that this is the way our first experience was going. Seeing me with my clothes off already.

"I don't mind," he tried to say politely.

I wrapped the towel around me as tight as I could and dripped my way into the bedroom where Spydawebs was already sitting on the floor-bed. My duffle bags were in the corner, so I snaked around him, grabbed a long baby blue dress with a plunging neck, and threw it on behind his back. I shook the miniscule amount of water off my shaved locks, wiped my naked face, and took a seat beside him on my bed. I could smell the grime even thicker on him, considering he slaved away above the grill all night. His dark, faded jeans were covered in stains, splotches, and Sharpie streaks. There was a knife tucked into his left pocket, and I just knew he was proficient in all the ways to use it. His brown leather boots were drenched in water, I'm assuming, but they looked more like clown shoes. Come to find out, they look that way because they're a size 14 boot. Size 14. You know what they say about big feet…

And his arms, oh! His arms! They were so thick, solid with muscle and power and venom, if necessary. He had solid black tattoos sprinkled all over; the words 'Blood' and 'Honor' sat below the bend of his arms. A cryptic Norse triangle surrounded with Viking runes had the words 'Strength' and 'Glory' wrapping around the sides. The Misfits infamous skull logo was on his forearm, while the other arm had some creepy face carved into it. I could see a few numbers lining the inside of his fingers, as well as little sayings on his wrists. I could see strands of his luxurious black curls falling out of his bandana and wanted nothing more than to rip that bandana off and let his hair tumble down all over me. I was diggin' it, to say the least. Diggin' every fuckin' inch of it.

"Sorry about the delay," I started, "but I can't handle that greasy smell!"

"Don't apologize," he said, staring me up and down, "you clean up nicely," he said, the red curls of his dark mustache coiling around his lip.

"Thanks! And quickly. It's a perk of having no hair," I winked.

"Yeeeeah, I guess that is a perk," he said facetiously. He reached his hand down into a brown paper bag and pulled out two tall boy PBR cans. "You ever had a PBR?" He asked.

"No, sir, I have not," I said, taking one of the cans from his outstretched hand.

"Well enjoy! It won a blue ribbon once. And never again. But it's still my blue ribbon." He joked. "You're not 21, are you?"

"Not quite. How'd you figure?" I smirked.

"Well, every college kid is proficient in PBR binging, but you haven't ever had one."

"Ahhh, yes, but my college is different! We're a bunch of ladies, right? Southern belles, at that! Mind you, alcohol isn't allowed on campus. If we want alcohol and parties, we just go down the street to Centennial."

"Well how old are you, then?" He pried.

"How old do you think I am?" I retorted.

"I already *think* you're older than I know you are, so just tell me," he smiled, eight inches from my lips.

"I'm nineteen," I said proudly, "and this is my very first apartment. I just moved in three days ago, so that's why it's so barren and boring."

"Yeah, I thought as much," he said, giving another whirl of the room with his eyes.

"So how old are you, then?" I asked.

"Well, tell me how old you think I am," he said, taking a sip of his can.

"Twenty-five?" I guessed.

"Cheers to that," he said, holding his can up to mine, acknowledging I was right. I glugged down a swig of that piss-poor beer and tried my hardest not to cringe as it went down my throat.

"So, tell me, what in the world is with that long-ass name you gave me in the restaurant?" I asked, nudging his arm.

"What part are you most curious about?" He asked me, trying not to let his secrets spill from his teeth.

"All of it! So, start from the beginning."

"Okay, do you know what the Necronomicon is?" He asked.

"No, I do not."

"It started out as a fictional textbook of magic. A book of spells, if you will, that famous authors started citing in their works. Over time, magicians began publishing their own real versions of the

Necronomicon, making it a slightly true work. Regardless, the origin of the name is derived from 'necromancy' which is just another word for sorcery, witchcraft, black magic, ya know?"

"So, you're telling me you're a high priest of black magic?" I asked, bringing myself closer to him.

"Yes," he said with a sinister smile turning up his mustache. I never believed much in the sorcery-bit. The voodoo and the chanting and the black cloaks and the black mass and the transference of bad intentions. But he clearly did, and I clearly wanted a piece of it. The allure of darkness is that the light overthrows it in a single flick of a switch. But the allure of his darkness was that it's deep-seeded, nursed, and unleashed on the world around him in a fit of murky Magick.

"So, do you have your own spell-book, then? Being a high priest and all," I said, stretching my body out across the bed to lie belly-down, sipping beer and gazing up at him like the king he thinks he is.

"I do," he nodded, "but you'll never lay eyes on it."

"That's what you think!" I squeaked. "Now, tell me about the next one. What was it? Wotanson?"

"Yes, Wotanson. Wotan is another name for Odin, the Norse king of the gods."

"Ahhhhh," I said as the lightbulb went off, "I never knew that one!"

"You're welcome," he chuckled, "but Wotanson is just another way of saying son of Odin. It's a tribute to my Norse roots and my Aryan blood."

"Aryan? Like, Hitler's Aryan?" I asked, intrigued.

"*Exactly* like Hitler's Aryan," he said proudly and emphatically.

Before I had time to respond to such a scandalous conversation, I heard Scarlette's footsteps clunking up the staircase in the foyer.

"There's Scarlette," I said, raising my eyebrows and darting off the bed to greet her.

"It's not like she can't get in!" He yelled, "You can just push the door and it opens!"

"Yes, I know!" I shouted back, "But you don't understand!"

Scarlette walked through the room, threw her keys down, and

hopped up into my arms with legs wrapped around my back, yet again. I twirled her a bit, per usual, and she showered me in loving hellos. She hopped down, threw off her coat, and asked,

"Where's Spydawebs? Is he here? You look gooooood!"

"Shhhhh!" I said quietly, "Yes, he's here, in the bedroom," I said, as he stared at us down the hallway.

"Oh! Hi! I'm Scarlette," she said walking through the hallway. "I've got a blunt rolled, y'all ready to smoke?"

"Wait, did I just hear you call me Spydawebs?" Sid asked.

"Yeah, it's because of that web tattoo you've got on your elbow," she said, excited.

"That's rude! My name's Sid." He tried saying without the offense showing in his voice. But it was obvious.

"What's rude about it?! It's endearing. We like your spider web tattoo, Sid," Scarlette flirted.

"It's rude to call attention to someone based off a particular piece of their physical appearance," Sid said, his eyes searching for a real reason as to why such a thing would be so rude.

"Well, what's it mean to ya?" Scarlette asked.

"The spider web?" He asked.

"Yeah. It's important to you, right? All of Lyla's tattoos have meaning. Multiple meanings, at that. So, what's yours?"

"If you don't know, you shouldn't know," he said coolly, clasping his hands together in his lap.

"I was always told it's a salute to prison," I butted in. "That men who have spider webs on their elbows killed someone while they were doing time."

Sid glared.

Scarlette's eyes lit up.

I realized I hit a nerve.

"Is that true?!" Scarlette turned to ask him as she lit the blunt.

"Yes, that's one of many meanings of the web," he said defeated, eyes staring at the ground.

"So you've been to prison then?" Scarlette asked unabashed.

"This is the conversation you wanna have?" He asked Scarlette. There was resentment and remorse in his voice, and I could tell how uncomfortable all the spider web talk was making him.

"How about we play a game instead!" I suggested.

"Yeah? What you got?" Sid asked.

"Let's play Favorites. Scarlette, you first. You're always the best at questioning."

For the next hour Scarlette, Sid, and I sat around in a triangle endlessly meddling one another about our favorite-whatevers. Favorite icecream, favorite color, favorite book, favorite movie, favorite food, favorite sex position, favorite alcoholic beverage, favorite season, favorite holiday—you name it. We asked it. Sid and I had more in common than I imagined, and it seemed with each answer he gave, my answer was the same. He was disturbing, troubled, and loved chocolate chip cookie dough icecream, and my instant attraction to him suddenly burst into fetishistic admiration. I could have watched his mouth move all night, the crooked teeth behind his red lips stained yellow from years of smoke. He was a downright hideous creature, and my, was I in Love like never before. His ride from one of the other kitchen boys arrived at 1:38 in the morning, and just like that, he disappeared out of my door like a ghost.

"Oh, Lyla, he's perfect for you, he's perfect for you!" She said, jumping up and down and clapping her hands together, "He's! So! Fucking! Perfect!" She stomped her boot with every word she spoke.

"I know, I know, I know!" I gushed, suffocating her in a hug and shaking her about. "But don't you dare jinx me! I'm gonna marry this one, Punk. I can feel it."

***

Thanksgiving Day. 6:47 PM. The plates in front of us were devoid of most food they held only a mere hour prior. Scarlette's still had scraps of steak on it and most of the vegetables. My vegetarian sensibilities kept me from the prime rib, but I couldn't get enough of the box-stuffing, green beans, and mashed potatoes. As our first holiday away from our families Scarlette and I spent Thanksgiving with our dashing coworker, Shelton, the likes of whom Scarlette has been eyeing since they day we met him. He's a 22-year-old blonde with a bronzed body of steel, an affinity for jazz and playing it, a fine home to host intimate evenings, and a mighty enthusiastic desire for psychedelia. The dessert was the only thing all three of us could agree on: a dish of magic mushroom caps and a bar of Hershey's milk chocolate, ingested only a mere twenty minutes ago.

Shelton and Scarlette worked together to clear the dinner table, fit with a candelabra, gravy boat, and empty wine glasses. Only droplets of cabernet sauvignon, Shelton's favorite, were left. His collared shirt matched the color of that bloodied wine, tucked into faded denim with a black leather belt to hold it all together. Scarlette wore her least-ripped black tights and a simple black mini-dress with golden geometric sequins sewn into it. I was wearing my favorite blue-grey patterned tights, periwinkle blue socks rising above my knee, an oversized white sweater, and a pale blue scarf. We couldn't be more different by looking at the three of us, but we certainly all ate the same drug that was setting in slowly and surely. Any minute now, it wouldn't matter what we looked like; we'll all just be blurred versions of ourselves.

"Music!" Scarlette demanded as she clapped her hands together. "I want music, Shelton. And do make it jazz, if you could."

"That's one of the only genres I can promise you, so we both win," he said, putting a jazz album in the stereo. Beside him I caught the gaze of a small white statue—a pale face, only visible from the nose down, holding out a hand and blowing a kiss. But the longer I stared, the less it looked like a face blowing a simple kiss, and the more it became a hand calling to pull me into the fourth dimension. She knows as well as I do that the third dimension can't possibly satiate my cravings for the Ineffable, the Infallible, and the Inevitable. She's reminding me that there's a way out if only I'd listen to the Piper and his march full of stars and of seeds. He's been calling me to join their army, but I always seem to miss his tune. He whistles in a pitch that my ears just can't catch, but one of these days, I'll hear it.

The shrooms are setting in. With each rip of the sax and ping of the piano the air began to swirl, bursting with pops of colors that aren't of this world. The human eye can only see so much in this realm, don't you know? Our range of colors is limitless outside of these wavelengths that we're so normally confined to. With the help of a little poison, one can see colors that haven't been named, motions that aren't usually apparent, and truths that aren't always told. Truth hidden in the delicate crystal of the wine glass, or truth hidden in the burning embers of the fireplace, or in the fuchsia wallpaper of the bathroom. Such things that are meaningless and baseless in the waking world somehow grow to contain the magnitude of divinity within them. And we only have drugs or God to thank for that. But I'll thank both.

    Scarlette sat on Shelton's lap in the plush velvet green chair across from me, and I could tell the shrooms were hitting them, too. Their hands were shivering slightly, their cheeks colored with splotchy red, and eyes full of tears, ready to leak. Scarlette's chest heaved up and down, and I knew her breaths were deep and unsteady. The air was pulsating, *breathing* like a living body. And we could see that body all around us. Pulsating, breathing, heaving, ebbing, flowing, throbbing, twisting, twirling. I got stuck watching the embers in the empty fireplace change from a chicken with a broken neck into a phoenix with wild, burning feathers. He was flapping and flailing, trying to escape the pile of rotted wood below him. He thrashed and crashed into the bricks, squawking a distress call that hurt my very soul to bear witness. Louder and more violent and hopeless until finally,

    "Lyla! Lyla, you wanna hear Shelton play some of his music, right? Say yes."

    "Oh, yes!" I said, giggling for nothing. "Yes, I'd love to hear your music."

    Shelton brought us to his bedroom where the piano plays. It only took ten minutes to drag us twenty feet down the hall. Side effects of not wanting to move, not needing to move, and not too able to move, really. I grabbed on to the ornate chair in the dining room, finding humor in the cabinet full of plates that nobody is allowed to touch. Finding humor in the paisley patterned carpet beneath my feet. Humor in the fact that I cannot locate my cell phone. Humor in the idea that the only person I want to talk to is Sid, Mr. Spydawebs. Humor that Scarlette is falling all over this piano-playing boy, kissing his cheeks endlessly and pulling him down to her by the neck. As much as I was enjoying the smooth tunes coming from Shelton's fingers, I had this overwhelming nag from a voice in my head telling me to find my phone. And once an idea hits you in a trip, that fucking idea refuses to quit until it's got every single one of your neurons chanting its name.

"I've gotta go find my phone," I mumbled into Scarlette's ear before exiting the room.

"Oh, won't you hurry back! I'll miss you," she said, grabbing my hands and still dancing beside piano-papa.

"No promises," I whispered as I stumbled my way out of the room and down the green tunnel of a hallway. Just as I reached the end, I heard my muffled ringtone crying out for attention. Luckily, it was in the very first spot I checked: hidden under a seat cushion. Whose name did I see calling me? Well, none other than Sir Spydawebs, and my fingers couldn't swipe fast enough to answer that call.

"Hello?" I said frantically.

"Heeyyyyyy," a smiling voice on the other end said. "How's it going? I liked the picture you sent me."

"Wait, what picture?" I asked.

"Oh, don't tell me you're so far gone that you don't remember sending me pictures of dessert!" He teased. "I once had a Thanksgiving like that, too. Only, there was much more involved in my desserts."

"Oh! That! Yeah, everything's a little swirly over here," I said, feeling compelled to leave the house. It's a stupid idea, really. It's fucking freezing outside and pitch black, too. But I twisted the handle to the door and let myself out into the brisk ice taking over the air while I listened to the shadowy voice from somewhere out there. The moon was nearly full, beaming down to me like a watchful sister. She started singing me a lullaby, but the song I heard through my phone was sweeter than what she could give me in my heightened state of passion.

"You're peaking right about now, aren't you?" Sid asked.

No answer.

"Lyla?" He asked.

No answer.

"Lyla. I know you're there, I can practically hear your heart beating, and it's beating heavily. Isn't it?"

"I'm here, I'm here," I said, "and yes, you caught me at the peak. I'm staring at the moon right now. She's trying to tell me something."

"I'm staring at the moon, too," Sid said, "but I have something to tell you that's much better than anything the moon has to offer."

"What is it?" I asked in a breathy daze, eyes nearly blind from staring at the light.

"That I want you. And I want to have all of you. I want your body, I want your mind, and I want your confidence. You can keep your heart and soul," he said with diligence.

"How generous of you to let me keep my heart. As for my soul, I think you're trying to steal it straight through the phone right now," I said with suspicion.

"Me? A thief? That's far below me, Lyla. There's more. Ya wanna hear it?"

"Oh, please, do tell me more," I begged.

"Ya sure you wanna hear it?" He taunted.

"Oh, I'm sure, I'm sure, Sid!"

Pause.

Deep breath.

Exhale.

Speak.

"You know I just wanna tease you. Please you and squeeze you. Torment you. Flirt with you, fight with you. Dance with you, make love to you, fuck you senseless, and grope you. I wanna lick you, kiss you, play with you. I wanna see the shock in your eyes when you're gasping for air. I wanna show you a man you've never had the pleasure of meeting before. I want to possess you. But don't worry. I won't keep you."

Speechless.

Breathless.

Helpless.

Helpless in his thralls.

Gasping.

"Ooohhh, Sid."

Deep breath.

Pause.

Speak.

"I don't think you know what you've done by telling me those things at such a time like now."

"Don't worry, mah lady. You know I only called you at the peak, because I knew exactly what it would do to you," he said with a touch of victory.

"Drive me mad, is the answer!" I squealed.

"Mad, you may be. But you can be mad with me. We're all mad, here, Alice," he joked.

"You know I won't be able to think of anything but you for the rest of the night, right?"

"My point exactly," he whispered.

"You're some version of a cruel man." I said lowly. I'll tell you that."

The moon's howling at me, and I can't help but cock an ear up toward the sky.

"You'll find out what kind of man I am Lyla. But it's high time you get back to your trip. Enjoy it. I'll talk to you tomorrow, little bird."

"You'd better."

CLICK.

The call ended, but I could barely see the characters on the screen of my phone. Instead of numbers and an alphabet I was seeing ancient Egyptian hieroglyphics. I shoved it in the front of my tights, glad to forget it for the remainder of the night.

"Lyla!?" Scarlette called from the doorway. She looked startled, scared. I can understand why; she found me standing frozen in the middle of the black street, shivering intensely and staring at something I've found in the radiance of the streetlamp. Truth, maybe.

"Lyla, get in here! What are you doing?" She pleaded to know. "It's so cold out here." Her voice was frail and meek, unlike usual. Those mushrooms take over and bring out all types of characters that you never knew existed inside of you. Perhaps this is what schizophrenia is like.

She took four steps outside the door without shoes before saying, "I'm not coming any further, you come to me!"

"I'm coming, I'm coming!" I said, stumbling slowly back to

the pathway. I could feel the warmth from Shelton's house pervading the entire atmosphere all the way to the street. Why, I felt like I could even see it! With each step, the heat pulled me closer and closer until I was within the safety and comfort of the sanctuary.

"Scarlette?" I said.

"Yes, darling?"

"Sid just called me," I said, staring into her smeared and dilated brown eyes.

"And?" She asked, reaching for my hand.

"And, well… I've got this uncontrollable feeling that this is happening to us. You and me. I mean, whatever this is with Sid isn't just happening to me. He's happening to us. Like, this Life is you and me together. Everyone else is just an extra. But I feel like Sid is here to change something, and it's something to do with us, Scarlette. Something to do with us…" I faded as I leaned up against the wallpaper, trembling in the heat and hysteria.

"I feel that way, too." She said, following me to the wall. "And I've felt it since that night at your apartment with him." Her eyes gleamed with heavy tears and the promise of a future only colored how we see fit. But in that moment, something, somewhere whispered that our colors can't be found in our waking world. We've got to brave the journey to far off distant lands in order to find the colors that will satisfy our longings. Whatever they may be. And here we are: in the distant land.

"What do you think it could mean?" Scarlette asked.

"I'm not too sure." I said, wrapping her in a hug. "But we'll certainly find out. Promise me something?" I asked.

"Anything."

"Promise you won't let me lose my mind over this boy," I chuckled.

"Oh, honey," she laughed, "you're already losing it. And it's okay. I'll be here for all of it."

She laid her sweaty head into my chest and squeezed tight. My chin sat on the top of her head as I grabbed tufts of her hair and pet her like the charm she is. We didn't speak; there wasn't any need. Together in that moment we understood truly how far we've come in our womanhood and in our mentalities. Without any kind of ceremony or even a conscious decision, we each placed a very important piece of ourselves within one another—a piece of ourselves that was once in danger of being degraded and lost forever. A piece that needs nurturing, sheltering, and calming within the comforts of another human. She holds onto mine, as I do to hers. It's a fair testament to the strength and the security that we've found within one another and where we are now: a tribe in the making. A team in the running. A duet in the showing. We're a goddamn pair, and whatever happens to one happens to the other. Sid was no exception, just a rare peculiarity—an odd blip swiped across the face of our friendship.

"I love you, Lyla," Scarlette said as she stepped back from the embrace. "You're the best friend I've ever had."

"Me too, Punky," I said with tears welling in my already wet eyes. "Me too."

Yet, another Truth found in the midst of Magick and Madness.

XVI: Autumn 2K13: The Bomb

Big Mick turned into a big fucking problem. As soon as my infatuation with Sid became sickeningly apparent, he decided to quietly take matters of revenge into his own hands; he began stealing money from my stash pile in the house. On top of that, he'd steal my credit card and debit card while I was sleeping, and use it at places like Subway and Domino's. I looked through his phone one night while he was sleeping on the mattress next to mine and found that he'd been bringing prostitutes to the apartment while I was at work. $80 an hour. Cheap tricks for an even cheaper man.

    I shook him awake when I read those messages and told him to get the fuck up. He denied everything, of course. Even though the proof was in the piddly pudding. I grabbed his twin mattress, flipped it on its side, dragged it out into the living room, and shoved it in the tiniest, darkest possible corner where the dining room was.

    "This is where the fuck you sleep until you find a place to go. And it better be soon. I have the right mind to call the police and kick you out this very second, so keep your mouth shut and don't fuck with me." I said, hands shaking with rage.

    "Dayum, gurl, I have just as much right to be here as you do!"

    "No the fuck you don't! Not when you're bringing filthy hookers over while I'm working! And have you paid me rent? For this month, or for last? No, you haven't. You have no right to be here. Especially after stealing my cards and money, too. Don't think I haven't noticed."

    "I didn't steal shit from you," he mumbled.

    "Oh? You think I misplace things? You think I'm Scarlette? Because I'm not. I'm Lyla. And I never fucking lose things. Especially my money."

"Blah-zay, blah-zay." That was his way of telling me to fuck off.

"From now on, all you do in this house is sleep here. That's it. If I'm here, you'd better not be. Go take a walk or something. I don't want you in my sight. You have a week to be outta here, or I will call the cops."

"You can't call the cops." He said, laughing.

"Why not?"

"You should brush up on your Sou' Carlina laws, gurl."

"What the fuck is that supposed to mean?" I asked him as he tucked his 'fro underneath the blankets.

"Nuthin, my Love. Nuthin."

This motherfucker. Homeless and friendless. Staying in my space, rent free, and yet, that's not enough. His own grandparents, the last family he knows, kicked him out and were happy to hand him right over to me. They didn't even have the decency to warn me about what kind of boy I was truly sheltering. When they dropped him off to me last month they brought him with two twin mattresses, and said,

"He's yours now," and hobbled out of the apartment. Nothing more, nothing less. I was the very last person on the face of this Earth to believe in Big Mick and give him every opportunity to pull himself out of a drab and meaningless existence. He was throwing that away with both hands, and now all I wanted was to throw him away. After six months, this boy had gone from a wandering gentleman to an entitled, bothersome thief. In all that time together, I gradually began seeing his true ugly colors. But now, I suddenly saw this bruised black skin stretched over his bones when I used to see soft caramel.

At 4:02 PM the next day, Big Mick came sauntering into the apartment after his shift at Bubba Burrito. Scarlette, Mia, and I were in my bedroom, piled onto that tiny bed and creating a list of all the fun house accessories we were gonna grab at Walmart. It was the first week of December, which translates into the horrid phrase: FINALS WEEK. Never will you ever see so much despair in sheltered youth than the week of finals on a college campus. The girls were sinking under the weight and needed a little escape from the endless papers and sculptures.

I thought I was very clear with Big Mick about his status in this house, but I guess I wasn't; I heard him walk across the tiles in the kitchen, open the fridge, and pour himself a glass of orange juice. *My* orange juice. I stared at Mia and Scarlette for a second of understanding before I jumped up from the bed, chased him into the living room, and detonated like Hiroshima.

"What the fuck do you think you're doing?" I asked, hips cocked and fists on my waist.

He took two big gulps before lowering the glass to show his smirk, rolling his eyes and saying, "Drinking juice."

"Yeah, my juice. The juice that I bought, right?"

"Yeah, you gonna put cho name on it?" He was swaying around, almost dancing. Not giving a fuck in the world that he was getting under my skin. In fact, that was his exact objective.

"Do you think I'm fucking around?" I asked, getting louder.

"I think you're fuckin' up." He said, laughing to himself through sips.

"I'm fucking up? Don't you think you're throwing away the good graces of the last person who will ever help you out?"

"Nope."

"Get out." I said, pointing toward the door. "I told you if I'm here, you'd better not be. You can sleep like a goddamn dog in the dining room, and that's all." I turned around thinking the conversation was over, but he proved me wrong.

"No."

"Excuse me?" I whipped around, earrings clinking violently against my neck.

"I ain't leavin'. You ain't my mama, you ain't my gramama, and you ain't my boss. You ain't got any power here, Lyla! What? Chu think all your shit talkin' last night wuz gonna change sumthin? Nahhhh, son, that ain't how it works."

He was still swaying and throwing his hands in the air like he was in an alleyway in New York City, sippin' Lean. My face was growing redder by the second, and my fists were curling into tighter and tighter balls. He was prodding me, and I wanted to fucking take a flame-thrower to his face for it. Mia and Scarlette came out into the living room to stand by me and try to convince him through the power of numbers. Scarlette, watching how helplessly enraged I was becoming, decided to try politely reasoning with him.

"Mick, come on, now. This isn't your house. This is Lyla's house. You're lucky she's even letting you stay here."

"Lucky?! You call this lucky? Shiiiiit, I haven't got any in months."

"Not even from the prostitutes?" Mia cut into him like the witty snapper she is.

"Bitch, shut the fuck up!" Big Mick yelled. Scarlette stood this time.

"MICK," she said with ferocity, "This isn't your fucking house. You have no right to disrespect anyone in here. So, shut the fuck up, and get the fuck out."

"Ya think I'm gonna listen to you? Scrawny lil twerp. I could break you in half."

With those words, Big Mick sealed his fate. You can fuck with me, but don't you dare think for a second you're gonna threaten my friends in my house. Standing three feet from him, I barreled toward his 6'4" body with a raging fist and clocked him square in the jaw, screaming,

"GET THE FUCK OUT OF MY HOUSE! Get out, you sorry piece of shit!"

The house fell watch to a shocking kind of silence while we all breathed heavily in our chests.

"You so smart, Ly!" He yelled as he shook off the blow and watched me walk toward the porch. "How da fuck you think you gon' call the cops on me now when you throwin' punches?!"

"Oh, please. Do you know where we are?" I turned to say, "We're in Darbyville, South Carolina. They're not gonna believe a little white girl threw a punch at an ugly black man like you."

"I'm beggin' you to hit me again, Lyla. Lemme call da cops for you."

"Get the fuck out of my house, Mick. Now. Or I'll gladly hit you again."

Mia and Scarlette stood wide-eyed in the living room, frozen for lack of knowing which step to take next. Big Mick stood five feet from them, still sipping that orange juice. He smiled, and with that smile he refused to move anywhere from the spot he was standing. But I was too tired of being in an uncontrollable situation with an ungrateful mongrel.

They keep prodding the alligator; bound to fall into the death roll.

So, I hit him again.

And again.

And again.

And a-fucking-gain.

Both fists flailing on the end of my tense arms. He wasn't throwing any punches back. Not even a petty slap. Instead, he took his nearly full glass of orange juice and dumped it all over my hot head. Dripping with vitamin C, I stopped and closed my eyes. I let it run all over my chest and down my back in an unusual calm as he stood laughing in front of me.

"You got a lil sumthin on your face, Ly," he said.

I said nothing. I turned away from him and walked toward my porch. I closed the door behind me, climbed up onto the railing, leaned my back against the brick wall, and spilled a few tears through the sticky juice. The frustration of not having control in my own house had brought me to the point of punching a black man and sobbing on an empty porch. Scarlette opened the door and came out to sit with me on the ground below, holding my hand without uttering a word. We heard the door to the complex slam shut and looked down to see Big Mick in his cherry red sneakers skipping down the stairs and onto East Main Street. Deep breath.

10:27 PM. Same night. The Skinnies and I returned to the apartment with bags full of floor-length blue-lace curtains, black curtain rods, a set of beautiful turquoise and brown dishes, an orange toaster, juices galore, and many more candles. You can never have enough fire. Scarlette sat down on my bed to roll a blunt for our nightcap, and Mia helped me figure out how in the world to hang a curtain rod on walls so thick we'd have to nail our way to China. Just when I thought we had one of 'em nailed to the wall, a loud knocking came to my door. I hopped down and ran over, peering through the eyehole. Three police officers in uniform, hands on their guns.

"Who is it?" Mia asked.

"It's the cops," I whispered to her, "go tell Scarlette."

A nervous spirit took over me, even though I knew I'd be lying with the prettiest façade of honesty wiped across my face. I opened the door halfway, and said,

"Can I help you, officers?"

"Yes, ma'am. Are you Lyla Calders?" The frontman asked.

"Yes, sir, I am. Is something wrong?" Be polite, be polite.

"Well, yes, there is. We've received a complaint from Mickey Branch about a case of domestic violence."

"What?" I asked, fake surprise in my voice and furrowed wrinkles of confusion on my face.

"Lyla didn't hit him," Mia said from the living room. "We were here with her the whole time."

"Well that may be true, but he's also saying that you're threatening to kick him out."

"Yes, sir, he's been stealing from me for some time now. He used to be a friend who didn't have anywhere to go, so I let him stay with me. But now he's stealing my things, and I don't want him here."

"Well, ma'am, legally you can't do that," the cop said to me with his face looking grim.

"What do you mean? He isn't anywhere on the lease, and he hasn't paid rent for two months."

"Ma'am," the officer lowered his head, "in the state of South Carolina there is a law that protects squatters against being thrown out on the streets. If somebody's things are in a home, legally you have to give them a court-ordered thirty-day notice that you want them gone. Until that happens, he is legally allowed to be here."

"What?" I said, tears nearly flowing from my eyes again. "So, you're telling me that because he has a box of clothes in my living room that he legally is allowed to do whatever he wants? Regardless of whether or not he's paying rent?"

"Unfortunately, ma'am, that's the law," he said with pursed lips.

My mouth hung agape and empty, for I couldn't find any words to combat the stupidity that they were spewing to me. What kind of a fucking state has a law to protect squatters? Mine, of course.

"But officer," I pleaded with trembling lips, "he's stealing from me when I sleep."

"And we're sorry about that. Next time he does, just come down to the station and file an official report. Once you have three reports, we can arrest him."

"Three reports?!" I squealed. Scarlette was behind me now, and she grabbed my elbow to let me know to simmer down.

"We're sorry about the circumstances, ma'am. But we've convinced him to stay somewhere else tonight to let things cool off before you see each other again. In the morning, I suggest you run down to the court house and get yourself a legal notice if you want him out of your apartment," he advised.

I stood shaking my head in disbelief and defeat. Anger began boiling in my veins again, and I needed a Loop now more than ever.

"Thanks for the information." I said quickly. "Is there anything else, officer?"

"No ma'am. Thanks for your understanding. Take care," he said, tipping his hat and turning away with the other men following him down the staircase. I shut the door, slid the chain into the lock, and turned to see Mia and Scarlette standing behind me in honest solidarity.

"Thanks for that back up, Mia. You didn't have to do that." I said pacing in the room.

"Oh, yes I did! Scarlette wasn't about to!" She laughed.

"I can't lie to the cops! My dad's a federal prosecutor! It's like looking my dad in the eye and lying. I just can't do it," she said shrugging and shaking it off.

"It's okay, Punk. Mia knew what she was doing. You got that blunt ready?"

"Sure do," she sang.

"Good. Because we've got ten minutes to smoke it, or I'll kill him."

***

December three. 9:42 PM. It's my last night at Bubba Burrito's, because it's also the last day before Annabelle's College lets her daughters out for winter break. Considering my mother still believes I'm writing a twelve-page report for my Hinduism class, I've gotta go back to Bloodmoon for Christmas to ensure the fortitude of this elaborate dropout-scheme. It'd give me three weeks away from Big Mick, thank GOD, ALLAH, YAWEH, SHIVA, ODIN, KALI, BUDDHA. But it's also gonna take three weeks from my gawking at the tantalizing Sid Bickley.

We spend most of the hours at Bubba Burrito pretending not to notice each other while taking turns at whose chance it is to stare. It's strictly against our employee agreement to fall into relationships with coworkers, so we had to keep our desires a secret to the taco familia. Whenever I found myself in the kitchen standing behind the boisterous chef, I could feel the very second when Sid's gaze fell on me. A shiver spun through my body while my face grew hot, and I sat with the discomfort to never let on that I was aware. But sometimes, I looked back. I had to feed the escalating addiction.

Around ten o'clock the biz slowed down. I started doing my chores, per usual, and sent Scarlette a message to ask about our nighttime blunt loop. I walked back into the kitchen to grab glassware, but Sid met me at the door right as I stepped foot inside. He had been waiting patiently.

"Hey!" He said, blocking my way so I couldn't get by him. Sweat dripped down his pale mug, and I had half a mind to stick my tongue out and lick it off.

"Hey, boy," I grinned.

"Hey, girl, answer me somethin," he said.

"What is it?"

"How do you feel about acid?"

"Like, LSD?" I asked.

"No, I meant acid rain," he rolled his eyes.

"Well I'm not fond of acid rain," I laughed. "But I looooooove some LSD," I said as my eyes rolled back for a very different reason.

"Yeah? You ever done it before?"

"Yes sir, twice," I lied. It was only once. But I for damn sure loved every second of those sixteen hours. I'd do it over and over again on repeat if someone would allow such a thing.

"Well, how'd you like to do it again? With me?"

"You serious?" I asked with an instantaneous smile spreading across my face.

"Dead serious. I wanna have a threesome," he smirked. "You, me, and Lucy."

"Well tomorrow is my last day in town," I warned him. "'My mom thinks I'm still in school, so I've gotta go down to Bloodmoon Beach until Annabelle's is back in session."

"You little liar!" He teased. "So, we're doing this tonight then?"

"It'd have to be tonight! Which I'm totally okay with."

"Deal," he smiled, brushing his fingers against my arm. "The acid's at my house, though. So, I'll get a ride home from chef when we get out tonight, get a shower, and then I'll call you. You think you can get Scarlette to let you borrow her car to come get me?"

"Sure, I don't see why not. She'll be down for the cause."

"Has she ever done acid?" He asked suddenly.

"Nope, never."

"Awwwhhhh, man!" He yelled, stomping his boot on the salsa-splattered floor. "I have an extra hit! We should all do it together at your place," he suggested.

"There's no way she'll be able to! It's finals week. And as of this morning, she still had two papers to write," I laughed. "But you let me know when you're all ready. I'll be waiting with her until then," I said while I discreetly squeezed his hand and walked away.

Game time.

10:38 PM. Scarlette's dorm room.

Annabelle's administration sure as shit had no problem getting rid of me the day I signed the dropout papers. Much to their own idiocy, they didn't even bother deactivating my access card! I could still get into all the buildings like a student could, no problem. After work I burst through Scarlette's dorm room, letting the hallway lights ruin the dark abyss she had created inside.

"Awh, shut the door!" Scarlette begged as she shielded her eyes.

"What are you doing in bed?!" I yelled, pulling the blankets off her.

"Stop it, Lyla! I'm so exhausted," she wept, kicking her feet at me.

"Did you get all your papers done?" I asked, flicking the light on.

"No," she mumbled.

"No?! Well what do you have left?"

"One for art history on Dali."

"Salvador?" I asked. He's my favorite.

"Yeah, that one," she said, sliding off her bed and stretching.

"Well what do you need?" I asked. "Do you need a loop? Do you need a back massage? What?"

"I need someone else to write this paper for me!" She screamed.

"Well I don't know if I can help you with that," I laughed.

"What do you wanna do? You wanna drive? We can loop." She said as she rubbed the sleep from her eyes.

"I need to ask a favor of you, actually," I said, biting my lip.

"What is it?"

"Can I use your car to go pickup Sid later tonight? He wants to do acid with me!"

"Uuuuuuggghhhhh!"

"What?!" I asked.

"I wanna do acid too! But I can't intrude upon your moment like that."

"Not to mention that Dali paper," I hinted.

"Does this mean you two are finally gonna kiss?" She sang, pinching my cheeks ever so slightly.

"It better mean we're finally gonna kiss!" I yelped, "I can't take it anymore! Day in and day out, pretending like we don't wanna know each other."

"Wait just a second," Scarlette said as she perked up and disregarded the conversation.

"What?" I asked.

"Let's make a deal." Her eyes were looking a little like they held tricks behind their twinkle.

"Okay, proceed," I said, climbing onto Mia's empty bed.

"You wanna use my car to go get Sid, right? Well, I don't wanna write this paper. I just wanna sleep. So, if you write the paper for me, you can use my car all night long. Do whatever you want with it. Go to Florida for all I care."

"Awh, man, what the fuck!" I said. "I dropped out, but I still have to write a final paper?!"

"Oh, please, Lyla! It'll be so easy!" She said, resting both of her hands on my knee. "You're so good at writing anyways. And Dali is your favorite! Right? Please, please, please. I couldn't do it, even if I wanted to."

I lingered for a long while, staring at her with my head facing down and glaring at the genius she's got within her. The girl always knows how to get exactly what she wants. And needs.

"Alright," I sighed, slapping my hand on my leg. "How long does it have to be?"

"Oh, Lyla!" She screamed as she hopped up into my lap. "Thank you, thank you, thank you!"

"Yeah, yeah, yeah," I laughed. "How long?"

"Only five pages! But it's a research paper. Make sure you cite it properly and all that shit, okay?"

"Ma'am, yes, ma'am!" I saluted. She tossed me her laptop while simultaneously tossing her body into bed. I began halfway plagiarizing a story about Salvador Dali while she snored sweetly through the click-click-clicking of the keyboard. Those five pages were the only things holding me back from my trip with a dear old friend and a new lover.

12:57 AM. Sid called to let me know he'd been freshly showered and had five tabs of acid in hand, just in case Scarlette showed up and wanted one of them. I let him know that I succeeded in getting the car, but was still two pages from being done with my end of the deal. He thought it was hilarious, all the school-girl stuff. After he got over the initial fear of me being a closeted lesbian, he found humor in things like research projects, cafeteria lunch, and dorm rooms. He had the opinion that I should have never quit school! But what would he know, really? He spent time on a few degrees online at some point, but that didn't prove fruitful. Not to mention he missed out on the college experience! Online test-takings are nothing like waking up surrounded by young women in their pj's.

1:43 AM.

Exactly five pages.

Bibliography—check.

Hit save.
Send email.
Shut down.
Go time.

On the night that I lost my virginity, I walked barefoot for four miles down an unlit country back road to get to a boy's house. He bet me that I wouldn't come over to see him, and being young and dumb, I bet him that I could prove him wrong. I snuck out of the second story window of my bedroom, got on the very edge of the roof, jumped, tucked, rolled, and disappeared. The whole way there I listened to my favorite music and felt nothing but elation for the moment when I would see that boy's face. I sang my songs to the nightingales, and they sang back to warn me of oncoming passersby. There was a certain high I felt, to be out amongst the black of a starry spring night in secret. But when I walked through the gates of his neighborhood and watched a rabbit scurry across the empty road, I felt my heart drop with anxiety; it wasn't until that moment that I had any inkling of the intimacy that was to unfold, and I was all of a sudden uneasy with that certain idea.

I felt like a virgin again with that same feeling on the way to pick up Sid. Once again, I've found myself trekking through the midnight hours to unite with a boy whom my fancy has fallen for. And once again, I've found myself anxious with the impending unfurling of his affection.

I pulled up to what I thought was Sid's house and waited outside, per my instructions. He's in between houses and was living with his aunt and uncle until he got himself established enough to move closer into town. No man in their twenties likes to admit that he's still living with some type of authority figure, so I went no further in my questioning of the scenario.

He was waiting for me. Not even forty-five seconds after I parked there was a bold, shadowy figure moving across the drive. I saw his ponytail dangling behind him as he hurried his steps faster and faster until his hand touched the door.

Open.
"Hey, shugah," he smiled.
"Hey, boy," I smiled back.

"You ready to do this thing?" He asked, fumbling with six different DVDs in his hands.

"Now more than ever," I said, putting the car in drive.

"I'm glad you said that," he said as he took a seat. He threw the DVDs to the ground and reached into the pocket of his jeans before saying, "Because we're taking it right now."

"Right now?!" I asked.

"Yeah, why not? It'll take an hour and a half to kick in. It's good shit. Made it myself," he said proudly.

"Damn, you know how to make acid?"

"I know how to make just about any drug."

"Does that mean I'll have an endless supply of acid from now on?" I teased. I couldn't let him know how impressed I was with his corrosive talent.

"Maybe you'll even learn how to make your own," he said, nodding. He held a tiny piece of tin foil in his hand where the acid tabs were kept safe. He pulled out the half-strip, and told me to park at the stop sign before the interstate.

"So, Scarlette won't be coming then?"

"No way, she's fast asleep. She's got an exam in the morning."

"Well, tell me. What's the most acid you've taken?" He asked.

"Two hits. And it was the perfect amount."

"Well, here's 2.5," he said as he handed me a small strip of milky white blotter paper. "It's good shit, though, like I said. So, don't you go crazy on me."

"Deal," I said, slipping the tabs under my eager tongue. It tasted just how I remembered: like shit. It doesn't have any sort of flavor. Rather, there's this metallic juice that becomes your spit when the tabs hit your tongue, and it's relentless. The first time I did acid, I threw up from slurping so much of my own odd-tasting saliva. Sid slipped his hits into his mouth, too, then told me to stop at the nearest gas station for orange juice. Thank Christ for a man who understands the bitter bite of acid's chemical corruption. He dived into this spiel about the science of how orange juice helps to give an extra kick to the trip.

But, maybe it doesn't. Maybe it's all in our heads.

We pulled up to my apartment after spending twenty minutes

scanning through the memories of our favorite firsts. As I parked, I remembered that there was a dirty scoundrel sleeping in the dining room, so I grabbed Sid's hand before he got out of the car to warn him.

"Hey, just so you know, there's a squatter sleeping in my dining room. I tried to get him out of here, but the cops got called and this whole big mess happened and—anyways. All I'm saying is not to mind the dude sprawled out on the floor." I said with hesitation. I didn't want Big Mick to be a big turn-off when Sid and I had just tuned it, turned on, and dropped out.

"I don't give a fuck," he shrugged and sneered, "let's get inside."
Perfect.

When I opened the door, there was a rhythmic wheeze coming from the middle of the apartment. It was Big Mick, and luckily, he was knocked out on his twin mattress. I tip-toed past him to the back of the house where the bedroom is, but Sid truly didn't give a fuck; he stomped right through that room, right past that sad man. When we got to the bedroom, I turned the lock on the door and took my seat on the bed. The room was dark save the few rays of moonlight pouring through the exposed glass. Shadows of the leaves swaying on the trees were the only form of decoration in the room, and I suddenly began to feel trapped.

"So what's the first order of business?" Sid asked as he took his black and red plaid jacket off to reveal the KISS shirt underneath. He put the DVDs next to my laptop, took off his boots, and sprawled his body out on the remaining piece of the twin bed. Lying on his back, he looked up at me from below and smiled. Only, this time the smile didn't make my heart flutter. It made my heart squirm and coil back in fear.

"Well, what kind of movies do you have?" I asked as calmly as I could, feeling the insides of my body start to rev and twist together in the wake of LSD poisoning.

"Ever seen *Point Break*?" He asked.

"Nope."

"What?! Well, that's my first choice. But I also brought *Alice in Wonderland, The Wizard of Oz, Charlie and The Chocolate Factory*. Ya know, some trippy classics."

"You say *Point Break* is your first choice, right? So, let's go with that."

He struggled to operate my laptop for at least fifteen minutes. I sat crisscrossed inches behind him on the bed, taking in his smell of cigarette smoke and sinister intentions. His luscious, wavy ponytail looked more like a white trash emblem rather than the Viking mane I usually see. The heavy body he possessed transformed into the body of an ugly village troll the longer I looked at his strong back, and I could feel my infatuation slowly sinking to a place of fear and disgust.

It's like the story of the old witch who uses the blood of infants to look young again, only in order to mystify and attain even more blood. She captures the unsuspecting and trusting children with her false attraction and promises of sweet treats or warm fire. But once they're lost in her grip, she morphs back into her natural state of hidden evil; the children see the overwhelming warts as they protrude from the skin, the dusty strings of gray hair as they replace the blonde, and the glass eyes that slip from their sockets after having been plucked out by ravens. The children know they've come to the wrong place; but it's already too late. She'll eat them alive.

In that room surrounded by nothing but old floorboards, I was certain Sid was going to eat me alive. The acid was strong, for sure, and it was coming on quick. Once he got the movie to play he started babbling about the different spells and rituals he's performed to psychically suck the Life out of someone until they can be readily manipulated time and time again. We got on the subject of his admiration for Hitler and the passion he feels for the Aryan race and ideologies. Conscious Lyla could hear him, but unconscious Lyla and all her other personalities had congregated in my spinning head and were trying to devise an escape plan.

I've always said that acid lifts the veil that usually clouds our mind and our judgement; as my veil lifted that night, I started seeing Sid for what he really is rather than what my own fantasies created him to be. When I peeled back the veil covering his face I saw his red lips twist into bloodied beds where his fangs lie. I started seeing the freckles on his ghostly face as tarnished reminders of meth-binges gone bad. His dark eyes that I loved so much had become an ominous black, and every time he twirled his thumbs around each other I was ready for him to choke me to death with those hands. I couldn't stop pulling at my own face with shaky nails, as if my skin had been tarnished by just sharing the air with him. I had to get out of that room, or I was gonna jump straight through the glass windows.

"I'll be right back!" I blurted out as he was in mid-sentence about the last Love spells he's cast.

I ran out of the room and closed the door behind me. I staggered through the hallway and into my empty living room.

Pacing.
Biting nails.
Biting skin around nails.
Pacing.
Staring out window.
Pacing.
Pacing.
Pacing. Pacing. Pacing.
Panicking.

I turned around from the window to see Big Mick lying face down on his mattress. I saw him as my way out of this—that maybe if I left Sid alone for long enough and he came out to see me lying next to Mick, he'd get the hint. Then I'd never have to talk to him again, right? I could take him back to his aunt's house, he could finish his trip in his temporary home, and I could finish my trip without fearing for my psychic well-being.

I walked back toward my room, raring my guts to tell Sid I didn't want him around anymore. We each just took 2.5 hits of acid, but I was gonna get him outta there.

"Sid," I said as I burst through my bedroom door

"What?" He asked, smiling and laying with his hands propped behind his head on the bed.

"This is hard for me to admit, but I don't want you here."

"Huh?" He asked, still smiling.

"Look, I'm just anxious. I don't think this was a good idea, and I'd really like if you could leave." My head was swimming in the LSD sea now, and I was trying desperately to hold on to the notion of saving myself from the danger of this ghoulish Dracula.

"You're anxious? What are you anxious for?" He laughed.

"I don't know, man, I just am. And it's not good when I'm anxious. Really. I want to take you back home before this stuff hits so hard that I can't drive."

"No." He said immediately.

"What?"

My whole body started tingling with rage and confusion. What did he mean, 'No'? This is my home, right? My home.

"No, I'm not leaving." He crossed his arms.

"Why not?"

"Because, Lyla, we committed to doing this, and you can't just shrug it off now. The acid's taken over. There's no way I'm letting you drive me anywhere."

Defeat. Utter fucking defeat, in my own house, by an unwanted man, yet again. I guess I really should start learning to not let them inside the walls.

"But, Sid. I can't do this with you," I pleaded. "The acid hasn't hit me that hard yet. There's still time to take you back!"

"Forget it," He said with his face half lit by the moonlight. "You can keep on being anxious and pacing out in the living room if you want. I'll stay in here." He wiggled around a little on the bed, making himself even more comfortable. Clearly, he wasn't going anywhere, which only means one thing: I've gotta go somewhere. I stared at him for two more seconds before turning to run out of the room again. Once I was in living room, I walked over to Big Mick and tried to wake him up.

"Mick," I said as I shook his foot. "Mick, wake up."

"Huh?" He groaned, slowly stretching out.

"Mick, can I sleep with you tonight?" I begged. I was desperate. So desperate that I'd beg the man who threw orange juice on me to let me cramp my body against his in a tight corner.

You see, I saw the ugly secret that Sid usually kept hidden, and I felt like my mind had been raped while my body had been totally and naively willing to bear witness to his sickness. It was as if he'd taken advantage of the walls that the acid was ripping down and tried planting a flower of evil right in my mind's eye. The seed had been planted, and all I wanted was to starve it so the petals won't ever grow.

"Whatchu wanna sleep wit me fo'?" He asked with an attitude. Shoulda known this wouldn't be such a piece of cake.

"I just wanna sleep next to you. Just one more time," I lied.

"Yeah, right, go on in your room and sleep on your bed," he said.

"I CAN'T!" I yelled. I was near snapping.

"Why the fuck not?" He mumbled.

"Because there's a man in my bed," I whispered back.

Big mistake.

"What da fuck did you just say?!" He asked. He threw the covers off his body and sat straight up as if he had never been asleep to begin with. "I *know* you didn't jus' say there's a man in my bed."

"Well, there is," I said, rising up from the floor.

"WHO THE FUCK is in that bed, Ly? Is it that troll-lookin' Nazi motherfucker? Huh?"

No response.

"Oh, I guess you just want me to see for myself, huh? Bitch, you outta yo' fuckin mind if you think that— "

I ran. I fucking ran. Big Mick stood up from his bed and threw on a shirt, rushing as fast as he could to reach the end of the hallway, pounding his chest with each step closer. As soon as he got off the bed I knew what was coming. And I knew that if I didn't wanna be around to trip acid with Sid, I certainly didn't wanna be around to trip acid while Sid and Big Mick duked it out. Two undesirable men couldn't cope with the fact that I wanted them out of my house; so, what happens when we can't cope with the circumstances of our own Lives?

We run.

We run until our feet hurt.

And then, even farther.

Slamming the door behind me, I shuffled down the stairs so fast that I thought I might eat shit on the staircase. I was barefoot, just like that time I wandered through abandoned backroads all those years ago. There was no time to grab shoes when a Neo-Nazi and, what he would call, a "Halfbreed" were about to meet face-to-face and erupt in my apartment. The only thing on my mind was fleeing; getting the fuck out and not coming back until my apartment belonged to me again.

I jumped into Scarlette's Jeep, flicked the ignition, and took one last look up at my apartment. My head was swirling and drowning in the dismal sphere that I'd caught myself in, but I focused my eyesight on the living room window and saw Big Mick screaming at Sid with his hands flailing in the air. Sid was smiling with his arms crossed, and just as I was about to look away, he got distracted from Mick's verbal assault and looked directly at me. Directly through the window, and through the windshield, and through my soul where I felt his cold spirit crawl through my limbs like an unwelcome disease.

I flipped the car in reverse and drove out of the Kangaroo parking lot like a bat flapping out of Hell's fury. I had to get to Scarlette's dorm room; that's the only safety in the world as far as I was concerned. I skirted through the back alleys and passed by the graveyard thinking that I'd never make it to salvation. The hounds of Hell were nipping the soft meat of my heels, and for a moment I swear the Earth was opening up below me to swallow my grief whole. I was racing the Dark, and its shadow was mocking me, threatening me, and gaining on me.

But the chase is far from finished.